Collateral Damage

Laughing Rabbit Books

Also by Susan Staneslow Olesen

Prisoner of the Mind series:
Prisoner of the Mind
Conflicts of Interest
Honor to the Emperor

Best Intentions series:
Best Intentions
Best Efforts
Broken Trusts
Best of Everything
Ancient History

Shorts*:*
Brain Splatter

One

Syron's Mercy was an ordinary transport ship equipped for thirty passengers, but Aila Perrin walked the halls with Masákh as if it were an abandoned derelict, expecting armed officers, or worse, her parents, to pop out of every shadowed corner. Sneaking off to Kerasím with a bunch of Kerasi nationals for a holiday trip and no government entourage had never been attempted by anyone before, but Aila had full faith in her mentor Masákh, in General Tokh, who had adopted her as one of his own, and in Emperor Nadigh, who had been trying so blasted hard to improve his world and solidify the fragile peace with the Planetary Union. Last year's massacre had been a little unsettling, but that was then and this was a whole year of progress later. Aila had promised General Tokh she would return for the New Year celebrations, and Mother not withstanding, she was going to keep that promise. Both Emperor Nadigh and the Union government had given their approval.

Once in their stateroom, Aila dropped her carry bag on the bed with a loud sigh. "I made it! I half-expected an official to be waiting outside our room, telling me I had to return."

Masákh placed his travel cases inside the small closet, as precise as anything else he did. Only Masákh could pack clothing, move it several billion miles, and have it emerge without a single new crease. He was full-blooded Kerasi, but like all *aghát* diplomats had been surgically altered to look more human, with a bleached yellowy-tan to his skin, two eyebrows, capped teeth, and the ridge above his eyes pared down to Human levels. "Knowing your mother, I would not say it was impossible."

Aila kissed him on his nose. "But I managed it. Lady Paranoia lost a round. We have a whole month of peace before we face the shitstorm we'll hit on return. Let's hope this trip goes smoother than the last." She dropped onto the bed.

1

Masákh's attention was deep in his hand unit, a gadget that not only provided communication on both local and interstellar levels but allowed him contact with the Kerasi ComNet and all the allowed Kerasi military databases, which were more extensive than the Union liked to admit. His reply was distracted. "No one outside the palace except Tokh should know you are coming. Therefore, nothing could have been planned unless there are leaks in communications to the Emperor."

"Hah! Caught you!" Aila crowed with delight. Masákh knew everything. *Everything.* And he thought about everything all the time, chastising her when she failed to spot the obvious. Rare indeed was the moment Aila could reciprocate. "Once we hit the border and they see our manifest, anyone could wave out who's on board. We're only safe until we hit the border."

Masákh lifted his head, but Aila could tell by his face she'd won. "That is truth. I will discuss it with the others and with the ship's captain. Perhaps we can make a request to have you listed under a false name."

"I don't care. The point is I thought of something you didn't. I won! For once, I won."

Masákh pocketed his hand unit and paused to kiss her on her head, a sign of affection but not of sex, a Kerasi obsession. "I will return. A number of us are gathering in one of the public rooms to converse."

"I'll come with you." Aila stood up.

Masákh flashed her his shy smile of amusement that said she was a cute little child spouting nonsense. "It is a male gathering."

"So because I'm the only female, I'm supposed to sit here alone the whole trip? That's not happening."

Masákh moved toward the door. "I thought you had something you needed to do? It might be better if I were nowhere near camera range. Nor do I wish to overhear the conversation." He gave her a tip of his head and left.

Aila's humor disappeared as her stomach twisted into a knot. The deadly thorn between the two of them for the last five years.

Mom.

Leila Perrin was so distrustful of Kerasi she'd spent much of the last year in therapy over it – most of it against her will. The final straw had been Aila and Masákh declaring an intent to marry last year, and

2

then living together. After a very public brawl between Aila and Leila, Ramden Perrin had insisted his wife get counseling to deal with her hate. The State Department had backed him up: get counseling, or get another job. Leila went, and though she was handling Aila's relationship better, she still questioned every stray hair and posture shift Aila made. Even as the paperwork slipped into place, Aila didn't pack until three days before the trip, lest she give off even a hint of travel. But Mom still needed to be informed why she wouldn't be around for the next month.

Aila sat at the room's com, took a deep breath, steadied herself, and placed a call home.

Her mother answered. "How are you, Darling? Are you alone? Do you need help? Where are you?"

Aila gave a soft laugh. "I'm fine, Mom. Yes, I'm alone, I'm free to go where ever I want, and I am more than fine. The only bruise I have is on my knee where I smashed the edge of the table at work, and there were three witnesses to it. I can show you." She put her foot on the chair, rolled up her pant leg, and held the spot up to the transmission camera.

"I believe you. So, what are you up to? I was just telling your father yesterday we should have lunch together. Do you have a day free this week or next?"

"Just me?"

Aila saw the flash of ire cross her mother's face, but Leila grabbed it before it rose too far, twisted it into mild sarcasm and stuffed it back down. "Yes, just you. You are still an individual, aren't you?"

"Yes. I was just messing with you." Their current "peace treaty" said that Aila would meet with her parents alone whenever schedule allowed, proving she was not being held against her will, and every sixth visit Masákh would accompany her, to ease her mother into tolerating him. Those visits were strained, but civil enough.

"I would love to, but I'm not sure when I could. I'm being sent on a mission, so I'll be gone for a little bit. I promise I will book the date the week I get back."

This time Leila's face clouded over. "Where are you headed? Back to Earth? Or over to Fornax again? How long will you be gone? I don't like you being on Fornax."

3

"Mm, I'm guessing one or two months, with travel. No sweat. Mostly just meet and greets."

"Where?" Realization dawned on Leila. She straightened as the truth came clear. "You're going back there, aren't you. After everything they did to you? Why, Aila? You want them to kill you this time? What hold does he have on you? I'm calling Hhani. You aren't an official diplomat. You can't enter their space without Union permission, so just sit back and let's think about this first."

"Yeah, that's true, Mom, but I've already got State approval, and I'm already en route. If I call you tomorrow we will definitely have pauses in the transmissions."

The screen went black as Leila hit end transmission.

Aila hit resend. The call went to mail. She ended, resent, ended, resent, then finally left a videomessage. "Mom, please just answer and talk to me? I'm not doing this to piss you off. I'm not doing this because I'm forced to. I promised Mímihn I would try to be there for their big holiday. I promised that when we left Kerasím. *I* promised, Mom. Not Masákh. Now I'm keeping the promise. I expect to be gone maybe six weeks. Figure two for travel, and that leaves me four to visit with various people, from government officials to Mímihn and Tokh. I'm already scheduled to meet with Ross, and I promised the Emperor last year I would meet with his daughter. That is my rough itinerary. You have my personal number; if you promise me you won't share it, I will forward you Mímihn's personal ID. Only for extreme emergencies though, okay? Only if you lose track of me for more than a day, and you can't get through on the official channels. I'm probably breaking laws by giving you it, but in a pinch you can call Ross Halian, and he'll know how to find me. Okay? Is that secure enough for you?"

Aila was just about to give up when the ship's computer buzzed.

"This is suicide and you know it, Aila. The first time they kidnapped and tortured you. The second time you were almost raped and killed. I don't know why you have this death wish, but there's nothing I can do to stop you, is there. Does he have some big insurance policy on you? Or that General?"

"The Emperor wants me alive, Mom. Very much so. I've done more for his cause than he ever dreamed. And Tokh's family would take any injury to me most seriously. If you'd just accompany me on a quick little trip, you'd see that."

"I'm not joking, Aila. What does he get if you die? If you don't know the answer, you don't know the man. What does he get if you die?"

Leila's face was caught half-way between anger and hurt, but the most overwhelming emotion that stood out was fear; Aila could see the tears coming, but they weren't there yet. Mom was being civil, and she was trying. That was huge. Aila thought about the scenario, knew how close it had once come to being true, and knew that her uptight and hopelessly dedicated partner had pretty much thrown away his entire life attempting to save her, insubordination and all. Tokh had filed it under temporary insanity. Aila knew the answer already.

"He gets a broken heart, Mom. He gets an irrevocably shattered heart."

Dinner was – interesting. Aila wasn't sure she'd ever seen so many *aghát* diplomatic officers in one place before, all looking so alike it made her skin crawl. Sixteen? Seventeen? men, all with dark hair, bleached skin, facial surgery, and a sculpted goatee instead of chin hank, just like Masákh, a convention meeting of store mannequins heading home for a holiday. At the ill-fated Accord last year they'd been mixed with a thousand other Kerasi, not gathered in a cluster. Aila was the only female passenger, though there were a few women on the ship's crew. Some of the *aghát* wore Union clothing, others still wore their uniforms, uncomfortable in anything else. Aila wore slacks and a modest sunflower-yellow tunic, and for safety's sake she wore gloves, as even accidental skin contact with another male could start trouble. Although every *aghát* officer was fluent in Union Standard – their very purpose as *aghát* – together, they reverted to Emperor's Tongue. Aila could follow about half of it if she concentrated.

She knew two of the other *aghát* well. Haghíde, General Tokh's third-ranked *aghát*, was the closest thing Masákh had to a best friend. He was stationed on Earth, while Aila and Masákh suffered the politicking of Alpha Centauri, the center of Union government. Aila trusted him as much as Masákh.

The other was Tokh's senior *aghát*, Mátokhan. Aila knew she should trust Mátokhan. He'd saved her butt at least once, but it didn't erase the fact he was the most conceited, demeaning, self-righteously pompous person Aila had ever met – and she'd met two Kerasi

5

Emperors, a couple of snooty former *fáhganids*, and an heir. Just speaking to him made Aila want to bathe. He spotted her and Masákh across the room – of course he would, he was *aghát*, he could probably recite the names of everyone in the room – and headed over.

Kerasi men ignored Kerasi females, unless it was with a roving eye, so Aila wasn't the least bit surprised when Mátokhan didn't so much as greet her, but spoke to Masákh.

"Masákh. You look well. I take it you bear success back to the Emperor. I see you've brought your – What are you calling her these days? Wife? Consort? Or do you also call her daughter?"

Aila made a snide face and spoke before Masákh could – terrible manners for a Kerasi female, but not so much a Union one. "Call me consort again and I'll inform the General you've slandered his name."

"The slander will fall on his unmarried yet openly bedded 'daughter.' Then what do you call him?"

"Partner. We are simply 'partners,' until we choose to make it legally binding, which will not be for two years yet. What we do or do not do as partners is not part of the term. We have chosen to share our lives with each other."

"Partner is the accepted Union term," Masákh agreed. "It is one we should use more often on Kerasím."

"Partner." Mátokhan rolled the word around on his tongue as if he'd just learned it. "I suppose that is accurate. There is no direct translation into Emperor's Tongue. 'Bedmates' might be closest, but I do not think you would approve of that."

"Stick to partner."

Mátokhan gave a nonchalant tip of his head. "Your choice. Better check with the legal department before we arrive, Masákh. Know what your rights are before trouble starts." He turned and walked away without so much as a nod of dismissal.

Aila shook her head. "I will never learn to like him."

Haghíde slid up to them. "You do not look pleased at his words."

Masákh gave a soft snort of discomfort. "I have never understood how someone who takes such delight in forcing others to be uncomfortable can be so successful at diplomacy."

"Short form," Aila said, "is that if he were lying on the ground bleeding, I would take my time finding someone to help him."

Haghíde flashed a brief smile. "Since we are to spend our time together at the General's, I suggest we ask General Tokh if there are assignments any of us can carry out away from the estate, or it will be a very long visit."

Aila leaned in. "He keeps that up? I'll kill him within a week."

Two

Even though she sat on the Union Council for Kerasi affairs, even though the *aghát* were used to dealing with Union women, Aila was ignored for most of the evening. Masákh made sure she was fed, and sometimes she got to sit with him and actually speak, but most of the time she sat by herself, or Haghíde would come over and speak with her. A few of the bolder *aghát* asked to take their photo with her; Aila was the darling of Kerasi-Union relations, close to the Emperor, and to have a photo with her meant the person would be seen as important, too, even if they never said a word to each other. Aila posed willingly.

She wanted to head back to their cabin, but even though the ship was full of *aghát*, she wasn't comfortable walking back to her room alone. The Kerasi were an extremely violent race, and the line between sexual assault, murder, and discipline was a very thin one. She, Aila Perrin, Union female, feminist, crusader for personal rights, determined individual who escaped Kerasi prisons and did not hesitate to beat on her captors or snatch their weapons, was afraid to walk the corridors without an escort.

Masákh noticed. He brushed noses, then kissed her softly in the little hollow just above her nose. "You are unhappy here."

"I'm tired. Let's go back."

"I can do that. There isn't much of importance being discussed. Everyone is still learning who belongs to which General, what their purpose is, and the politics involved on both sides of the border. It is more difficult remembering faces, as we all are similar. We will break for the night, everyone will do their research, and by morning we will all be on better terms with each other, and the conversations will have more meaning."

Aila stood up. "Thank you. Maybe you can tell me what everyone's talking about, since you left me out of most of the evening."

"We can discuss the general trends of thought." Not everything about work could be shared, on either side. It was a learning curve Aila was still mastering.

"Good enough."

Three *aghát* already waited by the lift; one of them was Mátokhan. They all entered the lift silently. The two strangers – at least to Aila – got off on the next floor.

Mátokhan stared down at her with a gaze that could have torn metal. "For all the praises sung, Masákh has failed you in his teachings. Six years you have studied our customs, our laws. People have fought and died for you, and you still don't understand. You are not his wife; you are not his legal property. You are an unbound female in the service of a male. You are thus a free servant, and can be claimed by anyone."

The lift opened and they stepped into the hallway. "This is not an argument for public debate," Masákh warned.

Aila stared back with her best blistering look. She shook the badge on her shoulder. "*Doh dahneg, tansohr Keralihn.*"

"Irrelevant. You are the female servant to a lowly *whátaral*, and you take the caste of your employer. Half the planet outcastes him. I outrank him, I out caste him, and there is nothing he can do or say to stop me should I choose to act upon it."

Aila fluffed herself up further. "By your own laws I am daras-Giláhn, at worst a *dihnarwharl* with *dahneg* privilege. I am under the protection of the Emperor himself."

"Tokh is not true to his word; a male of his stature and reputation would never allow a daughter to be an unbonded servant to a male. Protection of the Emperor is a legal term only; it means you have connections and will always have legal representation. Should you be seized by a person of high caste, the Emperor's office will step in and make sure you're released. His Majesty doesn't waste time on the whines of reprimanded females, nor can he hear your complaint with my *hihvat* stuffed down your throat." His hand patted her cheek.

It happened so fast Aila didn't have time to think about custom or protocol or even a sharp reply. Her hand hauled back and cracked Mátokhan so hard across his face he'd have a mark for the next half-hour.

9

Mátokhan's bleached face flushed a dark brownish yellow. Masákh seized Aila; one hand clamped over her mouth, his other arm locked around her and yanked her back.

"My apologies, Mátokhan," Masákh said, bowing his head. "I assure you, I will apply discipline and remind her of proper behavior. But remember you are dealing with a Union female, and she responds as such. It is appropriate on her world."

Mátokhan breathed like an angry bull, the hot air bellowing down on Aila's face as if she didn't exist. "She dares to strike a *nhásarwharl* with privilege. That is unforgivable, Masákh, no matter what her designation. She struck me once; I demand three stripes in return. The choice is now my hand or yours."

Aila squealed and tried to pull Masákh's hand away; Masákh twisted her to the side. His face was cold and serious, if not anxious – unusual for Masákh. "My apologies again, Mátokhan, but I don't feel this should be settled between us. We tread on interstellar law and cannot risk creating an incident. At the moment, the injury lies on our side. I suggest we allow Tokh to decide what is appropriate. She is his daughter. I agree to abide by his decision."

Mátokhan continued his angry breathing, but at last tipped his head. "Very well. But I will not forget to mention it to him. You can't keep her on the treaty line, Masákh. You need to decide if she is Union or if she is Kerasi. She cannot be both."

Masákh nodded. "Your words are truth, but they won't be decided here. Neither of us has the required authority. I'm interested to hear Tokh's solution." Mátokhan bowed his head, spun on a heel, and stormed down the hallway.

Masákh released her. Before Aila could say a word, his face twisted in anger almost as deep as Mátokhan's, and he shoved her hard enough to make her stumble. "To the stateroom!"

Masákh walked soldier-fast and focused, shoving her if she slowed down. Every time she tried to speak he raised a warning finger. It was a simple gesture, just a finger in the air, not even pointed at her, but Aila stayed silent. The sharpness of the movement spoke volumes.

Damn you, Masákh! She knew the coming argument and wanted no part of it. Yes, she knew better, but there was no excuse for

Mátokhan's obscenity, either. If only his threat could bounce back onto himself. Then he'd think twice.

Masákh allowed her to open their door, a motion calculated to force her to enter the room first. He shut it and locked it behind them.

"Could he have been any more of an ass?" she said, but stopped. Masákh's head was bent, arms half-raised, hands clawed, every muscle in his body locked with tension as if he were climbing an invisible wall. He held the position several seconds, then turned around and punched the door with a frightening bellow. A light dent pocked the metal skin. Aila took a step back.

He whirled back around, eyes cold, face dark, anger rising until Aila imagined she could see the air waver above his ears. Masákh didn't come at her like that. He just didn't.

"I should strangle you for that! You wouldn't have dared think such a thing five years ago! You are female! You can never strike a male!" He spouted a stream of Kerasi, too fast and angry for Aila to follow.

"I'm sorry! I was really mad. No one, male or female, may talk to another like that in the Union. No, I shouldn't have done that. It's considered wrong by Union law, but his remarks were obscene and offensive."

Masákh stuck his face in hers. "You aren't understanding. You struck him. You are under my claim: he has the right to demand you be punished, either by my hand or his. Depending on his temper it could be strokes with an incentive stick, he could assault you as he threatened, or he can legally demand the hand that struck him. Do you understand that? Your offending hand will be removed and given to him as reparation. Do you understand?"

Ice formed at the base of Aila's spine, creeping upwards in a grim frost until it made her hair crinkle. Her heart raced, but she didn't quite believe it. She knew the Kerasi were fond of cutting things off – like heads – but it didn't seem real. One slap, and lose a hand forever? One slap deserved retaliatory rape? It was so out of proportion to the crime it wasn't funny.

But there wasn't much the Kerasi did that was funny.

The *aghát* were supposed to be sworn to protect her, Mátokhan included. "I'm a *dahneg*, legal daughter of a *dahneg*-privilege, and a

11

Union citizen under the protection of the Emperor. Do you really think Tokh would let someone take my hand?"

Masákh's face still tread the line between anger and anguish. "Only if Mátokhan agrees to let Tokh decide punishment. If he waits, I would almost guarantee Tokh will sentence you to three strokes. The question is who will apply them. It is Tokh's right, as you bear his name, and I speak from experience when I say you do not want him striping you. He may grant Mátokhan the right, as the one assaulted. That is also not to be desired. Or he may order me to do it, as it was my negligence that allowed it. I must then strike you meaningfully, or I will be negligent in my duty. I have spent six years swearing to protect you from harm. I swore an oath to Admiral Perrin I would not harm you, and now I must either stand by and watch you be bloodied, or perform the task myself, against my will. Either way, I have failed. Which do you prefer?"

The reality of it didn't affect Aila as much as the pain in his voice. She reached out and hugged him. "I'm so sorry, Masákh. Please don't yell. You don't think twice of such threats; in the Union, such a threat is seen as a promise of assault, and treated almost the same. I'm so sorry to put you in such a position. I promise, I will think before acting next time. Perhaps Tokh could appeal to the Emperor for me."

Masákh stayed stiff in her arms. He shrugged her off. "You make everything difficult. I have much thinking to do. Please stay in the room, where I know you will be safe."

Aila nodded. Her heart squeezed in pain, seeing him upset, knowing she was the cause. She breezed around Tokh's men thinking she knew all about Kerasi, but everyone else was right: she didn't know a damned thing. She didn't have age protection anymore. Aila didn't even have a whole lot of diplomatic protection, either, but becoming a limp dishrag wasn't about to happen.

She watched him walk out the door with a sense of foreboding. If worse came to worst, she'd send an SOS to Ross Halian at the Union Embassy in Keranihn, and get him to intervene. Masákh worried her more. Hurting him hadn't entered her mind, and it was a long ninety minutes of gnawing regret until he returned. That night he held her close, kissed her head, but made no move to *push* on her, and that scared Aila's heart most of all.

Three

Masákh ate breakfast with the men, but Aila walked to the ship's vending room and grabbed herself a passable Centauri *simur* with milk and sugar and an imitation fruit pastry with some kind of thick topping. The *simur* was perfectly hot, not quite a coffee but functioning like one, more like a cinnamon-coconut-caramel tea. She headed back to the room with her cup.

Aila entered the lift. "Deck fi –." She stopped as Mátokhan slipped in behind her, blocking her escape.

"Deck five," he commanded, then hit the emergency stop after it began to move.

"Let me out!" Aila made a grab for the button.

Mátokhan flicked her arm away, splashing the *simur* under the cup's lid. "You will listen to what I have to say."

Aila backed into the corner of the lift. "If you think I'm bold for slapping you when you thoroughly deserved it, know that I won't hesitate to stab you just as fast, and I won't miss."

Mátokhan gave a soft snort of amusement, but the horrid disdain wasn't there, the arrogance down to tolerable limits, quite odd. "You are not that good. I didn't anticipate the strike, but drawing a weapon is far more obvious. You would be disarmed before you could aim. Enough. I have questions to ask you in private; this is the only place I can keep you alone long enough to ask. You claim your heart belongs to Masákh, no?"

Aila trusted Mátokhan about as much as a cockroach near a party cake. "Why?"

Mátokhan sighed. "Answer the question."

It took a pause, but Aila answered, "Yes."

"Do you consider yourselves to be husband and wife?"

Again Aila paused, not sure where the conversation was headed, and how he might trip her up. *Aghát* were very good at that. "In my heart I do, but it will not be made legal until I have finished my degree."

He nodded acceptance of the fact, as if he expected the answer. "Do you love him enough to keep information from him?"

"What do you mean?"

"Lovers share many secrets, sometimes ones they should not share. Masákh is newly Inner Circle. I have been Inner Circle for ten years. I know the situations he faces, and as Brother *Aghát*, I worry. Masákh is blinded by honesty and loyalty; he would die for an ideal. I'm not sure he is flexible enough for what might be asked of him. If I share information with you and only you, do you love him enough to keep the information strictly to yourself and not share it with him, no matter what you may whisper together?"

The wary feeling grew, but it eased some of her questions. "That would depend on the information and the situations involved. If I felt it was to his advantage to not know, or if it wasn't his business, then I would keep the secret."

Again Mátokhan nodded. "Then here is the secret. He would already expect some of it, but I tell you now in full. I will not be pressing charges at arrival. My orders were to push you –" He stopped at her horrified look and corrected himself. The common crude Kerasi word for sex translated to Union Standard as *push*. "No! Not that way. Forgive my choice of words. To," he searched his head, "cause stress and see if you would pull away from each other. In my opinion, as in my report, your connection remains strong. I had no doubts of Masákh; it was you I needed to test. No matter what you think of me or others, know that in six years, no one has given an order that supersedes Tokh's order that you not be harmed; that is scannable truth. That remains the primary goal of his *aghát*. Do not forget that. Even if you doubt Masákh, do not doubt that your back remains covered. Do you understand?"

Aila tried, but knew she'd never make sense out of it without an hour's deep thought. "I want to think so. Masákh is being tested as an agent to the Emperor, and what I think is going on at any given time may not be true, but even if I'm scared, not to worry because others are watching out for me."

Mátokhan smiled, condescending but not slimy. "Remember: our secret. He is not to know I spoke with you."

Aila nodded. The information was bland enough she had no issue with it. "Okay."

Mátokhan set the lift back into motion. "And watch yourself. You walk away intact having struck a *dihnarwharl-privilege* male, but if you do that on Kerasím, you will most likely lose the hand before the Emperor's guard can intervene. That is not an incident that will please the Emperor."

"I got it."

Sort of. Even if she worked with the *aghát* a hundred years, Aila would never understand them.

Four

The great palace of Derahl Nor at Keranihn, the world center of Kerasím, had lost some of its intimidation. It was Aila's third trip to the palace, and the process was becoming routine. The group disembarked at Emperor Khumroh Global Spaceport outside of Keranihn and boarded a helicraft that took them directly to the landing pad on the roof of the palace, the center of Kerasi government. The glorious building stretched six stories tall and almost half a mile long, covered in gleaming sheets of shimmering white stone, massive and intimidating.

Masákh and the other *aghát* sat reverently as the craft landed. The palace of Keranihn was the Holiest of Holies, a thousand years of history in one place, the home of the Emperor of the entire Kerasi Coalition, currently Nadigh Ramán Gol Suhr Zaghíl, and no one but the most privileged were allowed to walk the halls. Even the lavatory cleaners ranked no lower than *rhibani* in caste. The *aghát* would barely speak while there, afraid of breaking protocol, afraid of shaming their commander, afraid of never being invited to return. Nothing else in the universe could turn highly trained Kerasi warriors into well-dressed sacks of quivering jelly.

Aila, a human teen thrust into diplomatic duty long before her time, all but clawed at the glass of the transport window. At fifty feet from touchdown she was already out of the seat restraints, primping. She wore Kerasi-style clothing: a blouse and skirt that came below her knees, and a decorative sheer veil draped down her back like a ribbon from a tall veil-clasp, progressive but traditional. The craft touched, then settled with a small bounce. Aila grabbed the overhead rails to steady herself. The men stood up. Aila skipped for the door, her carry bag over her shoulder, but Masákh grabbed her arm and held her back.

A soft growl rattled her throat. He didn't speak, just gave her that indignant cold stare she was all-too-familiar with, the one that said she knew better and if she didn't behave properly unpleasant consequences would follow. It was easy for an *aghát* who never showed excitement in the line of duty. Screw protocol! She could see General Tokh waiting outside on the rooftop with a small contingent of officials, as well as a female that Aila was certain was his wife Mímihn. Tokh didn't like to wait.

The men went first. The other officers disembarked, greeted the palace official sent to welcome them, then Tokh's *aghát* left the ship, and only then Aila. How strange, being here as a nobody, without an official Union entourage and camera crews following her every move. The realization made Aila's stomach quiver. There were Union reps on the planet who knew she was here, but in the long run, there was no one from the Union accompanying her to back her up, advise her, or protect her. She was entirely at the mercy of the Kerasi Empire, something even the Kerasi wouldn't have allowed six years ago.

She bowed to the official, a colonel's rank on his shoulder. "Aila Perrin daras-Giláhn, Union Council for Kerasi Affairs. I come with the blessings of the Emperor."

The colonel bowed in reply "His Majesty Emperor Nadigh grants you full permission to visit his cities, under the responsibility of Grand Senator General Four Tokh."

Aila bowed again. "*Jihtar om mehi.*"

Masákh waited, and together they approached General Tokh, waiting with his newest *aghát* Ráhnif, who worked at the palace. At last she was allowed to step forward and be recognized, dignitary or not.

Aila bowed low. "*Triskaris-Bo* Tokh. I return as promised. You showed me great hospitality on my last visit. May I impose and request further hospitality for this visit as well?"

Tokh bowed in reply, still unwilling to shake her hand despite the fact he'd declared her his legal daughter. "You are of my house and of my name. You are expected." He stepped back and waved an arm behind him. "We have much business before we may return to Imahlva, but Mímihn has been keeping a surprise from you and refuses to let me rest until she is able to share it."

Mímihn came forward, holding a wrapped package in her arms. She broke into a wide grin, showing her perfect, yellowy pointed teeth. "Ah-lo, Ai-lah! I ham hahppy see yu more!" She ran out of Union words and switched back to Kerasi. The bundle in her arms was a white blanket.

"I'm sorry I kept the news from you. I wanted to be sure the surprise was real before I spoke about it. It was so very hard not to tell you!" She turned the package and the covering fell away. There was a small round sleeping face with a shock of dark hair, and a shadow on the tiny bump where an eyebrow would one day grow.

Aila's eyes almost fell out of her head. "Yours?!"

Mímihn squealed and bounced gently. "Yes! I birthed him! I did! No more am I a sterile consort. Ten years later, I'm a wife and a mother. Tokh took me to a doctor who said it was very easy to fix, and it was! His name is Thoren. He's ten weeks old. He weighs twelve *harach*."

"He's beautiful! I'm so happy for you!" She hugged Mímihn around the baby. "Masákh! Haghíde! Look! Mímihn's got a baby!"

Masákh craned his neck to confirm it was an infant. The *aghát* turned to Tokh. "To your strength, General."

Aila soured. "Excuse me? Who grew the baby? Who suffered birthing it? Who's feeding and changing it? Don't you think Mímihn deserves some credit?"

Masákh stared at her as if a potted plant had spoken. He flashed a small embarrassed smile and gave a short bow. "Of course. Fortunes grace, Lady Tokh." Haghíde and Mátokhan echoed a mumble.

"All this time, and you still haven't gotten it," Aila said. The Kerasi were trying to change, yes, but sometimes it seemed as if overweight snails moved faster. "Well, congratulations, General. That was a very noble thing to do for Mímihn."

Tokh gave a nod. "Come. We must attend to business."

They passed through security, and the officers surrendered their weapons. No one was fond of the policy – for a Kerasi soldier to be without his weapon was powerlessness, but there were only two exceptions to this rule: the Emperor and his heir. They headed downward in the lift, and Tokh left Mímihn and baby Thoren at a secured area for waiting wives.

"You will report to room 3491 for debriefing," Tokh told his men as he returned to the hall. "We will meet at the roof when you are done."

Aila began to follow, but Tokh put his arm out to stop her. "His business is not your business. We have other matters. Come with me." He set off in the opposite direction. Aila stayed close on his heels; there were more than three thousand rooms to Derahl Nor, more than three miles of hallways, and sections that were inaccessible from public areas. Her chances of getting lost were guaranteed, and chances of finding her way out slim at best.

After three long corridors, Tokh opened a door and entered. It was an ornate waiting area, the baroque details and gold trims rather silly for such a small space. A male receptionist – *whátaral* in caste – sat behind a simple table with a computer interface. Tokh bowed to him anyway. "Union Councillady Aila Perrin, as requested." The secretary tapped his screen without a word.

"You have been summoned to an official meeting. I suggest you answer all questions with truth, as you know where lies lead. I will be waiting here for you when you are done."

"What?" Aila felt her hair stand up. She could face anything if Tokh was by her side, but alone? Females did nothing alone on Kerasím. "What do you mean? Why aren't you staying with me? Who are we meeting with? What will they do? Is this safe?"

"I believe it will be. It is just an inquiry. If you do not attend, you will not be allowed to leave the palace. I was not requested and therefore not allowed in chambers. I will be here when you are dismissed." He placed his back to the wall, out of view, and opened the door for her.

Aila's heart stopped beating. Tokh gave her a last solemn nod. Her knees shivered, and Aila had to force them to bend, lift, and straighten again. She'd have settled for anyone she knew – well, outside of Colonel Kassán – standing in the room with her. Any friendly face.

A lone chair stood in the middle of the room, a regular chair, with no arms. Chair was good. Females were not usually granted chairs, and if that much respect was being given, it was fair to assume nothing horrible was planned. The door closed behind her, at the glove of a brown-uniformed *bhántim* guard. A grand table crossed the front of the room, white with gold trim, on a platform several inches higher than the floor. Five men sat behind it while one stood at their backs. The stander was an *aghát* Aila had never met, perhaps someone who

19

worked at the palace. Two of the sitters wore uniforms. Aila stood behind the chair and bowed to them.

The man in the center bowed his head. He tried speaking Union, but his accent was so thick Aila figured it was a memorized line, nothing more. "Uel-khome, Council Laydy Pehrrin. Seet, pleece." Aila bowed and sat.

His Standard exceeded, he switched to Kerasi. "Do you speak Emperor's tongue?"

"Some."

"If needed, my *aghát* will translate."

"Understood."

"*Doh* Nemutar, Minister of Foreign Affairs." He went down the line with introductions. "This is Revered Yulghan, Director of Internal Affairs; General Trannor, Revered Director of Union-Kerasi Relations; Supreme Reverence Durghid, Head of the Empiric Senate; and General Liehr, Revered Director of the First Imperial Court."

"*Galakh ris yar.* Your presence honors me." Aila took a steadying breath. Every one of them was highest caste, with total power over her, and Tokh as well. Durghid, she knew, was a brother to former Emperor Nághtas, Uncle to the current Emperor Nadigh. This was a panel of Empiric power. The second one was familiar; Aila was certain he'd been at one of the galas of the disastrous Accord of the previous year, but so much had happened afterward she couldn't be certain. The others were all former *fáhganid* in caste.

"You're the first Union female to visit Kerasím without a government party. You present a puzzle. We don't wish to interfere with your visit, but you present a security risk. We don't wish another incident with Union visitors. How long do you plan to visit?"

"I must return to Union space within three weeks."

"You will be staying with General Tokh, and he will swear to your security?"

"*Sukh. Reihot. Doh daras-Giláhn.*" Truth. It sounded strange, saying it that way. To give Aila legal protection on Kerasím, Tokh had claimed her as his biological daughter. Not a single person believed she was – it was genetically impossible – but it was legal. At the time, anyway. Maybe they'd closed that loophole.

"You are accompanied by Major Masákh gha Lil. It is known you have close ties to him. Within the Union, are you his wife?"

20

Ah. That was the concern. "No, I am not. We have no legal claim to each other."

General Liehr spoke. "But inside the Union, you share the same living quarters."

"Yes. It is by verbal agreement. There is no legal claim. That is allowed within the Union."

There was a fast mumbling between several of the panel which Aila was not able to catch. Nemutar tried again. "Are you his consort?"

"No. He does not own me."

The panel seemed stumped. The pause for discussion was longer, everyone leaning toward the center and speaking softly. After several minutes, Revered Yulghan asked, "Does Major Masákh bed you?"

Aila didn't flinch. It was a common enough Kerasi question, even if it was rude by Union standards. "Why is that information important?"

The panel stared back at her. Females did not question; they did as they were asked. Aila had broken protocol. General Liehl waved to the translator. Perhaps Aila had not understood.

"No dishonor is intended. You are the first non-Kerasi female we have met. We have many questions. Your ways are unusual to us. We don't know how you fit into our laws. You are not wife, you are not consort. We don't have a category for that. To grant you legal protection, we must know your relationship."

Aila spoke slowly. Sometimes Kerasi couldn't comprehend even something they understood. It also helped the translator. "I am promised to Masákh gha Lil. That is fact and truth. We *will* legally marry in the future, but are not married at this time. I remain daras-Giláhn."

The panel muttered to each other for several minutes. The Director of Union-Kerasi relations kept his hand over his mouth when he spoke. Aila didn't trust him. If he was the man she had met last year, he spoke better Union than the translator.

"A shadow-wife," the translator said.

"Please explain."

"A wife who lives in the shadows. A wife of spirit, not of law. A secret pairing without legal marriage."

Aila bowed her head. "If I understand correctly, *sukh*."

"You serve on the committee for Kerasím in the Union."

"*Sukh.* Yes."

"Do you have a political agenda while you are here?"

"No," Aila said. "That is truth. I am here to visit friends for the holiday. I will visit the Embassy as a matter of protocol. I will conduct several interviews while I am here. I am happy to do them. As always, I'm available to serve the requests of the palace. Otherwise, I have no authorization or plan to discuss politics."

The mumbling began again. They all seemed to check with each other, nodding, before Nemutar rapped on the table. "Very well. You are approved for a three-week stay under the protection of General Four Tokh dar Giláhn as his unmarried offspring. Your safety here will be his concern only. The palace will notify you if your presence is desired."

Aila bowed her head. "*Soyavoh*, Revered Ones. You give me honor."

From meeting with high officials, Aila's next stop was all the way down to the public first floor of the palace, for an interview for the Kerasi Global ComNet. She was used to news interviews; it kept up her popularity and kept her in good standing with the Emperor, and it didn't hurt the Union's image, either. Tokh reclaimed Mímihn from the waiting parlor so she could watch at the front of the crowd. A small sofa had been pulled before a well-known statue of Khumroh, the first Emperor. There were lights and camera crews, bystanders elbowing each other for a glimpse, a *tághinet* to apply eyeliner and bronze powder to her face, and a fantastically overdressed personality to run the interview. His hair was longer than most, slicked back on the sides of his head to a elongated point in the back, two great black birds' wings hugging his head and keeping him streamlined for running to interviews. His chin hank had been threaded with beads tight against his chin, then combed out in a perfect stiff fan and sprinkled with microglitter in an array of colors like a lacquered black Christmas tree, with a glittering personality to match. A palace *aghát* stood by for translation. After more than a half-dozen interviews, the questions never seemed to change. All fluff, no substance. Nothing about Union politics. Nothing about her experiences with interstellar travel – as if most Kerasi ever left their cities, let alone their planet. Nothing newsworthy at all.

"You've come back to visit with us!" he said, the wide pointed-toothed grin looking more like a large yellow paper cutter than a smile. He sat much closer to Aila than she would have liked. "Tell us, what brings you back? Is it our charming males?"

Aila smiled, keeping her lips closed. "I was invited to attend your New Year's celebrations, that I may experience a Kerasi holiday. Emperor Nadigh was most kind to allow me to return." Everyone got bonus points whenever she mentioned the Emperor.

"You will stay with the Emperor here at the palace?"

"I will visit, but I am staying with friends. I must also check in at the Union Embassy as well." Aila hoped it would spur him to ask more questions about the Union, get some real information out to the public, but no such luck. The rest of the interview centered around fashion, males, and whether or not she was married. Perhaps next interview, she would play coy and take the microphone, ask the interviewer the questions she wanted to be asked. No one would ever expect that. Thankfully, the interview lasted less than ten minutes, just enough soundbites to be exploited by a dozen agencies.

They returned Mímihn upstairs to the waiting rooms. The *aghát* hadn't finished their debriefing.

Aila sighed. Being at the palace was nice, and diplomatic nonsense was expected, but she hadn't traveled four days for it. All she wanted was to get to Tokh's, claim the beautiful room she'd stayed in last time, breathe the sea air and relax, and hold Mímihn's baby. "How much longer do you think it will take?"

"As long as needed," Tokh said. "They will receive physical exams, as no one in the Union is qualified to attend to their health. They will submit their reports as to their activities, and be given an itinerary of training they must update while they are here. They are no happier about their delays than you. But come. There is a more important interview you have been requested for, one that will have greater meaning internally." He headed back to the lifts.

They came to a door labeled only with a number. Inside was another small reception room. "You have announced an intention to marry a Kerasi officer," Tokh said. "The Ministries wish a deeper interview, as that situation presents difficulties. I will wait here until you are finished."

Aila's wariness returned. Tokh hadn't mentioned it until now, therefore he didn't wish to discuss it with her, so he was hesitating, which wasn't a good sign. He didn't approve. She stepped back. "I don't want to. Please don't leave me here. I don't even know where I am."

Tokh tapped the door and opened it. The room was sparse, a table, several chairs, some recording equipment, camera ports high on the walls. Two guards stood by; a recording technician sat by the equipment, and looming tall in the center was that Director of Union-Kerasi Relations from the last interview, General Trannor, not only in his well-decorated brown uniform but with a hip-length red cape like some overblown superhero. Nothing said upper castes like a cape, and upper caste meant power and intimidation. Red was the signature color of the *fáhganid* caste. Emperor Nadigh had declared the caste null and void, but a year was too short for such a huge change. All three upper castes resented it, and pretended nothing had changed. Aila's mistreatment of the previous year had been at the hands of a *fáhganid*, and her distrust of them made Mátokhan look like her best friend.

Tokh bowed to Trannor. "Aila Perrin, as requested."

"Thank you, Tokh. You are dismissed."

Tokh paused. "She is my recognized daughter. I do have right to witness."

Trannor straightened up, the dark eyes under his single eyebrow sharp and accusing, as if Tokh had just insulted his mother. "You were not requested. It is your right, but I will tolerate no interference, Tokh. For each word spoken, I will stripe you. Is that understood?"

Tokh bowed slowly. "Without fail, General."

"Clear him."

Aila jumped as the two guards all but leaped at Tokh, frisking him while Tokh held his hands high and allowed it. As expected, all his weapons were in security, but it still wasn't right. No one made Tokh powerless. No one.

Trannor pulled a chair to the center of the room. As Aila remembered, his Union Standard was better than Tokh's. "Please sit, Councillady. As you were told this morning, I am Director Trannor. It's my job to find out what reasons you have for wishing to marry into Kerasi society, thus becoming a Kerasi citizen. Our worlds have only the very beginnings of treaties; although we're working toward goals, we remain hostile to each other. Why would you wish to marry Masákh gha Lil, an enemy of your people?"

Aila took the chair. Trannor parked his hip on the edge of the table before her, commanding and at ease versus her anxiety. "I've worked with him for six years inside Union lines. We pleased each other, and discovered that our hearts had bonded."

"Why did your government tell you marry him?"

Aila frowned. "My government didn't ask me to marry him. Masákh asked me to be his wife. I agreed."

"That was not my question. I asked why."

Aila's confusion deepened. "I don't understand the question. They didn't ask me to. They didn't know of the arrangement at the time."

"Why, is the question."

Aila shook her head. "I'm sorry, your question doesn't make sense to me. You do mean the word *ghea*?"

"*Sukh. Ghea.*"

"Why do they allow it? Because it's my choice whom to marry. My government can't order me to marry or not marry anyone, unless they're of too young an age or too close a relation. Those are the only forbidden terms of marriage, the same as on Kerasím."

"Masákh gha Lil beds you."

"That's not open for discussion."

"All information is open to me. The purpose of this interview is to find truths, so we do not need to resort to stronger measures. You do not wish to visit the basement level. The information isn't secret. Answer the question." Trannor was icy cold. When Tokh had interrogated Aila all those years ago, he had been calm and patient, repeating things over and over as if she were addled and needed to be taught to answer. He was never confrontational, unless Aila had done something wrong. Trannor seemed out for blood. He knew the answer; this was a matter of controlling her.

Aila glared at him, but after several moments dropped her eyes and admitted, "Yes."

"As a Kerasi or as a Human?"

Enough. Aila snapped back. "Irrelevant! That is none of your business!"

Trannor's eyes bored into her until they hurt. "You will discuss what I tell you to discuss."

25

Anger rose up, and with it the foolishness that Aila knew was very dangerous. She'd stood up to Tokh, she'd stood up the *fáhganid Banukh*, she'd stood up to a whole slew of Union interrogators. Nope. She wouldn't fold this time, either. Certainly not in front of Tokh.

"Or what? You'll escort me downstairs to visit with Colonel Kassán? Kassán and I go way back. I can't tell you how many times he's messed with my head; you'd have to ask General Tokh. Been there, done that, doesn't scare me." She did something monstrously rude to a Kerasi male; she turned her chair around until her back was to him.

Aila didn't see the fury cross his face, but she heard his heels against the flooring, click-click, as he stepped forward and spun her chair around again on one leg, his face inches from hers. Aila couldn't help the small shriek that escaped as she clutched the chair to keep from falling. She twisted her head sideways to dodge a potential blow.

Trannor's words were slow and threatening. "I ask questions. You give correct answers. Do you understand?"

Aila couldn't keep the tremor out of her voice. "Yes."

"Yes, Director-General."

"Yes, Director-General."

Trannor straightened and removed an incentive stick from its holder on his belt. He extended it to its full length, three or four feet of thin telescoping metal rod, and laid it on the table for her to see.

"Beat me if you will. I will not answer questions about my bedding practices."

"How long have you been working to undermine Kerasi progress?"

Aila's face screwed up in confusion. "What? I've never worked to undermine Kerasi progress! I've done everything I possibly can to promote it! I just finished a damned interview for the ComNet to promote your progress!" The anger welled up again, and she jumped to her feet. It was impossible to look Trannor in the eye – he was probably ten inches taller – but she stared upwards at him anyway. "I have been your prisoner. I have studied your culture and language under force. I've fought to free your men from prison, I've fought to make the Emperor's wants known, I've fought for your treaties, I killed my own superior to save a Kerasi national despite having been brutalized and mistreated by your people. I've swayed your people and fought for your ideals while everyone told me I didn't know what I was doing.

You use my face in your advertising without paying me a *harim*. My belief in your cause and my love for Masákh has destroyed my family and made me suspect in my government. And you want to deny my loyalty? Go *push* your mother. This interview is concluded."

She stood and headed for the door. Trannor wasn't going to get the satisfaction of seeing her cry. With two loud thumps of boots and the ringing of metal, the guards stepped sideways to block the door, swords drawn and crossed. Nothing short of multiple lightning strikes was going to get her out of that room.

"Aila!" slipped from Tokh's lips, soft and unbid, possibly a warning, possibly a reprimand.

Both Aila and Trannor turned their heads to him, but the word held sway, breaking the tension of the moment.

If Trannor had scared her before, the look on his face at her name almost made Aila believe in evil incarnate. "I did not lie. Before me. And remove your shirt; uniforms should not be wasted due to poor judgment."

To Aila's disbelief, Tokh moved to the center of the room, unfastening his shirt. Aila had never seen him shirtless. He was well over his weight limit, with a sizable stomach Aila didn't find attractive, and it looked worse uncovered. His skin was bronze, light brown with a golden glow, covered with numerous brown scars from battles fought and won. Only the sparsest of hair speckled his chest, both black and gray; Aila had yet to see a Kerasi with extreme body hair, and quantity seemed to be a factor of age.

Trannor looked down his nose. "Tokh, you're farther gone than I thought. You have one month to improve, or you will be teaching fitness to recruits until you do. One word, one stroke." He reached for his incentive stick. The recording technician kept his eyes on his equipment.

"Don't you hit him," Aila warned.

"I allowed him to stay on the rule of one stroke for every word spoken. My word is law."

"No one hits General Tokh. Not even you." Aila stepped up to him. "As a Union dignitary, I strongly suggest you change your mind and show me just how far Kerasím's come in the quest to decrease violence."

Trannor lifted the incentive stick from the table. "The Union does not dictate military law."

Aila knew, under any and all circumstances, gender, caste, and rank, she could not touch Trannor, not even attempt it, so she slid between them to block Tokh. "No one hits General Tokh. You should be ashamed."

Trannor's face didn't twitch a muscle, cold blank space like an empty billboard. "Then I shall stripe you instead."

"You do that," Aila said. She turned so her back was to him. "Go ahead and stripe me. Leave marks so the Union will see them and ask what caused them, and I can say 'This is what the Government of Kerasím did to me when I refused to answer stupid questions that made no sense.' See what kind of mess that starts. The only thing that's kept them from pulling out of negotiations is me, because despite it all, I still see good in your world, and I think that can be fostered if the stupidity is weaned out. Because I... OW!"

Aila gave a shriek as the incentive stick connected with her backside. "OW! You sonofa-! Ow!" The thin rod cracked against her skin, a shock in itself before the pain caught up and blossomed across her buttocks, stinging with fury. A simple but very effective weapon.

Trannor collapsed the incentive stick and tossed it on the table. "One word, one stroke. That was my promise. Is she always this difficult, Tokh? You may cover that gut."

Tokh shrugged his shirt back on. "She's been confrontational since the first day. Only Major Masákh has been able to control her. She doesn't respond well to force."

Trannor nodded. "I've had enough of Union disrespect. Dismissed."

Tokh finished fastening his shirt, tucked it in, and shoved Aila out the door. She made it ten feet or so before twisting away and leaning against the wall of the hallway.

She grimaced and wiped her eyes. "Ow! Goddamn! Ow! That freaking hurt!" She shoved a hand down the waistband of her skirt and touched the spot. When she pulled her hand out, there was a smear of blood on her fingers. She waved it under Tokh's nose. "Son of a bitch. He broke the skin. Look at that! I'm bleeding. Do you know..."

Tokh seized her by the shoulder and pushed her down the corridor. They entered a door, Aila too absorbed in self-pity and swearing to bother looking for labels. It was a large room, ornate and masculine, with numerous sofas, tables, and cabinets. Tokh waved a finger to the waiting *nhásarwharl* servant and he left the room, leaving them alone.

"Where are we? What room is this?"

Tokh's anger simmered just below the surface, visible in his jaw and the way he began to pace. "A lounge for Senators. What were you thinking? You think I cannot take a single stroke? That I have not taken far worse? Do you know who General Trannor is?"

"Director of Union-Kerasi Relations."

"He is my direct superior! You have insulted me before my superior! Am I so weak you think I need the defense of a female?"

Aila's feathers ruffled, putting self-pity on the backburner for the moment. "Of course not. I saw no need for him to hit you. That was totally out of line."

Tokh's com unit buzzed and he answered it, mumbling softly in fast Kerasi while he paced before the grand windows at the end of the room; Aila couldn't make out a single word. After a minute he ended the call. "There is a washroom behind that door. You may examine your wounds there. Do not expect me to assist."

"I wouldn't ask."

Aila had finished patting the wound with cold water – a minor welt with a small split at the point of impact – and returned to the room when the door opened and Trannor walked in. She moved to the far side of the room.

He flapped the superhero cape before sitting himself on a sofa. "Have you finished your outburst yet, enough to have thoughtful discussion? Here. I promise not to strike your precious General again." Trannor removed his incentive stick, collapsed, and held it out to Aila. "Take it as a promise. Tokh, fill my hand with something better."

The General rushed to an elaborate display of fancy bottles and glassware, pouring a glass of bright red liquid from a square bottle. He handed Trannor the glass as Aila accepted the incentive stick.

Trannor sipped it. "Come. Sit. You may share my bench. I won't touch you. Let us discuss business without the benefit of recording devices. You are a fiery one, it's true. Not once have I seen an officer of any rank or caste jump to spare his commander from punishment, yet you moved without thought. Recklessness, or loyalty?"

Aila eyed him with open distrust. "No one hits General Tokh. Not you or anyone else."

"Of course I can. I am his superior. He reports to me. He fails, I discipline him. I could strike him now on a whim but you have my correction stick. So loyalty it is."

Trannor's whole demeanor had changed, stuffy and elite but much more genial and friendly. Aila wasn't buying it for a second. She made her face as blank as a Kerasi. "How long were you behind Union lines? How far in did you go?"

Trannor lost his smile. "That's a dangerous accusation."

"Not an accusation," Aila insisted. "Fact. All I'm asking is how long, and where."

"Why do you say that?"

"Because Tokh is quite fluent in Union Standard, and I know he was on Kye. You're even better. You don't get that by listening to broadcasts and news reports."

Trannor drew in a long breath and let it wear itself out. He put his glass down on a small table and sat with his hands together before his face. Aila stayed silent. Sometimes it took a while for a Kerasi to figure out what they could and could not say.

"The information is old, and much of it has been declassified, or at least not as strict. If I answer that, you must swear to answer a question in return, without temper."

"What question?"

The patronizing smile returned. "*Gah.* That you won't know until I'm finished. Yes or no?"

"As long as it's not about my bedding habits, I agree."

Trannor bent his head. "Accepted. When you came into Kerasi hands, where were you?"

Aila thought back. "I was on Fornax, then taken to Kye."

Trannor gave a nod. "The compound on Kye didn't appear overnight. Many of us worked years to bring it about. I was one of them. I was on Kye before Tokh was chosen, and that was ten years before it occurred. I've been in charge of three divisions of the project, including Kye, since its inception."

It was Aila's turn to be quiet. There was so much to think about – Kerasi living openly in Union space for more than ten years.

Unbelievable. And yet so peaceful nothing ever raised a flag. Was that good or bad? "So Tokh answered to you all that time?"

"Once accepted to the program, Tokh answered to me. You were not our target, but I was the one who told him to proceed anyway. I was the one who ordered you not be harmed. I was the one who approved punishment. Tokh merely carried out my orders."

Aila's head snapped around to Tokh. "That's true?"

Tokh nodded. "I was not allowed to use physical discipline without prior approval. I explained to you I was following orders. The orders were Trannor's."

Who's worse? The one who orders torture, or the one who carries it out? "I don't know which of you to hate more. I thought the orders came from the Emperor?"

"The project was conceived of by the Emperor. Twelve units were planned; eleven made it to completion. One succeeded. That, with great thanks to Tokh, was mine."

"Who did you answer to?" Aila dared. It would have been nice to know the puppeteers six years ago.

Trannor stared at her as if she were prying beyond politeness. "I answered to the *thósikh* in charge of coordinating the plan."

Aila scrunched her face while she followed the trail in her head. Tokh, a *dihnarwharl* at the time, answered to Trannor, a *fáhganid*, who answered to a *thósikh*, but the only *thósikh* was the Emperor or his immediate successor - The pieces clicked into place. Emperor Nághtas made the plan, his son Nadigh – now Emperor Nadigh – carried it out.

"I see. That's why you're chummy with Nadigh."

Trannor bored his penetrating stare again. "Why would you say that?"

Aila couldn't stop her eye roll. "Anyone could see it last year when we were here."

Trannor reached for his drink. "Now you must answer my question. You marry Masákh gha Lil. An exceptional officer. As loyal to Tokh as you. Don't make a lie; lovers share secrets they would never share elsewhere, no matter how many oaths they have sworn. That is what passion does, loosens tongues, which is why a good consort can be a powerful weapon. What is to keep you from telling the Union things half-understood and best left unsaid? What is to stop him from demanding secrets from you that might put you in jeopardy?"

Aila flashed a nervous smile. "That's a valid question, isn't it. The one everyone seems to be worried about. There's only one problem with it, which I can't get anyone to understand. You assign me far too much power in the Union. If you doubt my word, call Ross Halian right now, as we sit, and ask him the same thing. I'm nothing in the Union. I have no power – less now than I did six years ago. I'm seen as nothing but a... a... cadet granted a seat on the Royal Senate. I anger people because I've been given a rank without working for it. I'm a member of the council only because they couldn't deny my knowledge and experience, something they didn't have at the time. Otherwise, I have no certification, no education to let me have the position. I have no political ties. I'm a 'mascot.' Do you know what that is?"

Trannor and Tokh both shook their heads. "It's a symbol of something greater. If the emblem of your sports team – your *rahl*-ball team," she said, referring to something they'd understand, "is a snarling *ghoosh*, then I am that *ghoosh*. People walk past me and pat me on the head and say 'Oh look! The team *ghoosh*! It's not a part of the team, but it makes a wonderful face to cheer people on.'" Understanding hit the men, and they nodded.

"I'm hated for what I am. *Hated.* Those with experience and training see me as someone who has no idea what they're doing, even when I know more than they do. There are those who don't trust me because I've been too long in Kerasi hands. There are those who think I'm crazy for defending Kerasím. They worry I'm being manipulated. No one – bloody no one – is going to tell me any secrets. I have no power, and no supervisor with power. People are angry that I was kidnapped again last year and it cost the government money to rescue me. They see me as a liability, not an asset. My own mother won't speak to me. If I told them a secret, no one would believe me. You built me for the task, but the method destroyed any chance of power, because my world doesn't see me that way."

"Yet you manage to do the job," Trannor said. "That shows great ability."

"Only because the Kerasi demand it. I'm your mascot even more than the Union's. My face adorns your ComNet screens; my face smiles out from store windows wearing clothing I have purchased. My face decorates your political ads, urging females to take up learning and males to see their wives as partners of their household, not servants.

The only difference is that Kerasím is more welcoming. My answers won't change, even if you send me to Colonel Kassán."

"Kassán is busy with other tasks," Trannor said. "And if you were worth some of that effort, you would know it is forbidden."

"Forbidden?"

"The second signed treaty forbids use of memory investigational equipment on Union personnel. So far we have honored that bargain."

"Oh. I knew there was a second treaty, but I must have missed that section."

"Then you have work to do. I will expect you to know it next time we meet." Trannor's com unit went off. He glanced at a message, then activated it. He didn't bother to move from the sofa. *"Vesbar."* He listened for well over a minute. *"Zooshkama. Soyavoh."*

Whatever he'd been waiting for, the report was excellent.

Trannor stood up. "I am finished. Thank you, Tokh, for the hospitality." He held his hand out to Aila; she returned his incentive stick. "I will go over the rest of the information and give His Excellency my full report, which will be favorable. Congratulations, Councillady, on your choice of husband."

"Thank you, Director-General."

"I meant what I said about fitness, Tokh."

"I will begin today," Tokh swore. The three of them set off on a ridiculous round of bowing, until Trannor left.

"Let me summon my men and retrieve my wife," Tokh said, reaching for his com. "Get us home."

Five

Tokh's home stood regal and proud, halfway down the exclusive Imahlva cliffside of *Chuhri Terat Hasihl*, which translated roughly to Beautiful View Street. The street lived up to its name, overlooking the long inlet of the Aretvohs Sea. The view faced west, and although the opposite shore was visible just three miles away, it lent for some glorious sunsets reflected off the green water.

Entering Tokh's house felt as if she'd never left. Zhenihda, Tokh's first-wife, bowed in greeting first to Tokh, then to the four *aghát* – Ráhnif had accompanied them back to the estate, then at last to Aila.

Aila knew better than to grab Zhenihda; she was old-school conservative and a bit cantankerous, her sharp eyes taking in every person, every movement, and judging them with suspicion, but Mímihn claimed she had mellowed and almost never picked at her anymore.

"Great Lady Zhenihda, thank you for letting me return. You honor me."

Zhenihda looked down her thin arched nose, and an actual smile broke out, small but sincere. She spoke haltingly. "Ahlo, Ai-la Pehrrin. I ham vehrry khappy to see you. Uel-khome tu mai khome."

Aila felt her jaw drop, and her stare caused Mímihn to giggle. "You – you speak Union now? Zhenihda! I am so honored!" She grabbed Zhenihda's hand and squeezed it.

Zhenihda; stuffy, sharp, caustic Zhenihda beamed with pride, and she bowed. "Tokh say I learn. Little much. Laydies verry *kéro*."

Aila frowned and turned to Masákh for translation.

"To be brown is to be jealous," Masákh said. "To have so much emotion the face turns brown."

"That makes sense. I am very happy for you," she said to Zhenihda, slow and overenunciated. Zhenihda bowed, pleased to understand.

Footsteps pounded down the stairs and a blur of brown hair sped toward Aila. It stopped just long enough to give a formal bow, then sprang and hugged her. "Great Lady Aila! I ham so khappy to see you a-gain! Welcome back to Imahlva!"

Aila hugged Kesseh, Tokh's only biological daughter, just as hard. "You speak so beautifully!"

Kesseh grinned. She wore a frilly blue dress and her hair was done up pretty, but Aila got the feeling it was for the benefit of the company and not from choice. "Father makes Faelihn and me learn. I have nine years now. When I am a laydy, I can speak like you. Jora is at school now. He has more lessons, and he speaks good."

"Joralan will be more than a year ahead next year, because I insist he speak at home," Tokh explained. Joralan was Tokh's third son, now twelve and preparing to enter the military academy later in the year. "He is the only one of his school to have met a Union person."

"You're a visionary, General," Aila said with respect. "They will be guaranteed employment the day they graduate. They will always be in high demand."

"That is my goal."

"Khome! See!" Mímihn said, and led the way up the stairs with Kesseh bounding after.

Aila rushed behind her, eager to unpack gifts that she'd brought for everyone. The joy, the rooms, the people, the friendships - everything was exactly as it had been.

She'd come home.

Dinner lasted hours, old friends who hadn't seen each other in a year catching up, men on one end of the table and women at the other. It was near midnight by the time Aila collapsed in her room, drained by time changes and travel. She snuggled close to Masákh in the bed, nose to nose, petting his goatee. He held her, but made no other move.

"You were so quiet tonight. That's not like you. You're always at your loudest when you're with your team. You're not still mad at me, are you?"

"No," he said quickly. "Mátokhan was kind enough to listen to reason, and dropped his request for punishment. I owe him a favor for that, I'm certain."

"Did your debriefing go all right?"

"Yes. My health is perfect, despite eating Union foods. My paperwork was submitted, and I will be called to discuss it within four days. I was given my training update schedule."

Aila tipped her head up. "Did they grill you on why you wanted to marry me?"

Masákh sighed as if the question brought up a bad memory. "Yes. The issue was discussed privately."

"Who did it? Was it that General Trannor, the head of Union Relations? He's a real psycho son of a bitch, let me tell you. I hope you never have to deal with him."

"I spoke with Grand Revered Minister Nemutar and General Five Whemarg. They were quite thorough."

Aila's forehead frowned and she sat up on an elbow. "But they said it was okay, right? I mean, they've got two more years to get used to it, but they said yes, right?"

Masákh flashed a brief smile. Aila knew it was truth, but not a comfortable one. He kissed her above her nose and pushed her back down, but still made no attempt at anything further. Even though the pressures were now gone. Even though Mátokhan had publicly taken her off the hook. "Yes. I have official permission."

Aila kissed his jaw. "Don't you want to maybe fool around, then? Now that you have government approval?"

His smile was much broader this time, much more himself as he settled down into his pillow. "Not yet. I will wait for sunup. I will finish out the year the same way I will start the new one: by making you scream with pleasure."

Aila poked his chest with her finger. "You better, Mister."

Six

When Tokh mentioned a New Year's celebration, Aila had a picture in her head of a group of friends gathered around the table for a festive dinner, maybe music in the background, people talking and laughing, children playing games, and some sort of official clock counting down the calendar change on a viewscreen with everyone toasting a new beginning. That's generally what happened around the Union. Obviously every world had a different New Year and different customs, but that was pretty universal, except on Korulan, where the New Year was treated with suspicion because they believed that the resetting of the calendar could reset good fortune, too. The Korulans stayed inside with doors and windows shut tight, fasted, weren't supposed to speak until after sunset, and prayed for the coming year. Korulan was just weird.

Aila dressed and opened her door to a flurry of activity. The wives as well as Shanohr the housemaid were putting final touches on the spotlessness of the house. Outside, Thrit the handyman was stringing party lights and hanging various decorations across the courtyard. Mímihn, with her weak eyes partially restored after three years of blindness, was glued to her lap screen, confirming orders. It was a high holiday, second only to Emperor's Birthday, and the servants would have the evening off; Zheníhda had arranged for catering. Masákh was already up and carrying out tasks for General Tokh. Aila rushed to gulp a handful of breakfast and help.

"Here," Mímihn said, handing her baby Thoren. "He just woke up. Play with him, so I can work."

Aila heart jumped. "I would love to!"

"I can watch him!" Kesseh said, reaching for him. "*Ama* lets me play with him all the time."

"You have tasks to do," Mímihn warned. "You and Faelihn will play with him later."

37

Guests began to arrive before the last of the lunch dishes were put away. Tokh's son Kitras, a captain in the army, had two days' leave, and he and his wife Dalo and their three children appeared, people Aila also considered good friends. Faelihn was a little darker and a little taller than Kesseh, but just as adept at Union speech. Faelihn was technically Kesseh's niece, but with just five months difference between them, they were much more like sisters. Lanag was eleven, and his baby brother Niboh just two and obsessed with climbing the grand staircase. A man arrived with two women who were well over forty. He was taller and thinner than Tokh but still resembled him: he was Tokh's father-brother Kaloh, ten years older. Aila knew only of Tokh's current family; never for an instant had she wondered about parents or siblings, and she stared in awe. She pulled Mímihn aside at the first opportunity.

"Oh yes," Mímihn said easily. "His father died just a few months ago, but his mother is still living. He has two older brothers from his father's first-wife, and a younger sister and brother from his mother. Kaloh is the only one who could make it here this year."

"His mother does not travel?"

Mímihn laughed, but it wasn't a sound of pleasure. "*Gah, ka!* She was here for several weeks after his father died. If she stayed another day, Nihda would have killed her, and I would have brought her the weapon. Her head has gone to the spirits before her body, and she is most difficult."

Aila had enough trouble with straight speech; idioms were much harder. "Her mind is gone because she is old?"

Mímihn's cheerful face stayed curled in a frown. "*Sukh.* She is also mean from the heart, but Nihda says she has always been like that."

Aila never paid much attention to gossip – something Masákh yelled at her for, for gossip often provided important information not otherwise leaked – but she resolved to stay nearer to the older women, and hope they broke into discussion of Tokh's mother.

It still amazed Aila that terrifying General Tokh had wives, children, and grandchildren. Tokh having a mother – obviously he must have had one – was even weirder.

Tokh's two final *aghát*, Tótoghar and Ghírandar, arrived amid a free for all of backslapping. Tokh's high officers, Colonel Dahven and

Colonel Khaním and their wives, Major Khagán and his wife and son, Colonel Kassán, Justice Whateghan, a rotund, high-ranking former *fáhganid* of bilious complexion who lived in the house just above them, and his wives Arshmuhn and Gahna. *Dahneg* Oghil and his wife and son from one house below and one over on the cliff, arrived soon after. Oghil was the statistical analyst for the Imahlva city governing council, the only reason he'd managed to gain a house on the cliffside of the city, even if it was just five small rooms end to end and accessible only by a flight of stairs and walkway. Gilmaneg, the neighborhood busybody across the street and one up, was having his own drunken revelry, relieving Tokh of the dishonor of not inviting him. His loud music drifted down the street and into Tokh's yard.

Aila had been to a few diplomatic gatherings on Kerasím: the guest lists had been carefully screened, castes had been allowed to mingle and both sexes had been allowed, but separate, under the sharp eyes of the imperial guards. To her surprise, this, a relaxed party among old friends, was not much different. With the servants gone for the night, almost everyone was of the same caste or only one apart, save the *aghát*, who, by their nature, functioned outside of caste laws. The front courtyard had been swept and arranged with two circles of chairs on opposite sides, one for the men and one for the women. Thrit's lights glowed overhead, along with a dozen flaming torches along the cliff wall. Buntings of red and gold, imperial colors, hung from the balconies and over the side of the stone wall at the end of the courtyard, overlooking the cliff and houses and inlet far below. Music played from speakers hidden around the courtyard, not the growling hot-tempo'd popular music heard on broadcasts but something melodic; more upbeat than the somber wailing tunes played when Emperor Nághtas died but pleasant for alien music. Fancy cloths draped the tables, and shimmering gold streamers reflected all the lights, dancing to the music in the breezes that blew up from the ocean below. Tall potted bushes had been dragged from the side patio and placed as decorations, draped in twinkling colored lights like surrogate Christmas trees. It was a scene that would be perfectly at home anywhere in the Union.

There was only one serving arrangement for all, on long tables across the front of the house; without word the wives filled plates for the husbands and carried them over, then the women served the single men, then the children, and only then the wives and women. Zheníhda and Mímihn served Judge Wahtegahn and his wives, as they were higher-caste and could not be expected to wait on themselves. Aila glanced at Masákh, but he stared back with his two eyebrows raised: he expected her to serve him as wife.

Aila sighed and grabbed a plate. Their arrangement said when on Kerasím she was supposed to follow Kerasi rules; inside the Union, Masákh had to follow hers. Fair was fair, even if she didn't agree with their customs. She got her own food at last, and went to sit with the ladies.

Mímihn was perhaps her best friend anywhere at the moment, alongside Thayer, her best friend inside the Union. Aila also considered Dalo a good friend from her last visit. She'd met Judge Wahtegahn's wives on her last visit, too. Arshmuhn was a good ten years older than Zheníhda and eighty pounds heavier, while Gahna was perhaps thirty years younger than Arshmuhn, two generations by Kerasi standards, but they had made their peace many years before. Aila headed to sit with Mímihn and the younger women, but the older crowd called to her.

"*Ka! Ka! Great Lady Aila Pehrrin!* Come sit with us! Please, give us your honor!"

Aila glanced at the back of Masákh's head, wishing she could sit with the men and their far more important conversations, but she spun and smiled at the older ladies. Tokh's sisters in law had not met the stranger from the land of the enemy, the Union female whose face had sold more clothing than any Kerasi superstar; the Union female not afraid to greet every caste the same. Zheníhda dropped her sharp gaze and bent her head with a polite smile, thanking her silently for doing the right thing.

As much as Aila enjoyed the party, it was difficult, too. The wives didn't speak Union, and Aila's grasp of fast conversations by many individuals was less than stellar. Too many speakers, too much background noise and it was hard to concentrate on the words.

"Masákh, please come here," she called yet again.

He came back, but the look on his face said she'd crossed a line. His words were short but still polite. "It is inappropriate for you to keep interrupting me."

40

"I don't understand what Gahna is saying. I need help," she said, but her temper got the better of her. "If any of you truly practiced what you're supposed to be preaching, we'd all be sitting together and I'd have eight translators available without effort. Therefore, blame Tokh for not integrating everyone like the Emperor says you should."

Masákh straightened taller, and Aila knew she'd hit a fact he hadn't considered. That was two this trip! Either he was completely distracted by something, or she was getting better at arguing.

"Revered Lady Wahtegahn wishes to know which of the Fortunes you favor."

"Please tell her I do not favor any particular Fortune as of yet, but I would gladly make an offering to the Mother fortune if she will make my mother a calmer, happier person."

Masákh translated her words, and the ladies all laughed. "I suggest you find easier topics to discuss or accept the fact you will not understand all of what is said." He didn't even apologize, just spun on those hard *aghát* boot heels and went back to the men.

Faelihn and Kesseh ran up before Aila could get too angry. Kesseh bowed and tried her very best Union. "Grrreat Laydy Ailah, will yu teach us to dance like Yun-yon laydies?"

One distraction was as good as another. She smiled back. "Yes, I can."

As midnight approached, the party moved inside around the giant wallscreen in the great room for the official palace broadcast. Cameras had been set up in the palace's private Temple of the Fortunes, where the ancient Forecaster for the coming year sat in a special alcove. A carved stone disk whose age was debated to be somewhere between seven and eleven hundred years old, its face was divided into ten sections, one for each month, each corresponding to a specific Fortune. There was a section for honoring motherhood, a Fortune for luck, marriage, fertility, one for good harvest, for charity, battle, frugality, and more. This year had been a Year of Good Harvest, and if accounts could be believed, most regions had reported good crop yields.

Official music blared and Emperor Nadigh appeared in full ceremonial attire, a glimmering gold suit with white *gallor*-fur trim, and his ancient metal ringlet on his head. He smiled at the screaming

41

crowds, raised his hands, waved, and made a good show. Tokh knew, and the rest had a good guess, that the crowd was hand-picked and pre-screened. Nadigh made very few public appearances that weren't security-assured. While the program hosts bantered back and forth, Nadigh approached the stone circle. The Master of the Temple handed him the polished stone forecaster from its official resting place with a reverent bow. Nadigh held it up and gave a short speech on the tradition, the previous year, and his hopes for the coming year. When he finished, he dropped it down onto the circle with a twist. It spun and slammed its way around the circle, spun into the section for charity, then slowed in the section for frugality, a dire portend signifying a bad year of foul weather, bad crops, poor economics, and a bad time to be spending money or making plans.

The videobroadcast hosts gave a collective gasp. *"Ka! Ka! Ka! Everyone, blow to roll it out of there!"*

With its last inertia, the forecaster made a final flip and rested in the section for marriage.

Nadigh raised his hands to the crowd. "The Fortunes have spoken. The coming year will be a blessed year for those wishing to marry. Following tradition, all fees for registering new marriages will be waived. May the Fortunes bless everyone, and may this year's marriages be long and happy ones." He waved once more to the crowd, then departed, leaving the commentators to prattle on about whether the Emperor would take a seventh wife.

Mímihn gave a squeal and hugged Aila. "A year for marriage! That's Fortune telling you to marry Masákh!" The gathered ladies were quick to agree.

Aila smiled and shook her head. *"Ka.* I promised *Ama* two more years. I will marry when I am 21."

Mímihn squeezed her hands. "You have the whole year to think about it. You don't know what the Fortunes will say two years from now. The same blessing two years in a row doesn't happen often."

"Living with him is enough blessing for me."

Oghil and his family left, as did Judge Wahtegahn and his wives. The remainder of the party flowed back outside, where the chairs were pulled over to face the inlet. Downstream at the harbor, and every so many towns up and down the inlet, fireworks were sent up from barges. Thrit had gone out for the evening and come back; he sat up on the aircraft landing pad with Shanohr and three other servants from the street, drinking their own supply of *lunahl* and *muhr* and watching the same spectacle.

"A lovely evening, General," Colonel Dahven said. None of the men was feeling much pain; Colonel Khaním snored readily from his chair, oblivious to the booms and crackles of the fireworks, and Colonel Khagán wasn't far behind. "May our year be filled with moments such as this. May all the artillery we hear be from celebrations."

Mátokhan's voice rose in song deep against the night. Tokh joined him, Colonel Dahven, three or four of the officers, and most of the wives. Khaním gave a great snort and mumbled the last two lines without really knowing what was going on.

Happy New Year to you and yours
A thousand blessings on your head
May your table always keep you fed
Warm and soft to be your bed.
May you never lack a female's care,
May your pocket never be left bare.
Emperor's blessings and cheer to you here,
May we live to do it again next year.

Mímihn had been usually quiet, sitting in her chair. She couldn't see the intracasies of the fireworks, just occasional bursts of color against the black. She didn't like nightfall or being outside in the dark; it reminded her too much of being blind, and if she wasn't with Tokh, she slept with a light on, so if she woke she knew she could still see. The conversation drifted to silence as they watched the show.

"The more I think about it, the more I insist," Mímihn said into the silence. "This is a year for marriage. You need to marry Masákh. If you marry him in the Union, I won't get to see it. Tokh, you can marry them. Marry them right now. This can be their celebration."

Dalo had been sitting in Kitras's lap. "Oh you must! While we're all together! There's no better night of the year. You'll always have celebration for your anniversary."

Tokh had been dangerously close to sleep. He struggled to sit up. "I can do that."

Masákh stood up. "I am willing."

Aila's heart sank. Had no one heard a word she'd said? Masákh of all people should have known better, and she stared at him in disbelief. "How could you? You know the answer to that. I'm not. It's not that simple. Even if I said yes, and I already said I won't, I'd have to get approval from my government, as it ties a council member to a hostile government. I probably also need formal permission from your government. Does that make me an automatic citizen? Do I lose my rights as a Union citizen and become nothing more than a Kerasi wife? Will Masákh have citizenship inside the Union, or will they reserve the right to throw him out if relations go bad? All those questions must be answered before a wedding can take place, and since there has never been a Union-Kerasi wedding, there's no protocol. It'll take time to get answers. I wouldn't marry anyone without speaking to my embassy first."

Tokh rubbed his eyes. "She is correct. I would not dare without permission from the palace."

"They are aware of our intent, and have given preliminary approval," Masákh said.

"It is past time for me to find a wife as well," Mátokhan said. "I can't say I'm not well-established. If I wait much longer, I'll never find a desirable one."

Haghíde swirled the drink in his hand. He'd lost count of what number it was, or even what it was. "We've all wasted too much time on duty. I dare each of you – No, let's make it a pact. All of us *aghát*. Before the year is out, we will all take a wife. The last one... *Gah*, we'll think of something. Name a child after us or such. Swear to it, Brothers."

"Agreed," Mátokhan said.

"I like that," Ghírandar said. "We could marry as a group. We'd be inviting the same friends anyway."

"I don't have anyone in mind," Tótoghar said, "but as long as I have the year, I will inquire."

Ráhnif didn't look happy. "I'm not Lieutenant-Two yet. I can't afford a good enough apartment for a wife."

"You work at the Palace," Mátokhan said. "I'm sure with everyone here, we have enough pull to get you a deal."

"*Gah*. I was barely an L-1," Tokh said. "It will work out."

44

"And we had nothing," Zheníhda reminded him. "The entire apartment could have fit in our kitchen here. You were never home."

"Did I not purchase you a house in time? Not this one," he said, waving his arm toward the estate. "The last one. How many *dihnarwharl* can say they own a house?"

Ráhnif spoke before an argument could start. "I will keep my eyes open."

Colonel Khaním laughed. "You need to keep your pants open." The men howled.

Aila's voice snapped. "I hope you have a happy year, but count me out. I told you I won't marry for two years, and that is my word."

Mímihn couldn't see in the dim light, but she turned in Aila's direction and gave her a hard look of disapproval, a rare thing for Mímihn. "We are doing something joyful, Ai-la! Why must you be a moldy cakelet?"

The group erupted in a wave of taunting and harassment. "He's drilling you into the bed, but you won't be his wife?" Colonel Dahven said. "That doesn't say much for his performance." A great howl rose up, right down to Zheníhda. Masákh shot Aila a glare that burned right through her.

Aila bit back the retort she wanted to give, more irate by the second. She stood up. "Fine! If you want my parents to disown me, I will go and contact my government right now and ask what paperwork is involved. Is that enough?" She bowed to Tokh. "Thank you, General, for a pleasant celebration. May *your* New Year be one of joy." Aila spun on her heel and stalked into the house without saying goodnight to anyone.

Masákh followed minutes after. "You were angry with Lady Tokh. That is not like you."

Aila sulked on the lounge in their room. "I said what I meant, and I meant what I said. I get screamed at enough by my mother. I'm trying so hard to keep the peace between us, and if the easiest way to do that is to wait two years to get married, then I will keep my word. I don't see what's so wrong about that. Mímihn gets all these fancy dreams in her head but she doesn't understand why they can't work. I mean, do you understand? Do you agree with me at all?"

Masákh began unloading his pockets onto the table under the wallscreen. "I would be happiest if we could settle the marriage issue soon, but I am willing to wait. I agree, keeping your mother calm is perhaps the most important thing we can do. If all she requires is time, then we should allow it." He wrapped his arms around her and kissed her neck. "We spend the majority of our time inside the Union, so it is only right we use Union rules."

She kissed his chin in return, just above his goatee. "Thank you for understanding. Your support is everything to me."

He lay back on the plush lounge, squeezing in around her. "Let us see what the governments decide, and then perhaps we can reexamine the issue."

"She might not see it otherwise," Aila said, "but my mother is not the government."

Seven

The table was full of guests at breakfast, so Aila joined the women serving the men, eating bites of her own meal between passes like the wives. Mímihn didn't say a word to her, didn't even look in her direction when Aila was in range. Never had Aila seen Mímihn lose her cheer so long.

Tokh's brother Kaloh gave a deep chuckle. "In my day, it was bad manners to refuse an offer of marriage. It showed poor breeding, and gave the female a reputation of being disagreeable. Once a refusal, always a maid, they said."

Masákh tipped his head politely, but Aila knew the patronizing tone of his smile. "Forgive me, Lord Kaloh, but Aila has not refused to marry me. She has only refused to marry me without proper approval or paperwork. Ours is a complicated situation that will take time."

"Diplomatic issues should never be rushed," Haghíde added.

Mátokhan raised his cup of *raffin* to Masákh. "If you knew her mother, you would never rush Masákh into such an arrangement sooner than he must."

Tótoghar seconded the toast. "No, you would not."

"Have you placed a call to your people?" Tokh asked.

Aila flicked away a tear before it could be seen. Masákh, brave bold Masákh, standing up for her in front of so many men who out ranked him and outcasted him, as well as his *aghát* brethren. He could so easily have made a joke, put her down, made it seem like it was her problem and he should be given sympathy, but he didn't. He defended her against ridicule before all those Kerasi. And the *aghát* backed him up. *They backed him up.* Her heart coated itself in another layer of love.

"I was waiting until after breakfast was cleared. I didn't want to leave the ladies without enough help."

Tokh stared back, immobile and unflinching as a dark night sky, the piercing stare that used to scare the daylights out of her, threatening nothing and everything possible at once, daring her to displease him. "You told Mímihn you would place the call. A promise to my wife is a promise to me. You will not eat another meal until you do."

Old fear melted any steel in her spine. Aila bowed with apology, eyes down. *"Of course, Triskaris-bo."*

Aila sat in the bedroom, personal com in her hand, but it wasn't activated. "I have no idea who to call," she told Masákh. "If I call Secretary of State Halian, he'll just about kill me, because he knows my mother will come after him. And she will find out. She always finds out. She'll go through some channel or other and start a war to stop me. Who else do I call? The legal department? The Council for Kerasi Affairs? They'll forbid it until legal thinks it through. Do I speak to the Council for Non-Union worlds and ask them the details? I want to obey, I just don't know how! You have it easy. You ask your commanding officer, he asks the proper supervisor, they get the okay from the Emperor, and you're done. We don't have one such person."

A knock on the door disrupted them. Haghíde entered.

"Forgive my interruption. I was hoping to speak with you before you placed your call." He stood stiff and uncomfortable, even though Masákh claimed him as the closest friend he had. "I am not unfamiliar with Union diplomacy, holding an office on Earth. I know Lady Tokh wishes to celebrate your marriage, but I do think caution is best. Knowing the disruption your mother can create, and knowing the power of Admiral Perrin within Union government, I fear that unless your mother will give approval, it could damage the treaties we have all worked so very hard to create. Perhaps we can return again next year, and Lady Tokh can celebrate then."

"Thank you, Haghíde," Aila said. "We've already been thinking about that. I can't even figure out who to ask for advice."

There was a silent, sad pause before Haghíde said, "If I were in the Union and wished to clarify a Kerasi law or procedure, one that was not specifically military, I would contact the Kerasi embassy inside the Union. I have done so on several occasions. Have you tried the Union embassy?"

Aila's head lifted. Masákh met her gaze. The obvious had been right at their fingertips. "Of course! Ross! Ross can give me advice without anyone else knowing about it. Why didn't I think of that! He can work both sides of the fence." Aila jumped to her feet and headed for the door. She stopped long enough to pat Haghíde on the shoulder, daring for a female. "Haghíde, if you weren't Kerasi, I'd give you the biggest damned hug right now."

He turned as she ran out the door. "I would not refuse it."

Aila bounded down the stairs and into the courtyard, where Tokh, Kitras, and the *aghát* were bidding goodbye to Colonel Khaním. Mímihn saw her; her mouth pinched up and she turned away.

Oh, get over it, Mímihn. You don't understand.

Aila waited until Tokh turned to address her. "Have you received permission?"

Aila stood firm against Tokh's glare. "I'm trying, General. I've never broached the question to my government, so I don't know procedure. It can't be solved easily. May I meet here with a representative to discuss the issue? I don't trust the airwaves. You've met the Ambassador, Ross Halian. I'll ask him my questions and he'll be able to guide me to gain the clearances with full privacy."

Tokh chewed his lip, no happier. "Very well. I grant permission. But I will expect an answer."

Aila bowed. "I'm doing my best to comply."

She sent Mr. Halian a text. *Urgent I speak with you as soon as humanly possible. Not critical, just priority.*

Not a minute later her com rang. She hit privacy even though she was alone, and held it to her ear.

"What's up?" Halian's familiar voice was serious but calm. "I can be there in forty-five minutes, thirty if I push it."

"No no. I'm fine. I didn't mean to scare you, I just didn't want you to forget to call me. I'm sorry to bother you on a holiday. I do need to speak with you in person as soon as possible regarding potential legal issues, protocol, and government things. Is it possible for you to visit me?"

"That's okay with the General?"

"Yes. I cleared it. He's aware of the situation."

Aila could hear the relief in Halian's voice. There was no immediate danger. "Okay. I will be there at one past the quarter-mark."

49

"Thank you, Mr. Halian. I'll see you then."

The craft bearing both Keranihn and Diplomatic identifications settled onto the courtyard as Tokh's craft sat on the 'pad. Ross Halian, Union Ambassador to the Kerasi Coalition, disembarked. He wore official attire to emphasize he was here on business, not a social call. Tokh, Mátokhan, and Aila met him outside.

"If you will permit me, Ambassador," Mátokhan said, and frisked Halian. Halian stood still, arms out, but carried not even a pocket knife.

Tokh tipped his head. He'd met Halian once or twice; they were on polite terms, but the trust was still formal. "My apologies. I was fooled once; I only wish to know what I am up against."

"Understandable." Halian bowed before Tokh. "General Tokh. I am honored to visit your home again. Thank you for hosting me on such a holiday. May the new year bring you nothing but good fortune."

Tokh bowed back. "May it bring greater peace between our people. She wished to discuss matters. I will not stop her."

Halian turned to Aila. She smiled and gave him a familiar hug, which he returned. Ross had been the person to rescue her from Kerasi clutches the first time, and he still kept friendly contact with her. His sandy hair was an odd color for Kerasím, but his skin was tanned from the Kerasi suns and he'd grown out a shaped section of beard to make a passable chinhank. He looked more Kerasi than the *aghát* did. "Thank you for coming, Mr. Halian."

"If you will come this way, my wife has prepared refreshments for you," Tokh said.

"I was hoping perhaps to take a walk with Mr. Halian first," Aila said. "Show him the beauty of the neighborhood. Walk and talk. That kind of thing."

"Is that safe?" Halian said.

"It should be," Aila said.

Tokh studied Halian, then reached for his holster and handed Halian his energy pistol. "You will not need it, but I offer it to you for her defense."

Halian accepted it with a bow. "I am honored, General."

"It is my opinion, but when I am in need of privacy to find my thoughts, I find a long walk on the shore to be most helpful, south past the docks. It is the most private place I know."

Aila frowned. His words were slow and measured. No doubt he meant something she wasn't thinking about. She gave a nod anyway.

"Perhaps we may sit together and enjoy your hospitality when I return," Halian said.

Tokh bowed. "I look forward to it."

Eight

Aila led Halian out the gate and down the steep street. There was road access to the house below Tokh's, and three houses on the other side of the street. *Dahneg* Oghil's clung to the cliff down a walkway behind another home. A heavy barrier was embedded at the turnaround at the end of the street where the road became cliff. From there, steep stairs led the rest of the way down the hillside, another hundred feet or so to the narrow beach and the waves of the inlet.

"I take it this is something you didn't want to discuss before the General?" Halian tried on the stairs.

Aila held a finger to her lips. "Isn't the weather simply lovely? I love walking the beach in the morning. By lunch it's getting too hot, and if I wait until after dinner, the sun has already set over the opposite hill, and it would be too dark by the time I got back."

Halian caught on, and they bantered meaningless gibberish down to the water and to the three docks where several of the residents had pleasure craft tied up. Aila waited until they were at least a hundred feet beyond the docks, a place where the beach sands gave way to broken rock and where the cliff rose straight upward with no houses, and parked herself on a stone slab. Little waves broke six or eight feet away, reaching her feet with the finest of sprays.

"There. If I read the General right, this place is clean. Nothing listening. I've never considered him to be paranoid, but he knows the houses and the politics better than I ever will."

"What's up?"

Aila sighed long and hard. She twisted her forehead on folded hands as if praying for strength. "Ohhh, I am in a mess of trouble. I don't even know how to approach this. I'm screwed no matter what happens, and I don't mean that in any good way. I need you as a third party, one to tell me honestly what my options are, if it's even possible, and how to deal with it if it isn't. And most of all, you must swear upside down and sideways to make sure my parents get absolutely no wind of this, until I know for certain what's going on."

"Okay," Halian said. His eyes followed a pleasure boat cruising up the inlet. "Tell me."

"You know how the Emperor declared it a year of marriage last night? Well, Mímihn got it in her head that Masákh and I should get married. Now. They wanted to do it yesterday. I claimed I had to clear it with my government. I promised, promised, promised my mother I wouldn't marry Masákh until I was done with my degree. I meant that. I don't know if it's even legal. I don't know if the palace would allow it, I don't know what the protocol would be for the Union – does that make Masákh a Union citizen? A dual-citizen? Do we have that with the Coalition? Is it then legal at home? I need a ton of guidance, here, Ross. I'm scared. I'm scared because I don't know where that leaves me – if I marry Masákh under Kerasi law, I lose my voice; he gets full control over me, and I won't allow that. I don't fear him; I live with him, I plan to marry him in a few years, it's doing it here on Kerasím first that worries me. Everyone's been very good, respecting me as a Union citizen, but that's their choice. On Kerasím, I am legally Tokh's daughter. Masákh and Tokh could be signing papers as we speak, making me very legally Masákh's wife and giving him total control over me, and there isn't a thing I can do about it while I'm here. That's Kerasi law. He can send me somewhere, lock me up, medicate me, forbid me from speaking to you, forbid me from leaving. I knew about the law last year, but I never gave it a thought until now. "

Halian cut her off with a wave of his hand. "Come back with me. Right now. Stay at the Embassy until we get some grounding on this. I don't want to have to do a third manhunt for you."

Aila pulled her feet up as a stronger wave came close. She shook her head. "No. It's just, Mímihn got everyone riled up to make it happen, and if I try to back out, I'm afraid it's going to bring down some very bad feelings between me and Tokh's family. Tell me what to do."

Ross closed his eyes and grimaced. "Shit. I have no idea. And you're right; the last person I want to find out about it is your mother. How bad are you being pressured?"

"It's heavy, but not unbearable yet."

"What does Masákh say?"

53

"He prefers to marry now, but he understands my rationale. He's the most patient out of anyone. I do trust him, Ross. He's never not listened to my wishes yet, but then, we've never been married on Kerasím before."

"Do you feel safe? Do you want to come back with me until we get some answers? Masákh can stay with you, but under Union law."

Aila thought about it. "No. I trust them. It's just kind of tense right now. You know how the Kerasi see honor and insult."

"Okay. Let me take the heat for you. I'll talk to my contacts at the palace and find out what the legality is. I'll put in a call to Bindai the second I get back to Keranihn. I need at least 48 hours to put it all together. If they want to be angry, let them be angry at me. Play innocent. Tell them we're requesting permission, but you can't move until we get word. I'll make sure your parents are not to be informed at all about the inquiry. Can you hang on a couple of days?"

"Yeah, I think so, as long as they know it's not my decision."

"Okay. Let's go talk to Tokh."

Downhill was easy; walking upward eight hundred feet, some of it almost vertical, took a half hour. Aila let them into the house. Masákh entered the room, anxious for news, and Tokh left his office to greet them.

Halian handed the weapon back. "Thank you, General. It was a most peaceful walk. You live in a lovely community."

"Did you make progress on what you wished to discuss?" Tokh asked Aila.

"We did, General."

Halian stared briefly at Masákh, then focused on Tokh. "I will ask permissions from the Union the moment I get back to Keranihn, but be aware: the issue is no longer in Aila's hands. Permission and approval is now the business of the Union government, just as much as it is your duty to clear permission from the Palace. Is that understood? We are aware of the situation, and you will agree to abide by Union law regarding this matter or I will consider the Councilmember to be under threat and remove her immediately. I won't hear of Aila suffering disapproval for permissions she cannot give. I would hope to have a reply within two days."

Masákh frowned. "No threat to Aila has ever been implied. I have taken great care to respect Union law since the beginning."

Halian bowed to him. "Aila insists everyone has been most honorable. I wish to make certain there are no misunderstandings."

Tokh bent his head, but Aila could tell he felt a sting. "Very well. We will wait for the diplomats to make their decisions. Until then, come. We can discuss other matters." He led Halian to his office and left Aila in the dining room, out of the conversation.

Aila watched them go with a snort as Masákh slipped his hand into hers. *Men.* Kerasím had a long, long way to go.

The holiday wound down. Kitras returned to duty, and Dalo and the children returned to their home on the other side of town. Tokh's officers left, Ráhnif returned to the palace, and Ghírandar returned to his current assignment on a lower council. Tótoghar hung around as Tokh's officer of the week, carrying out orders as needed. Masákh, Haghíde, and Mátokhan were due back in Keranihn.

Aila knew better than to hang on Masákh in public, so she clung to him half-dressed in their room. "You can't leave me here! I've never been alone on Kerasím! Outside of the kidnapping last year. But that's what happens when you leave me."

"You knew I must spend a week or two in retraining. I must be recertified in my field training, weaponry, and procedures. I will have at least twenty hours of new training to keep me current on politics, law, and military policies, as well as several meetings with officials to discuss my work on Centauri."

"Take me with you. I've lived on Centauri longer than you have."

He held her face and gazed at her with the softest of smiles, his eyes the warm black coffee she adored. It was the man behind the duty, a little shy, a little unsure of himself, so unlike the hard, lethal, analytical machine he'd been trained to be. "It does not work that way on Kerasím. You would be relegated to a ladies' waiting room all day. I don't know what they do there, but I don't think you would like it."

"I don't know. Unless Mímihn gets over her snit, it might be more pleasant. You'll be back tonight, right?"

"Yes. This is day-training only."

Aila let him slip through her fingers. "Fine. But I won't like it. Dalo wanted me to visit. Maybe I'll see if Thrit can bring me to her home. Maybe I'll go to school with Faelihn and Kesseh, see what their lessons are like now."

"You will like that more. But be safe. I know you don't approve, but please wear a veil in public. Your face is known, and that presents danger."

Aila meant it when she said, "I know."

The call came in the early evening, pulling Tokh from dinner. He returned just a minute later. "It's official. You have approval from Derahl Nor to marry a Kerasi officer of your choice."

It wasn't exactly what Aila wanted to hear. Perhaps the Union would say no until after she left Kerasím, saving her. She played along anyway, hoping to lighten a strained meal. "Choice? I have a choice? Excellent!"

Masákh sat straighter with an indignant glare as Aila glanced up and down the table, pretending to examine her "choices." Haghíde lifted his head.

Mímihn's mood brightened, and she laughed. "Now the truth will come out! Maybe she's changed her mind, Masákh."

Aila smiled at his blank stare. "No. My choice is made."

Masákh relaxed, though he didn't look pleased.

Mímihn squealed and reached over to squeeze Aila's hand. "There! See? Now you have your permission. I'm so glad! Because Zheníhda and I have a surprise for you." Mímihn looked about to explode, holding in the secret, but she deferred to First-wife, as was proper.

Zheníhda put down her glass. "With Tokh's permission, we wish to give you a grand wedding party, fit for a *dahneg* daughter."

"That is most gracious of you, General," Masákh said. "It was not necessary, but I thank you."

"Thank you!" Aila said. "You are too kind. I still don't have permission from my government, though."

"It will come," Tokh said. "This I know. If we said no but the Union said yes, then it would continue conflict and worsen relations. The Emperor will not allow that. If we say yes and the Union says no, they will be dishonored. The only possible diplomatic answer would be yes. It becomes a symbol of progress that both sides need. Neither of my older sons chose to have a party, and it will be some years before Jora and Kesseh will be ready to marry, so it is a good time to earn the

56

favors of friends and associates. Masákh, if you think they would attend, you may invite your family. If they are formally invited by the palace, will the Union allow your family or some of their dignitaries to attend?"

Aila gave a deep sigh. They'd gone from two people standing before a commanding officer to a Galactic Gala of the Century in the space of two minutes. This was *not* what she wanted, for a wedding she promised she wouldn't have. "Oh gosh. I didn't want my parents to know about it. The only way my mother might come is to assassinate Masákh. I would need some sort of guarantee of transport and security from the palace. They would need a place to stay, or at least permission and escorts to travel from Derahl Nor."

"I will see it is arranged."

"It's going to take time to pull that all together – at least two weeks for travel allowance alone," Aila said. "My papers are only good for three weeks. They'll need to be extended. I'll need to call my mother and warn her, give her time to calm down before she has to leave, if she comes at all."

Tokh gave a nod. "We will make the wedding in three weeks time, then. I will have your papers extended, and you may place a call after dinner."

Aila sat in Tokh's office, alone. All she had to do was push the button to start the call, but her arm wouldn't do it. This was never her intention, not even in a tiny secret back drawer of her mind. She didn't want some major event that would be tied to politics no matter what she did, and she didn't want in any way to break the news to her mother.

"Hi, Mom," she practiced to the black monitor. "You know how things get out of control really quick? Well, I did it again."

"Hi Mom! You know how you loved all those big parties when Dad was campaigning?"

"Mom, you were right all along. I'm over my head, I have no idea how to get out of this, so could you pleeeease come to a party in my honor? No, not another award. This one's a wedding party. Yeah. The kind I promised I wouldn't do."

Aila let her head hit the desk. *How the hell do I get myself into these things?* Her finger hit the *connect* button and she lifted her head to the camera.

"Hi Mom!" Aila said. She didn't want too much enthusiasm, or Mom would think it was all faked and Aila had been lying to her the whole time. If she was too subdued, Mom would think she was unhappy and being forced. On the other hand, Leila was going to freak out either way.

"Where are you? Are you okay? Have you left yet?" There was a long pause in the transmission back and forth. A little static played on the wave, and every so often the picture would flicker and jump.

"I'm here at Tokh's house," Aila said when her turn came. "I'm very well and happy. Mom, can I have a reasonable discussion with you without you freaking out? And no, it's not about anything bad. If you don't want to reply immediately, that's okay, but could you please listen?"

"Aila, whatever you say is going to antagonize me, because that's what you do. You don't listen to me, so why should I upset myself?"

"Please, Mom? I know you don't believe me, but it really does mean a lot to me. I'm trying, I'm really trying to keep you involved. I don't want to lose you, no matter what you think of me. Please?" Three minutes pause seemed like thirty when so much rode on the answers.

Leila's reply rebounded. Her eyebrows arched upward in a sour attitude. "Just say it, Aila. Stop the games and just say it."

"It's not a game, Mom. I'm dead serious. Please don't yell until I finish, okay? I have already messaged Mr. Hhani for travel permission, but the rest is up to you. I promised you I would not marry Masákh until I was finished with my degree. That is true – within Union space. But my friends are bugging me to hold a Kerasi ceremony for us here in Imahlva, and General Tokh would like to invite you, and Dad, and Ramie, and a few select officials to be present. You will get a formal invitation in the next day or so. You are not required to be here, you are free to leave at any time, I have permission for you to stay at the palace or only aboard your ship if you prefer. I have a letter signed by the Emperor guaranteeing your safety while on Kerasím. Remember, Kerasi law is not valid inside Union space; it doesn't break my promise to you, but while I'm here, it's a logical move. If I'm legally married, I have rights – including personal safety – that I don't have as an unmarried female. It will help many things. I've thought it through very, very carefully. Ross clarified points for me, and we both feel it is in my best interest if I plan to visit Kerasím again. You've been to the palace. You've met the Emperor. You've met Tokh's family. You know you'll be safe here. It's in three weeks, and I really, really want you to be here. That's it. That's all." The minutes ticked slowly, waiting on the reply.

Leila laughed. She glanced left and right with interest, as if searching for something behind Aila. "I can't see who's holding the gun to your head, but you're just stupid enough to come up with that on your own. Have fun playing house, and let me know when you finally grow up, okay? Because I just can't play the game anymore. Nothing's that simple, Aila. I truly do hope you wake up and see the danger before it catches you, and I hope your friends are actually there to support you when it does, because I can't do it. Good luck." An *end transmission* label appeared across the screen. Mom had closed out.

Aila heaved a heavy sigh. It still hurt, but the conversation had gone much better than she'd hoped. She felt bad for Bindai Hhani, who would take the worst of Leila's wrath, besides her dad. As Secretary of State for the Planetary Union, Hhani knew the implications of such a marriage, even if it wasn't legal in the Union, and would be pushing her parents to attend. He himself would most likely come, as a high-level statesman. He was on speaking terms with General Tokh and the Emperor, and the palace would make a huge deal out of his visit. If it went well – All the Deities of Earth and Kerasím make it go well! – it would be a major achievement for both governments, the kind of boost they both needed after the horrific disaster of the previous year. They had just a few days until they would need to board a ship; all Aila could do now was wait.

Nine

Ross Halian's message sat on Aila's queue the next morning. *Hhani says if I think it's safe, and you think it's safe, then you have the Union's blessing. The Union will examine the law and make resolution as to Masákh's status later. Hhani and four officials will arrive the day before and meet w/ the Emperor at Derahl Nor. Your father has agreed to come; he and Hhani swear your mother will accompany him if she must be shipped cargo. Nix on your brother.*

Fair enough. Dad was figuring they'd all die, so leaving Ramie out would let him carry on the family. No doubt Ramie was throwing a tantrum over that, and she'd get his irate call later.

Why does this stuff always happen to me?

She tiptoed down to the dining area. Aila held up her personal com. "It's official. I have Union permission."

Zheníhda's face lit up, a strange glow instead of her usual caustic demeanor. It took years off her appearance. "Praise the Fortunes! I was getting worried."

Mímihn shrieked and gave Aila a fierce hug and a kiss. The noise startled Thoren, napping in his carry basket, and Aila rocked him until he drifted back asleep.

"We don't have a moment to lose." Zheníhda fetched a lap pad. "One of you keep the notes, but write them simple so I can read them. We must make menus, decorations, and decide on guests. Tomorrow we can ask Tokh to lend us an officer to take us to the city so we can find you a dress worthy of a wedding."

"There's nothing fine enough for Aila in Imahlva," Mímihn decided. "We must go to Keranihn."

Zheníhda looked down her nose. "Imahlva is an upper caste city. *Dahneg* is the least they sell."

Mímihn printed her words as if writing for a preschooler. It was for Zheníhda's benefit, but the large clear symbols were easier on

Mímihn's damaged eyes, too. "Aila is Union, and Union must have the very best. Besides, she is Tokh's daughter, and he will be inviting people from Keranihn. It'll reflect well on him if she is as *bhisroti* as we can make her."

"Very well. Just not too extravagant, or someone will cry foul."

"Nihda, that's old thinking. They're all *dahneg* now, so no one can object."

The truth of it struck her. Zheníhda nodded. "Then we must do it. I'll tell Tokh to bring us to Keranihn tomorrow."

Mímihn could barely contain her eagerness. She reached out and squeezed Aila's hand. "Are you excited?"

Aila broke into a nervous grin. "I've been living with him almost a year and it never bothered me. Now I'm scared. You make it sound so important."

Zheníhda waved a hand in the air. "The ceremony is three *fasim*. The rest is just a celebration party. I was a very sheltered girl; everything at my wedding was new and wonderful to me – the foods, the people, the dancing. You're used to the palace; it won't be as special for you."

"Of course it will. I have no idea what to expect, and knowing you are the people giving me the party will make it very special."

"You'll enjoy it; I promise," Mímihn said. She leaned closer as if telling a secret. "In truth, the party is for me. I didn't have a party for either of my weddings. I had to make my own dinner for the first one. Zheníhda made me a beautiful dinner for my second. Just once, I want to see a wedding party."

Aila smiled for her. A thought turned in her head, until she gave it a voice. "I know you are the ones inviting the guests, but am I allowed to invite someone?"

Zheníhda paused. "We included your family and several Union diplomats. Is there someone we forgot?"

"Maybe I'm crazy, but I wish to send an invitation to Her Royal Majesty Heir Apparent Rimas. She has been most kind to me. I think it would be a good gesture on the part of the Union."

Zheníhda's eyes grew huge, making her pinched nose seem even narrower. Even Mímihn drew back in shock.

"She's Royalty! We couldn't possibly…"

"I... suppose we could send her an invitation," Zheníhda faltered. "Even if she personally reads it, it's most unlikely she would accept. She's far too busy with palace business to attend the wedding of a *dahneg*."

Mimihn's breath came in nervous bursts. "Of course she wouldn't. But you're right; it would be a very nice gesture from the Union, honoring her as a guest welcome at the wedding of one of their females. It is only appropriate. We must invite her."

Zheníhda and Shanohr had begun the breakfast the following morning when the bellow shook the walls of the house. Mímihn was nursing Thoren; he let go of her breast at the noise.

"NIHDA!!!"

Tokh fled his office as if the room was on fire and his wife had set it. "What did you do!"

Zheníhda frowned in confusion. She placed the bowl of *hyrak* eggs on the workspace. "What's wrong?"

"There is a message on my queue from Derahl Nor. They will be sending a preparation team out tomorrow to examine our house and address security issues for a potential visit of the Heir! The day of the wedding!"

Zheníhda turned a sickly yellow. "What!"

Mímihn's jaw fell open in shock. "What?"

Tokh looked as if his heart was about to stop. He held himself up with a hand against the wall. Desperation fogged his eyes, and he breathed hard through his mouth. The glass eyes of the stuffed *dhastal* head hanging over the door had an amused glint. "Eight *fáhganid* aren't enough of a worry. You invited *thósikh* royalty?!"

"Me." Aila stepped from the kitchen and approached the table. "I'm afraid that was me. I asked to invite Rimas, as a State gesture. If it was wrong, it's my fault. I thought it was the right thing to do."

"It was a gesture!" Zheníhda stammered. "A politeness of Aila as a dignitary. We never thought she would accept!"

"Did you not look at the guest list?" Tokh raged. "We invited the neighbors as a politeness. That includes that wretch Gilmaneg! His wives are welcome but I fear he will bring that beast of a consort. He will embarrass us before the palace!"

"Can we not find a way to uninvite him? Perhaps I can talk to his wives," Mímihn said in a small voice.

Tokh pressed his lips together, cornered by too many social demands. "No. First I'll find out for certain if Her Royal Majesty is planning to attend. Then I'll explain the situation and ask if the Royal Guard will keep him in their sights, scare him hard enough to make his shit run yellow. I won't allow him to create trouble."

"I'm sorry, General," Aila said. "I thought I was being polite. I thought she would just send an official letter of congratulations. I never, ever expected her to say yes."

Tokh seemed to accept her apology. He let go of the wall and stood up. "Even I would not have had the *khatas* to invite the Heir."

Aila shrugged. "I don't have *khatas*. Rimas doesn't have them, either, so she probably didn't see why she shouldn't accept. Females don't need *khatas* to make decisions, we just do it."

"That is exactly the problem."

Giving in, getting all the permissions, stabbing her mother in the back – Aila thought all the issues had been fixed. The wives were happy, Tokh was happy, the governments were happy. Never once did she think about the men.

She and Mímihn were giving Thoren a bath in the kitchen when the shouting started in the sitting area.

"You're acting without thinking," Haghíde said, his voice loud above the ComNet screen playing on the wall.

"What's done is done," Masákh said. "It can't be changed. To back out would bring down anger from the palace."

"You're being used! They're using you to push their agenda. When she's by your side, she's a symbol of Kerasi honor. You marry her, you condemn her to our laws, and they'll manipulate you to do their will. You'll be placing her in danger. Prove to me how that shows care!"

Aila came around the corner in time to see Masákh take a warning step toward Haghíde. "Lower your voice! Your topics are not fit for every ear." Behind Aila, Mátokhan emerged from Tokh's office, and Tokh himself appeared at the top of the stairs.

"What's going on?" Aila said.

Masákh cut his intimidation long enough to give her a glance. "A matter that does not concern you. Please return to your activity. Haghíde is creating a scene."

"Not half as much as you will create when they pull the platform from under your feet," Haghíde spat.

"Stop!" Aila ordered. Masákh and Haghíde did not fight. They just didn't. "Stop, right now. Mátokhan, stay with Masákh. Haghíde, come with me. I feel better outside with an escort. Please."

They gave each other one last foul glare, and Haghíde turned. "Only because you ask."

"I apologize if the loudness of my voice has upset you," Haghíde said. "I did not mean to create a disturbance in Tokh's home. I'm certain he will speak to me about it later."

Aila said nothing yet. He escorted her to the far end of the property, past the pool to where the land sloped dangerously steep beyond the wall, but not as sheer as the cliff by the courtyard. Somewhere beyond the stone outcropping lay another home accessible from another, unseen street. The last glow of twilight was fading into darkness. Up and down the inlet warning lights blinked their colorful patterns, house and yardlights glowed with increasing power, and the lights of many boats shimmered on the dark water. When they were far enough away from the house, Aila turned to face him.

"Just come clean, Haghíde. Say what's on your mind. You're Masákh's very best friend, a brother *aghát*, and I don't want to see you come to bad blood. This wedding is upsetting you and I will know why, now. I promise you won't anger me, and if you prefer I won't tell Masákh that you told me, or anyone else."

Haghíde's lip pinched tight with tension, and he looked away. "I am happy for you both. He is a good man."

"If you don't tell me, I'll ask Tokh to come out here and order you to speak truth. You're upset with me. I heard it."

The tension worsened, and Haghíde looked for any escape. It took a full minute before he spoke. "No. I am not upset with you. I'm upset with me. I..." Haghíde wrestled with himself, daring the words to both be said and remain unspoken, until he looked as if he were fighting off a sudden wave of pain.

"I wish it were me marrying you. No, not exactly," he corrected quickly. "I am not blind with love for you, like Masákh. He truly is; I know that. I wish I'd had the *chance* to find out if I could be love-blind for you. I enjoyed working with you very much. You didn't laugh at me when I tried to understand your concepts. I learned more from you than you did from me – Do not tell me different; I know that's truth. I ask questions because I want to know things, but it's seen as a weakness, and people think me a fool."

Aila's heart went out to him. He was out of uniform but wore a long-sleeved shirt; even though she was gloveless, she dared to reach out and lay her hand on his arm. "I never once thought you a fool, Haghíde. Your curiosity is what I like most about you."

He gave a snort of self-pity. "I wanted to say more so many times, but Masákh was so *perfect*. At everything. I never had enough nerve to find out if you could like me like that. I am angry at my own failings."

"Don't be. It's not your fault. I will always consider you one of my dearest friends, next to Mímihn. You make me laugh, in the best ways, and you have always been strong by my side. Your heart is your strength. Please don't be mad at Masákh, either. If it's one thing I've learned about him, it's that he's that perfect because he's so afraid of being wrong. It's fear that makes him work that hard. From when he first entered the Academy, they scared him into perfection, that he had to live up to his General's faith, that horrible things would happen to him or his family if he didn't. And that's how they led him to be what he is. And they promoted him to Inner Circle, and that scares him most of all. If he fails now, they won't just demote him. They'll kill him. Some nights he's so worried he can't sleep. Don't envy him. Seeing his stress makes me want to cry."

Haghíde's tension faded, and he gave a nod. "I've seen it, too. I apologize for increasing his stress. I wish you both only good fortune."

Aila smiled at him. "I'd hug you, but I don't want you to take it the wrong way. You'll find a female who makes your heart sing, who'll make you blind with love. You just have to look for her."

Haghíde made eye contact at last. "I will. But I swear an oath to you: should anything befall Masákh in his duties, I will take care of you, wedded or not. That is a blood-pledge."

A nervous snort escaped Aila. Haghíde had spent six years working inside the Union, but he still thought like a Kerasi. Widows had few choices on Kerasím: be taken care of by a son, remarry, return to her parents if possible, become a servant to a higher caste, or throw herself on the mercy of the sex industry, which wasn't a mercy at all. Haghíde had just offered to marry her immediately should she become a widow, even if it meant taking a second wife. "That's a little too creepy for me, but I know it comes from your heart. Thank you, Haghíde. That's a great comfort to me. Friends?"

He hesitated, but gave a nod. "Yes. Friends." Aila clapped her hand on his shoulder, the male equivalent of a hug. Haghíde grabbed her wrist, ignoring the implications of skin contact. The grip was unbreakable; if it wasn't Haghíde, Aila would have labeled it a threat. "As I said to Masákh: be very careful after you are married. It is not the same here as in the Union. Your rules will not apply. You are a political liability. What each of you do will affect the other, and they will not hesitate to control you both."

It was too dark to read the intent in Haghíde's face, but his voice was worried enough for both of them. Aila gave a somber nod. "I promise."

Ten

Aila understood that Tokh was a Very Important Person. He was a Level-Four General, with a team of fifty personally chosen officers and a cadre of enlisted that held at 200, with 30,000 troops available at his command if needed. His official title was Adjutant to Diplomatic Securities, as well as serving on His Majesty Nadigh's senate council, which met for two weeks every eight to discuss issues. He sometimes worked from home, but when he didn't he had a lengthy air commute to his office in Keranihn. When he arrived home he was exhausted, but still tried to find time to meet with his children, discuss their studies, quiz them on what they were learning and direct them to know more. To Zheníhda's disapproval, he taught Kesseh basic weapon proficiency, though he put more of an emphasis on self-defense and hand combat. And now he had baby Thoren to think of as well, besides two wives and a household. Like now, he sometimes had a houseful of guests if his men were staying with him, or Dalo and his smallchildren.

And yet, with all the chaos of the moment, with his men about, with a high-risk foreign dignitary staying with him, with all the last-minute preparations for a wedding, every night felt like a party. The *aghát* were in and out, attending to duty or visiting others: Mátokhan came and went on his own schedule; Haghíde spent six days with his parents, Masákh was held in Keranihn for five days, Ráhnif or Tótoghar had accompanied Aila on several excursions to the palace for interviews. Tokh's lead officers might stop by if in the area, or perhaps neighbors. It was a different crew every night, but always the same. The wives and children would gather around the large viewscreen after dinner and watch various entertainments, laughing and talking. If Tokh was not involved in business, he might join them for a while. If he had associates, he might stay at the table drinking and talking or playing a vicious game of Tabs.

Aila loved the hominess of it. It was another planet, another culture, another species, yet when she sat back and observed, it seemed so familiar and natural. She loved watching it unfold from the sidelines. Even when Masákh wasn't there, even when she didn't always understand the nuances of the culture or the words of the language, Aila felt safe and content, which was why, after two weeks on Kerasím, her uneasiness was driving her up a wall.

Masákh entered the room to find her sitting on the lounge, comm in her hand, staring at nothing. "You should never sit with your back to the door. You didn't even look up when I entered. That is most dangerous."

Aila twisted her mouth sideways. "Hmph. Sometimes, when the risk is low, you just don't care."

"That's a bad habit to accept." He loosened his clothing and lay behind her on the lounge. His hand reached around and snatched her personal com from her grasp. Aila glared at him while he looked over the contact information.

"Who nominated you Minister of Security? Do I search your comm?"

"I am sworn to keep you safe; your security on Kerasím is my business. Your brother. Your mother. Dalo? Dalo again. A Union number, no identification. A call with Earth's location tag – I assume your school friend. For someone who wanted very much to return to Kerasím, you don't seem happy."

Aila continued to sit like a lump; Masákh pulled her down next to him and she spooned in on his arm. "It's very peaceful here, when Mímihn's not mad at me. But I went from Mímihn being mad to my brother calling me yelling that it's not fair he's the only one in the family who hasn't been here and no one has the right to keep him away, and why aren't I doing more to try and get him permission; to my mother leaving screaming messages about what a liar I am and she doesn't care what happens anymore since I don't; to my father trying not to yell, but you can tell he's really angry, too, because he has to listen to my mother, and asking me question after question after question. Thayer's pissed at me because I didn't invite her, despite the fact she'd never get travel permission. Then I've got Hhani on my ass asking me the same questions as my dad, pretty much, and demanding to know about security measures beforehand, and palace stuff I can't begin to answer, and Ross calling to make sure I'm still okay. At least he doesn't yell at me. My ears can't take anymore yelling."

She wiped her eyes on his shirt before he could comment on her tears. "It's supposed to be a happy time. None of them are even here and they're making me so damned miserable. And Mímihn and Zheníhda keep whispering around me like they've got some big secret and they won't tell me, so I'm worried about that as well. I have no idea what your customs are. I'm afraid of what they'll try to do and how bad it will look if I refuse."

"First, you will stop answering calls, unless they are from here. You do not deserve to be yelled at." Masákh shut off her comm and tossed it under the lounge. He slid down and nuzzled her hair. "Second, I will inquire about the whispers with Second-wife Tokh. I will decide if it warrants worry or not. Third," his hands slid over her body, pulling her against him while his lips explored her neck, "I am concerned about your report of Secretary Hhani being on your ass. I do not look forward to fighting with him, but it is my place only, being on your ass. Which is exactly where I want to be right now." He pressed his hips forward against her backside.

Aila burst out laughing. She twisted around until she faced him. "Very good! That was actually really funny." She kissed his nose. "But I don't think so. Tonight you're going to be on your ass, with me on your lap, while I ride you to the moon and back."

Masákh feigned surprise. "You know this as fact?"

"Scannable truth," and she kissed him until he gave in.

Aila understood she was under a lot of stress. She would have left the week before if it wasn't for this crazy wedding idea, and had needed to get extensions to her visitor status from both sides of the border. She didn't want the wedding – she did but she didn't, because of the extreme issue it was causing with her parents. If it was two years from now, or her mother was cool with the idea, it would be a supernova experience. But it was now, too soon and unexpected. And probably it was just Aila misunderstanding language and culture, hearing things and interpreting things as they would relate in the Union, not on Kerasím. Despite her years of experience, despite the best work of the *aghát* to teach her, Aila realized she didn't have a lot of actual understanding of the greater culture – the function of a family, yes, but

69

not the people as a whole. And surely that's what must have happened, overhearing Mímihn and Zheníhda giggling together – Zheníhda didn't giggle. Not stuffy, uptight, haughty Zheníhda. But they were giggling together, and when Aila stared at them funny, Mímihn laughed back and simply said, "*Kavirhwhan!*" as if *wedding* explained everything, when it explained nothing. Simple enough, but it sat wrong with Aila, and left her wondering the rest of the night.

The third time, Aila snapped. She was polite, but her face conveyed her annoyance. "Why do you do that? Why do you laugh and then stop when I walk into a room? What secrets do you keep from me?"

Mímihn gave her a coy little smile that Aila didn't trust. She kissed Aila on her cheek. "You're getting married. All you have to do is keep yourself as beautiful as you are. We will take care of the rest." Zheníhda smiled her practiced thin smile that might have meant "I'm very happy for you," or "I can't wait to toast marshmallows while you burn at the stake."

Aila cornered Mímihn that night. She snatched Thoren from his basket and refused to give him back. "Not until you answer my questions. Why are you laughing at me? You are being cruel. What should I know that I don't?" She turned her back and hugged the baby close.

Mímihn's face fell. "We don't keep anything from you, Aila. You already bed him, so it's not like you don't know what marriage means. I'm happy because Zheníhda and I are working together without fighting. We're enjoying all the planning and surprises. Tokh has had parties, but never this big. He has invited a hundred guests; important people. We want everything to be perfect for you and for him. This is how we earn our glory."

Aila turned around and allowed Mímihn to take her son. "Then why do I feel so bad?"

Mímihn kissed her cheek again. "Because you're getting married in less than a week and you are full of stomach-shivers, like every young girl."

Aila nodded. "I am." But the feeling didn't go away.

Eleven

With two days to go, the six *aghát* reassembled at the estate. Tokh's son Kitras and his family arrived early in the day. Zenak and his wife Avalihn, the son Aila had never met, were due toward evening; their sons were half-way through military school and would not join them. Joralan would head to Nar Rhede military academy with his cousins at mid-year. Kitras's son Lanag, less than a year younger than his Uncle Joralan, shadowed him, no less set on upholding the family name. Kesseh and Faelihn hung around Aila, practicing their Union for the coming guests – some of whom would be Union ladies.

The evening fell into a giddy reunion of old friends, males at the table and females running back and forth serving them and socializing. Avalihn, though almost double Aila's age, was quite pleasant, more traditional than counter-culture Dalo but no where near as rigid or old-fashioned as Zheníhda. They took turns attending to the men growing louder and more raucous with every round of drinks.

Aila served alongside the Kerasi females. She refilled her own *lunahl* glass and went back to the circle of women, just as they burst into laughter. Aila grinned in good humor. "What joke did I miss?"

A final laugh escaped Avalihn. "You will understand, once you are married."

Mímihn put her arm around her and tried to hug her. "Just two more nights! You mustn't sleep with him until then. Pretend he isn't here. You'll be happier for it. Take my bed."

Aila's smile faded faster than the sun behind a storm cloud.

"Why can't you be honest with me!" She said it loud, and in Union. The volume garnered the attention of the men, most of whom knew enough Union to understand her. Aila's nerves reared up, the anger, the fear, the foreboding. The glass of *lunahl* sailed from her hand to hit the wall near the men, and they ducked as it shattered. All conversation stopped.

71

"FORGET IT! I'm DONE! I don't know what you're planning, but I'm tired of pretending everything is fine. I call this wedding off! There will be no wedding. I will not marry Masákh. Not now. Not here. I'm sorry for the inconvenience, General, but I won't do it."

Tokh stood up, quiet and imposing. Before he could speak, Aila pointed at him. "Don't. Just don't. I don't find this funny. I will return to Keranihn if I have to walk there myself. If you will present me with your expenses, I will see you are reimbursed."

Tokh pointed to his chair. "You will sit."

Aila fought a losing battle against her tears. "No, General. This time I will not."

She stormed out the front door and across Tokh's yard. Masákh followed her, several seconds behind. Aila heard him and stopped short, away from the cliff. She wouldn't be a stupid 'accident.'

He waited behind her, not touching. "You cannot call off this wedding. Not after Tokh has gone to such lengths to provide us with a celebration."

"I can't do this, Masákh. I love you! I all but panic when you aren't next to me, but I don't trust this. I have no problem being married to you inside Union territory, but every ounce of my being is telling me don't do this here. That something is going on here everyone else seems to know except me. Haghíde tried to warn me. I think the ladies were trying to drop me hints, but were afraid to say it. It's like there's a joke and everyone's giggling at me but they can't laugh out loud until after I'm married, when it's too late. I can't do it! I look at you and my heart soars, but the back of my head can't stop reminding me how much older you are, and how much you know, and how much you aren't telling me. You may not even know it, because everyone is hiding something. Tokh is hiding information from you, his commander is hiding things from him – I'd have to try to squeeze information from the Emperor himself if I wanted to get anywhere. You shade things, you downplay things, you steer me away from topics – I would take a bullet for you – I killed a man for you! – but I can't eliminate the warning lights going off inside my head. Not here. I don't think I've ever understood what it means to be a Kerasi female until this very night. And it scares me so badly, I think I'm going to call Ross Halian and stay at the Embassy. No offense to Tokh."

72

Masákh listened to her rant in silence. He started to reach out to her, but stopped himself. No-touch was always proper, no matter what the intimacy. Instead he bent over the wall at the cliff edge and rested his forearms on it. He gazed out toward the ocean. The air was slightly hazy, and it wasn't possible to make out the blinking lights on the far shore.

"I have no agenda for you except to make you my legal wife, manager of my estate, and mother of my children, should we have them, and to spend the last of my days with you. That is my scannable truth. Wherever our work takes us, I want to be with you, and have you with me. I don't know what else to say to you. You have redefined my concept of love, Human or Kerasi. My commission is my life, and has been since the day my parents signed the papers. And I was content, until you appeared.

"In your culture, it is considered extreme dishonor to soil oneself with feces, no matter how uncontrollable it may be."

"Yes."

"On Kerasím, it is such a dishonor for a male to cry that there is not even a word for it. The word for tears, *bragh*, can only be used for females, not males. If an elder male has lost his thoughts and is seen crying, one must say his spirit is leaking. Everyone turns away, will not bear witness to ease the shame. It is far less a shame for a male to soil himself than to be caught with leaking eyes. It can cost your community standing, affect your child's marriage opportunities, cost you your employment, even your life. If it cannot be prevented, it must be a most private thing, with no witnesses. When we were on our way to Tokh's last year and you were taken from me, I disobeyed a direct order to hunt for you. Do you understand what that means, for a Kerasi officer to disobey a direct order? When I realized it was a most foolish attempt, I knew I had lost both you and my life. I had nothing to live for. I knelt in the dirt and lost my spirit. I had stopped when they found me, but Gurih isn't stupid. He turned his head from me; he knew. When we reached Tokh's, my spirit leaked again as he striped me, because I knew without my rank and position I would never find you. It stopped my breath, thinking what you might endure. In all my life, I have never been so helpless as that moment. Tokh knew I had shamed myself irreparably, I know he did, but he said nothing. He berated me and told me to get back to work. He holds my life in his pocket and can destroy

73

me at any moment. And after much thought, I know I would give it up if you would remain by me in my shame."

Aila seized him in a tight embrace, which he returned. "We can write our own marriage ceremony all we want, but it doesn't mean it will take all the legal issues into consideration. This world will always be against us."

"What if we consult with Ghírandar?"

"What good is it? Someone orders Tokh to order you to do something, and he will, up to the Emperor himself. A lawyer will simply tell me, 'This is Kerasím, this is the way it is'."

Masákh didn't answer, just held her to him, his cheek pressed to her head. After a moment Aila stiffened and pulled back. "Maybe that's where I need to start, then."

Masákh frowned. "The Emperor?"

"No. He can change his mind at any moment, depending on his needs. Someone better." She pulled away and hurried inside.

Mímihn stood before Tokh with a very repentant look, as if she'd just been chewed out. The other ladies stood behind her in a group, sad and silent. She stepped forward before Tokh could say a word.

"Ai-lah, we're sorry if we made you angry. We didn't mean to. The other day, when you found Nihda and me laughing, we weren't laughing at you. We were discussing Tokh's private habits, a conversation wives may have but it wouldn't be for other ears. Nihda and I don't often have friendly conversations, and I was enjoying the moment."

"It was not something that could be shared with you, or anyone else," Zheníhda confirmed.

"And now – if you were Kerasi and about to married, we would gather around you and speak about bedroom things, tell you things we know, tell you what to expect, what to do in situations. Sometimes females find much friendship and support in sharing circles. Sometimes young girls don't get such talks and have very bad marriages because they know nothing, and don't know to ask."

Dalo broke in, "What things a husband likes, what to do if he wants to do something weird, how to put fire in your pants." She shook her hips as if wagging a tail. "How to avoid teeth."

Mímihn said, "You've been in his bed for many months, so you already know. We were disappointed we didn't get to have such a talk, so we were having a bit of it anyway. That's why we were laughing. We're very sorry if it made you angry."

Aila's hurt hung in the air so thick she could have punched it and it wouldn't have dissipated. At least she knew the knife was in her heart, not her back. "You were wrong. I don't know. And I would very much liked to have had that conversation with you."

She turned to face Tokh, whose burning glare promised violence if the situation didn't resolve itself. Female spats were not the concern of males, and Aila had embarrassed him before his men. She bowed low in supplication. "General, may I place a call from your office?"

Tokh's displeasure came out in his words. "Is it to cancel your wedding?"

"Not yet. If it goes right, it will save it."

He waved permission. "Then you may call."

Aila consulted her palm com for the address. It would look more serious coming from Tokh's identification. A male secretary answered.

"May I please request a communication with her royal highness Rimas, Heir of All Kerasím, at her earliest convenience. The information on your screen will show that I have a priority clearance assigned by her highness herself. It is in regard to a ceremony she is attending."

The secretary must have been a former *fáhganid*. He glared at her as if she hadn't bathed in a week and he could smell her from three hundred *nalis* away. "You will wait."

After a minute or two Rimas appeared on the screen. Her face wasn't hostile, but it didn't exude friendliness, either. "Aila Pehrrin. You couldn't wait until tomorrow to speak with me? My time is not yours to demand."

Aila bowed her head and kept her eyes to the bottom of the screen. "I am most deeply sorry for the interruption, your Royal Grace, and I beg your forgiveness. However, if you cannot answer my questions, then I must cancel my wedding. You are the only person I trust to give me truth."

"All of Kerasím would be most upset if you canceled your wedding, including my father the Emperor. Your wedding is a symbol of the progress between our cultures, a victory the people are looking forward to with great excitement, and it would not bode well if it were to fall through."

Aila hung her head. "I understand the importance of my actions, but I remain firm. Your Majesty, I request truth: what is my standing on Kerasím if I, a foreign official, marry a Kerasi subject? Am I subject to Kerasi law, or Union law?"

Rimas's official face disappeared. Her eyebrow slipped downward over her nose as she thought. "That has been a matter of much debate. By law, you become the wife of a Kerasi male and are subject to his authority. However, we are trying very hard to prove to the Union that we are willing for females to increase their independence. If there was an issue, we would take Union law into account for you."

"That is most gracious, your Majesty. However, I fear that my voice could be silenced by lower courts who would not be aware of my privilege and not grant me such rights. Before I allow myself to become a Kerasi subject and wife to a Kerasi male, I need more guarantees than that. I want your public vow, my most Royal Lady Majesty. I want your word you yourself would represent me in legal matters, as the representative of all Kerasi females. I want a written guarantee that while I shall be loyal to the Emperor while on Kerasím, I remain a citizen of the Union, and must be granted the rights of Union females when dealing with matters of law. I need your written word, my Lady Majesty. I have great fears about my position should my marriage become formal, and I need that reassurance. Most importantly, I want a guarantee that I will always have the right to leave Kerasím, with or without my husband's permission, as my duties to the Union may require it. I also want a guarantee that I cannot be kept from contact with my government or its officials here on Kerasím."

Rimas sighed, weighing scenarios in her head. "We are used to ambassadors from other worlds, but not Union ones, nor female ones, and not ones who will be married to Kerasi citizens. What you seek is not impossible. I will bring your concerns to His Majesty my father, and give you an answer after."

Aila bowed until only the top of her head remained in camera frame. "You are most gracious, my Royal Lady."

Twelve

After the guests had retired, the ladies climbed the stairs, Avalihn and Zheníhda bearing trays of food and beverages, and Dalo lugging Thoren in his carry basket. Mímihn went down the hall to knock on Aila's door. She opened it before Aila answered, and the women filed in.

Aila sulked in her oversized room, checking her com in hopes that it would buzz an answer into her hand. Tradition banished Masákh to the close eye of his crewmates, away from his bride, leaving her grumpy and alone.

"Pleasant evening, Aila. You said you wished we had given you a wedding-talk, so we have come to share our wisdom. But be warned: we will want to hear your stories in return."

Aila sat up and slid her hand com into her skirt pocket.

"Gah! Look at her face darken!" Avalihn said as she took a seat on the second lounge. She reached out and squeezed Aila's knee. "She's still much a girl!"

There was *lunahl* on the tray, and *bohjis*, and *harfa* punch made with *flehdan* and *varvet* that went down smooth and sweet and then roared upward until Aila felt as if steam were rising off the top of her head. It didn't take long for all of them to be screeching with laughter, and it was a dry comment from Zheníhda – Zheníhda, Queen of All Things Snooty, that made Aila choke and *lunahl* pour from her nose with a searing of her sinuses, making the ladies laugh even harder. Avalihn pounded her on her back as she coughed and laughed more.

"Now tell us," Dalo said with such seriousness it seemed as if the question was highly classified information. "Tell us what Union males look like under their clothing. Kitras says they must have *hihvats*, because we can bed each other. But do they work the same? Are they bigger or smaller? They do only have one, don't they?"

The ladies gave a collective *"Gaaaaaaah!"* a nervous sigh that said Dalo had breached politeness. In a flash Aila realized the ladies were just as curious about Humans as the Humans were about Kerasi, even if they couldn't acknowledge it in public. Whatever information she shared would spread quickly among other wives, not only the Imahlva neighborhood but back in Nar Rede, where Avalihn and Zenak lived, and over the mountain to the apartments where Dalo lived, and then around half the planet. Aila blushed, but admitted, "Of course they do. They do not look exactly alike, and the *khatas* do not move upward. Actually, they tend to hang a bit." Four pairs of eyes stared at her, watching her lips to see if her words actually formed a picture.

"How do they differ?" Dalo said.

Aila heaved a great sigh and pulled out her pocket com. "I can't believe I'm doing this. I swear to you, I have never done this before. Never." She called up beefcake photos of various nude men from the universal databases on her hand com, and passed the photos around.

Zeníhda pulled back. "So much hair, even on the young."

"Sometimes." Aila took the com back, shook her head at her own gall, and dug deeper until she accessed video of two humans having sex. She'd never set out to look at porn before, and after the briefest of glances to confirm that's what she had found, she passed the com around again. "There. Just like Kerasi."

By the gasps and stares Aila could tell neither Zeníhda nor Avalihn had seen such videos. Dalo watched with rapt attention, taking notes with her eyes. "Kitras looks much happier than this. This male looks bored. She's not even *pushing* with him."

"Because it is a manufactured video for entertainment, not real," Aila said. Dalo passed the com to Mímihn, but she passed it immediately back to Aila.

"I cannot see such a small screen," she explained with a sweet smile.

"I can zoom the picture for you," Aila said, and tapped the controls.

Mímihn pushed her hand away. Her voice was brusque and commanding, strange and disturbing for Mímihn. "I said, I can't see that small a picture. I saw the photo; that is enough for me to believe you."

Aila shrugged, confused by the change. She shut off the com and put it away. "Okay."

It wasn't okay with Mímihn. The room held a silent pause. She took a deep breath, and her chin fell to her chest. "Forgive me for being loud. I didn't mean to ruin the party. I have seen enough of that. I don't want to see more, even if it's not Kerasi."

Aila threw her arms around her in a hard hug, careful not to disturb the baby in her lap. "I'm so sorry, Mimi. We forget about your before-times. I did not mean to make you sad." Her daughters-in-law – both older than she was – jumped forward to comfort her as well. Zheníhda didn't crawl across the lounge, but the *hyrak*-face softened and a motherly empathy took over.

Dalo rubbed her back. "You have a good husband now. Tokh's really nice for a male."

Mímihn nodded. Her carefree face folded up and she struggled for a moment, but the tears remained inside. Her voice shook with repressed pain. "I get so scared sometimes. My life is better than I could ever dream, even as a little girl. Tokh will be in retirement when Thoren comes of age. My first husband Maghentor – he was older then than Tokh is now – he died not long after he sold me. Tokh could be sent to battle, his aircraft could fail, he could be hit by a vehicle on the streets of Keranihn – what would I do? If Joralan isn't old enough yet, or if he refuses to acknowledge me, it will be fourteen years before Thoren is old enough to speak for me. I can't do that again. I can't."

Avalihn squeezed her hand. "You're a wife with a child. That wouldn't happen."

Dalo hugged her. "Kitras is Joralan's brother; he would beat him if he doesn't accept you. Thoren is also Kitras's brother; I'll ask him tomorrow if he will ask Tokh to be Thoren's regent. We would ask for a Widow's Payment and get a bigger apartment. Lanag will be going to Academy next year anyway. Don't worry. Thoren and Niboh can grow up together."

Joralan and Kesseh were Tokh's children by his second wife, Umara, who had died three years previous. Although Tokh had assigned Mímihn to raise them, Joralan wasn't bound by law to support Mímihn after his father's death. He would only do so if he had bonded enough with her to feel she was indeed like a mother to him. After Tokh's death, Zheníhda would be taken in by Zenak, her oldest son, as was law, but Kitras had no such responsibilities unless his brother died before his mother.

Aila grabbed Mímihn's chin and turned her face to hers. "You hear my words! If Tokh dies, you run to his office immediately and send a call to me! I will come for you. I will take you to the Union to live in peace until Thoren is old enough to return, or forever, if you wish. I will not let harm come to you."

"Gaaah!" Zheníhda spat over her third cup of *harfa* punch. She waved an arm through the air. "All that wailing and whining, for what? 'I will save you!' 'No, I will save you!' 'No, I will!' The solution is much more simple. We will ask Tokh's superior to order him not to die until then. The flesh will rot from his bones before he breaks such an order. Problem solved."

Mímihn's shriek of laughter broke the melancholy moment. There was a sly glint of satisfaction in Zheníhda's smirk. "You are very right, Nihda! He would never do that."

Aila woke to bright daylight in the middle of a sweaty pigpile of Mímihn and Dalo in her bed with her, Mímihn curled protectively around Thoren in her arms, one perfect golden-brass breast hanging out of her blouse from a sleepy feeding. Aila groped for her hand com, still in her pocket, and checked the messages. One was available, and she sat up in a flash.

AN EDICT FROM THE ROYAL PALACE OF DERAHL NOR:

By decree of his Royal Majesty Nadigh, Emperor of All Kerasím, let it be known the following is now law:

1) Non-Kerasi females who marry Kerasi citizens and reside on Kerasím as Kerasi must follow Kerasi law.

2) Non-Kerasi females with diplomatic status must be granted immunity to Kerasi tradition and be held to the laws of their society, providing they do not harm Kerasi society.

3) Non-Kerasi females with diplomatic status cannot be denied contact with their sponsoring governments by any agent of Kerasím and must be allowed to leave Kerasím at their request.

4) Union Females may not be borrowed, sold, or traded to any other persons for reasons of assault, servitude, consorting, or marriage, as their laws state.

All jurisdictions note: This is my word; this is my law; follow and obey from this day forth.

Nadigh Raman gol Suhr Zaghil, Emperor of All Kerasim and its Territories

Aila gave a squeal of delight, waking the other ladies. *Thank you, thank you, Rimas!*

"The wedding is go!"

Thirteen

This was it. The com had been quiet – only Dad had called to say they were in orbit – but no doubt the shit was about to hit the proverbial fan. Aila waited inside the security lounge on the roof of the palace with General Tokh as the Union shuttle made its landing. Outside was the official greeting assembly – General Trannor, Minister Nemutar, Ross Halian and two of his aides, a palace translator, and six heavily armed security guards. Nine Union representatives disembarked the carrier, including Bindai Hhani, the Secretary of State, and both of Aila's parents.

Mom actually made it.

Aila bounced on her toes, eager for the formalities to be over. They still had to pass through security. To ease the situation, Aila had requested Masákh not accompany her. The fact Mom had made it planetside was a miracle; there was no need to ruin it. Yes, Aila wore Kerasi clothing, but nothing outlandish – silky wide-legged pants she'd borrowed from Dalo, and a conservative blue shirt. They could have been leisure clothes from home. Mom shouldn't mind.

She greeted Secretary Hhani warmly as he cleared the checkpoint. "I'm so sorry about this. It was never my intent, never. I'd planned on being back home by now."

"Sometimes the best meetings are the unscheduled ones," Hhani said. "The fact Nadigh is willing to meet with us and have some discussion is a good sign. Even if all we discuss is how to proceed with intermarriage, that's still progress." He patted her hand as he held it. "You're still forging policy ahead of itself. If I had a dozen of you, there'd be a lot more peace in our galaxy."

Aila gave a sarcastic laugh. "I don't think you're going find eleven more people who want to go through what I did. They tried that, remember? I'm the only one who survived undamaged, and everyone's resented that fact ever since."

"Not if we put General Tokh in charge of that program, no?" Hhani bowed to Tokh. "It's a pleasure to meet you again, General. I thank you again for your outstanding care of our councilor."

Tokh bowed sharply. "It is my honor, Secretary. It is no longer duty. Now it is personal."

"We're very glad to count you as an ally."

Admiral Perrin cleared the checkpoint, wearing official uniform despite retirement, his white hair still regulation-short. Aila attacked him with a fierce hug. "Daddy! I'm so, so glad you came. At first I wasn't even going to tell you, and then I thought I'd explain it later, but then Mímihn and Nihda went and made a big deal of it and insisted they had to invite you as protocol. I know how you feel about everything; I didn't expect you to come, but I'm really glad you did. I think you'll enjoy this visit. I hope you will, at least."

Ramden Perrin put his hands on the sides of Aila's head and squeezed in feigned ferocity. "Child, I don't know what to do with you. You're going to be the death of me yet. If I can't talk sense into you, I better be next to you so I know exactly what you're getting into. I know you think you know what you're doing, but I still know more than you."

"I know, Daddy. Mom!"

Leila Perrin cleared the checkpoint, but Admiral Perrin grabbed Aila's arm, stopping her rush. "She's here under great protest, Aila, and they've got her on medication to help deal with it. You watch what you say. Don't make this worse."

A huffy sigh of annoyance escaped Aila. Did parents ever stop treating people like three year olds? She got more respect from Tokh. "I know that. What do you think I've been trying to do?" She pulled away to give her mother a gentle, apologetic hug.

"Hi, Mom. Thank you so much for coming. I know, I know, I know you don't agree, and I swear to you I did not plan this, but maybe we could sit and I could explain why?"

Leila didn't offer any type of greeting, didn't so much as raise a hand to return even a portion of the hug. She stared straight ahead in deliberate disregard of her daughter. Her voice held a bitterness that promised a vicious retort if given a private chance. "This isn't the place, Aila. I'm here at the request of Bindai, and as a special favor to President Rill. All I have to do is show my face. I'm not in the service of the military, I'm not a diplomat, and I do not have to socialize with anyone, even you."

"I'm not asking you to, Mom. I'm just very glad you came. Thank you."

The rest of the Union visitors cleared the checkpoint, including Secretary Hhani's wife, Chonda, the only other female in the group. Her curly gray hair and mahogany skin were certain to amuse Kerasi females. She glanced back at the checkpoint and the armed soldiers. "So far so good. You're certain this is safe?"

"You're royalty here," Aila said. "Nadigh's greatest fear is a repeat of the events of last year, and he will take every possible precaution to prevent it. The security checks are a pain in the neck, but it's to ensure your safety and everyone else's. They're always quite thorough; they make a mistake, they die. Be cautious, certainly, but there's really no need to worry. Ask your *aghát*; they're literally standing around itching to show off their knowledge for you. Ask my Dad; they survived their last visit without a scratch."

"You'll be staying on Union soil," Ross Halian cut in. "We've made arrangements for you to stay at the Embassy with me. It's much more like home."

"My home is also open to Union guests," Tokh offered with a bow. "It would be my honor."

Aila took her mother's hands. "Actually, Mom, I was hoping you'd come back and stay the night with me. It's the night before my wedding, and I want to spend it with you. You've already met the ladies; you already know the *aghát*. You can stay right in my room with me. Zheníhda would be thrilled beyond reason if you did. It would send her status off the charts with her neighbors. You can see Mímihn's baby; he's just adorable! I'm staying with you guys until Tokh heads back home later this afternoon. Please come back with me tonight?"

Laila pulled her hands back, distant but polite. "I've barely set foot off the ship, Aila. I've not seen where we're staying, seen an itinerary, or had time to use a ladies' room. I'm not ready to make decisions yet."

Aila flashed an embarrassed smile. "Fair enough."

Aila accompanied the group throughout their day. There was a grand private reception on the fifth floor, hosted by Trannor and Nemutar and perhaps a dozen of the top cabinet members. Aila stayed in the background and tried not to interact with Trannor at all. Now that she knew who he was, she wanted to observe him. Despite his claims of decency and having been the driving force behind her good treatment, she didn't trust him. Making decisions from several lightyears away, even several hundred miles, was not the same as being friends with a person, and Aila had a long way to go before calling him friend. She'd merely decided he wasn't an immediate threat, despite having the power to do a lot more than spank her. The reception lasted an hour, followed by a tour of the palace.

Tokh assigned Ghírandar to be Aila's personal guard. He'd been a raw recruit when Aila had been kidnapped the first time, just twenty-three and on his first assignment fresh out of *aghát* training. He hadn't been allowed to supervise her alone, except occasionally as escort, and any of his educational lessons had been supervised by others. Aila knew his forte was Kerasi law, and that he had a law certificate behind his *aghát* title. Ahead, three palace *aghát* accompanied the small group behind an official tour guide.

"You look distracted," Aila told him.

Ghírandar gave a faint smile. "I'm trying to pay attention to my job and be a tourist at the same time."

"You've never toured the palace?"

His eyes examined a painting in the grand hallway, a massive framed work depicting cavorting around the occasion of a successful *dhastal* hunt, with woodland females dancing with joy and males already chasing them with lust. Ghírandar's head then snapped back to survey the party ahead of them, the hallway, the marked exits, and count the number of people in sight, ever vigilant. "Just the little bit last year, never in this part, or with such high-ranking guides. I am humbled by the history and glory of the Empire."

Aila had been through Masákh's breakdowns over the privilege of walking through Derahl Nor. "You're a *nhasarwharl*, if I remember."

"Yes. Caste doesn't matter to *aghát*; we are considered equal, but outside of duty, I outrank all Tokh's *aghát* except Mátokhan. Mátokhan is *nhasarwharl* with *dihnarwharl* privilege, so he has a slight advantage. If that is negated, however, he still outranks me."

"You're Captain now, correct?"

Ghírandar nodded proudly. "I made Captain One three years ago at twenty-six. That's hard to beat. Tokh was Captain Two at twenty-five, but they skipped him C-One entirely. His was a unique situation."

"Mímihn said he was wounded in a major battle. Why did they move you up so fast?"

Ghírandar glanced at her with amusement. "I would have thought Masákh would have explained it by now. The expected rule, if you serve regular duty and do it well, is five years for each half-rank, or ten years for each whole one. Do a poor job, receive reprimands, and it will take longer. Take risky positions or take on extra training, you earn at a faster rate. Off world? Faster rate. Hazardous duty? Faster rate. Battlefront? Faster rate. I served more than a year off-world, behind enemy lines, was taken prisoner, and then helped negotiate a preliminary truce. I served one more year behind enemy lines as a diplomat. I sped through an entire half-rank at triple-speed. With Tokh's recommendation, I was promoted to Captain just three years after joining his men. Now I am on regular duty, so I will hope to make Captain Two in two more years, and Major by thirty-six. That is still a significant accomplishment."

Aila's smile shared his pride. "You earned every bit. You have much more confidence in your duties than you did five years ago. No one would guess your age."

"I am very confident today. May I share a truth?"

"Please do."

Ghírandar took a deep breath. "*I – was – terrified*," he confessed. "I was one month past my certification when Tokh chose me. That alone was prestigious. My first assignment, and it was highest secrecy, off-world, in enemy territory, and incredibly dangerous. Thank the Emperor Mátokhan was not often with us; I was more intimidated by him than by Tokh. I was so afraid of making a mistake. I did not have just one commander to please but five *aghát* above me, who could give me unfavorable recommendations at any moment. I had great difficulty even speaking to you, because I was afraid I would use a wrong word, or you would not follow my requests and I would be forced to use physical direction that I would have to explain."

Aila burst out laughing as the group stopped to listen about a large statue in an annex. "That's so funny! I was so terrified of you! I mean, not as much as Masákh or Tokh or Sóghar, but you were so quiet, I didn't know what you would do if I acted up. I felt bad for you when you taught me lessons. Your lessons were fine, but Masákh or Sóghar would always be there as well, and I could see the sweat at your hairline. It made it very difficult to focus on your words."

Ghírandar gave a chuckle. "I knew they were observing and rating me. I did not know my fear was visible."

"We both survived, didn't we."

Leila Perrin's voice rang out from the back of the group. "Aila, I thought you said you'd be with us? Haven't you spent enough time with your little friends?"

Aila raced forward until she was side by side with her parents. Her hands landed on each of their shoulders and she jumped a little when she made contact. "I'm right here. Excuse me for talking to someone. Don't be mean to Ghírandar. He's a decorated hero. He was a prisoner of war, once, too. But you should know that, because we were the ones imprisoning him."

Her head turned around to Ghírandar behind her, and she winked.

Leila Perrin wouldn't make a huge scene before the Kerasi or Secretary Hhani – not that she hadn't ripped his face off before – but she couldn't get past the security and the only other way off the roof was to jump. Aila did feel bad. She knew that look, a sense of imminent death and no possible way to escape it. It was a horrible feeling, and not what she'd meant to do to her mother. She held tight to Leila's hand as her mother gave a final "I can't believe you're making me do this" glare at her father.

"I'm only an airwave away. I will see you tomorrow," Ramden Perrin repeated.

"You have my sincerest promise, Lady Perrin, you will be given highest respect," Masákh said, and tried to turn Aila to the aircraft. Aila pulled on her mother, who finally relented.

Leila paused to speak just loud enough for Masákh to hear her over the building engines. "If you want to keep your tongue, I suggest you stop speaking to me."

"Mother!" Aila shoved Leila into the aircraft.

It was a quiet flight. As much as Aila wanted to throw herself around Masákh's neck, sit on his lap, laugh with the men, this was not the time. Tokh kept the mood professional, speaking quietly with Ráhnif, Ghírandar, and Masákh, and Tótoghar piloting the craft. Aila ignored her mother's mood, pointing out the various shore-towns they passed, explaining the layout of the towns on the hills, the styles of housing, the geography of the inlet as much as she was able. Aila realized with a start just what she was doing. This was only her second visit to Kerasím – second, and already she was so used to traveling the coast and with the structures and the people she was able to discuss the damned geography of the region. She couldn't do that on Centauri, and she'd been living there more or less for seven years.

Maybe it was because she never wanted to be on Centauri in the first place. She hated leaving Earth again, and her former friends, just to follow Dad on his quest for a political appointment. Maybe it was because she was young – twelve or so when they moved – and took it all for granted. Maybe she just never had anyone to teach her about it. Being held captive on Kye had made her grow up fast. Being on Kerasím itself had given her maturity. Aila felt a little glow burning inside her, a little pat on her back that she was on the right track, doing the right thing, growing up. Suddenly it didn't seem so weird to be facing a marriage ceremony. Yeah. She was ready for this.

Zheníhda and Mímihn met them as they disembarked, Kesseh and Faelihn alongside. Despite their overflowing eagerness, the girls stood still like little *dahneg* hostesses in their best dresses and fancy hair, desperate to impress the new lady, a diplomat lady, whose husband was a great and powerful Admiral in the Union Space Fleet. Aila introduced everyone.

"*Well-khome, Laydy Pehrrin,*" Zheníhda said with a formal bow. "*Thank yu for vizit ing. We hahppy yu here.*"

Mímihn stayed reserved, within the lines of proper behavior, but she grasped Leila's hand, something she knew was appropriate in the Union. She had a much more useful vocabulary, thanks to Aila. "*Ama* Aila! Well-khome! Well-khome! More hahppy see!"

"They speak Union?" Leila whispered to Aila.

"Most of the men here will. Tokh's required the girls to learn it, and the women have been trying as well. Dalo is best at it."

Kesseh couldn't wait any longer. She stepped forward and bowed perfectly. A huge grin lit her face, though her eyes strayed as she fought to remember the proper words. "Ah-lo, Laydy Pehrrin! We arr very pleased to meet yu. Well-khome to Imahlva. Please enjoy yur visit. We arr here to serve yu."

Faelihn burst out, "Ah-lo, Laydy Pehrrin! Mai name is Faelihn. I am very khonored to meet yu."

Leila couldn't help but smile back. "Thank you, Faelihn. I am honored to meet you, too. You speak very well."

Faelihn couldn't smile any harder. "Thang kyu, Laydy Pehrrin. I study speaking."

"I study, too," Kesseh said. She slid a step to the side, blocking Faelihn.

Leila squeezed each of their hands. "You must both study very hard." Neither of the girls understood every word, but they caught *You study very*, and took it be a compliment. They giggled and bowed again before Zheníhda waved them off.

Aila followed the women into the house, Leila close behind. Masákh carried her small luggage case up the stairs.

"Where's he going with that?"

"Up to our room, Mother. I promise, he's not going to go through it and judge you by anything nasty you may have in there."

Leila glared hard. "Stop it!" she hissed through clenched teeth.

Zheníhda already had an assortment of refreshments on the table. She waved a hand. "Please, to eat, and to talk."

"Thank you, Zheníhda," Aila replied. She explained each item to her mother. "*Lunahl* you've had before, it's a mild wine. The water here is good enough to drink straight; it's clean, but if you're ever in doubt, ask for hot *raffin*. Say the word: *raffin*," and Leila repeated it. "It's perhaps the most common non-alcoholic drink, served hot or cold, always appropriate, and if it's hot, you know it's been boiled and is safe to drink. You can add anything to it – fruit, whipped toppings, alcohol, syrups, sugar – *zahnot*. Think of it like a coffee." She handed her mother a cup with sugar and whipped topping, then made one for herself.

Leila took a tentative sip, careful not to burn her lips. Her eyes said she wanted to spit it out, but managed a swallow. She smiled at Zheníhda, who bowed in honor. "That's a unique flavor."

"It's not bad once you get used to it and find a combination you like."

The *aghát* had shed their uniform jackets and gathered around Tokh. Tokh's men were familiar with his younger son Kitras, but few of them had met his older son Zenak. The men weren't drinking *raffin* but various spirits, while Mímihn offered delicacies from a tray. The men spoke loudly, pounded each other on the shoulders and arms and laughed, quite unlike the stoic reserve a good *aghát* always presented. Aila had grown used to it, but it still made her shake her head each time. *Aghát* were prim, proper, precise, not "normal" men. *Never confuse the officer with the person.* It was a lesson Aila still struggled to understand.

Leila's eyes kept shifting back to watch them. "How much do they usually drink? You're sure we're okay?"

Aila took a deep breath, but it didn't help. She'd tried. She'd tried so hard, had such hopes and dreams for this moment. The fact her father and Mr. Hhani had helped her pull it off said they thought it was a good idea, too. If only her mother would just pull her head out of her ass for one second to see the truth.

She put her cup of *raffin* on the table. "Nice move, Mom. You just insulted your host. Tokh promised you would not be harmed. The one thing you never, ever doubt in this world is Tokh's word. It's stronger than yours. I was so happy to bring you here, to be with my friends who are closer to me than my family is right now. I wanted you to gain that relief of knowing where I was and who I was with when I'm here, so you can relax about it. But you're just not willing."

Aila's anger surged up, but the hurt came out as tears that twisted her face and burned her nose but didn't yet spill over. *Kerasi don't cry.* Her words grew louder, until the men quieted down and stared, even if the women didn't. No one offered to translate.

"I guess I'm the stupid one. I always had this dumb fantasy of you working alongside me, pointing me in the right direction, helping me to change the rights of suffering women here. I had this – crazy game I used to play in my head, where you would sit down with Ghírandar and discuss laws, because he's an interplanetary lawyer too, just like you, and you could work out what we had in common and what we needed to fix, so that if I was ever stuck, you'd know their laws and could help me. I've seen you rip the head off the president and scream down his neck, but the second I mention Kerasi, you run and hide. These people see you as royalty, they are truly honored to have you in their presence, and you can't see it.

"You know why, Mom? Because you've never needed to. You spend hours with me and Masákh, and you don't say a single word to him. Maybe because you've never needed to depend on him for your very life. That's how I learned to see through the propaganda. My very life depended on them. So maybe that's what you need. Let your life depend on them, and see what you learn. Instead of just bitching about the problem, maybe you should be trying to fix it."

She turned and strode out the door without a single look back.

"Aila!" Leila Perrin commanded. She took two steps in the same direction. "Don't you dare do this to me! Get back here!" But Aila was gone.

Fourteen

Aila was gone, and Leila was alone, on a planet that terrified her, with violent people in a strange unknown place, a long flight from her husband. Her breath fought to enter her lungs until she felt dizzy from lack of oxygen. She spun to face the room, not trusting them for a moment with her back.

Mímihn put down her tray and rushed over. She grabbed Leila's hand and patted it. "*Ama* Aila! Laydy Pehrrin! Vehry sorry! Vehry sorry! Pleece, *kuhmra doh sis?*"

Masákh approached the dining table and bowed before her. "Lady Perrin. Lady Tokh wishes to know what she may do to help you."

Leila's fear gave over to anger. She stared at him with her lips pressed tight before speaking. "She got her way, didn't she. I have no choice but to talk to you now. Was that her plan all along?"

"If you prefer, I will have one of the other *aghát* translate. You are acquainted with Haghíde. He will be happy to assist."

"No. I'll stick to the evil I know best."

Masákh understood the insult, but his only response was to nod. "Truth, she did not wish to invite you. She knew it would upset you, and she did not wish to do that. She has tried hard to avoid the ceremony. It was Tokh's wives who insisted. They considered it improper not to invite you. If you chose not to attend, their honor would still have been fulfilled."

"I didn't have much of a choice in that, either."

"*Igra, jiht.*" Tokh waved the other men outside to the patio. He walked to the table with a slow and deliberate gait and sat down, intimidating without meaning to be, gesturing to the chairs opposite. Masákh pulled one out for Leila and invited her to sit before standing between her and Tokh, the closest he'd yet been to her without some sort of verbal attack.

"Nihda, get our guest something stronger than *raffin*, then sit with her, please." Zheníhda wouldn't understand any of it, but females felt safer in clusters, and she was closest to their guest in age. The grand inquisitor whose fortune had been made wresting information from people, willingly or not, focused on his task.

"I have spoken extensively with Admiral Perrin. We have buried the worst of our disagreements and come to understandings. I accept his daughter as one of my own. I open my home to his wife, as it is of greater luxury and security than that of the Union embassy, where you can have private conversation with your daughter and the company of other females. You are not pleased with this arrangement."

Leila stayed silent for several moments, wrestling with herself, and it wasn't clear if anger or fear would win. She had borne an incredibly strong spine when her daughter had been kidnapped; it returned now, when she needed it. "You – you yourself – stole my daughter from me. You held her, tortured her, maimed her, and last year your people tried to rape and murder her. No. I am not happy with this arrangement. What guarantee do I have that you won't do the same to me?"

"The same guarantee I gave to Admiral Perrin. Not one of my men will touch you, simply because of your rank and position, mother of a *dahneg*. I would personally execute anyone who attempted it. I'm sure you have been told, your daughter was never our target but seized in error. Had we realized then that she was in the wrong place because she could not obey orders, we would have returned her immediately. She placed us at extreme risk. Yes, I carried out punishment, but on the order of a superior; as the wife of an Admiral, I believe you understand following orders. I stood witness to make sure nothing occurred more than necessary, and that she was not harmed. The procedure done to her speech would have been reversed had she not been seized back unexpectedly by the Union."

Masákh added softly, "The incident of last year was proven to be orchestrated in part by Union Secretary Omi Kel. While Kerasi officials were involved, Kel had the opportunity to prevent Aila's mistreatment at any point. General Tokh was directly responsible for preventing the second assassination attempt, and providing the security for Aila to recover in peace."

Zheníhda patted Leila's hand, then rubbed it as if reading her mind. "*Goohd, Laydy Pehrrin. Yu goohd.*"

93

Leila was not convinced. "I don't know what hold you have over my daughter, but I don't like it. In six years, she has never recovered to her former self, her former outlook, her former person. You destroyed my daughter. You even adopted her, to where she thinks you're better than those who raised her. I'm upset about that."

"That was never my intention," Tokh insisted. "No subliminal ideas were implanted. No change should have occurred. All we did was instruct facts, as a teacher presents lessons. More than that is her understanding of the lessons. Putting her under my name was a risk to me, not to her, and was done as a protective measure. By giving her my name, she has protection under Kerasi law. If you were familiar with our laws, you would understand. It was never to replace her Union family. That is truth."

"I strongly disapprove of this marriage, for many reasons. Aila promised me she would wait until she was twenty-one and finished her studies. She can't do that if she is running back and forth across the galaxy. She needs to grow up first. She's gone two weeks, and suddenly she insists she must get married this very week, but she will wait so graciously until we get here. I can't believe a word she says." Leila was all steel now. Her words were clipped and sharp. Her unflinching glare stabbed at Tokh with a hatred that welled up from her very core.

Masákh translated that bit to Mímihn, who rushed over and grabbed Leila's arm. "No! No, Laydy Pehrrin. I!" She launched into a long apologetic paragraph. Masákh translated it whenever she stopped to take a breath.

"It was me, Laydy Pehrrin! I demanded Aila must get married this year. I didn't know if she would ever return to visit, and I wanted to see her be married. She is my treasured friend, and I wanted to make her happy. Do not be mad at Aila or Tokh! It is my fault. I am most sorry, Laydy Pehrrin. She was very afraid of your anger, but I wanted to give her a party. Please forgive her, Great Laydy. I miss her when she isn't here." Mímihn's whole face pinched up in sadness.

Tokh nodded. "That is truth. The Emperor declared it a special year for marriage, and Mímihn took it to heart. I did not demand it. We did not know if the Emperor would allow it, but he rewrote laws at Aila's request to ensure her rights as a double-citizen. She has moved most cautiously. You would know this, if you allowed her to speak. I have always found it more difficult to make her stop speaking."

Leila's steel weakened. "Where is she now?"

Tokh paused. "She would not leave the compound by herself. She is on property."

Leila fell silent, Mímihn still rubbing her arm in consolation. It was difficult to be angry with Mímihn, even if she had no business trying to convince Aila to get married. No matter how much she still thought Aila was off her rocker, either her friends were experts at lying or Aila was telling the truth. "Aila said I was staying in her room. May I wait there for her to return?"

Masákh translated, and Mímihn jumped to her feet as her tears evaporated. "*Gah*, yes! Yes, khome! Khome!" She tugged on Leila's arm until she stood up.

Leila paused. "May I see a copy of the laws that were rewritten for Aila?"

Tokh nodded. "They were sent to all officials. I will have a printed copy brought upstairs."

Leila bowed her head. "Thank you."

Aila looked at the gate posts at the street-end of the property, but knew she couldn't cross them. Tokh's aircraft stayed locked to keep the children out; she couldn't hide inside it. No doubt Tokh could track her on grounds with his security system; she wanted to get off-property, but didn't dare. Once outside, without a male escort, she was free game. Tokh had warned her about the creepy guy across the street and up one. He had a long balcony on his house from where he liked to keep his eyes on the neighborhood and know their business. Tokh said to consider him dangerous. A shame, because she would have loved to walk along the tranquility of the beach until her anger lifted.

The vehicle shed. There was a skinny little path around the far side, just enough to peel back the hillside so it didn't touch the building, enough space to walk around it for inspection. She slipped along the ditch, one hand on the building while her feet had to walk toe to heel until she came to the far end of the building, probably the most invisible space on the entire property. Aila squeezed into the ditch to sit with her back against the building and her legs crossed, knees pressing into the dirt.

Oh, Mother.

Yeah, she'd listen to Holy Hell later, but it was what Mother needed. She'd have to settle down and talk to Masákh or Tokh; no one else would understand. She'd have to rely on them, the same way Aila'd had to. *They aren't evil, Mom.* Sure, they had some issues – she'd seen Tokh murder men who'd screwed up, and Haghíde and Masákh, for that matter. She never, ever, wanted to see Masákh truly angry at her, but so far their good had always outweighed their bad. Especially Tokh. Mímihn had seen a lot of ugly bad in her life, and she couldn't praise Tokh enough. On the other hand, when your whole life depended on someone else, you weren't going to be quick to criticize them. But Aila knew it to be true; Tokh had been exceptionally kind to Mímihn, freeing her from slavery at his own expense and getting her surgery to allow her to see again. Not many Kerasi men would have done that. Even the creepy guy across the street and one up, who owned his own sex slave, hadn't blinded her like Mímihn's owner had done to her.

Open your eyes, Mom. Open your heart. Stop being such a

Aila jumped, heart in her throat, as a face popped from around the very back of the vehicle shed.

"Great Lady Pehrrin? You walk, but you not come out."

Aila calmed her breathing. She was never sure whether Thrit's incomplete grammar was due to a language issue – he could have been raised with a local dialect, and not Emperor's tongue – or something else. He certainly wasn't stupid, so it wasn't an intellectual disability. He was *ghinadín*, lowest of the lowest castes in all of Kerasím, so maybe it was just lack of education. Few *ghinadín* ever saw a day of formal schooling. Or a real house, for that matter. He was tiny – shorter than Aila by at least two inches, light as a bird, with thin gray hair and a wrinkled amber-gray face to match, and small branding scar high on his cheekbone to remind the world he was *ghinadín*. Tokh had hired him for Mímihn when he acquired her, a castrated servant who could be trusted around a female, provide protection, and work for pennies a year. He was old – not even Thrit knew his actual age, but when Mímihn no longer needed him, Tokh kept him on as hired help, a trusted escort for his females, a groundskeeper, a handyman, and an extra pair of eyes. By law he couldn't be paid more than a small maximum, but he had two furnished rooms to himself over the vehicle hangar, and all the leftover *díhnarwharl* food the housekeeper could feed him; far more luxury and independence than most *ghinadín* servants ever had. Aila didn't know their arrangement, but Tokh treated him with an unparalleled amount of respect and trust for his position, and she knew Thrit would lie down and die on Tokh's command.

It was rude of him to speak to her; even if Aila collapsed on the ground in heart failure, their caste difference was so great Thrit couldn't touch her to give assistance, even with gloves; he would have to run and find someone else. She put a finger to her lips. "*Shu.* I wish to run far away, but I cannot go alone. This is my run-away place. No one will find me."

"Lord Tokh know."

Thank you, Colonel Obvious. Aila rolled her eyes to him. "Yes, but he will let me sit until I am ready."

"Wedding tomorrow. Guests arrive tonight. Major will come for you."

Aila sighed. Had she ever been out of sight around Kerasi? *"Sukh, Thrit. Behspa. Tavi fasim, koormaht ka."* Five minutes to sulk, that's all she wanted. Better to rescue Mom before she got too hysterical. She was probably on the com to Ross Halian to come and get her right now.

"T'rit wait in front."

She tiptoed up the stairs after thanking Zheníhda and Mímihn for looking after Mom. Aila didn't apologize, just stood quietly in the room until her mother looked up from whatever she was studying on her com.

"You win. I was forced to speak to them. You got your way."

"The only 'way' I got was to stop your snit," Aila replied. "You weren't going to listen to anything I said, so I simply stopped talking. Do you like the room? It's their best guest room. Mímihn's room is next door on the end. Did you get the grand tour?"

Leila shook her head. "What I've seen is lovely. So how do they make that work, with two wives? Do they all sleep together in a pile?"

Aila laughed. "Goodness, no. Zheníhda would lose her mind. It's up to each family, really, but here both wives have their own rooms, and they take turns in Tokh's room, a week at a time. A smaller house might have one room for wives, and the one not busy will have the room."

"What about the consort nonsense?"

Aila shrugged. "I don't know. When I knew Mímihn as consort, she had her own space in Tokh's quarters, but his wives weren't there. They're property, so where they sleep and how they sleep is up to the owner. Mímihn said before Tokh made her secondwife, Zheníhda made her sleep in the housekeeper's quarters. They work it out."

Aila took Leila's hand and pulled on her. "Come on. I'll give you the grand tour. It's an amazing place. You can walk anywhere in the house or yard without worry. If you want to explore the road or go down to the beach, you just have to take one of the men with you. Any of them will do it, you just have to ask. If you don't want to speak to Tokh, Zheníhda or Mímihn will assign someone. You'll catch on. Come on."

Fifteen

Aila woke up to the sun filtering through the grand curtains. Today was her wedding day. She, Aila Lissette Perrin, nineteen years old, already a member of the Union Council on Kerasi Affairs, was getting married – willingly – to a Kerasi national, on a world that just five years ago was the grand enemy of the Planetary Union, and Aila's personal enemy then as well. Life was weirder than anyone ever imagined.

Leila Perrin slept next to her on the bed, quiet for the moment. Five years ago Mom slept next to Aila, too, in their own apartment, a panicky doze from which she opened a worried eye every time Aila moved or sighed too deeply. Yes, Aila'd had some nightmares when she'd returned home from a year in Kerasi captivity, but the worst anxiety had been Leila's, terrified her child would disappear again in the dark of night, never to be found. When cornered, Aila would admit she'd had a little difficulty settling back in to a normal life, but the greater trauma had been Leila's.

This moment was a miracle.

Mímihn, Dalo, and Avalihn burst into the bedroom carrying trays of extra-fancy breakfast, waking Leila. "Today! Today!" Dalo said.

"You must eat," Mímihn said. "Then a bath, and I will make your nails and feet pretty for you."

How is this any different than life in the Union? The only thing missing was her friend Thayer, but Mom and Thayer got along worse than Mom and Masákh.

Aila's comm signaled her as Mímihn buffed her feet.

I have not held you in three days. I am in a most dire situation without you.

Aila burst out laughing. Leave it to Masákh to send the most unromantic sex message ever.

If someone will distract Lady Tokh, younger, I will meet you in the hall closet.

Mímihn eyed her laughter with suspicion and snatched the com away. She squinted at the text, but it was in Union. "You aren't talking to Masákh, are you? *Ka ka ka!* You're not supposed to speak to your husband to be. He's supposed to be a surprise. You've already ruined that, bedding him." She returned to coating Aila's feet with a thick cream, then rubbing it in with a rough towel.

"You knew Tokh before your wedding," Aila said with a good amount of sass. "Did that ruin it for you?"

Mímihn blushed. "No." She stopped buffing for a moment. "It's different after a marriage. It feels different. It feels... I don't know. More meaningful. You know that happiness is there to stay. It can't go away tomorrow. At least, in a good marriage. In a bad one, that's the saddest thought." Her voice trailed away, remembering her awful first marriage. She brightened again a moment later, and gave Aila's foot a final swipe. "But you have a good marriage."

"Yes, I do. A *very* good marriage." Aila's words held a lecherous note. Mímihn let out a screech of laughter, Dalo joined her, and even Avalihn blushed with a smile. Aila glanced at the bathroom door, checking it was still closed. Some things weren't meant for moms.

Aila was kept sequestered, much to her annoyance, relegated to minding baby Thoren while Mímihn ran about the house, or keeping the girls out of the way unless needed. One of the women stayed with her at all times. Leila was allowed to leave the room, but not Aila, lest she be seen by Masákh, who, when not given a specific duty to keep him out of the house, was kept isolated in Tokh's room. To make it worse, the *aghát* took delight in taking turns guarding the upstairs hall and making great pains of themselves. Mátokhan went up and down the hall every hour, banging on the doors and shouting the time, followed by "All accounted for!" Haghíde knocked on the door; Aila let him enter. He took up a guard stance just inside the room.

"Did you want something?" Aila asked.

"No. I am here to make sure all is well and the honorees stay separated. I am also here to offer my assistance to anyone changing into their evening clothes." He snapped his heels together and bowed.

Thank goodness Leila wasn't in the room. Aila rolled her eyes and tried to stuff him out the door. "Go!"

Haghíde pulled out his com unit and held it up. "Then I bear Masákh's request that you remove an article of clothing so I may bring him a photograph he may think about."

"No!" Aila wrestled him out the door with no help from Avalihn, who couldn't follow the conversation. "I know what you people would do with that picture, and that's disgusting. Get out of here." She closed the door as Haghíde took several photos of her shoving him.

From the balcony, Aila watched the yard transform as hired people set up tables and chairs and strings of lights. A cargo truck backed across the courtyard, bringing mountains of flowers that Zheníhda inspected and directed. A quartet of men arrived; Shanohr showed them to the grassy area, where they began to set up instruments and a small canopy to shelter them from sun or rain. Caterers examined the layouts, observed the workspace they would have in the kitchen, and set themselves in motion.

Leila stood next to Aila on the balcony. "I have to hand it to them. They are certainly going all-out for this. I'm impressed. This must be costing a fortune."

Aila nodded. It was humbling, having this much honor thrown at oneself. "When Mímihn said wedding party, I figured the Kerasi equivalent of pizza and beer and loud music, and dancing 'til dawn with Mímihn and Dalo. I never dreamed of anything so grand and formal. Ever. Even at home, I never expected this. They're the best friends I'll ever have, past behavior included."

"Maybe they're trying to make up for that."

Aila turned to stare at her mother. All Aila'd ever wanted was a truce from Leila. She didn't have to like the situation, she just needed to stop being so rabid and hostile about it. Never once had Aila expected exoneration. "Does that mean you're forgiving them?"

Leila's voice bit back. "Oh no! But I admit they are not entirely bloodthirsty murderers, and I see why you might want to fight to save your lady friends from their own society. I can't trust them, not even Masákh, but if I can't keep you away from it, I might as well try to make it as safe a place as I can for you. At least I know who to hold responsible if something happens."

101

Aila hugged her mother as hard as she could without snapping ribs. "Thank you, Mom. That's all I ever wanted in the first place."

The grandeur of the preparations still bothered Aila, and she messaged Mímihn to ask Tokh to speak with her. Mímihn had helped him bathe and Zheníhda trimmed his hair and chin hank, then helped him into his dress uniform – no longer straining at the buttons, with Trannor's enforced fitness regimen. With all of his medals and pins and ribbons and trims and sword in place, he looked like a king on parade.

"Please be brief. My time is in great demand."

"I will," Aila insisted. They stepped into the hallway for privacy. Tokh's eyes stayed focused out the open doors to the balcony over the front door, watching servants and hired help scurry across the courtyard. "I wish to say I am humbled by your efforts for my wedding, General, and I am in your debt. Thank you, from the sky to your heart. Your kindness is extreme, and will be widely publicized within the Union."

Tokh held his hands behind his back. The faintest of smiles nudged his face, and he nodded absently. "I am pleased you are pleased, but I admit it is self-serving. It is to my benefit to host neighbors, friends, and superiors with events. I do not do so often enough, not on a large scale. Your wedding is good reason for impressing those whose *khatas* I must stroke. You are designated *dahneg*, daughter of a *dihnarwharl* with *dahneg* privilege. *Dahneg* is now the highest caste below *thósikh*. We stand equal to the brothers of the Emperor." His voice faded off, as if still in awe of the fact. "That requires appropriate decoration." He turned to her and gave a full smile. "You are merely my excuse."

Aila bowed her head. "Then I am happy to be of service. May this day bring you great honor. Thank you, *Triskaris-bo*."

He didn't lavish her with affection as he did his wives and daughter and smalldaughter, still kept an uneasy politeness between them, but he patted her shoulder. "We will climb higher tonight. Both of us. You will see."

Sixteen

In the blink of an eye, time became short. Dalo dressed the girls while Mímihn fed Thoren one last time, then turned him and Niboh over to a hired woman for the night. Zheníhda waited until she thought no one was looking and poured a worthy amount of *flehdan* into a juice drink. Aila helped her mother into a fancy dress, one Aila had never seen before, paved in silver-white beads and coming just above her knees, sure to be all the rage in Keranihn the following week, as well as her freshly-blonde hair.

Nerves crept up and seized Aila's middle. It was silly; she and Masákh had been living as husband and wife for a year. This was a simple ceremony; it changed nothing. It wasn't legal inside the Union, where they spent the majority of their time, so why was she so edgy?

Mímihn helped her slide into her dress, then noticed the two tears on Aila's cheeks. She beamed like a ray of sunshine. "Silly female! You're still like a maid, after all this time. It's just a party." She kissed the tears to make them disappear.

Dalo elbowed her in the side. "A few more hours, then you can get back to the fun stuff." Her single eyebrow arched high in the middle, and Aila couldn't help but laugh.

Leila's face was all glare. "Aila, if you're having any second thoughts at all, step out of the dress. Let them wait an hour or so while you figure it out. Get Masákh in here if you have to."

Aila shook her head with a laugh. "No. This is what I want. I'm just overexcited. It's not the ceremony, it's the size of it. Everyone is so beautiful and so excited, and it's all because of me. I'm just – overwhelmed. I'll be okay once I see Masákh."

A light knock sounded at the men's door. Haghíde opened it wearing his dress uniform, impeccably polished and presented despite his altered *aghát* appearance. His eyes went wide, and he fell into a nervous bow. Mímihn stood in the hall, perhaps the most gorgeous female Haghíde had ever laid eyes on. Her hair was piled high on her head, only to fall in a cascade of jet curls down to her shoulder. Individual sparkling crystals had been glued onto the curls, giving flashes of rainbow when she moved her head. She wore a sweeping silver-gray gown with a single soft ruffle flouncing over her hips, and her makeup accented every perfection of her face. Silver-gray gloves came up past her elbows to complete the effect. Mímihn glowed from within. Perhaps it was because she was calmer than usual, the flighty amusing child-wife replaced with a sophisticated grown-up female who exuded *dahneg* charm and power, a wife any male would be proud to claim.

"Lady Tokh!" Haghíde stumbled, and bowed again.

"Is Masákh in?"

Mátokhan had been aligning and polishing the citations on the front of Masákh's dress uniform, but Masákh approached the doorway.

Mímihn's hands clasped behind her back, and she glanced up at him with a saucy grin, much more herself. "Honored Citizen, I come to inform you that the lady you should marry will be clothed in green."

Masákh bowed his head. "I expected so. Says my friend, or says my foe?"

Despite all the finery and image, Mímihn giggled, her excitement one breath from exploding. "Sayeth your friends, Honored Citizen." It was a common game, seeing if the groom could find his chosen bride among a cluster of veiled females. Not picking the right one was seen as an ill-fated sign; sometimes the females were all eligible and the groom was forced to marry the one he picked. That was often bypassed by someone leaking the color of the bride's dress to the groom, but if one of the persons needed out of an arranged marriage, or someone was sabotaging the pairing, he could be fed the wrong information. Friend or foe was a cue for true or false. Masákh never doubted he could pick Aila out of a crowd, but now he knew for certain.

"Then I shall join them soon."

The air outside began to hum, swelling into an overpowering thwapping noise as three large helicraft approached the house. With the number of people gathering, there was no room for more than one to land at a time, the yard decorations straining in the draft. Mímihn took one look at the craft hovering just past the courtyard and gasped before rushing back to the room.

"She's here! She's here!" Mímihn screeched. She grabbed Zheníhda by her arms. "Her Majesty Heir Apparent Rimas is here!"

Zheníhda paled gold. "No!"

Faelihn and Kesseh burst into the room. "*Ama! Ama! Dihnama!* There's aircraft from the palace! The Heir is here!"

"I recognized the seal, and I read the words on the side," Faelihn told Dalo. "Airfleet of the Emperor, Derahl Nor!"

Zheníhda gasped for air. She clutched her chest as if her heart was stopping. "I never expected her to come. It was a politeness. We only meant a politeness. Even when they said she would, I never dreamed she actually would! What do we do? What if we don't honor her enough? Mímihn! We'll be shamed before royalty, and they'll destroy Tokh!"

"*Shu!*" Aila commanded. "*Hoxt!*" She snapped Mímihn's trembling chin up with a finger. Pomp and circumstance frightened her; Rimas didn't. "Stop, now! You doubted the word of the Heir? Rimas is a lady of honor, and she has come to honor me and honor Tokh. She is only a lady of honor. She knows she is attending the wedding of a mere *whátaral* to a Union female, and yet she comes. Treat her with respect, but let her be a Lady. Believe me, Rimas isn't the type to hold things against you. If anything, I think she'll enjoy just being able to be herself."

Zheníhda nodded. "I can't know all the rules in advance; I must just hope we're able to please her."

"I'm sure you will." Aila turned and gave her mother the short form of the issue.

Leila nodded. "I'm used to dealing with government and dignitaries, if I can help at all. I don't know their protocols, but I can try."

Aila translated back and forth. "Zheníhda says she appreciates your offer, but you are also a special guest, and she can't ask that of you. But it can't hurt to rub elbows, if you know what I mean. Daddy's seen as a very important Union person, far more than he actually is, so being his wife gives you great stature. It wouldn't be wrong at all for you to speak with her."

Leila flashed a faint smile. "Okay. I am trying, Aila."

Aila kissed her cheek. "You're doing wonderful, Mom. Don't think of them as Kerasi, just as people. Just like being at a Union function."

"I can do that. There aren't going to be any Korulans, are there?"

Aila burst out laughing. "No! I can guarantee that."

Avalihn ran in. "Hurry! They don't want to keep the Heir waiting long."

The room jumped all at once, a dozen hands primping and pressing themselves and each other. Mímihn draped Aila's veil carefully over the fresh flowers in her hair. Zheníhda led the procession, her long veil down her back as she was not participating in the choosing. She wore a gown of royal purple that faded into blues and pinks at the highlights, and the front shimmered with matching purple crystals. It was by far the most fashionable – and youthful – thing she'd ever worn. Her precious *habivend* earrings hung from her lobes, and a thick, shimmering choker of clear *nemsihl* and purple *gallah* stones circled her throat.

They marched out the front door as the sun set over the water, and the *taghinet* quartet began to play a soothing processional as soon as they saw them. Tall torches lined the property, giving soft light wherever people walked. Colored lights had been set inside the pool, making it glow a soft gold. Pots of white and gold flowers had been placed around the walls, reflecting the light from the torches. Small globe lights had been thickly strung across the main patios and dining areas, but still it would not be bright enough for Mímihn, who would have difficulty seeing beyond her table.

Zheníhda took her hostess place at the main table; Leila walked to the section for the Union guests, to stand by her husband Ramden. General Tokh stood before the pool in his dress uniform, under the trellis of red *whenir* flowers, his slayer sword hanging at his hip, the line of *aghát* stretching out to his side, Masákh at his elbow, Haghíde next to him. They stood at attention as the females approached.

Avalihn, Aila, Mímihn, and Dalo slid into the cluster of perhaps a dozen other females, waiting to the side, all with their veils down. Aila knew nearly a hundred people were in attendance; friends, associates, neighbors, and superiors of Tokh's, Masákh's family, her family, and the small crew of Union delegates; a collection of some of the most influential people of two galactic governments in one place, and hopefully no bloodshed. The security craft patrolling the coast and the city were not a whimsical show of power but a deadly threat to anyone breaking the no-fly zone around the Heir.

The music stopped, and the guests quieted down. Tokh stood taller and took a deep breath.

"I dislike speeches. I asked General Trannor to do this for me, but I was told I was the reason for everyone being here, so it was only right that I do the honor. So I will do it. Seven years ago, I chose a team of men for a mission, a squad most excellently trained. Their task was to instruct a Union diplomat to be a liaison for the Emperor. Through fate, I was handed a female Union child. We assumed the worst, that we had failed. Instead, the female was the best hope Kerasím has ever had. She was highly educated, learned her tasks well, and when needed represented the Kerasi to the Union in a way they understood. A female so honorable, I was proud to claim her as my own kind. In the process of working together, the female caught the heart of one of my men. He has pursued her patiently by Union rules, and won her affection in return. Today, we witness the legal bonding of one of my *aghát* to that female, perhaps the very first Kerasi-Union pairing in the history of both peoples. *Aghát* Major Masákh."

Masákh stepped forward.

"You have served the Empire above and beyond the call of duty, and it is only right you be entitled to the pleasures of a wife. Major Masákh, choose your wife."

Any nerves Masákh may have had were hidden under his *aghát* look of detachment. The people expected a show, and he didn't deny them. He stopped before a tiny, frail female, elderly hands strangling the stem of the flower in them to keep them from shaking. He leaned over and inhaled the scent of her veil, the audience inhaling with him. Then he shook his head and stepped onward down the line. He came to Mímihn, all silver-gray beauty under her veil, with sparkling silver shoes on her dainty feet. She was the same height as Aila, roughly the same size, but he already knew what she wore. He smiled his forced diplomat smile and bowed his head to her. The crowd gave a gasp, but he moved down the line.

Masákh reached toward tall Dalo in frilly black and orange, paused as the onlookers whispered, then leaned around her and pulled forward a female in a green gown and veil. He lifted the shimmering veil with confidence. What he found made his eyes widen, his pupils dilate. *Aghát* training could not stop the smile that broke out and the nervous snort from erupting, blowing his image of cool composure.

Aila's dress was a rich shade of emerald green, but a modern style fit for *bhísroti*. Sleeveless, it clung to her body like a second skin all the way to her knees, where it flounced outward in gentle waves of soft fabric, sweeping back into a short suggestion of train. The top of the dress consisted of nothing but two long pieces that crossed over her chest, over her shoulders, and down her back like long flat twin tails, secured with invisible netting. The one that crossed over the other was embellished with a sprinkling of crystals that made her hip shimmer. The front V'd scandalously low, a *bhísroti*-only depth, and the burgundy *jama* and *nemsihl*-stone necklace Masákh had given her the year before, a promise of intended marriage, glittered at her throat. Green gloves completed the dress. Mímihn had pulled her brown hair upward and braided it in what was known as a Wedding Weave, with white and yellow flowers threaded through the braids. At Mímihn's direction, Dalo had plied Aila with cosmetics in full Kerasi style, a heavier accent on the lower lid, sweeping wide past her eyes. The upper lids were touched by shadows of browns and greens and outlined by crystals, making her seem otherworldly and mysterious. Masákh's nose caught the scent of a Daghnahn perfume, stirring up memories of his homeland. He gave a longer nervous snort, almost a laugh, and his whole body shivered. Aila smiled at him, and her face seemed to glow in the setting sunlight.

Masákh stepped back and dropped to a knee, bowing to her. Aila couldn't bend well in the tight dress, and if she bent too far she could feasibly lose the top, but she bent over in half before him, arms pressed against the dress. The guests went wild with shouts and knee slapping.

Masákh took her hand and led her to Tokh.

Tokh tipped his head at both of them. "*Aghát* Major Masákh gha Lil, you claim my daughter, the Union female Aila Lissette Perrin daras-Giláhn as your wife?"

Masákh's uniform was text-book perfection, surpassing not only his inspection but the hyper-criticism of his five *aghát* brethren. *Aghát* wore no chin-hanks, so he couldn't decorate himself with fancy clips or braids or flowers, but the number of citations and awards on his blue-gray uniform – several of them high-level – made it seem as if a party

108

was already taking place on his chest. His eyes burst with pride when they found hers; he fought hard to maintain an official face and not smile when he said, "*Sukh.*"

"Do you promise to serve her as a proper husband, share with her all your property, ensure her health and safety, and treat her with the same respect you would wish to be given? Do you swear on your honor to respect her under Union law as well, never to use violence or force in your discipline, never to restrain her or keep her from her people, to allow her to pass freely across the Union-Kerasi border, and to allow her the right to refuse your requests when it violates Union laws and beliefs she has sworn to, until one of you joins your ancestors?"

Masákh gazed down at her. He wasn't happy with the changes to the public vows. There was nothing in them that couldn't have been done with a private contract. Allowing a female to demand no violence decreased his image among his peers, but Aila insisted it be witnessed. "I do swear."

"Aila Lissette Perrin daras-Giláhn, Union Junior Councilmember, Emissary to Kerasím and sworn to me as daughter, do you accept Masákh gha Lil as your husband?"

"*Sukh.*"

"Do you promise to serve your husband as a proper wife, protect his property, care for his children, and tend to all his needs, whether in sickness or in health, to carry out his requests to the best of your ability, until one of you joins his ancestors? Do you swear on the honor of your Union to uphold the laws of Kerasím when you are within its borders, to show respect to the Emperor at all times, to allow your husband to cross the Union-Kerasi border without objection, and allow him to continue his duties as long as they do not violate laws inside the Planetary Union?"

Tradition be damned: Aila had made Tokh change the wording on her oath, so it did not say "obey your husband's every command." That was not a trap she would allow herself to fall into. She was the wife of a Kerasi, but she would never be a Kerasi wife.

Aila beamed at Tokh. "I do promise."

Tokh lifted his head to address the crowd. "So says the wife; so says her husband. By the law of the Emperor, you are now joined."

The crowd gave a loud cheer. Haghíde removed Masákh's gloves; Mímihn removed Aila's. Masákh took her bare hand, skin to skin, and raised their clasped hands high for all to see. The crowd roared again.

The five remaining *aghát* moved to form two lines. Tokh took the spot vacated by Masákh.

"Ghit!" Tokh barked the order to attention, and the *aghát* snapped straight. *"Khe su, hataan!"* In perfect unison, the officers reached to their sides and grasped their swords. *"Khe na jotesh!"* The swords were drawn and pointed at the officer across, the tips of the swords exactly even with the wrist of the opposite officer, a triple barrier to the couple. Masákh had explained the ritual to Aila, the swords representing the barriers of life.

"Khe hakh!" The swords rose high in unison to form a bridge, the cutting of difficulties that would then float away, that the couple might pass through life trouble-free. Together Masákh and Aila passed under the bridge, to thunderous leg-slapping applause.

The music resumed as the sun disappeared. Masákh led Aila to where Rimas stood before all the other guests. Her table, covered with a gold cloth, was raised on a platform a foot higher than the others, and covered by a gold carpet. Royal guards stood impossibly straight at the corners. The couple knelt before her.

Rimas smiled down on them, wearing a grand gown of blue and silver satin with a shining silver capelet trimmed in feathers. "My father, Emperor Nadigh, sends you his warmest wishes on your day of uniting. May the blessings of the Fortunes shine upon you all the days of your lives, and may your union be a symbol of peace and friendship between our people. What two people can achieve, so can two governments."

"We thank you most graciously, Your Lady Majesty," Masákh replied. "Loyalty, Duty, Honor to the Emperor."

He helped Aila to her feet, and they stopped before Masákh's parents. Had this been a normal wedding, both sets of parents would have been at the front table. Having a third set of parents made it strange; having one set of parents as dignitaries who didn't speak the language made it stranger. They sat Aila's parents with the other Union guests so they had someone to talk to, and Masákh's parents, the lowest-caste invited guests, at a table to the front, but far from the Heir.

Masaruhn gha Lil's sun-leathered face cracked a huge smile. He clapped his hands on his elder son's shoulders; Masákh returned the gesture.

"Masákh! So long we waited for this day. I'm so very happy for you. I know why you waited; you were hunting for the very prettiest one." He pinched Aila's cheek. "Welcome, welcome my daughter." Her shoulder was bare, untouchable, so he settled for patting the green tails.

"Thank you most kindly, Citizen Masaruhn," Aila replied.

Masákh's mother kissed his forehead, mumbling praises, not quite keeping the tears in her eyes. "You are most lovely, most lovely," she repeated to Aila. "Thank you for making my son so happy! He is a most honored son; he deserves the best wife." Namig's hands darted up and down, wanting to touch her new daughter but well-aware of caste restrictions. The gha Lils were only *rhibani*. To have a *dahneg* provide a wedding for their son, with the Heir Apparent present, was unimaginable. Aila reached out and grabbed her hands, skin to skin, as she had not yet put on her gloves.

"You are now family, mother of my husband. You are always allowed to touch me." Namig struggled, afraid of reprimand, but she stopped fighting the touch and bowed several times.

"You are so very beautiful, even if you are not Kerasi," Namig mumbled, eyes down. "Your dress is fit for the wife of an Emperor."

"Or a Lady-Emperor," Aila said, since the word Empress didn't exist in Kerasi. She dragged Namig's timid hand and placed it on the fabric, holding it there until Namig stopped trying to pull away. "Please! Please enjoy it." Namig gave in and hesitantly petted the dress.

"Beautiful! Most beautiful! I'm so very honored to have you as a daughter, someone so important."

Aila grasped the hand again but was unable to make eye contact, something a *rhibani* would never dare do to a higher caste. That battle would wait for another day. "No. It is I who am honored to have you as a mother."

Greeting the Union table was a bit easier. The group cheered as they approached.

Ross Halian returned her hug. "You have to be one of the most charmed people I've ever met. I don't think I've seen such an event outside of the palace. Happy with the way everything turned out?"

Aila couldn't smile harder. "Yeah. Everyone's been pretty incredible. Thank you so much for your help."

Halian gave her hand a squeeze. "Call if you need me."

Secretary of State Hhani shook her hand and kissed her cheek. "Congratulations. It may not hold in the Union, but let's hope it helps things here. You're a wonder, my lady, daring something that was unimaginable six years ago. I wish you both the very best of both worlds."

"Thank you, Mr. Hhani!" Aila kissed him back. "Thank you for everything!"

Mrs. Hhani grasped her hands. "You are the most beautiful bride I've ever seen. Congratulations!"

"Thank you so much!"

Admiral Perrin got his chance to kiss her. "You couldn't look lovelier anywhere in the universe," he said with pride. "That was a very nice ceremony. Not too long, not too short, not too flowery. Congratulations, Sweetheart." He shook Masákh's hand. "Congratulations, Masákh. I'm still holding you to your promise. Hurt her, and I'll hunt you down and make you beg for mercy."

Masákh bowed his head. "It is a promise I intend to keep."

Aila kissed her mother. "Are you okay?"

"If I understood it, it was lovely," Leila said. Her voice was restrained, but not sarcastic. "I hope you'll be happy. That's sincere, Aila. If I can't wish anything else, I wish you happiness."

It was as close to a truce as Leila could make. Aila hugged her tightly. "Thanks, Mom. That means everything to me."

Leila seized Masákh's hand, and the grip wasn't friendly. Her face was sharp, and the flickers of torchlight made quivering highlights on her pale hair until it seemed it was sparking along with her temper. "I will hold you to every word you said. You now belong to both and neither: you are a galactic government of your own, and you must make your own rules of engagement with the outside world. You will make her protection your first priority, and you must never, ever hurt her."

Masákh's head tipped as he considered her words. "You have uncovered a new truth. I swear on my honor, Lady Perrin, I will do my

112

best to please your daughter and keep her safe. If I suspect she is in danger, I will return her to you for further protection."

Leila released his hand. "Then I accept you. I don't trust you, but I accept you."

Leila's fight was over. Masákh bowed before her. "Thank you, Lady Perrin. You do me great honor."

They took their seats after dozens of photographs with various important guests. The last weak rays were fading across the water and the torch-lights were taking over. Aila took a moment to observe the party, from one end of Tokh's property to the other. Happy people had merged together for an evening, from the very top caste down to *rhibáni*, Kerasi and Union. The air was fresh and damp from the inlet far below, the scents of Zheníhda's gardens and the mounds of cut flowers wafting a sweet perfume on the currents. The lights and ribbons and strange but soft music lent a fairy-tale feel to the moment. These were her friends and family, this was her wedding, and there was not a more beautiful moment in time than this.

The band slowed their tempo. The servants delivered food to the tables. There would be seven courses to the meal, and three courses of desserts. First was a small plate of five tiny eggs, the size of Masákh's thumbprint. They had been painstakingly boiled, sliced in half, scraped from their pink shells, mixed into five different flavors and colors, and artfully poured back into the shells with a tube, then placed in a nest of crunchy vegetable strings. A light *hyrak*-broth soup with shaved sheets of vegetable followed it. Third came thin slices of eel wrapped around a soft-cheese center, topped by an artful squiggle of a spicy-hot brown sauce. Aila could barely manage a bite of the stinging sauce, while Masákh chewed each one whole. The fourth course was Zheníhda's idea, in honor of Masákh's homeland, Daghnahn, and his town of Kinas Dagh: roast *bagresh* slices with a crust of *fum, rinbanar*, and *pelov* spices, and a side of crispy pearled *tapoor*. A dish of golden poached *patigha* fruit came next – the twin spheres of *patigha* being a symbol of virility. Whole roasted *nabaka tho*, stuffed with grains and standing on a thin bed of toasted bread crumbs to mimic sand, followed that. *Nabaka tho* were a Daghnahn sand lizard, and although Aila accepted a bite of Masákh's, she could not bring herself to eat a cooked lizard with two baked berries for eyes. Protocol be damned; she just couldn't do it.

Last came a salad of thin shredded vegetables and greens in a tart vinegar and *harfa* dressing. Aila wished they had started with the salad. No matter how she tried, she just couldn't fit more than three bites into her overloaded stomach.

Masákh was halfway through his salad and Aila on her third glass of *lunahl* when Haghíde stood up and stopped the quartet. He took the seven-stringed *tahgta* from its musician. "In honor of the couple, whom I have known since the start, I wish to give them a song. Here is my wish for you, my brother *aghát*."

Aila glanced at Masákh; he was smiling with as much embarrassment as she felt. Haghíde was full of *varvet* and *ghor*, and not feeling much pain at the moment. Haghíde was well-trained on *tahgta*; Aila knew that from way back when he'd tried to teach her to play and she'd pretty well refused to learn, but was he coordinated enough at the moment? He plucked the strings for a simple melody.

"The first time I met her my khatas gave a leap."

Aila understood the words, and her hand smacked her forehead. General Tharkis's *aghát* would be translating for her parents, and she waited for the strangled scream to cross the courtyard. Masákh laughed out loud and slapped his leg.

"The second time I met her, my heart began to beat."

The men began to whistle and catcall to each other, but Haghíde's clear tenor never paused.

"The third time I met her, I was in trouble deep
And I knew she was the one for me...
The first time I pushed her was on our wedding night
She did not put up a fight
I spread her wide
On the inside
And kept it up all night..."

Aila closed her eyes and shook her head. By the third verse many of the men had joined in. Haghíde carried the song out for eight verses, position to position, until the randy bastard in the song was too sore to carry on. The applause was deafening.

"You have every right to be jealous!" Masákh shouted across the courtyard.

"I am jealous," Haghíde said as he walked back to the table. "Had you been less perfect, it might be me sitting there. I have decided it is time I also found a wife. I am thirty – how many years do I have? Thirty five. I have thirty-five years, with a solid career and a small fortune saved, and it is long past time I should have found a wife."

"You should find a Union one," Masákh said. "Then they can complain together." Aila pinched his leg under the table, where no male could see.

"You'll find someone deserving of you," Aila said. "You just have to stop working and start looking. You'd make a most excellent husband for any female. I will swear it for you."

Mímihn pulled him from his seat with a gloved hand. "Come! Come with me. I'm hostess. I'll find you someone right now." She dragged him by his sleeve across the yard and pulled a female from her seat. She ushered them to the Union section.

"No one will complain about you sitting together here. Haghíde, this is Fahni. She's delightful. Speak with her, and let me know your thoughts."

First dessert was being cleared when Masákh pulled Aila to her feet and was about to speak when a light appeared in the star-riddled sky, growing brighter by the second. A thrupping noise grew louder as it sped toward them. Four smaller craft flew nearby as escorts. Tokh and his officers stared upward with alarm; no craft should have been entering the no-fly zone.

The main craft hovered overhead, aligning with the landing pad, and the reason became clear: the bottom bore the symbols of an Imperial craft. The no-fly was by order of the palace; of course the palace could violate it. It must have been the craft come to retrieve Rimas.

Six guards exited the craft, wearing gold imperial uniforms. They unrolled a carpet behind them, gold with red edging, then stood along it at attention. A camera crew popped out after them, running to film the craft. Guests ran forward, elbowing each other for a better view of the spectacle. The crowd fell to silence as a guard shouted, "All kneel before his Royal Majesty Nadigh, Emperor of All Kerasím!"

115

The quartet of musicians paused to gasp, then broke into playing the Emperor's March as loud as it could.

Tokh was none too steady on his feet, toasting with his guests, and he dropped to his knees so fast on the hard stone he would be limping the next day. The whole assembly fell to their knees; Masákh had to help Aila before bending himself. Somewhere behind them Mímihn gave a strangled shriek. Aila couldn't see, but expected Masákh's mother had passed out by now.

Nadigh stood before them, tall, regal, imposing, wearing a gold tunic but only blue pants. The three-person camera crew followed him, filming every move. He waved the party up with a hand. "Everyone, rise. This is a celebration; I wish to see celebrating. Since I had to send a craft to retrieve my daughter, I thought I'd come and congratulate the groom myself. And the bride," he added. "Tokh, escort me."

Masákh and Aila stepped forward, bowing. "Congratulations, Major. You have achieved something I never imagined, a marriage between two hostile parties. May your names be revered as a spirit of the times. May the Fortunes bless you on this night, and always."

"You are most gracious, your Majesty," Masákh murmured, his head bent.

"May I congratulate your bride?"

"You honor us both, your Majesty."

Nadigh wore gold gloves, but they lacked the metallic luster of his tunic. He stroked the shoulder of Aila's dress. "That is a most exquisite gown. Did you bring it from the Union?"

"No, Your Majesty. It was purchased in Keranihn."

Nadigh smiled. "You do us such honor. It pleases me that a Union female can appreciate Kerasím as well as you do. I am in your debt. You are as beautiful in that gown as the finest of Kerasi females, and an inspiration across our world. If I may." Nadigh placed his hands on her jaw, and planted a kiss on her forehead. Masákh stood straighter, but Tokh's hand fell on his shoulder, a reminder of who stood before them.

No one can refuse a request of the Emperor. No one.

Aila blushed and bent her head. "You honor myself and my husband too well, Your Majesty."

"Bo!" Rimas strolled up, General Trannor at her side to avoid her billowing cape. She'd drank as much of the spirits as the men, and looked as merry. On the other hand, she was taller and perhaps stronger

than some of them. "You would kiss a stranger before your own offspring?"

"Working my way to you, my daughter." He kissed her by her eye, most proper. "Have you enjoyed the celebration?"

"It was a most joyous evening. I asked Trannor to serve as my escort. I fear I have spoiled his evening, making him pay attention to me instead of running wild with the other officers."

Trannor, all-powerful boss of Tokh and member of the Imperial Council, bowed in half. "It has been my pleasure, Lady Heir. It is my duty to serve, and the conversation has been most entertaining."

"Good. Tokh, I would greet the parents of these heroes."

Tokh led Emperor Nadigh across the yard to the gha Lils. They had been to the palace the previous year on Masákh's invite; it was almost more than they could bear then. Now they were presented to the Emperor himself at the wedding of their son. Masákh's father's voice was so soft and reverent it barely carried across the space between them; Masákh's mother would not lift her head, and could not manage more than nodding.

Aila's parents were far easier. They had met the Emperor at the previous year's ceremony, and they were used to foreign dignitaries. Leila grasped the Emperor's hand as firmly as her husband, and while she bent her head, it didn't stay down. She looked Nadigh right in the eye, something no one but his wives were allowed.

"You gave my daughter a promise to protect her while she is under your flag. The Union will hold you to that promise. Harm to her will be seen as a serious incident."

Nadigh patted her hand. Whether he meant to be condescending or comforting couldn't be determined. "Understood. General Tokh keeps her close. I have great confidence in him." He spent longer speaking with Hhani and the other representatives before gathering Rimas and Trannor and heading for his craft.

Masákh held Aila back by the corner of the house as the crowd surged after the Emperor. "Get upstairs. Immediately. If anyone asks, tell them you must urinate."

"What?"

"This is a moment where you must not question but just do. Now!" he ordered in her ear. "I will join you in one *fasim*." Aila nodded and slipped into the house through the kitchen.

Masákh started to follow the crowd, then darted into the house through the front door and up the stairs.

In her absence, Aila's room had been decorated with garlands of white and gold and pink flowers, with loose petals strewn across the bed and the carpet. Gifts mounded on the lounges. Warm oil candles burned on the clothing drawers and shelves, and a tray of exquisite tiny pastries and spirits waited for them. She turned as he entered.

"Isn't it beautiful!"

Masákh removed his dress jacket in a hurry and tossed it on a chair, a dishonor he never allowed. "It is. We will enjoy it after." He unfastened his shirt and shrugged out of it. "I'm afraid this will be rushed, but I will take time to please you later."

Aila frowned. "What do you mean?"

"This has been a most calm and orderly wedding for Kerasím, probably because of the presence of royalty. They are now leaving." He turned her around and located the fastener for her dress. "In the lower castes, it is an outdated custom among some for the guests to observe the first mating, to assure it occurs. In the case of my teammates, they'll deliberately annoy us into frustration. Unless you prefer an audience, we must do this as rapidly as possible and put it behind us while there is a distraction."

Aila's dress fell to the floor, and he stripped her of her undergarments. "What! But we've been doing it for months!"

"It doesn't matter. It's our wedding, it's expected, and I know neither of us wish my father or Mátokhan critiquing our performance."

"Absolutely not! I forbid it!"

Masákh proceeded to kiss her, urgently and without passion. Aila helped by caressing his *khatas*, but she would always remember the moment as something with about as much lust and intimacy as two people trying to wash each other clean of leeches. He bent her over the side of the bed and *pushed* her as if racing a clock.

They could hear the shouts outside in the courtyard before he finished.

"Where are they? Masákh, you *trixahg*! We want to witness! Who was supposed to be watching them? Where's Haghíde? He better not be trying for second call. Togha, pull that table over, boost me up to the balcony."

Bottle-stoppers pinged off the balcony doors. "Masákh! We know what you're doing up there!" A louder shout of laughter followed, as the guests wandered back to the tables.

Masákh finished his race with an unsatisfied grunt. He didn't need to wait to uncouple from a human, but paused from habit. He pulled out as the shouting grew louder, flung open the doors and stood on the balcony stark naked. The railing and buntings blocked the worst view from below.

"Your spirits may leak, my friends, but you're too late. I've claimed her as mine, and I will not share."

"You worm-tailed *nunu*!" Tótoghar pegged him in the shoulder with a dessert nut. "We were trying so hard, too. Nadigh messed us all up."

Ghírandar hummed himself a note, then broke into a song. The other three *aghát* – Haghíde was nowhere to be seen – joined him, in four-part acapella harmony. After a minute, Aila crept out to stand beside Masákh, wrapped in the bedsheet. The guests gave a shout of delight. Crying was a shame on Kerasím; sex was not. Thankfully, her parents had left for the Embassy.

"What's it about?" she asked softly.

"A ballad about the pleasure of love. Not the physical pleasure, but the pleasure of the heart."

"It's lovely."

The *aghát* saluted them when they finished; Masákh returned the salute, but Aila slapped her leg with the rest of the guests.

"Thank you, guys. That was incredibly beautiful. I don't know what it said, but it was beautifully done. Thank you!"

Masákh raised a hand for the attention of all the guests. "It's been a most joyous party, friends, and I – *we* thank you for joining us, but I bid you pleasant night. I have better things to do." He gave Aila a lingering kiss over her throat while the crowd roared, then turned her toward the room and locked the balcony doors behind them.

Seventeen

Aila woke to a nuzzle at the base of her neck, followed by the pressure of two warm lips against her skin. Masákh was spooned against her, and she turned her head to smile at him.

"Bright morning, *falahndi*. Great Lady Masákh gha Lil." His eyes had that weird dreamy look to them, a look that didn't belong on a Kerasi, let alone the most infallible, hard-nosed, rule-abiding *aghát* she'd ever met. When he got that look she could never tell if he was mooning over her or about to devour her in a psychotic obsessive fit.

She smiled wider at the title. No longer partner, but a full-fledged wife. *Wife*. That was weird. Mímihn was right. Sex did feel different after marriage. Maybe because it didn't feel as if Mom was going to burst through the door any second with a blaster. "Am I still Great Lady? Aren't I now *whátaral*, and just Honored Citizeness?"

"I will have to make an inquiry. I don't know. You have title as no other Kerasi female."

"Besides Rimas," Aila reminded him.

"Besides the Heir," Masákh agreed. His lips found hers, once, twice, and she nibbled on the corner of his jaw. He gave a grunt of pleasure and rolled over on top of her; her legs wrapped around his hips.

Aila kissed him twice, then pushed his head up. "If you don't let me pee first, you won't like what happens."

"Gah." He stole one more long kiss before the door slammed opened and four *aghát* strode in. Masákh's head whipped around; Aila screamed in his ear.

Masákh rolled off and sat up while Aila snatched the bedcover and jerked it over her head like a Champaign-gold ghost. "I thought you locked the door?!" she screeched.

"I'm glad you're finding marriage to your liking," Mátokhan told Masákh, "but there are more important things at the moment. We allowed you to pound half the day away; now you must dress."

"I've been granted two weeks' leave," Masákh reminded them. "Unless the General's health has collapsed, emergencies must be managed without me. As senior *aghát*, that duty's yours."

"Haghíde is missing. He hasn't been seen since last night. All the other guests have left; he was not among them, nor was he found in any room of the house. We checked the property and over the cliff wall. We tried his comm unit; Thrit found it inside the vehicle shed. There's no sign of him anywhere."

"When was he last seen?"

"He was with us before the Emperor left," Tótoghar said. "Then we lost him in the crowd. The last guests left about four hours later."

"He was seen speaking to a female not long after you left," Ráhnif said. "He didn't return to the room last night."

"Perhaps he escorted the female home and was seized on the way. Could he have been held by authorities? What about medical clinics? Could he be at a discretion house? Did he leave with the Heir?"

"Tokh is working on that," Mátokhan said. He slapped Masákh on the arm. "Come. Clean the stink from your thighs and help search."

Aila felt the motion as Masákh stood up. Her arms waved under the cover, emphasizing the ghost image.

"Hello?" her voice said. "You're off duty? Remember me? This is our first day of marriage?"

Masákh knelt on the bed and pulled the cover from her head; Aila clutched it tight to her chin. "This isn't duty; this is Haghíde. If Haghíde were on leave and you were missing, do you not believe he would give up his leave to help search for you?"

Shame burned Aila's cheeks. "Of course he would. Find him fast, yell at him for me, and get right back here."

Masákh kissed her once. "Without fail. Please urinate before I return."

Aila washed and made her way downstairs, already past lunch.

"There she is!" Mímihn teased. "You're walking rather well. Perhaps Masákh was not pleased. Let us see! Come, come!"

121

Aila blushed, but she held still while Mímihn pulled the pretty gold and black scarf from her neck, revealing at least ten bruising passion marks. Damn Kerasi men and their need to bite down on something at release!

Mímihn gave a squeal of delight, and even Zheníhda gave a pleased smile. "Ooooh, someone had a very wild night! Good for you! What a shame they didn't leave you alone. I yelled at Mátokhan, and made Tokh yell at him, too. That wasn't fair."

"Is there news? Did they find Haghíde?"

"No word yet," Zheníhda said. "Tokh has pushed his authority on all the security offices, but they deny having contact with him."

"You don't think something bad could have happened?"

Mímihn's pause said otherwise, but she smiled. "Of course not. It was a wedding party. I guarantee he took a walk with a bottle of *durwah* and fell asleep somewhere. He might not know where he is when he wakes up, but he'll find his way back. They always do."

The mood in the house grew more brittle by the hour. *Aghát* went out, followed possible leads, but came back with nothing. Yes, he'd spoken with a female, but Mímihn distinctly remembered her leaving with her family – without Haghíde. If he was at a discretion house, there was no way short of an edict from the military to find him there, if at all.

An hour before dinner, the security monitor in Tokh's office sounded.

"Visitor arriving. Visitor arriving. Visitor arriving."

The house scrambled to its feet. Tokh opened the door and found himself face to face with his missing officer. He hauled Haghíde into the house by the front of his shirt and spun him around. "Major! You were given no leave from duty! No communication in more than twelve hours? Explain yourself!"

Haghíde kept his eyes on the floor. He writhed so much from nerves he could have been tapdancing. "General, I bear sincerest apologies. I will explain in detail. First, I wish to introduce my wife, and beg that you will let us stay a night or two while I find housing."

The room silenced. No one had noticed the female still standing in the doorway. She was tall, almost as tall as Zheníhda but not spindly, somewhere in her late twenties. Soft waves of dark brown hair hung to

122

her shoulders, topped by a short bronze veil over the back. Frightened dark eyes stared out from a pretty face. A colorful shawl crossed over one shoulder and tied at her hip over a dress that said upper-caste.

Zheníhda breezed forward and pulled her inside. "Come! Come in! My apologies for not greeting you immediately. I am Zheníhda, firstwife of the house."

Mímihn greeted her with a kiss. "Fahni? Did I hear him right?"

The conversation ended as Tokh's bellow deafened the room. Anger turned his face a dark brown and the top of his head looked ready to blow off. Aila wasn't standing close, but she took two steps back, ready to run. The patio doors were a clearer exit than the front.

"You abandoned your post for a female?! You wasted the time of an entire team, pulled an officer from his wedding bed to hunt for you, because of a *female*? On your knees, soldier! I should take your head! Remove your uniform."

It was only then Aila realized Haghíde's dress jacket hung open, a serious public dishonor. His face was bruised, and the dress shirt beneath his jacket was stained and torn. Haghíde had not just been out walking with a girl. He fell to his knees. It took only a second for him to shrug out of the jacket. The instant he did, Tokh drew his incentive rod from its holder on his belt, extended it, and delivered three harsh, rapid strokes to Haghíde's shoulders. Haghíde gave a grunt of pain.

The new girl gave a jump and a shriek and covered her mouth with her hands.

Tokh handed the whip-like metal rod to Mátokhan. "Once each."

Aila counted in her head. Eight? One was like fire; eight was unimaginable. She stepped forward but didn't dare get close. "You can't! You'll cripple him! Masákh!"

The anger in Mátokhan's face made her step back again. The incentive stick gave a frightening whistle and crack as it laid into Haghíde's broad back. He jumped and grunted, but said nothing. Blood seeped through his shirt. Mátokhan passed the rod to Masákh, who didn't spare his strength, either. Aila watched in horror as he, too, drew blood from his best friend, and she felt sick at the thought of ever having to face Masákh if he turned violent. She wouldn't survive.

She couldn't watch. The sounds enough were making her ill, the whistle and smack, Haghíde's snorting grunts of agony. The new girl was crying, but she, too, didn't dare move closer, and from behind her came a higher-pitched cry of terror.

A small child clung to her skirt, perhaps all of five. No one had noticed him, either.

Ráhnif handed the rod back to Tokh.

"That is for leaving the grounds without permission," Tokh snarled. "That is for not leaving word of where you were going. That is for not making contact afterward. And once from your team for wasting their time and efforts trying to find you." His hand raised, froze in furious indecision, then gave in to the feeling and slammed Haghíde in the side of the head so hard he fell over.

The girl shrieked again and ran to him. Mímihn grabbed the child. She called up the stairs to Joralan. He and Kesseh appeared at the top, and she waved them down. "What's your name?" she asked the sobbing boy.

"Vihren."

"Vihren, this is Joralan and Kesseh. They will take you upstairs to where the toys are and you can play with them."

Jora sneered. "He's a baby. Why do I have to play with him? That's the work of females."

Mímihn's eyes flashed fire. "Because someday you will be host in your own house, and this is good practice. This is not the time to anger your father."

"Do you like to play swords?" Kesseh said. Vihren sniffed and nodded. "Then come on. We've got lots to pick from." She pulled him up the stairs, though his head turned to watch his mother. She nodded permission, and he followed Kesseh.

Haghíde's wounds bled in a steady brown ooze, soaking his shirt and running into the waist of his pants. Zhenihda brought a basin of warm water, a cloth, and several ointments. Aila took his jacket, and she and the new woman helped him remove his shirt. Aila, as a married female, couldn't touch another male, so she merely handed the woman whatever she needed as she wiped and dressed the fearsome wounds as gently as possible. The *aghát* had been both vicious and merciful: their strokes cut, but each was spaced away from the others, so as not to leave compound wounds. They may have been angry, but the beating was from Tokh's command, not their hearts. It was still a terrible thing to see.

Tokh stood before Haghíde, fierce and powerful. "Explain. Explain the word wife. You're Colonel Aegarr's daughter, are you not?" The girl nodded.

Haghíde gave a nod and kept his head down. It suggested submission, but Aila was close enough to catch each hidden flinch and grimace as the injuries were tended to. She had no gloves with her, so she wrapped her hand in a dry cloth and squeezed his shoulder in an unwounded spot.

"Lady Tokh introduced me to Fahni last night," Haghíde said. "We spoke all evening. I found her most pleasant to converse with. After the Emperor left, we walked around the grounds and found ourselves in the privacy of the vehicle shed, where we wound up sampling each other, which led to the deeper conversations that accompany such activity. We found each other quite compatible. She was widowed four years ago. She didn't want to leave with her family. I offered to escort her home later, but they insisted on her accompanying them. I followed them. I understand I should have informed someone, but if I paused, I would have lost the direction. When I reached for my comm, I realized I'd left it in the vehicle shed and I couldn't give my location.

"I located which room of their apartment was Fahni's, and we spoke together the rest of the night. I promised her I would marry her the next day. I left, waited around for the shops to open, bought her a necklace, and returned to present it to her and ask for her father's signature."

"It's a lovely necklace, Haghíde," Zheníhda murmured. "She has your heart, for certain." Fahni blushed as she finished rubbing an anesthetic cream into the last of the wounds and covered it with a thin healing film. Around her neck she wore a choker of blue and green gemstones interspersed with silver beads; every fifth stone was a shimmering *nemsihl* gem. It was an envious and no doubt very expensive treasure.

"That was when the trouble started." Haghíde remained on the floor; Tokh had not given him permission to rise. Fahni took his shirt and draped it over his bandaged shoulders, then kissed his cheek.

"Her Colonel father has had her keep his accounts for him. With care, she is able to enter the numbers into the proper columns in the computer. For that, he gives her room and board for her and her son. He didn't want to lose his personal accountant and refused to sign the marriage certificate. She also has a small inheritance from her husband. By law her father cannot touch the accounts, but he has invested the money and skimmed off the interest."

"That's illegal," Ghírandar said. "The interest should remain hers. When he comes of age, if there is any remainder, it goes to her son."

"Agreed," Haghíde said. "We discussed it. We argued. We raised our voices, but he refused to sign. I admitted to bedding her. Still he would not sign. Fahni pleaded with him. He screamed obscenities at her, accused her of untrue things, then started beating her. That's when I behaved poorly, and I fear my actions may yet cause issue."

Tokh frowned. "What did you do?"

Haghíde's head remained down. "I drew my sword and held it to his throat. I told him if he hit my wife again, I would see that he breathed nothing but blood."

Tokh's eyes grew wide under his brow. "You held a sword to the neck of a *dihnarwharl* colonel?!"

"Yes," Haghíde said softly. His marriage would be brief, perhaps a day before the authorities came for him. He would spend the rest in prison, until they executed him, unless he was able to somehow make it off world in the next few hours and demand asylum inside the Union, never to return. "He signed the marriage certificate, but he refused to allow her to take her son. That was the next battle. I threatened to call in the authorities, as decorated officer of the Emperor's *aghát* and an Ambassador to the Union. I know it carries no authority, but it sounded very strong and he didn't know for certain, so he allowed the boy to leave with her. Then he refused to sign over her inheritance. At that point the situation was most unstable and I chose to leave without further discord. I didn't marry her for an inheritance."

"He has no right to it," Ghírandar said. "It's a simple thing to present before a justice. I'll write the plea for you today, and you may have him summoned in the morning."

"We came here as soon as I could hire a vehicle. I beg you allow us to stay the night, and I will find an apartment for her tomorrow."

Tokh gave an unhappy sigh. "Did you invoke my name at all?"

"I don't believe so."

"Then we may have a little time. He knows you're an *aghát*, but he may not know who you're attached to. He can ask to run names, open

126

the database. He'll see your name, see you're attached to me, and come after me. That'll take time. Ghírandar, what's your take?"

Ghírandar's face looked grim. "It may be possible to sidestep the caste-crime. As *aghát* you operate outside of caste. You have spent the last five years working inside the Union, which is caste-free. You returned for a wedding and forgot to pay attention to caste. It's possible they will take that into account. As *aghát*, as an officer who works toward the Emperor's goal of female rights, as someone who, inside the Union, must defend females who are in danger, you acted to protect the female before taking into account where you were. When you threatened him, had he already signed the papers? Was she legally wed to you at that moment?"

Haghíde's voice went soft again. "No. It was before."

"Then she was not legally your wife. If she was, you were within your right, but she was his concern at that moment. Even if the other all went away, the crime of rank will not."

A tinge of hopelessness carried over in Haghíde's voice. "I am aware of that."

Silence fell over the room until Mátokhan spoke. "Aila, when did you plan to return to Centauri? How fast can you request a ship?" A cloud of hope rose around the room.

Aila shook her head. "I don't know. I was supposed to give a week's notice. I then have to clear it with the palace, get permission and escorts through Kerasi space, and they'll send one from Fornax, the closest territory. A week, if all's right."

The cloud evaporated again.

"The embassy," Aila said suddenly. All heads turned to her, but she spoke in Union for clarity, and the women could only hope it was for good.

"I would assume it works the same here as everywhere else. Embassy property is sacred ground, a piece of home away from home. Inside that property, the law is that of the homeworld. Inside the Kerasi embassy, they're free to follow all the laws that the Union objects to. The Union has no choice; it's under the government of the Emperor. If that holds true here, then we just have to get him to Ross. He claims status as a political refugee and he can stay there under Union law as long as he doesn't leave. Keranihn can't touch them without an interstellar incident. It'll buy time."

127

"That is the agreement," Ghírandar said with relief. "She's correct."

The women smiled as the room relaxed. Haghíde explained to Fahni and she leaned forward and kissed him again.

"Rise," Tokh said at last. "Here is my plan. Aegarr's a cantankerous dried *aakan*, still angry because he lost a rank thirty years ago and had to work through it again. He doesn't win many friends. I'll find out his commanding general and explain the situation to him, cut Aegarr off before he can make trouble. Then I'll invite Justice Wahtegahn down and present the problem to him. Aila, you will contact your Ross Halian, explain it to him and demand his assistance."

"I can have Haghíde there inside an hour, if necessary," Tótoghar volunteered.

"No. You want Ross to send a ship," Aila said. "His ship counts as diplomatic exemption. They'll think it's me and Masákh on board. They won't know otherwise."

Tokh gave a nod. "Good. Mímihn, find them a guest room for now. The child can stay with Joralan."

"Thank you, Lord Tokh," Haghíde said. "You are most merciful."

"No, I'm not," Tokh growled. "I'm saving my own skin."

Aila got hold of Ross and put him on standby. He could have a vehicle dispatched and waiting nearby, but four hours on a road was far riskier than a fast 45 minutes of flight. Aila hadn't forgotten her disastrous 22-hour road trip of the previous year; she wasn't going to risk another female's safety.

Tokh entertained Justice Wahtegahn in his office while the wives readied the meal. Aila came down the stairs and joined them, now fully their equal.

That was strange.

She was still subservient to Firstwife and Secondwife, for she was still a daughter of Tokh's, but she was now accountable for guests just as they were, and could order servants around. And now there was a fourth.

Oh Haghíde. It's not your pants that got you in trouble, it's your heart, as always. This had to work out right for him. It had to, if Aila had to plead it all the way up to Nadigh himself. She formally introduced herself to Fahni.

"You are the bride from last night's wedding," Fahni said while she bowed. "You were the most beautiful bride I have ever seen, and that was a most wonderful wedding. I'm so grateful you invited me."

"Thank Mímihn and Zheníhda," Aila said. "It was like your wedding party, too, I guess, but no one knew it then."

Fahni smiled. "I didn't know it, or I would have enjoyed it even more." She leaned in close to Aila. "Do you know him, my husband? Was it a good choice? Is there anything I should know, anything not to speak of, anything that might anger him? Is he very rigid about things, or is he relaxed? Should I fear his anger?"

Aila seized Fahni on both sides of her head and kissed her nose. "You have married the best remaining male on all of Kerasím. If I did not have my husband, I would choose Haghíde over everyone else. I have known him six years, as teacher, and protector, and friend. His heart is bigger than his head. You will love him very much. He will be the best of husbands for you. He is brother-*aghát* and brother-friend to my husband Masákh. We will see each other often."

Fahni hugged Aila as if she could consume her. "Thank you! Thank you for your words! He took my heart the moment he sang to me."

Aila burst out laughing. She had no trouble at all picturing the scene. "That's Haghíde!"

"My first husband, Olet, he was a good husband, but he never made my heart leap with song. He was a lieutenant. He didn't die in battle, though. He wasn't looking and walked in front of a vehicle on the base. His head was always in the clouds."

"Haghíde will make your heart leap every day," Aila promised.

Aila's own words stayed in the back of her head. *Like your wedding party, too.* While the dinner was cooking, she ran upstairs and pulled the flowered garlands from the walls of her room, draped them around her neck, and grabbed one of the large flower bowls and carried them down the hall. Kindness between females went a long way on Kerasím.

She knocked on the guestroom door. Haghíde answered it. Tokh wanted him out of sight and silent, so that even a spy drone wouldn't know where he was. He wasn't allowed to come out even for dinner.

Aila knew better than to enter the room. Haghíde was Haghíde and she feared him no more now than she did alone with him in a room at the State House back on Centauri, but this was Kerasím, and now they were both married to different people. She handed him the bowl of flowers while she unwrapped the garlands from her neck.

"Tonight is your wedding night. I thought maybe Fahni would like her room to be decorated, too."

Haghíde bowed gratefully. "Thank you, Aila. That is very kind. She'll be most pleased."

Aila handed him the last of the flowers with a smile. "Nice job, Haghíde. She seems very sweet. I wish you both every happiness. You'll make a wonderful husband for her."

Haghíde stared at the flowers in his arms. "I'm afraid it will be far too brief. It's wrong of me to make her a widow again so soon. I've given her false joy."

"She won't be. I have Mr. Halian on standby. I can have you to safety in a flash. Don't worry. The Union will keep you safe."

Haghíde's *aghát*-control cracked, and Aila felt terrible at the distress she saw between the edges. He gave a soft snort far too close to hysteria for Aila's comfort. "*The Union.* Six years ago they were our greatest enemy. I would have killed someone on sight and received promotion for it. Now they'll save me from my own people. I don't always understand life."

Aila squeezed his arm, keeping to his sleeve. "You don't understand life, Haghíde. You just live it."

The strain drained the life out of the house. Fahni stayed upstairs with Haghíde and Vihren, and everyone crept upstairs early, unsure of what the next day would bring. It wasn't inconceivable that authorities would come to seize Haghíde in the middle of the night.

Masákh's head was distracted. He didn't suggest sex or point out her mistakes, just sat brooding on the lounging sofa. Their room looked out over the gardens and hillside; he couldn't see the courtyard or gate to know if danger was coming.

Aila slid her hands over his neck and kissed his ear. "Hey. Remember me? Day one of married life? I hope this isn't how the rest of our life together is going to be."

His eyes didn't shift. "I can't understand why he would throw his life away over a female."

Aila chuckled and kissed him again. "Like you never did? Did you not disobey a direct order to chase a female?"

Masákh snorted irritably. "Yes, but I didn't threaten to kill a superior officer in the process. Tokh can't make that charge go away."

"Have faith. Between Tokh, Ghírandar, and Ross, they'll make it work out." A scream sounded through the door, a female's high voice.

They must have come for Haghíde.

Masákh and Aila scrambled off the lounge. Masákh grabbed his pistol from the bedtable. Aila grabbed the door to run out but he elbowed her aside as the screams rang several more times. She followed him, undaunted. The hallway was empty; he proceeded out, weapon raised, checking over the rail to the floor below, but all downstairs was dark.

Mátokhan, Tótoghar, and Ghírandar flew out of the dormitory room in various states of dress, also armed, as Tokh exited his room with sword in hand, followed by Zheníhda, her hair down. Mímihn sprinted down the hall in a dressing robe, Thoren wailing in her room.

It wasn't like Haghíde to beat on a female. Perhaps he'd received bad news on his comm. Mátokhan took position outside the door, weapon ready, and pounded a knock. "Major? Status report! Is there a problem?"

Haghíde opened the door part way. Aila gave a yelp and turned away. Haghíde was stark naked, shocked and surprised to find an armed contingent at his door. He smiled nervously. "My apologies for the disturbance." He glanced behind, then leaned farther out the door and lowered his voice. "She has not been *pushed* in four years. She's overly pleased. I'll make her stay quiet."

The words sank in, and Mátokhan began to laugh. He backfisted Haghíde in the stomach. "Only you, Haghíde. Make the Emperor proud." Haghíde closed the door and everyone trailed back to bed, the tension broken.

Eighteen

Haghíde was ordered to present himself to tribunal at half to noon. Tokh asked for the location to be changed to Keranihn due to his work, and it was granted. He had more pull in Keranihn, and more options at his disposal. It also meant Haghíde was only a few *fasím* from the safety of the Embassy.

Tokh mustered his officers for as large and impressive a show as he could. He wore his dress uniform, and had his *aghát* dress as well. Ross Halian and at least one advisor would meet them there, as well as several of Tokh's command officers: General One Brinkh, Colonel Khaním, Colonel Kassán. It was a powerhouse of intimidation.

Aila was forbidden to accompany them.

"Not even as a character witness? Not even as someone who can verify he works inside Union lines, under Union rules?" she begged.

"No." Tokh was firm.

Masákh hugged her. "A female would not be allowed in. You'll have to trust Tokh."

Aila put her head on his shoulder. "I'll be absolutely sick with worry, and if I feel that way, imagine how poor Fahni will feel. You call me the second there's a verdict! You hear me? Promise!"

Masákh's lips nuzzled her ear. "Keep your comm with you," he whispered. "If I'm allowed to keep mine, I'll open the link between us. You'll hear everything as I hear it."

Aila kissed his lips. "Thank you. If all else fails, get him to the embassy at all costs."

"I will do my best to honor all parties."

Fahni tried. She tried so very hard to be an honorable wife, making sure her new husband, whose importance she hadn't begun to understand, looked his absolute best, that he ate well and wanted for nothing, and that she never had less than a smile on her face. She almost made it, until he moved toward the door.

"Ka. Ka. Fanor rahx! Fanor rahx!" Fahni's face collapsed in desperation, her heart shivering so hard it made her body shake. She threw herself at him, holding on, and the harder he resisted the tighter she clung, until Zhenihda stepped in to pull her off. Fahni didn't try to stop the tears.

Zhenihda watched them cross the courtyard to the landing pad, then shut the door. "It's anyone's guess. If I walked into a room and saw all of them staring at me with their strong-faces, I'd slip out and pretend I was in the wrong room and forget about my complaint. It's at least half-half, I guarantee."

Aila and Mímihn dragged Fahni to a sofa and let her cry. Vihren sat in her lap and hugged her, frightened without knowing why. Fahni should have been entering him into a school, but there was no point unless she knew she still had a husband and somewhere to live. She would have to beg her family to return, if they would allow it, or perhaps Haghíde's family, once they were told he had married.

The men had left early to arrive early, and it was ninety minutes until Aila called everyone over to the table and told Shanohr to take Thoren and Vihren outside for an hour and keep them quiet.

"Come! Masákh is going to open a link so we may hear exactly what's going on, but we must be quiet. They can hear us if we're too loud."

The women flew to the table and joined hands, nervous as a séance that promised to raise departed spirits. Just two minutes late, Aila's comm chirped. She hit the receive button and turned up the volume. In her head she could see Masákh, ram-rod straight, chin high, his face cold and his dark eyes even colder with intimidation. She knew the look well, and in her younger years it scared her so much she couldn't breathe before that look. Even at her angriest, that look could fold her up fast.

Colonel Aegarr had brought his wife; she was excused to wait outside. A wife couldn't testify for or against a husband unless she brought the charge herself, as her testimony would be suspect, and he'd brought no one else with him. The justice introduced himself, General Three Garshughan; Aila could hear the formerly *fáhganid* superiority in his voice. Most *fáhganid* she knew were neither pleasant nor young, and her head invented his looks.

Aegarr stated his grievance, that Major Haghíde had dishonored his daughter, forced her into marriage, threatened the Colonel's life, and stolen his smallson as well. For this he asked justice.

Tokh introduced himself. He introduced his men, man after man after man, all of good reputation and high decoration. Ráhnif was wearing his insignia that allowed him to work at the palace, as was Kassán, in addition to Tokh's Senator status. The Union Ambassador himself stood by, ready to testify as to the accused's duties inside the Union; a powerhouse of palace ties.

"We will bear witness that Major Haghíde's story differs from that of the Colonel's, and that justice should be minimal."

"How does his story differ?" asked Garshughan.

Footsteps echoed away from the comm, so the room must have been quite large and without carpeting. There was a rustle of paper. "*Aghát* Captain Ghírandar otta Paiéhr, Advisor for *aghát* Major Haghíde Kitáhl. This is my client's statement. There are extenuating circumstances as to why he acted as he did, which are reasonable, lawful, and to be expected."

There was a silent pause that seemed to last an hour as Garshughan read through Ghírandar's carefully worded statement.

"Colonel: speak," said Garshughan. After a single sentence he stopped him. "Major, do you agree with this statement?"

The first statement was about Haghíde arriving at Aegarr's house as he was ending his breakfast. "Yes, I do."

Garshughan walked them through their stories line by line, picking out the facts that were in disagreement. Ghírandar didn't allow Haghíde to argue, but substituted laws and allowances for each disagreement. Aegarr's huffiness waxed and waned depending on the disagreement. After half an hour of microdiscussion, Garshughan cut them off and sat back to think.

"The charge of forcing your daughter into marriage is dismissed," Garshughan said. "Your daughter is a widow with child. The charge of dishonor does not apply unless she is under age, or of age and not yet married. The dishonor is on you, Colonel, refusing a marriage offer on a daughter who is nearly thirty. She's lucky to have such an offer. Your duty was to find her a suitable husband so that she didn't fall into the

134

misfortune of not having someone to care for her later in life and relying on the Emperor's charity for her welfare. That's a gross failure on your part. Accountants exist for a purpose: to make money to support themselves. That is also reprehensible. By making your daughter keep your accounts, you have denied a male the income he needs to support his own family. I'm not liking your character, Colonel. Your daughter is past an age where you have say over her; you have no right to beat her at will. She has the right to bring charges against you, and on seeing the photos the Major has provided of the bruises left by you, I will charge them for her in her absence. You have no claim to your daughter's dowry or the interest on it; it's her first husband's estate and should pass on to his son when he comes of age. That must be surrendered before you may leave.

"The final charge, that of threatening a superior officer, cannot be dismissed," the Justice said.

Ghírandar's voice spoke up. "Revered Justice, may I point out that Major Haghíde was not on duty, nor the Colonel, and the dispute was a personal one not involving military order."

There was a shuffling of feet and a pause for inaudible conversation. Ghírandar spoke again. "If it may please the Justice, what is the amount of the dowry involved?"

Colonel Aegarr's voice said, "Approximately fifteen thousand *dakra*."

A sizable fortune, considering Fahni's husband had died a Lieutenant-Two. Ghírandar continued, "Major Haghíde wishes to know if the Colonel will drop all charges in exchange for keeping his wife's dowry."

There was a long pause. A distant grunt sounded like an agreement.

"In the name of the plaintiff's smallson, I cannot grant more than half the dowry," said Justice Garshughan. "Major, are you willing on charge of this court to replace half of said dowry from your own accounts, to replenish the inheritance of your wife's son?"

Haghíde's voice was firm and clear. "I am, your Reverence."

There was a loud bang as Justice Garshughan cracked his control stick on the strike block of his desk. "Then it is settled. Colonel Aegarr will drop all proceedings against Major Haghíde, in exchange for one-half of his wife's dowry. On order of the court, Major Haghíde agrees to replace said half of dowry, valued at seven thousand five hundred *dakra*, by the child's fifteenth nameday."

Aila's hands shot up in silent victory. Mímihn and Fahni covered their mouths to keep from crying out, while Zheníhda's smile shone proud, never doubting her husband's power for a moment.

"However," Justice Garshughan continued. "The charge of threatening a superior officer, even if caste is discounted, remains a serious offense, even if the colonel chooses not to press charges. I cannot ignore this. General Tokh, did you discipline your officer when you discovered his misconduct?"

"I did, Revered Justice. He was striped without mercy, eight lashes, and kept isolated until today."

"I will observe." There was a rustling of chairs and clothing as Haghíde stripped to his waist before the Justice, then a pause.

"You are correct about no mercy," Garshughan said without emotion. "That's a punishment that will remind him for weeks to come. Very well. Major: you will not receive such leniency again. I will allow General Tokh's punishment to stand, with the addition of a permanent reprimand in your file. It will state that you did threaten a superior officer, but during a personal off-duty dispute and not related to command or orders."

The control stick cracked the desk again. "Complaint is dismissed. Please see the secretary to receive your paperwork."

The link clicked out, but Masákh buzzed her back a few minutes later, while Tokh and Haghíde and Ghírandar were busy signing the agreements. "Did the link hold?"

Aila was beside herself with joy, but not nearly as much as Fahni. "I love you! It worked perfectly! We could hear almost every word. It helped Fahni so much. I know you don't want to hear she's crying for joy, but she thanks you from the stars down. I'll thank you in a very personal way when you get back," she teased.

In her head, she could see his eyes searching to the sides, seeing if anyone had possibly overheard the comm pressed to his ear. "I look forward to it."

The men arrived back in Imahlva at dinner time, every one of them, save Tótoghar flying the craft, well past the point of inebriation. They strolled into the courtyard in a raucous mix of drunken shouts, and the congratulatory shouts of the wives and children. Aila forgot to bow first and tackled Masákh in a bear hug that almost knocked him off his feet. Her kiss lingered on his lips to the catcalls of his crewmates, and she flashed them an obscene gesture.

Fahni ran to Haghíde just as hard, but he put his hands out to stop her. The wounds on his back pulsed in excruciating agony, and her touch would put him over the edge. She kissed the side of his throat without any other contact, then set about removing his jacket and shirt right there in the courtyard. Spots of brown blood were still seeping through his liner shirt. Vihren hugged his legs.

"New *Bobo*! New *Bobo*! You came back!" Haghíde looked down at the boy as if just discovering his existence. No one had ever called him father before. Two big eyes black as *orak* stones and an adoring grin shone back at him.

He reached down and ruffled Vihren's shaggy black hair. "I couldn't forget about you."

They stumbled into the house, several of Tokh's command officers still with them. Tokh pointed to Masákh. "You have a marriage leave. Go! Get out of my house by tomorrow." He pointed at Haghíde. "You have caused me too much grief. I grant you a week's marriage leave; get out of my house by morning."

He pointed at the rest of the *aghát*. "You have work in Imahlva. You have business to attend to. You: you have assigned duties, and you – go practice what you do. I want my house to myself tomorrow. But tonight –" He looked around the gathered crowd through wavering vision. "*Push* the Lord of Fortune all the way to the skies. There was a wedding yesterday we haven't celebrated, and we are already half-way there. Nihda, make it a party for dinner."

Zheníhda bowed her head with a patronizing smile that Aila read as nothing short of 'I'll kill your drunken ass in your sleep tonight.' "As you wish, my Lord."

Nineteen

Kinas Dagh, Daghnahn, Kerasím.

Aila wasn't prepared for the heat of Masákh's homeland, a brutal furnace that beat down on the people and baked their souls from them. Kinas Dagh was in the middle of a desert, twenty thousand people and nothing but empty space and a straight, flat road to the next city, twenty miles away. There wasn't so much a low-caste suburbia as a thinning of the buildings at the edges, and then an abrupt end where the public utilities stopped. Sand... So much gray-brown sand, and gray-white dust wherever there wasn't sand.

Four caste-sections divided the city, each with its own open spaces for tiny public parks with shaded, raised desert gardens and low-moisture trees with greasy trunks and sharp rays of golden leaves that grew in giant sunbursts, shading benches below them where much of the city sat to socialize at lunch. Some roads were paved, many weren't, and with all the drifting sand it wasn't easy to tell which was which. Each residential street had spaces for gardening under billowing canopies; every family had a small plot to supplement their food, and the females traded different crops among themselves. Without much for landscape views, the people made up for it with colorful awnings and flapping flags and banners everywhere. It was lively and bustling, just baked and dusty.

They stayed three days with Masákh's parents. As far as Aila was concerned, it was two days too long, but she bit her tongue and smiled and made the best of it.

Masákh's parents lived in four spacious rooms on the third floor of an upscale middle-caste apartment building in the Kirzaka district, just *rhibani* and *whátaral* living in good harmony. There was no lift for the four *rhibani* floors; higher floors meant higher standing in society, and it was only with Masákh's help his parents were able to acquire a third-floor one. Owning two successful stores was not prosperous enough. The kitchen balcony was just large enough for two people to stand on and overlook the street, but it let heat out of the kitchen and breezes in. Often Masákh's mother Namig cooked over a small two-burner stove out on the balcony, to spare the apartment.

Aila realized that despite her familiarities, she hadn't really experienced life on Kerasím. She'd spent time among the privileged, where females were a little freer in their closed luxury compounds and had a little more power than their lower caste counterparts. Without privilege, it was an entirely new set of rules. Masákh was off duty. *Really* off-duty, not just sitting around in his shirt with his jacket hung up, or lounging in his liner-shirt. He hadn't even brought his uniform with them; it stayed clean and pressed and waiting at Tokh's, though his identification and weapons had accompanied them. Only twice had Aila seen him without some sort of uniform: when he wore prison garb after the Union captured him, and last year when he went undercover to escort her to safety, a disastrous five days that put them in increasing danger each minute they were gone from Imahlva. In six years, that was it. And here he was, lounging about in light, loose clothing, a thin poncho-like cloth called an *apo* over his clothes when he went out, an item all the men wore to help keep their indoor clothing dust and dirt-free – as well as keep them cooler in the heat. Aila delighted in irritating him by calling it his man-veil.

And veiled she was. Fashion was not forward in Kinas Dagh. Aila was used to Tokh's, where his wives considered veils nothing more than a fashion statement and his daughter-in-law wore hers anywhere but her head. Even the Heir Apparent wore only a functionless remnant on occasion. Here almost every female wore one, and they wore them down. Aila's new Kinas Dagh veil was lovely – swirls of red, black, gold, and brown, with fringes and metallic threads and clinkity antiqued gold metal beads on the fringe – but it came down past her shoulders, almost to her elbows. Outside, it held the heat on her head and made her face sweat more. Inside the apartment his father still required her to wear it, flipped down her back where it made her neck and back sweaty, and pulled her hair when she sat.

Ugh.

Both times Aila had met his parents, they were intimidated by her *dahneg* status and her position as Councilmember. Here, in their own home, things were even more confusing. As daughter by law, she was subservient to her husband's parents, but Aila was in a sort of limbo –

139

she was *dahneg*, but now married to a *whátaral*-with-privilege, which meant she took her husband's caste, but she was still a foreign diplomat, and even the palace hadn't figured that one out yet. For now, she was a *dahneg* dignitary, married to a *whátaral* who somehow had *rhibáni* parents. Aila would offer to help Namig with something and Namig would accept, then remember the *dahneg* and return Aila to the sitting area. Masákh's father, Masaruhn, stared at her wordlessly, until Aila felt like pulling her veil down. His parents spoke the local dialect; their Emperor's Tongue was heavily accented and Aila had difficulty understanding them. The food was not the same as in Imahlva, though the *lunahl* was good and flowed just as plentifully. On the first night, Masákh's brother Nárukh and his family joined them and stayed well past dark, keeping the conversations going.

Alone at last in the guest room, Masákh stole Aila's nightwear from her hands before she had a chance to slip it over her head. He kissed her throat. "You will not need that."

She tried to push him away. "Are you kidding? Your parents are on the other side of that wall! Your father will have his ear against the door."

"It is not unlikely, but this is Kerasím. They will be pleased by the sounds. They'll wish to know you're pleasing me, and that we are happy. You don't protest at Tokh's."

"Because there's usually an empty room on either side of us, and he's too busy *pushing* his own wives to care. Your parents are four feet away from us."

Aila lost the battle. This was their official newlywed week, and *pushing* was the main item on the itinerary. She couldn't relax and enjoy it, no matter what Masákh did. Half-way through the second round, raised voices were audible through the wall, a female voice wailing, and a male voice raised and unintelligible.

Aila lifted her head, any possible remnant of interest gone as her heart stopped. "Are they fighting? Does your father hit your mother?"

Masákh's pace slowed as he listened. "No. My father is younger than Tokh. I suspect they are doing the same thing we are." He resumed with a sudden hard thrust, knocking Aila off one of her elbows.

Aila let her face drop into the bed, any possible hope of pleasure gone. Having sex when you knew your husband's parents were listening was awful enough; having to listen to your husband's parents having sex while you were having sex, and they knew you were having sex, killed everything.

Welcome to Kerasím.

Day two was somehow worse. Aila ate breakfast with his parents, knowing everything from the night before. As eldest son, Masákh had family business to attend to. There were family accounts to keep track of, and he had to make sure his father's businesses were up to par with taxes and legal codes and the myriad things needed to ensure success. That was his duty as eldest son, even if he was off world more than he was on it, even though his brother was in charge of half the business, even though his brother lived there in Kinas Dagh. That was law. To Aila's horror, Masákh left her home with his mother for the day, where good *rhibáni* females stayed.

Great Galaxy, give me strength.

The moment the men left, Namig cleaned the apartment. Both beds had to be changed, the furniture and cushions all beaten and fluffed, the dust shook from the draperies and wall hangings, surfaces wiped, and then the floors cleaned. Robotic cleaners were forbidden by the Emperor – they took jobs away from the lower-castes, but cleaning was easy; Aila understood it and knew how. She could feel Namig's eyes judging her, but in the end Namig seemed satisfied Aila would give her son a clean home.

Once that was done, Namig made two steaming cups of spicy-sweet *raffin* and a plate of cakelets, and they sat together and watched a drama program on the Kerasi ComNet. It was a global program broadcast in Emperor's Tongue, and Aila was able to follow the majority of the dialogue.

From what Aila could figure out, the plot line covered the storylines of six families, a *fáhganid*, a *dahneg*, a *nhásarwharl*, a *whátaral*, a *taghinet*, and a *solahrin*. The *fáhganids* were the primary focus, and everyone else was caught in their shadow, from their *solahrin* maid to the *taghinet* musician who played at the restaurant the *fáhganid*'s owned, to the *nhásarwharl* who ran the establishment, to the *dahneg* commander the *fáhganid* was blackmailing. Aila wasn't one for gossip; her problems were never like anyone else's, but after two hours of watching the maid's misfortune, the *dahneg* putting his career on the line for the *fáhganid* by bribing a hospital worker to get him drugs that were then given to the *nhásarwharl* to pay off a Justice, the *taghinet's* wife being assaulted by a neighbor who knew he wouldn't be home and her fear of telling her husband, and, at the end, the cliffhanger of the *nhásarwharl's* small child coming upon the stash of narcotics and opening a container – Aila was sucked into the stories, and knew she was looking at something that was a little overblown perhaps but most likely not far from the truth of how ordinary Kerasi society worked. She made note of the title, *Inside Connections*, and planned to point it out to Ross Halian. Someone in the Union should be watching it to learn about society, and no doubt that properly marketed and overdubbed into Union, people would watch it in droves out of curiosity.

When the drama ended, and Aila was mad at herself for worrying about a fictitious child getting into fictitious poison, Namig decided they needed to go shopping. She told Aila to ready herself, then called to the office of the apartment building and asked to hire one of the building's escorts.

Aila pulled her dreaded veil over her face when they reached the street. It was light enough that she could see through it fairly easily, as if watching people through a sheer window curtain. People looking at her might see where her eyes or her mouth were located, but not clearly enough to identify her. The mid-day heat was so intense it made Aila's skin shrivel under her sleeves, but the veil trapped the moisture from her breath and kept her nose from bleeding.

They walked two blocks to a commercial street – most cities had residences going one way and businesses on the cross streets, so females didn't have to travel far. An empty lot on the corner was crammed with street vendors under awnings, those of lesser means who couldn't afford the rental on a storefront, or perhaps a traveling vendor who went town to town, or a husband or son selling items hand-made by family females. A display of simple wire bracelets caught Aila's eye.

"*Ama* Namig, may we look?"

The public escort cost by the hour, but Namig smiled and bowed her head. "For a few *fasim*."

Aila wound up buying herself a group of a dozen jangly metal bracelets, shoving six onto each wrist. At the next stall, Aila lifted her veil and flipped it down her back.

"What are you doing!" Namig gasped.

"There is much dark; I cannot see," Aila said. "I am still wearing it." Namig's head looked like a green and purple lampshade.

"You will be a target!"

"For what?" Aila sniffed. She pointed to her *dahneg* badge and her Emperor's pin, neither visible with the veil down. "I am *dahneg*, and I am under the Emperor's guard. I do not fear." She moved to the next booth.

Namig stood still, wanting to argue – no, it was her *duty* to argue with this daughter-by-law – but frightened by the *dahneg* status. Unable to decide, she simply followed. Aila's fate was in the hands of the escort.

They admired a vendor of hand-blown glass lamps, then stopped at a perfume stall. The first one Aila sniffed reminded her of dirty feet, and the second was a heavy, murky floral scent. The third one she tried was intriguing.

Namig sniffed the contents of a pumpkin-colored globe. "*Ahhhk!* Smell this!" It smelled spicy, like a warm kitchen. Like cooking in a kitchen while wearing an evening gown. The scent made Aila think of Namig. It fit her.

"You should buy that one," Aila said. "I think it smells like you."

"Me?" The green-purple lampshade laughed. "What would I do with perfume?"

"Wear it."

"No, no." Namig put it back and moved to the next vendor.

Aila looked about the table for the price marker; if *dakra* were the same here, it was a steep price for a small luxury. Perhaps Namig couldn't afford it. Aila purchased her own perfume and a matching skin cream, then pointed to the globe. "One of that, also. Can you paper it for me, please?"

The vendor's eye fell on her *dahneg* badge, and bowed his head. He handed her the two items, then wrapped the last one in colored paper like a present. Aila paid him and slipped them all into her shopping tote. To be fair, she purchased a jar of exotic treats for Masákh's father at another vendor. Better to keep things even.

They left the vendors and went to a food market, where Namig purchased fresh items for the evening meal.

At the end of the market, a group of older teen boys were looking at the displays of *muhr*. One noticed Aila, half a row from Namig and the escort. He poked the others, and they blocked her way. The boldest one spoke to her, but with the dialect and accent, Aila only caught every third word. He reached out and flicked the edge of her veil.

"???? display ???? for me, consort? ??? me your ???" A second youth actually grabbed the back of Aila's skirt with both hands and scrubbed the fabric across her backside in a cha-cha while the third one laughed.

Masákh had taught her what to do if cornered, depending on the caste of her attackers, and these were just pesky little *nhásarwharl* bullies. If she were a plain *whátaral* she would have been in trouble, even if just *nhásarwharl*, but she was wearing her *dahneg* badge, and she knew how to use it.

Commit to act, then do not stop unless you are dead. She grabbed the dagger she wore in the waist of her skirt and flicked it out with a twist of her wrist. It pressed against the throat of the leader a scant second later. Aila leaned forward until she was nose to nose with him.

"Do you have eyes? Do you see the rank on my shoulder?" Aila bellowed loud enough that everyone in the market stall heard her. She grabbed her blouse and shook it with her free hand. "*Dahneg*! That says *dahneg*! Do you see this one? That says Emperor! You are messing with the Emperor!"

Dahneg and *Keralihn* were two words that crossed all language. The two friends backed off, while Aila's victim raised his hands in surrender. A wail sounded in the background; Aila didn't turn, but assumed it was Masákh's mother. Oh, there'd be hell to pay for this. Good wives didn't attack their attackers. The grocer hurried down the row with the escort and a law officer, chattering.

Aila released her attacker and slipped the knife up her sleeve. She turned to the officer, shaking her pins. "My husband is Major Masákh gha Lil – Major – of the Emperor's *aghát*. I am under the protection of the Emperor. These no-*hihvat* babies touched me with plan to assault. I am *dahneg*, and I want justice."

Namig petted her arm, muttering calming words, but Aila held her evil glare. She dug out her comm as the officer tried to placate her, pulled up a photo of her standing next to Emperor Nadigh and showed it to him. The officer was a *nhásarwharl* lieutenant; his attitude

144

changed completely. He reached out and seized the leader by the back of his clothing.

"What do you wish, Great Lady?"

"Three stripes each, and a written warning not to assault females again."

The officer bowed to her. "It will be done, Great Lady." He chained them together with a cable from a pouch on his belt. "Does your husband have an address so we may report the final outcome to him?" Aila gave him Masákh's com linkup, and the officer led the grumbling teens out.

Namig's face flashed fire, and she steered Aila out of the market none too gently. "*Embarrassment!* Are you happy now? Maybe now you will pull your veil down! You dishonor my son, threatening a male!"

Aila glared back. "Who do you think taught me to fight? Maybe now they will leave females alone!"

Aila didn't know a lot of the words Namig threw at her on the way back, but she held her tongue. They returned to the apartment, where Namig set about preparing the supper and called Aila in to help. Aila made simple things at home – Masákh knew full well how to cook anything, but stubbornly insisted it was a female task – but she had no idea how to cook Kerasi foods. She wasn't much help, and after cutting up some items and stirring others, Namig sent her out of the kitchen. No doubt many of the words Namig uttered weren't very polite, and the slamming of cookware underscored it. Aila was overjoyed when Masákh returned, and she explained the day to him before Namig could – and Namig did, in a very rapid and unforgiving tone, with lots of hand gestures. Aila sat at the table and pretended not to hear. Masákh, to his credit, defended her to his mother, and not with the politest words.

"She is a qualified diplomat. She does the same job I do. She goes among government officials and speaks with them, tries to get them to make peace," he argued. "She does not spend her days trapped inside. Our very own Emperor has given her his approval."

"All the more reason!" Nadigh spat. "Only a fool wakes a poisonous eel!"

145

Namig's world was spent avoiding the notice of higher-ups who could cause trouble. *Aaka* flowed down hill, and *rhibáni* bore quite a bit of it. Meeting the Emperor had been a thrill of a lifetime, but the implications sank in later. If the Emperor knew her son, then he knew where his parents lived, and if the son had issues, they could bounce back onto the parents; that was Kerasi fact, and one that ate at Namig in the dark of night. "A wife worthy of her husband doesn't bring attention to herself! Why! Why would you give her a weapon? You're asking for trouble, Masákh! If they don't kill her, they'll discipline you for giving it to her! You are tempting Fortunes!"

"That isn't true for Keranihn, *Ama*. Females show their faces in Keranihn. They show their legs. They show their arms. And they appear in public that way. Upper caste females carry weapons. If you would come with me to Keranihn, I would show you."

Namig waved him out of her face. "*Gah!* I won't go where wives dress like consorts. Power brings nothing but trouble."

Masákh *pushed* Aila once that night, then stopped. "Your heart isn't with me at all. You don't even look at me."

Aila brightened quickly, though the room was dark. "I love you more than yesterday, and less than tomorrow. I missed you today."

"You have greater conversation with Zheníhda, a difficult female, than you have with my mother. Today created more tension than it relieved."

"I can't always understand her. She has an accent I'm not used to. She speaks more local than Emperor's Tongue."

Masákh sighed, and the arms of impenetrable strength wrapped around her and held her close. "I feel the difficulty. I haven't been part of my family since I was of nine years. That's when they took me for training. I returned eight weeks a year, but after a year or two, my family were strangers to me. Their lives continued, but I wasn't part of it. I wanted very much to be back home, not because I disliked the academy but because I wanted to be with my family. After a while I no longer mattered in their daily lives. I was a relative who lived far away and visited. By the time I graduated, my achievements were bringing them pride. They could brag about me, and my success brought them favors. I am most dutiful; I use my position and income to get them luxuries they would not otherwise have. I will take care of my mother if

146

needed, but I don't feel special affinity for her. I have a vast education. I've been deep into space, been held prisoner in other star systems. My father was born here, my mother two cities away. They were sixteen and fifteen when they married. This is all they are, and all they'll ever be. They were born and lived their entire lives under Emperor Nághtas's stability. Change is not easy for them. I look at them and I see what I was supposed to become, and it gives me great fear. I didn't know at the time what a gift General Saddík gave me, choosing me."

"You make it sound so miserable." Aila hugged his hands against her. "They seem happy enough. Your father has his own business. Your mother has friends and grandchildren to care for. They're ordinary people."

He sighed and thought before speaking. "Perhaps that's the issue. They are too ordinary. I was born a humble *rhibani*, recasted *whátaral*, then *whátaral* with *nhásarwharl* privilege, and due to my position I have spent much time in luxury settings far beyond my birthright. I am what you would term, 'spoiled'."

"That's not a word I would ever use to describe you. I'm not old enough to be that spoiled yet. At least, I don't think so. If anything, I'm spoiled by power. I'm used to cutting to the top and getting changes made, or getting my points aired. When I was fourteen I kicked a galaxy, and it turned its head to look at me. Even important people can't do that easily."

He tensed all his muscles and pulled her against him, squeezing until Aila feared she might pop out the other side of him. When he relaxed, he kissed her jaw. "Tonight we will just sleep. I will plan something enjoyable for tomorrow."

Twenty

Masákh hired a private vehicle and driver after breakfast, and took Aila sight-seeing. If Kinas Dagh was the middle of nowhere, they drove an hour past nowhere to the tourist stop of Armig Ghan Bihl, an active archeological site of a cliff-dwelling people six thousand years old. The cliffs themselves were breathtaking, hundreds of feet high, a gray-white stone streaked with soft rainbows of mineral colors shining through, and the hundreds of excavated cave-homes carved into the cliffs were rich with primitive paintings made from the ochres. From there Masákh had the driver take them another hour and a half to Sahr Dagh, the capital of Daghnahn.

In Sahr Dagh, Aila understood Masákh's shame. Sahr Dagh was a metropolis of two million people, built on the shores of a large lake. There was a sizable, functioning upper-caste presence, as the lake provided vacation destinations and exclusive living for those of the desert. All the upper castes brought office jobs, and office jobs brought inhabitants, and inhabitants needed commodities. Sahr Dagh's markets competed on a global level; anything available in Keranihn was also likely to be found in Sahr Dagh. Here the people were more educated, and perhaps three-quarters of the females had bare heads. Here were the fashions of bright colors and sleeveless blouses and skirts that crept well above knees, and shoes of every outlandish decoration. Here was the food Aila had grown used to. They passed a pleasant afternoon walking about the city and poking into attractions, hand in hand, relaxed and happy, not running from unseen dangers or getting funny looks from passersby, even though Aila had removed her veil and tied it around her hips.

They returned to Kinas Dagh, but not to the apartment. Masákh took her to a restaurant that catered to *nhásarwharl* and *dihnarwharl*. When the doorman sneered at Masákh's mere privilege status, Aila thrust her shoulder out with her *dahneg* badge on it, and the man let them in with a grunt.

It was dark by the time they left the restaurant. Aila clued in: Masákh was dragging it out until his parents would be asleep, and they wouldn't have to interact with them.

Masákh had other ideas. They hopped a local *eel*-bus to the far edge of town, where the *eels* reversed direction. At the second-to-last building, he rented a large, pre-filled gearsack.

"What are you doing with that?" Aila asked.

"Hiking."

"Hiking? In the dark? To where?"

"Nowhere."

"No, seriously. Where are we going?"

"I'm being as precise as possible. Nowhere with a name."

Aila stopped walking. "Now you're scaring me." *Darkness... desert... no witnesses... a bag of tools...* That scene never ended well.

He turned back to eye her in the pale light of the distant streetlamp. "Do you trust me or not?"

"I'm not positive at the moment."

"We will both be back at mother's by morning. That is fact."

Aila played along. Masákh wouldn't say a word, and she knew if she pressed him he would take the secret to his death. They walked along the highway by the small circle from a tubelight, spotting at least two other couples also out walking in the dark. In the distance were the flashing lights of communication towers and observation stations, blue dots of light at ground level, and the glow of far-off cities. Overhead were the omnipresent twinkling lights of aircraft. Empty land, but not uninhabited.

Masákh left the road at random, and they walked awhile over the super-fine sand. At last he stopped and turned off the tubelight. It seemed crazy to look around. Here in the center of nothing, the only difference between Kinas Dagh and outer space was gravity and the feel of ground beneath you. Aila's eyes adjusted slowly; the dead blindness gave way to shades of black, and she could make out his blacker outline against the deep purple-black of the sky, or the silhouette of her hand in front of her face. Just as she got used to it, he activated the tubelight and dug in his pack, blinding her again.

He pulled out several pieces of plastic tubing, connected them, stuck a large knob on the top, and drove it into the sand until it stood four feet high. With the flick of a switch, the knob on the top began to flash blue. "It's a warning, so random vehicles will know to avoid us."

They had passed blue lights on the walk. Aila lifted her head and now realized just how many. In the distance, in every direction, faint blue dots were everywhere, perhaps hundreds, spread far across the night. While Aila was staring about in wonder, Masákh set up a simple crude tent.

"We're sleeping here?"

Masákh knelt in the sand and dug through the bag. He placed a tiny solar lamp in the sand, activated it, then turned off the tubelight. The soft glow made just enough light to see each other by. "Yes. You wanted to get away from everything. I wanted to show you what it means to be Kerasi. That is tonight."

Aila scanned the darkness. There were no walls, no security, no privacy. No bathrooms. The twinkling blue lights said they were surrounded by others, and all the horror stories of Kerasi abuse popped back into her head. They'd kill Masákh, and she'd be the centerpiece at the next stag party. "Isn't that dangerous?"

"No more than anything else." He sat down and found his tote bag. From it came disposable cups, a bottle of *lunahl*, and a box of dessert bites. "Sit with me." Aila sat in the sand next to him and accepted the cup he poured for her.

"This is a night city. Kinas Dagh is small. The people know each other. You may not know the person directly but know their name, or their business, or a relative. It makes running a house of discretion difficult, but there are many square miles of open desert. When darkness falls and the temperatures drop, night cities appear. You may occupy any space you choose, as long as you are not in sight of another occupied space. Here is where lovers meet in secret. Here is where the hunted may hide. Here is where dark deals are made. Here is where anyone may come to be alone. It's not in anyone's interest to commit crimes against the campers; there are more campers than lights, and criminals can be dispatched and buried without a single witness. Come daylight, this city disappears, only to reappear after dark, with different inhabitants in different locations."

150

"So, in theory, anyone who doesn't have an apartment could work during the day, then just find a spot out here every night."

"Yes."

"Oooh! What's that?" Glowing dots bounced near the ground. The more Aila looked, the more she saw, and it wasn't because of the *lunahl*.

"Starflies. Some call them glowflies. They are harmless insects with a clear skin and luminescent blood. They are attracted to the moisture and sugars in the *lunahl*. When they cluster together, it looks like a miniature night sky."

Aila made several grabs to scoop up some of the magical creatures, but they scattered at her movement. Masákh wet his fingers with *lunahl,* then held them out. Soon his fingers were covered with a little blue-green-white scintillating cloud. He raised his hand slowly for her to observe.

"Oooh." Aila marveled at them until Masákh shook them off and cleaned his hand with a splash from a water tube.

Masákh took off his shoes, placed them inside his tote, and let his feet dig into the sand. He fell backward on a cloth before the tent. "Come. Lie here with me."

They lay under the stars, Aila's head on Masákh's chest, feeling it rise and fall with his breath. "I've never seen such a beautiful sky. I know you can't see Centauri or Earth from here, but which direction is Union space?"

"That way," Masákh pointed. "That is the constellation of the Pendulum. The star at the top is what you call Kye. That one there – the bright star? Count out one, two, three, four, and then off to the sides? That's the Great Dhastal. That star at the far right horn? That's Onigar, the star you call Vega."

"Wow. I've been in space how many times, shuttled around by you or my dad, and I don't think I've ever seen a more beautiful sky. I don't think I've ever seen so many stars at once. You can see the clouds of entire galaxies. It's gorgeous."

Masákh stared upward with a dreamy expression. "This. This is where I feel the heart of Kerasím, not Keranihn. Not the military. Here. Put your hands out." He flattened her hand in his and burrowed them under the sand. "Can you feel it? The heartbeat of the entire planet, pulsing beneath us. You can almost feel it turning toward daylight. There is nothing but you and space. No parents. No army. No commanders. No duties. Just time itself."

Aila smiled. It didn't take a lot of imagination to feel the ground vibrate with life. "You're being poetic! I didn't think you had it in you. There's like – no tension at all in your body. I've never seen you so relaxed." He looked beautiful like that in the starlight, all the *aghát* precision out of his system for the first time until only the man remained. Aila leaned over him and kissed his lips.

He returned the kiss, then more, until they swapped positions and he was above her. His hands crept under her blouse, then pushed the fabric up to her shoulders to kiss her breasts. Aila tried to pull it down.

"Not here! There's a billion eyes all around us."

"Just glowflies, and they do not judge or speak. This is perhaps the most private place on Kerasím. No one can see us, no more than we can see anyone else. Since I first dreamed of you I have wanted to *push* you here beneath the stars. Now we can." With his foot, Masákh kicked sand over the little lamp, burying the glow. It was just the two of them and the darkness and the stars as he lifted her skirt and moved his kisses to her thighs.

He *pushed* her, or maybe she *pushed* him. Aila wasn't sure. There was no up or down, no top or bottom, just stars and darkness and a pleasure so deep Aila wasn't sure she hadn't died at some point and no longer existed. Not even Masákh had brought her that intense a release before, and judging by his own grunts and cries, it was an exceptional experience for him as well. Seven? Was it seven times? Not counting the time she had climaxed twice before he finished, her heels digging deep into the sand while he pinned her shoulders down as she thrashed beneath him, stabbing into her as she cried for more while the stars and sky and time spun into one blur. For all she knew they'd *pushed* for six hours without stopping, and she was weak and shaky and sore and physically exhausted by pleasure. She slept with her cheek on the cloth under them and Masákh heavy on her back where he'd collapsed.

"I hate you for making me love you so much," Aila murmured. Her mouth was dry and she was too exhausted to speak. "No one should be that good."

"You are the Fortune-Spirit of my dreams," he mumbled back, so slack-jawed Aila could feel his spit sitting hot upon her back. "I have no choice."

You moved the heavens with your hihvat. *You win, Masákh.*

Twenty-one

There was a mass exodus at sunrise, hundreds of people leaving the sand and trudging back to the city. The air was joyous and jovial; it was no walk of shame. Some of the females were veiled, most were not, and everyone was disheveled and slapping sand from their clothing. Aila had wrapped her veil around her head like a scarf, but she took it off and tied it around her waist, and no one said a thing.

Masákh's mother wasn't surprised at their appearance, just offered them *raffin* and a small breakfast and ordered them to bathe to rid themselves of sand. Masákh played dutiful son and escorted his mother to a dozen places she needed to go, Aila's hand in his, quiet and submissive as a perfect wife was supposed to be, until at last they were able to nap while Namig went to the wife next door to watch an afternoon drama (the fictional child of the morning drama had been saved in the nick of time by someone who stole the stolen goods for himself, to Aila's relief).

When they woke, Masákh checked his com. "Would you mind if we left and traveled somewhere else?"

"Wherever you want to go," Aila said with a shrug, but inside her heart was doing cartwheels. "Where did you have in mind."

"To Morruhg, in the mountains of Kilif. We've been invited to visit Haghíde at his family home."

Aila beamed. "That'd be awesome!"

Aila presented his parents with the gifts she'd bought. His father seemed pleased, bowing and smiling and patting her cheek. Namig stared at the perfume with misty eyes, as if she now regretted causing arguments. She bowed and thanked Aila several times, then kept her head down. For all the issues, the parting seemed to be on decent terms.

A military flight took them north, back to the northern continent, a short three hours. They sat on plastic shipping crates in a cold and loud cargo hold with six other soldiers, but the flight was free.

They arrived at the end of sunset, and Aila's heart wept at the beauty of it. Morruhg was high in the mountains, many of them snow-topped, breathtaking on its own but the last orange and red rays of the setting sun turned the sky and the mountains to fire. The land flamed all at once and then the fire went out, cooled by deepening greens and blues and black.

Haghíde's family lived in a sidebyside, a row of narrow two-story apartments that were connected side to side, not stacked, that ran the length of the street. Tall buildings would ruin the views, which ruined property values. Buildings were limited to three stories by law, making land very expensive.

Haghíde's father Háhkon answered the door, overjoyed to see them and greeting them like old friends; Haghíde unleashed. He bowed repeatedly to Aila, his hands wanting to touch her but not daring, until they wound up flapping in the air.

"Welcome! Welcome to our home! We are most honored to have you! We have never had a Union person in our home – we have never seen a Union person. Or a dignitary. Only one other time has a *dahneg* been to our home! We have seen you on the ComNet. Sometimes you even stood next to our son. Thank you for coming. We are most honored! Most honored! Please, tell us anything you may need." Haghíde's mother continued to smile and bow until it looked more like she was exercising than giving honor.

Aila put her hands out, then hugged her. That seemed to help the females. "I am more honored to meet you, the parents of my friend Haghíde. I am married to a *whátaral*; please, treat me as *whátaral*."

Mrs. Háhkon returned the hug with relief. "Thank you! Thank you! We were afraid you'd be unhappy with us."

Aila squeezed her hand. "I cannot be unhappy when I am with friends."

She hugged Fahni next. "How are you? How is your marriage going?"

Fahni hung on for privacy. "Very kindly. I'm liking him more and more. He has a wonderful family. Everyone is very kind to Vihren."

"I told you!"

Vihren danced in circles around them, dying to be noticed. "You were at the big house! I got a new *bo*, and a new *dihnama*, and a new *dihnarbo*!"

"You were at the big house, too!" He held still long enough for Aila to beep his nose. "I hope you like your new *bo*."

"I do."

Masákh went to clap Haghíde on the shoulder, but Haghíde kept him at arm's length. "I accept your greeting but I still suffer your wrath, and I'll break your arm if you upset the healing."

"That's fair," Masákh said. "I'd doubt it's disturbed your celebrating."

"We've had great success despite the difficulties," Haghíde admitted, and Masákh laughed and punched his unwounded arm.

"Come, sit!" Hahkon waved them to the sitting area. "Come! Falahn will fill the table while we talk. Please, tell me all about life in the Union."

Falahn – Haghíde's mother – pressed a glass of *flehdan* into Aila's hand, packed with minty leaves and ice and a large whole *harfa* fruit, after offering one to Masákh.

Men first, always.

And unlike Masákh's house, where the silent pauses stretched to minutes, while his father fell asleep in the sitting room and his mother ran out of things to talk about, Haghíde's parents never stopped moving or talking. Aila and Masákh replied with a single sentence and Hahkon was off on a new topic. Hahkon's curiosity knew no bounds and no one outcasted him – unless his guests wanted to throw around their privilege – so no one could tell him to shut up, and they spoke until too late into the night.

In the morning, Haghíde took Masákh and Aila, with Fahni and Vihren, on a tour of the mountain. With Masákh's *nhásarwharl* privilege, they were able to get into places even Haghíde had never been. The mountain views took Aila's breath away – not to mention some of her nerves, pressed against metal railings over drops four times the height of Tokh's cliff. Hahkon returned from work early, Haghíde's twin sister Raghída arrived with her thirteen year old daughter Gharil, and within ten minutes of his return, Haghíde's baby brother Gharant arrived.

156

Wearing a blue uniform.

Aila stared. Gharant was much younger, a little shorter, not nearly as muscular as Haghíde, who enjoyed lifting weights. Haghíde and Raghída looked like their father; Gharant looked more like their mother. There was no mistaking the bleached skin, the two eyebrows, the goatee instead of a chinhank, or the tell-tale insignia pins on his chest. There wasn't a crease on his uniform, and when he smiled, his teeth had been filed flat.

Haghíde stood behind his brother and clapped both hands on his shoulders. "Surprise! I haven't told anyone. I've been guiding him for the last ten years, telling him what to study and how to be perfect so no one could overlook him. The *aghát* program isn't accepting as many applicants even as more apply, so it's more difficult to be accepted, but it worked. He was sworn in six months ago."

Masákh bowed; Gharant bowed back. "Congratulations, and welcome to the Brotherhood. Yours is the first family I know to have two sons pass *aghát* training. Where is your assignment?"

Gharant's smile never wavered, better at hiding things than his older brother. "I haven't been chosen yet, but I do have two parties bargaining for me. The Palace thinks I would be perfect for working with upper caste females, while General Rahken is lobbying for me as a foreign diplomat."

"Rahken has been jealous of Tokh ever since Rahken's team failed and Tokh succeeded on the Emissary Project," Haghíde said. "If Tokh has me, then Rahken will take my brother if he has to pay bribes to the entire committee."

"If you're at the palace, you could very well work with me," Aila said. "That's a long wait for placement. I thought *aghát* were in high demand right now."

Gharant's smile froze, and he searched for an answer.

"You can speak truth," Haghíde said softly. "They are good friends."

Gharant bowed again, uncomfortable. His smile became apologetic. "I am *hivex*. It will not prevent my placement, it has just taken a little longer."

Masákh shifted feet. Aila whispered, "What does that mean?"

"He beds only males."

157

Aila smiled. "Then you must come work inside the Union. You will earn your promotions twice as fast."

"Then I will request to join General Rahken's team, if he will send me to the Union."

"I look forward to working with you. I can give you the names of people you will want to know, what they do. I'm sure Haghíde has already told you most of them, and to watch out for my mother, who eats people like a *dahrkuran*. I think she will like you, though." *Dahrkuran* were huge carnivorous sea-dwellers who ate anything in their way – including swimming Kerasi.

Masákh bowed. "The brother of my friend is also my brother. My connections within the Union are different than Haghíde's, and many are higher up. Do not fail to ask me about them. You will go into your position already in control, without having to learn as we did."

"Thank you," Gharant said, returning the bow. "I am most grateful."

"No else 'connects' with the Union as you do, Masákh," Haghíde said, and he jerked his chin toward Aila. The two men burst out laughing. Aila deciphered the joke and blushed.

"I'm still your commander," Masákh said. "If you weren't already wounded, I would discipline you for that."

"*Gah.* No one can fear truth. Come. I'm anxious for Mother's good food."

They huddled at the table for hours, chatting and laughing and picking endlessly at the fifteen different dishes Falahn and Raghída and Gharil had prepared. Aila tried her trick of pulling back, of looking at the moment as if through a window, and she adored what she saw. Here was the future of Kerasím: here were the people already wanting the greater of their society, who lived it behind closed doors already, waiting for the Tokhs and Trannors to set them free. Freedom would come to Masákh's family, too, but they would resist, afraid of such a big change all at once. Aila's heart soared with hope.

Gharil, Haghíde's niece, stared at Aila in awe, and Aila spent an hour sitting with her, showing her and Raghída photos and videos on her comm of Union girls the same age. Raghída's husband, Bathar, a *nhásarwharl* geologist who lived one mountain over, joined them for dinner. Their son Sirahd was sixteen and in his last year of schooling.

He'd been accepted to a career academy and would be going on to study botany and conservation later that year. The house rocked with laughter; no one would have guessed that half the people had never met before.

Haghíde's parents' apartment had five rooms and three bedrooms, the open lower floor dominated by a glorious spiral staircase with a white metal rail, the sides carved out in a filigree of leaves and vines. Masákh and Aila were given Raghida's old room to sleep in, while Haghíde and Fahni slept in his old room and Vihren slept downstairs on the sofa. Eventually Raghída and her family left, and Gharant, and the house settled down for the night.

It took patience, as there was only one bathroom for the seven of them. Aila caught Haghíde alone in the hallway while he waited for the room to empty. She had her gloves on, so it wasn't a total sin to reach out and touch his arm.

"How's it going, Haghíde? You met a girl and married her twelve hours later. I know things can be a little crazy on Kerasím, but that's insane. You almost lost your life for her. Is it working out? I mean, she seems happy enough, but you went from lonely soldier to a family of three instantly. Do you at least like her?"

Haghíde looked away, and a little smile broke out. It was possible he was blushing, but no doubt it was the shadows of the hall. "I thank you for your concern, but I do like her, very much. I'm not sure why I married her, only that I enjoyed speaking to her so much I didn't want her to leave me. Every time she speaks, I find myself coming to love her. I love her voice, and her words, and the way she cares for her son. She's very intelligent and not afraid of conversation. Her laugh is a beautiful sound to me. I know I should have thought more about it, but something told me never to let her leave. I am very relieved to have found a wife. It's been a great worry of mine. There is a narrow time between being well-established and being so old as to be seen as undesirable by females. Captain is the common rank for marriage, but I was off-world for most of my captaincy. Being made Major, I was afraid I would be too old. Now my worries are gone." Haghíde bent close. "Do you think I did the right thing? Did she tell you if she is happy? She seemed pleased, unless she was just pretending."

Aila nodded. "You're a good man, Haghíde, and I think you did the right thing. I think she is truly pleased with you. She's a sweet person, and I think she'll make you a magnificent wife. And I do think her pleasure is real."

The light made it seem as if he were blushing again, but his smile said he was relieved by her words.

Twenty-two

They headed back to Tokh's as a group, friendships bonding deeper. Haghíde's back had healed to where it no longer bled but itched to drive him mad, and Fahni spent much time rubbing it with creams. Aila and Masákh had filed their paperwork to return to the Union, and their itinerary was expected to be approved within days. It would take a week for a ship to arrive to retrieve them, and they would leave Kerasím for an unknown length of time.

Haghíde had a tougher fight. He'd filed his paperwork, but now had to get travel permission for Fahni and Vihren not only to leave Kerasím, but to enter the Union. He had filed on his second day of marriage, but the request was still under consideration. He had tough choices if permissions didn't come through in time: stay on Kerasím with his new family and give up his exclusive position inside the Union, or go back and leave them set up on Kerasím, and hope to be able to retrieve them as soon as possible. He checked his comm every quarter-hour, hoping for news.

Tokh was in Keranihn when they arrived, but Mímihn greeted each of them warmly. "I don't care if Tokh liked the quiet; I missed everyone."

Aila grabbed Thoren from her. "I can't believe how much bigger he got in a week! He's huge! Look at him watching everyone!"

"He's almost four months now," Mímihn said. "I don't know where the time's gone."

Aila cuddled him close and kissed his black hair. "I'll miss him when I leave."

"I'll send you a picture every day," Mímihn promised. "You must hurry back for his nameday."

"I doubt I can. My government is getting nervous because I've been here so long. They want me back fast. You'll have to come and visit me."

Mímihn laughed at the impossibility. "If I could! This time I'd know I'm inside the Union, and now I could see it."

Ghírandar had been left in charge of the house and the females. Ráhnif returned from his tasks late in the afternoon. Tokh and Mátokhan returned at eveningtime. With four wives and a maid, dinner was prepared in a flash and everyone sat recounting their wedding travels. To Haghíde's surprise, Tokh had already known about Gharant.

"He has excellent credentials, but my complement is full and none of you has expressed interest in changing commanders," he said. "I also don't feel it prudent to have two officers from the same family in my ranks. It can create many difficult situations, both with command and with morale. It's better to keep family separate. That's why Kitras isn't among my men. My heart wants him by my side, learning what I know, but he'll learn more if he learns from another commander and then I temper it with what I know. Rahken's a good leader, but he's holding off retiring, hoping to make General Four. I know he's trying to get his foot in the Union, so maybe such a placement would be to everyone's advantage. I have backed his bid."

Haghíde bowed his head. "Thank you, General. I know Gharant will not disappoint."

Aila woke in the morning to the Imahlva sunshine. Masákh was bathing, so she threw open the balcony doors and drank in the fresh air, wrapped in one of his casual shirts. Beneath her, Mímihn and Zheníhda were setting breakfast out on the patio.

"Bright Morning, ladies!" she called over the rail. "I'll be down as soon as Masákh lets me in the bath."

"You are late, new-wife!" Mímihn giggled. "Nights don't last forever. Hurry, or the husbands will leave before you can say goodbye."

Aila washed in a flash and flew down the stairs to the smirks from Ghírandar and the other *aghát*. Mátokhan actually put his hand on her head and tipped it, examining her neck for bites.

"One, two, three, perhaps four? I thought a new husband would have more stamina than that." The smarmy superiority overflowed.

Aila jerked her head away and stared him down. "Perhaps you should examine Masákh instead, to see how many I left on him." The room erupted in catcalls and hoots. Masákh didn't say a word, but he smiled just enough to say he had secrets he wouldn't tell. Haghíde pulled the collar of his jacket up to hide his own neck, but Fahni was too new to harass.

The wives hung back from the table, serving husbands and officers, as there weren't enough patio chairs for everyone. Some of them had nibbled while making the food; the rest would eat after the men had left for Keranihn. Both Masákh and Haghíde were back in uniform, their honeymoons officially ended.

Haghíde finished eating, pushed his chair back from the patio table, and pulled Fahni onto his lap, whispering and nuzzling her ear. She buried her face in his neck and stayed there. It would be the first time they had parted in eight days. Fruit pits began to fly across the table at them with accompanying hoots from the *aghát*.

"Jealousy does not become you," Haghíde said, and threw a pinch of his bread round back.

"Stop!" Zheníhda waved her hand so it whapped against Rahnif's. "You are teaching the child bad manners." Fahni reprimanded Vihren, who was laughing and throwing chunks of food across the table. No one dared criticize Tokh's wife, not even Mátokhan.

Masákh grabbed Aila and pulled her onto his lap. She wrapped her arms around his neck and kissed him. She was his, and they knew she was his, and they could go jump the cliff for all she cared. It wasn't dignified for an *aghát* to give public displays, but Masákh did nothing to discourage her.

Tokh watched them with a cold expression. "I'm feeling distinctly left out in my own home, despite having twice as many wives as anyone." As Zheníhda reached for his glass to refill it, Tokh yanked her onto his lap and held her to him, making humming noises of pleasure. Zheníhda screeched, pushing and slapping at him as he tried to gain access to her neck. Zheníhda kept her face averted in disgust, but despite her struggles Aila caught a glimpse of a suppressed smile, then another. Mímihn stood at the end of the table shrieking like a choking bird on her laughter.

Tokh released Zheníhda with a swat to her backside and stood up. Zheníhda straightened her clothes and touched her hair back into place while glaring. "Fool! Fifty-eight years old, father of a newborn, and you act like you're twenty."

"I know how old I am, Nihda. Perhaps you should stop acting your age."

"Gah!" Zheníhda flapped her hands and headed back to the kitchen. The remaining officers stood up and went inside to get ready to leave. Masákh let Aila up and they followed while Shanohr scurried out to clear the table.

Mímihn's pocket comm beeped while they were still laughing. She pulled it from her skirt pocket and answered it without looking. *"Sukh?"*

Hello, Mímihn. Where'd you get the baby? I rammed your lihx until it bled and you didn't conceive. Or does his blind consort nanny for him, too?

Mímihn's golden face faded until she was almost as pale as Aila. Her eyes took on a look of profound horror, and she stopped breathing. "I... I don't think you have the right link," she said faintly.

Oh, I know I do. I loved your voice all nervous and scared like it is now. Next you'll start pleading with me, and my ring will get hard just hearing it. I saw you on the broadcast with him. I don't forget the name or face of someone who stole my consort. Now that I've found you, you tell him I'm coming back for my property. And I'm not going to play some cheating game to do it.

Mímihn jammed her finger on the *end* button and began to scream. She threw the comm as if were burning her hands; the housing fell off it as it bounced on the floor tiles. Her screams were tortured and terror-filled, and they didn't stop. Her hands shook so hard she had trouble bringing them up to cover her mouth. All conversation stopped as the room stared at her.

"Mímihn? What's wrong?" Aila laid a hand on her elbow.

Zheníhda's scowl softened as the tone of the scream worked its way under her skin. "Who was that? Did someone die?"

"I did!" Mímihn's screams turned to explosive tears. "I'm dead!" She tried to run across the kitchen but didn't make it, vomiting onto the floor before the work sink. She stayed bent over, shaking and screaming and gasping.

Tokh strode across the room and yanked her upright. "Who was on the comm? Tell me now!" Shanohr put dishes on the workspace and dove between their feet to wipe the floor.

Mímihn's trembling wouldn't stop. She reached down and fumbled with the belt strap where his sword hung, but he wasn't wearing it in the house. "Get your sword, Tokh! Get your sword and take my head! If you care for me at all you'll show me mercy! Get your sword!"

Tokh shook her. Mímihn resumed a high-pitched morbid keening and melted in his hands. "MÍMIHN! WHO WAS ON THE COMM?"

"Him!" she gasped. "He-who-was-my-owner! He said terrible things to me. He says he's coming to take me back and he doesn't intend to pay you. Please, Tokh! Take my head. Just take my head! I won't go back to him! Not ever! I'll throw myself in front of a vehicle! I'll take poison! I'll throw myself over the wall! I won't go back. I won't!"

Tokh's arms tightened around her until it seemed as if she'd be torn in two. He glanced over at Haghíde, trying to snap the plastic housing back onto the frame of the comm unit. "Don't touch that! Don't lose the settings. Give it to me." He rubbed his face over Mímihn's hair. "*Shu, shu, falahndi.* I won't allow that to happen, not for the Emperor's treasury. No one will be taking your head or any other part of you. I have an entire division of men at my disposal. I can ring this house with guards six men deep. I can take you elsewhere. I'll chain you to me if I must. I don't tolerate threats against me or my family. *Shu.*"

He held his hand out; Haghíde placed the comm in it. Tokh thumbed several screens, but the calling ID had been blocked at the source. He shook his head and sighed. "We're going back years. He was the son of General..." Tokh's mind blanked. It was more than six years previous, just before he shipped out on his Big Mission, and the mission erased trivia like that from his head.

"Engmar," Mímihn gasped against his chest. Some horrors ran too deep to forget. "General Engmar. But he was always kind to me, Tokh. It's not him I fear. Don't make me say the name of his son. Don't make me. Please, Tokh! Don't make me! Don't make me."

"*Shu, shu, falahndi. Shu.* You're a free female, married with a child. He has no legal claim to you." He petted her hair, kissed her several times, and passed her off to Aila. "I know who he is. A cowardly *trivarid* not fit to own a pair of shriveled *khatas*. Let me investigate. I'll find him and I'll gift you with his *hihvat*, which you may set on fire or any other way you wish to dispose of it. Everyone is

165

aware of your past, and your present. You are my wife and you're safe here." He took the comm unit and went to his office.

Zheníhda took Mímihn from Aila, to her surprise. She held her close and petted her hair. Mímihn sank against her like a sobbing child. Aila didn't know what was going on yet, but no doubt Masákh would fill her in.

"You can't be serious. How? How did he find you?" Zheníhda asked.

"He saw me with Tokh on the Emperor's broadcast of the wedding."

"I've seen Tokh angry when others have wronged me. Don't fear. When he's done, there won't be enough of the Evil One left to feed to a *jappa*. And he meant it about the *hihvat*. I had to dispose of a *khata* once." A nervous laugh burst from Mímihn, high and thin and slightly less hysterical, and her tears began to slow.

The ruined morning became a long unsettled day. Mímihn could not, would not leave Tokh, even when he yelled, even when he threatened to discipline her. Her breath came in gasps, and she couldn't stop crying. He gave in on the order she was not allowed to cry. Mímihn packed up Thoren and accompanied him to his office in Keranihn for the day, and Tokh left Tótoghar in charge of the house.

When he reached his office, he backed his secretary against the wall. "You sit before a security door all day. No one is to pass that door today without their ID. If they forgot to bring it, they do not enter. If someone has an interview, they will submit to print and DNA before entering that door, and someone must accompany them at all times. If two people are crossing that door, then each one must scan their ID and enter separately. I don't care if it's General Trannor. The only exception I will allow is Nadigh himself. I'm declaring highest security alert today. One person, just one, passes that door without me knowing who it is, I will have your head as you sit in your chair, before you can apologize a word. Is that understood?"

The secretary turned yellow as a *patigha*-tree blossom. He nodded rapidly. "Absolutely, Lord General."

Aila had never been in Imahlva without Mímihn. The heart had gone out of the house, leaving it huge and dark and empty. The breakfast was cleared away, and Shanohr refused to have a guest help with the upstairs work. Vihren was temporarily enrolled in a school for mid-castes on the other side of the mountain; Thrit brought him and Kesseh and Joralan to their schools. Zheníhda made herself a cup of *raffin*, put her feet up in the sitting room, and settled in to watch *Inside Connections*. Aila hadn't realized Zheníhda was caught up in it as well. She thought about joining her – it had to be more pleasant than watching with Masákh's mother – but Aila's heart was tight with the morning drama, and didn't need more anxiety over a made-up crisis when real ones were happening. Aila had nothing to do, so she wandered outside and leaned over the cliff wall, watching the ocean far below. She wore a gauzy layered white skirt and a brilliant blue tunic; gusts of breeze wafted up the mountainside, flapping her clothes and hair out behind her.

Fahni came up beside her. She copied Aila's stance, resting on the top of the wall. "Do you know what happened, this morning? Is it something to worry about?"

"It shouldn't be our worry," Aila said. "If I understand, it's Mímihn's business, and I don't know how much is her secret. I met Mímihn six years ago; I have known her well for two years. She is my most great friend. I can say this: Mímihn married too young to a man who was very bad to her. Then he died. She has been married to Tokh for three years, maybe? He loves her very much, and she is now very, very happy. If I understand, the call was from someone in her past who wants to take her from Tokh. She is most frightened. She has Thoren to worry about, too. Imagine if someone threatened to take you away, or to kill Vihren. Imagine your worst bad time, and imagine you had to live that over and over, every day, knowing your son was dead." Aila didn't know Fahni well enough to know her secrets, but everyone had a nightmare somewhere, even if it was only a bad dream.

Fahni took a shaky breath. "I would die inside."

"That's what scares Mímihn."

Tokh and Mímihn and his crew arrived before the sun set. Mímihn was jumpy but calmer. Her smile was back, and she let the new wives play with Thoren and give her a break. Tokh had held onto her comm

167

unit all day, but there'd been no other calls. No one said a word about it at dinner, but the ghost of a *dhastal* hung heavy in the room, and not just the giant stuffed head over the door. Tokh ordered the children to play upstairs or outside, but leave the adults alone.

In the morning Mímihn slept as late as Thoren would allow, fed him, washed him, dressed him, and made it downstairs to catch the end of breakfast. Her nerves were a little steadier, and her sweet smile danced upon her face as she bid everyone a pleasant morning. Aila swooped in on Thoren and picked him up, delighted to find him awake and playful. She held him so Mímihn could eat in peace.

Aila shoved the baby at Masákh. "Look at him! Isn't he adorable? Look at that face! He's looking right at you."

Masákh's face was as blank as a corpse's as he studied the infant. He didn't reach out to touch him, not even pinch a round gold cheek. "It is good to know that his eyes work well."

Aila pulled the baby back to her shoulder. "Ugh! You are so dull when it comes to babies! How can you claim to want them if you can't begin to interact with them? Maybe you're not as educated as you claim."

"Creating offspring doesn't mean I must reduce my intellect to that of an infant."

"Their intellect is no less than yours," Aila said. "It's their communication skills that are lacking. I can see we're going to have to teach you a thing or two about infants before we have one."

The argument was cut short by the chiming of the perimeter sensor. Mímihn looked up in alarm; Tokh pulled out his com unit and observed the camera feed. A courier approached the front door and touched the call sensor. A chime sounded inside the house.

Tokh waved Shanohr away and answered the door himself.

"I have a delivery for Mímihn daras-Giláhn," the *solahrin* said. He held out a large brown envelope.

Tokh held his hand out. "That's my wife. I'll accept it."

"I'm ordered to deliver it directly to her."

Tokh's face slid downward in impatience. "Ordered by who? Who sent it?"

"I don't know, Lord. That was the order given to me by my supervisor."

"Very well. Mímihn, take this." Mímihn reached for the envelope., Before her fingers could close on it, Tokh seized it from her. He spun away and tore it open, holding it so no one else could see the contents. When he spun back, his sword was drawn and the *solahrin* was pinned to the doorframe with the blade at his throat. The man's face said in another minute he might need a clean uniform. Fahni gave a scream from the back of the room. She grabbed Vihren and buried him in her skirt.

"Who sent you!" Tokh thundered. "My shoulder reads General Four, and the *dahneg* on my chest is by order of the Emperor! Speak truth or I will have you taken to Keranihn and your mind flayed open until you shit yourself and call it lunch!"

"I don't know!" the *solahrin* screeched. His copper skin had faded to a rancid mud-color, and sweat broke out across his nose and forehead as they watched. "My supervisor, *rhibani* Edmarikh nan Prisporkhan! Owner of Burgas Speed Delivery in Burgas City Center! I have worked for him for two years and five months! I do what he tells me and I earn my pay! That's all I know! I swear it! I have a wife and three children; I need my pay! I don't look inside things! He doesn't tell me where things come from, just where they go!"

Mímihn used the distraction to snatch the papers from Tokh's hand. She danced back toward the kitchen and looked at the pages. Her eyes widened impossibly large. She choked on the scream that caught in her throat, and it came out as a strangled moan before she blacked out and fell to the floor.

"Mímihn!" Zheníhda gasped. She ran to her side.

Aila whirled, baby still on her arm. She seized the dropped pages. They were large photographs. Aila glimpsed a close-up of a teenaged Mímihn's badly bruised face, covered in fresh yellow male fluid. The second was of Mímihn, tears on her face, hands bound, while two men gratified themselves with her at the same time.

Aila's heart stopped beating for several seconds, and the air that made it into her lungs felt like melted ice. Her stomach squeezed tight around her breakfast, and she wanted to be sick and to cry and to beat something up all at the same time. Gentle, kind-hearted Mímihn! Masákh stepped toward her, but Aila clutched the photos to her chest and moved next to Zheníhda. "Here, Zheníhda. No one but Tokh sees them. Understand? No one."

Zheníhda nodded and slipped them behind the waistband of her skirt. She continued to stroke Mímihn's cheek.

Tokh glanced at the activity, then turned back to the hapless delivery man. With two deft flicks of his sword he left minor gashes in the man's cheeks, then seized his chin hank and sliced it off, marking him. "Go! Go back to your supervisor and you give him this message: General Tokh wants the name of the person who sent this package, and if I don't have it by sunset, I will request a team from the Imperial guard and I'll hunt down your owner of Burgas Delivery and he will answer to them. Is that clear?!"

The man's jaw moved several times before any words came out. "Yes! Yes! General Tokh is sending the Imperial Guard to find the sender! But it wasn't Javen the delivery man! It wasn't!"

"Remember it! Now go!" Tokh lowered the sword, and the man ran across the courtyard as if Tokh were at his heels.

Tokh shut the door.

Mímihn gave a guttural groan that seemed to come up from the stone floor, a moan of pain that came not from her body but from her being, an agony of waking up to find oneself still alive when they had sought the mercy of death. The noise was high-pitched and spooky, a storm-wind fighting to get through the closed shutters of her throat. Mímihn held the note a hideously long time, took a whooping, wheezy breath and keened it out again, rocking on the ground. Aila handed Thoren to Fahni and joined Zheníhda in trying to comfort Mímihn.

Tokh growled at them. "Enough! Give her a double-glass of the rum."

Aila glared right back. "She has an infant! You can't give her spirits; it will poison the baby!"

"Then feed him something else! Get a wet-nurse! Get some orphan-milk! I can't work with that noise!"

Tokh's face wasn't angry, wasn't annoyed. Aila had seen those emotions on him. If she dared – she didn't, because that emotion just didn't exist in the great Lord Tokh – she would have said he was frightened. He put his hand out before Zheníhda, and she handed him the pages and envelope.

"Where's Thrit? Get the children out of here. Now. I don't care if they have to wait for the schools to open." He turned the envelope over in his hands. "No markings. This game stops now. Now I don't want *khatas*. Now I'll settle for no less than a head. *Aghát*, follow."

Tokh sat at his desk and activated the ComNet. He tapped the controls for General Trannor, and made it priority. The *aghát* stood at attention behind him, visible on camera, so Trannor knew they were not alone. Trannor answered after two minutes, a short time for a response from him.

"Tokh? What's so great you must disrupt my breakfast?"

"My apologies, General Trannor. You know I wouldn't bother you unless I had no option. I am under attack, and I request a greater assistance at finding the source. I need a head, and I need permission and greater access to find it immediately."

Trannor sat up with a frown. "Attack? How? From whom?"

Tokh bowed his head briefly. "You are aware of my younger wife's history, General. Yesterday my wife received a call from her former owner, stating that he was coming to reclaim her without my permission, even though I have the papers he signed deeding her over to me, and the signed papers freeing her from bondage are filed there in Keranihn. My wife is mortally upset and fears for her safety as well as that of our son. She recognized his voice, but the call has so far proved untraceable. Now, just twenty *fasim* ago, my wife received a courier delivery of an unmarked envelope. It contained several photos of her being violently assaulted. My wife's now not only humiliated but disabled by terror, neither of which she deserves. Another incident and I expect her to die from fright. I've had no response from General Engmar, and his son no longer lives at the last address on record. I want the son, and I want his head, for my wife's peace of mind, if not my own safety or that of my infant son. I don't need to remind you I'm entertaining guests." Trannor knew exactly what Tokh meant. The Union's greatest demand was the end of rampant executions; an assassination in the presence of a Union dignitary would not go unnoticed.

Trannor laced his fingers behind his head and leaned back, silent. It was a long pause before he spoke. "I don't involve myself in personal affairs, Tokh. This isn't a matter of governmental importance, and I trust you are capable of seeing to your own safety. However. I realize threats to your family and property are a priority, and I need you

171

focused and available to me. Send me the information you have. I'll reply in twelve hours."

Tokh bowed his head before the camera. "I am in your debt, General."

Aila and Zhenihda all but carried Mímihn to a sofa. Zhenihda made her a cup of hot *raffin*, and poured a sizable shot of *durwah* in it. She held it out but Mímihn refused to drink, lying flat, staring into space sobbing, while Aila stroked her arm.

"Do you want your son?" Fahni said, and held Thoren out. "He loves you more than anyone."

Mímihn gave a sob, pushed herself up, and took the infant. His head turned and began to root against her blouse. She looked down at him lifelessly, opened her blouse and attached him to a perfect golden breast. "He loves me now. He will hate me later, when he learns what his mother is."

Aila pounced on the self-pity. "His mother is the wife of a Level-Four General, whose great honor bought him *dahneg* privilege."

If it was possible, Mímihn looked even more morose. She pulled Thoren from her breast and handed him back to Fahni as he cried at the loss of his meal. "There is orphan-milk and a bottle in the cabinet. I can't. I can't even feed my son. I can't have even a baby touch me like that. I'm a shame to my husband." The sobs welled up for a moment and she started to shake again. Aila hugged her.

"It had faded," Mímihn mumbled in Aila's arms. "Most of the time I forgot. It was hard at the start, with Tokh. I couldn't see him. I didn't know him. I didn't know what would happen. I just accepted each day, tried to please him so he wouldn't hurt me. He never did. He was so kind I didn't trust him. But day after day, he was still kind. And no others came. No one hurt me. And still I was scared. Thrit was my eyes; I asked him many questions. I knew men came and went, but they didn't come for me. Just three times. Three times he shared me, and he apologized for each one. I relaxed. My heart started to feel. After we came here, after I knew I was still safe, and that even with two wives he still was kind to me, my body started to feel again. And I let myself be happy. When he gave me my eyes back, I knew the Fortunes had forgiven me. When Tokh married me, I thought I could put all the bad behind me forever. I was the wife of a very powerful General. I was in a dream. When I gave birth to Thoren, I thought no one would ever know the bad again. I could forget forever, because the bad person no longer existed. There was nothing to prove she ever did. And now someone has made her come alive again, and I have died in the effort."

Aila hugged her harder. "No you haven't. You're just scared."

Zheníhda stroked Mimihn's hair. "Tokh will make it right. He always does, and you will be pleased with the result. Don't be surprised if he asks you if you want to be the one to take his head. Do you have that in you?"

The depth of hatred that darkened Mímihn's face pulled the very light from the room. Sweet Mímihn, who never stopped smiling. "Oh yes. I could take his head blind, but I will stare into his eyes while I do it. And I'd do it slowly, taunting him as I took his life *fasim* by *fasim*, watching the fear and hatred in his eyes. And when I was halfway in, and he was still alive and voiceless and choking, I'd cut off his *hihvat* and force it up his *aaka*-hole, then cut off his *khatas* and force them down his throat until he had no air, and then I would go back to sawing at his throat until the blood went everywhere, and then I would start on his neck-bones. Only then."

Zheníhda stared. "And Tokh lets you near his children."

Aila rolled a sharp eye toward Zheníhda. "*Tokh* should never be allowed near children."

Fahni stood back, holding Thoren over her shoulder and patting his bottom. She didn't make a sound, lost and unsure.

Mímihn noticed. "Kah! Stop it! Stop staring at me!" She launched herself from the sofa and got in Fahni's face. Poor Fahni took a step back. "What difference does it make? You're the only one here who doesn't know. No doubt Haghíde will tell you at some point. You might as well be able to make faces and spit at me when I look away, too."

"That's not fair, Mímihn," Aila said. "Not one person does that to you."

Mímihn shot a cruel eye to Zheníhda. Her voice was taunting and venomous, but it was unclear if she meant to hurt Fahni or was stabbing at herself. "I was a consort. A seventeen year old consort after a failed marriage, passed around like a sweet on a tray. Lying there naked before his wives and friends on his dinner table, pretending to enjoy it with a smile on my face, no matter what they did or how they hurt me.

And when I kept smiling, he blinded me. And kept hurting me. And I kept smiling. Until Tokh took me away. And when his secondwife died, he freed me and made me secondwife, and he made the doctors give me my eyes back so no one would suspect he had married a consort as filthy and pissed on as a public toilet. And he allowed me to pop a son he didn't need out of my rancid dirty *lihx*, to complete the illusion that his wife is anything but a *ghinadín* for the taking. Now stop staring at me unless you plan to *push* me!"

Fahni stood stone-still, afraid to blink. Mímihn's anger disappeared with her words and her anguish took over again. Her scream kept to a wail as she fell to her knees. Aila dropped next to her and squeezed her, rocking as Mímihn clawed and clung to her as if she were drowning in more than just tears.

"I'm sorry! I'm sorry! I didn't mean that!"

"*Shu, shu, shu, Mimi!*" Aila crooned, holding her tight. "No one here thinks of you that way. No one! There's a roomful of officers in there that would protect you with their lives. Mátokhan is so foul I want to bathe just from his breath on me, but he gives you nothing but respect. That's the hurt speaking, not truth. No one has ever looked at you like that."

"Nihda," Mímihn gasped from Aila's chest.

Zheníhda looked pained. "We made our peace. I apologized. I haven't mentioned it; I've defended you for the last two years."

Mímihn cried harder, but she nodded. "Truth!" She seized Zheníhda's hand and squeezed it almost to breaking. "I'd put it behind me. I tried to be the wife I pretended I was. But he's bringing back all the pain. All of it! And I can't bear it again. I can't. I don't want anyone to know. I don't want them to think of me like that. I just want to be Tokh's wife. I can't. I can't bear it. Let me die. Please! I can't bear it again."

Zheníhda knelt and rubbed her arm, murmuring. "He wants you afraid. He wants you to fear. You can't let him win. Draw him out, and Tokh will eliminate him once and for all."

Fahni still held Thoren, weeping silently. She put her arm around Mímihn and her face on her back. "I don't care what you used to be, Mímihn. I do know that beauty comes from the heart, and there's no way a bad heart could birth a baby as beautiful as yours. He's more beautiful than my own Vihren was, and that's from the mouth of his own mother. Don't lie to yourself to cover your pain. There is nothing but beauty inside you, and that's all anyone sees. Most females share your fear, so don't ever think you're alone."

The group grew quiet, lost in their own truths. No one knew Fahni well, but Zheníhda had her own private nightmares, and Aila's close call last year left her screaming in terror for three days. Their minds stopped at their own fear; to empathize too much would be to drown alongside Mímihn.

Thoren gave a hungry fuss; Mímihn wiped her eyes and took him. She had birthed him. He was hers. He was a beautiful baby, and that wasn't just his family's opinion.

Tokh canceled the day's plans and locked himself in his office. He could do as much research from home as he could from work, with Khaním feeding him anything else from Keranihn. He spent most of the time on the comm, reassigning officers and speaking to a dozen different possible leads. The *aghát* were sent out to track down various people and interview them, using whatever means necessary – not excluding a private escort to the basement level of Tokh's Intelligence building, to the room where memories and thoughts were extracted by force; Khaním was on standby to take custody of prisoners. Three *aghát* terrorized the office of Edmarikh nan Prisporkhan, owner of Burgas Speed Delivery, but the owner had already left town, and the only records Mátokhan found was that the transaction had been in cash. A female in a veil had made the order, and the male accompanying her had stayed outside the door. No cameras were in use in the delivery office, so there was nothing but the terrified squeals of the clerk to go on; the trail died.

Tokh didn't appear for lunch; Zheníhda brought him food wordlessly while he conferenced. It wasn't until dinner had been held an hour that he dragged himself out of his office with a hard sigh. "Nothing. No one has seen a thing. General Engmar hasn't been seen by neighbors for four months; they thought he had moved, but the apartment is still in his name. I asked the local officers to run a safety check, make sure he hadn't died; they found no one inside, and no fresh food. No one has been there in a while. No one knows where the son is; his last known address is from three years ago. I would need to access bank accounts or tax records to dig further; I don't have that authority."

"Does that mean you can't catch who's trying to hurt *ama*?" Joralan asked.

"*Gah!*" Tokh doused his meat with a sweet-vinegar sauce. "I've been in this business thirty-five years. It's only two days into an investigation. I'm nowhere near the end. They can't get off-world; they can't even take an aircraft: I got a no-fly put in place for both men. If they're seen, they'll be held for questioning."

"What about private craft?"

Tokh conceded. "That we can't control. Money can buy privacy, but not entirely. Unless they're landing in an empty field, air pads can still stop them. I'll keep tightening the circle, and eventually they'll have to come up for air. Then they're mine. Everyone, rest easy."

Easy was a relative term. Masákh sat on the lounge in the suite, busily working a lap pad late into the night. Aila sat on the bed, her com in her hand. "What do I do? My travel orders are up again. I need to go back, but how do I leave Mímihn in peril? I know Tokh will win in the end, but I feel like every hand is needed right now, even mine."

Masákh never looked up from his work. "It probably is. Ask for another extension. Tell them I am engaged in a task and cannot leave for two weeks, and it is unsafe for you to leave without me."

Aila gave a slow nod. "Okay. That might work. I'll put it through. Why are they doing this? Why would someone try to hurt Mímihn? She's never hurt a fly."

Masákh lifted his head for a moment. "I don't know the details of the situation, but it is known that her previous owner was abusive and ill-tempered, and that's what prompted Tokh to win her freedom. He succeeded, but the owner didn't take the loss well. Tokh believes he's after revenge, and that the attacks are directed at Tokh, using Mímihn as the weapon. The owner is trying to shame Tokh and ruin his position, but Tokh's reputation is most excellent, and those at Derahl Nor know the situation of his wife; I believe, at best, the attempt is futile. Most persons who want revenge that badly make foolish errors. It will be only a few more days.

Aila crept off the bed and hugged him from behind. "Thank you for helping her, Masákh."

Twenty-three

No alarms disrupted breakfast, and the morning had a tense but normal feel. Mímihn finished the last of her *raffin* and stood up when her com chimed where it sat in the center of the table.

Mímihn stared at Tokh in terror as the room froze. He raised a palm to calm her, and gave a nod. Mímihn activated it as if it might explode.

"Sukh?"

Hello, Mímihn. That's a pretty blue dress you're wearing.

Mímihn went pale, and her eyes went so wide they seemed entirely white. She placed the com on the table and put it on speaker.

Her voice shook so hard she could barely form words. "You are mistaken. I'm wearing a white blouse and skirt today."

No you're not, you blind lihx. *You're wearing a blue sleeveless dress with a red pattern on it. Disappointing, really. I bought you prettier things. Where's the baby? You really should keep a close eye on him – haha! I'm sure Tokh might get a little upset if you lose his son. Gah! A blind trixahg keeping an eye on a baby! He really is stupid, isn't he. It won't matter soon. It will give your little diplomat friend something to talk about. How much longer is she staying?*

Mímihn took a brave breath. "Why don't you come here in person and ask her? Or are you afraid of me?"

Tokh gave three sharp movements of his head; three of the *aghát* sprang into action. Masákh ran upstairs; Mátokhan ran out the side door to the patio; Tótoghar moved to peer out the draperies by the front windows. As they moved, Tokh snatched the com. Haghíde grabbed Mímihn and the baby and ushered everyone into the back hallway, away from all windows.

"What do you want!" Tokh bellowed. "Show your face, you cowardly *trixohran*! I know who you are, and when you are seized, you will regret the day you ever saw my face."

Tsk tsk. Tokh, privilege isn't the same as full caste. You can't speak to me that way. I'm not military; you can't touch me under current law.

"Accidents happen."

The speaker chuckled. *You might want to think carefully about that, Tokh. You have five smallchildren. If you don't care about your baby, perhaps you care about them. The little female's going to be quite the prize in a few years. Your daughter's not too bad, either. First one, then the other.*

The words crept under Tokh's skin. Spit flew several feet as he yelled into the com. "You will die a most painful death if you continue to harass me. That's a fact. I will personally see to it you are turned over to an authority who does not care about rules!"

The voice suggested it was losing patience. *Gah, Tokh. You can't win this one. Just give her up and we'll call it settled.* The com clicked off. A second later, weaponfire made them jump. Something moved outside the window.

Mátokhan ran across the courtyard; Tótoghar burst out the front door, followed by Tokh, then Masákh pounding down the stairs. Aila ran after, but Haghíde kept the females and children inside the house.

Mátokhan gazed down over the cliff wall. He handed Tokh his com, with a photo pulled up. "A spy drone, General. That's how they could see in the house. I shot it, but it may have landed in the water. The range isn't far on those; it had to be from a boat somewhere in the inlet."

Tokh eyed the water in futility. "There's a hundred boats in the channel at any given *nali*, at any given time, plus the shore. I'll see if there was satellite coverage we can use. In the meantime, I want a four-person armed escort to bring Dalo and the children here for safety. No games. I'll inform Kitras. I'll have personal guards posted for the boys at school; the girls are not to leave the house. Pull six of my best investigators from Keranihn; I want them working on this. My patience is gone. I will have answers, today." He strode back to his office without a word.

Tokh made a beeline to Keranihn and got an appointment to speak with Trannor, but outside the buildings. He chose a little window café around the corner from Trannor's office. The eatery was exactly that: a window with a counter that folded up over the glass when closed, with three tables set up around the corner on the side of the building, but the food was fast and excellent. He ordered four *farallesh* and two bottles of *muhr*. Just two acquaintances, sharing a lunch break.

Trannor didn't acknowledge the hospitality. He sat at the commoner's table without making a scene, but didn't so much as take off his gloves. He took the side of the table with his back to the building, leaving Tokh vulnerable with his back to the street. "Since when do you not trust my office, Tokh? Is there something you know that I don't?"

"I trust nothing at the moment. Not when I'm under threat. Here, we're unofficial. If you're being monitored without your knowledge, we're free of it. If you're monitoring my conversations without my knowledge, I hope I'm free of it. If there's something you might tell me off the record, with no proof but my own imagination, this is safe ground for us to discuss it."

Trannor grasped his bottle of *muhr* and held it out; Tokh opened it for him, and Trannor drank a good swallow. "You're not normally so troublesome, Tokh. I told you I will not be involved in personal issues."

Tokh picked up a *farallesh* – ground *bagresh* meat and spices and sautéed vegetables stuffed inside a raw bright yellow *farad*, a thick-walled, fist-sized peppery fruit – and bit into it. There was a fine line to be tread: Trannor was former *fáhganid.* He was a highest-level interrogator, and part of the Emperor's council. He could be nagged only so far.

"I've been doing quite a bit of research these last several days. My sources are pointing me in a disturbing direction. Either you know information relative to my issue that you're not telling me, or I have information you're in need of knowing. Of course, I don't want to burden you with personal issues, so I'm not sure I should say anything, especially if you already know."

Trannor's stare would have made a lesser man shrivel in fear. Tendons stood out on his neck as he held back his rage. His mouth pursed ever so slightly, the bottom lip pushing upward just enough to make his chinhank twitch outward. "Speak it now, Tokh, or I will demote you and remove these privileges you're abusing."

Tokh returned the stare with perhaps too much accusation, but once fired it couldn't be corrected, so he held it. "Threats and surveillance as I've experienced take large streams of cash, even for a *dahneg*. Every legal search has ended at a blank wall. The numbers for his business don't add up, and some of the associated names have dark shadows. My sources keep pointing me to rebellion money. Is this correct?"

Trannor held his face, but Tokh knew the subtleties of body language and Trannor's breath told him he'd hit on a sore spot. Trannor knew it, and nursed his *muhr* as if they had all day. It was a common middle brand, good to the low and middle castes, but to Tokh it reminded him of the sour smell of *bagresh* piss. He'd said what he wanted to say, so he stayed silent, waiting.

Tokh finished his first *farallesh* and started on a second. Not the best, but rather tasty for street food. Trannor bent his head at last.

"Tokh, you are a trumped-up General hired to oversee a diplomatic mission. You succeeded beyond expectations. You were allowed to continue to oversee diplomatic missions because of your experience and relationship with the prime Union diplomat. Because of your rank and security clearance, you were given a choice Interrogator Three position. Because of your unfailing loyalty, you were granted a seat in the Senate. You excel at what you do, and you've been given an ample list of rewards far above caste because of it. With that said, you are treading outside of your area of expertise. If you pull the wrong chinhank, you will find yourself in a far more perilous predicament than you are now, both physically and employment-wise. Am I clear?"

Tokh smiled with false amusement. "I knew that as fact when I woke up. My wives stroke my *khatas* just as sweetly, but only you can answer my question."

Trannor's nostrils flared, and his great eyebrow squeezed itself downward. He breathed heavily for a full minute before folding his hands before his mouth and keeping them there. "Tokh, what you ask is outside my area of expertise."

Tokh continued to eat his lunch. "You know the answer, but don't trust me with it."

Trannor's eyes moved downward to stare at his knuckles. "Tokh, there are truly things outside my sphere of influence. I deal in galactic affairs, not domestic ones. If I question too far outside my reach, I will

180

attract attention, which will lead to investigation. Yes, even I. There are forces at work you don't understand. I understand, but I don't know details enough to judge or know what's being done. I only know an issue exists. This is truth, even under your demon Kassán's thumb."

"The answer to my question?"

The eyebrow squished down again until, from where Tokh sat shorter than his Superior, it appeared to mash against the knuckles. "Without facts, my instinct is yes."

The news was no surprise. Tokh gave a thunderous belch after swigging his *muhr*. "Can you trace the account to give me the location?"

"No. Entirely outside my access." Trannor closed his eyes momentarily, then lifted his mouth from his hands. "Tokh, don't think I'm unsympathetic. I've met your wife; I find her to be a delightful hostess and excellent at conversation. She's no cloud-fluff. I wish her no ill will at all, but I can't get deeper into this, and I mean it when I say to tread carefully. Some things are best left undisturbed."

Tokh's patience faded. "General Trannor, we've known each other for more than fifteen years. You either trust me or you don't. I understand your position and your reach, and you understand I will not sacrifice my wife or my son. You may or may not be aware the emissary has alerted her Embassy to be on standby for her safety if needed, which means they're aware there's an issue. If you can give me even the most vague of backgrounds to the problem, perhaps we can engage in a little mutual handshake, and both be better for the deal.

Trannor's mouth slipped behind his hands again, and he thought long and hard. "The crisis of last year has not disappeared. Nadigh angered a great many powerful cabinet members when he dismissed them; some of them family, some of them favorites of his father for generations. Many would prefer to see Moragh on the throne, but Moragh will have none of it. I know this for fact, because I did his interrogation. Much money flows to cause unrest, to draw Nadigh out where he could be vulnerable politically and physically. He's aware of this, and does have forces tracing insurrections. However, he can't move until he has undeniable proof on a great many at once. If he fails, instead of making them run in terror, he'll appear a tyrant and stir them into greater power. This I also know as fact. To pry into the situation without permission could be a warning to those he hunts. I strongly urge you to pull back."

Tokh stroked his chinhank. "All I want is a head, without politics. If I can get the head, I don't need to upset anyone."

"What I should do is order you off-world until it settles down. I don't favor those who crush my *khatas*."

Tokh blinked. The threat was real and he had no ability to decline, but he didn't rise as high as he had by bending. He kept his voice low and respectful. "I understand you are privy to things I'm not, General, and you must do what you feel is right. However, I can't back down on my request. I require a head, and I will utilize any means I can to achieve it."

Impasse.

Trannor nodded, and his hands dropped. His mind was set, and he was done. He stood up; Tokh jumped to his feet. Trannor turned a shoulder to him. "I don't have direct access to the information you seek. However, if it's possible to send you a correct channel to follow to achieve the same result, I will do my best to find it."

Tokh bowed. "I would be eternally grateful, General."

Trannor gave a tip of his head, then departed without another word. Tokh glanced at the table; two of the *farallesh* remained. He knocked twice on the table and left.

From behind the building two scavenging *ghinadín* youths darted forth, grabbed the *farallesh* in their serving box and the bottles of dregs and disappeared again, table cleared.

Twenty-four

While Tokh conducted his business, the *aghát* had theirs.

Today would be more debriefings; not only Masákh, but Mátokhan and Haghíde, who had also been in the Union for the last year, as well as four other *aghát* from three other generals, also serving inside the Union. Some of it seemed too close to interrogation, but there was plenty of open discussion, too, not only between the *aghát*, but with the Ministers. There was no set agenda; meetings were called when questions were thought of, when the government needed information clarified. Today might be a discussion of protocol for various Union worlds, to avoid insulting future delegates; tomorrow might be to discuss information about something overheard on spy satellites, and how it might pertain to Kerasím. Any *aghát* spending much time within Union boundaries was expected to be an expert on the Union.

The morning debriefing went well, a thought-provoking debate on the role of independent worlds as neutral territories, the idea of a mutual ban on using them as military outposts. The *aghát* unanimously felt it would be a favorable idea to the Union, and well-worth pursuing. They broke for lunch, the seven officers dining at a public cafeteria on the first floor. Divine smells drifted from the private grand dining room for ministers farther down the hall, but except for two or three *dihnarwharl*, almost all *aghát* were *whátaral* or *nhásarwharl*, and at the palace, even the floor scrubbers ranked *nhásarwharl*. Janitors did not eat with Ministers. It was at the end of the meal when a palace page approached Masákh with a folded paper.

The *whátaral* bent and whispered in his ear. "Your presence is requested in room 3406."

The whisper meant it was not public information. Masákh thanked the messenger and glanced at the paper. It was merely the number, written down for his convenience, with an official stamp. He tipped his head to the table. "Brothers, duty calls me elsewhere. Please continue."

The palace had lost none of its holiness to Masákh. Each and every footstep was a breath-stealing treasure. To walk the halls with nothing but a paper for escort – unimaginable! He walked a good distance down the public floor, took a lift to the second, and stopped at the security block. Parts of the second-floor were public – the upper balconies to the Senate chamber, several lesser meeting rooms, and sections of the museum – but the entire northern wing was not. The hall was sealed off by a security checkpoint, with impact-proof glass, armed officers, and a chamber that could trap a suspect until subdued by gas or stunners. One did not access the third floor or higher without crossing the checkpoint – unless entering from the checkpoint on the roof.

Masákh showed his paper, showed his identification, and submitted a thumb for printscan. He passed through the security lock, nervewracking on a good day, and was escorted to the lifts. Another guard met him at the lift on the third floor and accompanied him to the correct room. Masákh didn't know if such security had been standard under Emperor Nághtas or if Emperor Nadigh had installed it upon his father's death, but it was certainly effective.

He opened the door, not knowing what to expect. It was a small conference room with no outer vestibule, empty for a lone figure. Masákh knew its back was to him only by the position of the hands; it wore a loose black robe and a black veil over the head, blotting out all identifying features. It was average in height and average in shoulder, a formless shadow looking out a window.

"*Aghát* Major Masákh, as requested." His voice seemed too loud for the room, too abrupt, too rude. In training he would have lost points, deserving or not.

The figure didn't turn. "Masákh gha Lil of Kinas Dagh, graduate of Ghar Hamín Academy, currently of General Tokh's division. You have been assigned duty at Crater Ridge on the Union world Centauri and recently took a Union female as wife. A key player in assisting the Emperor with routing out traitors during last year's uprising and assassination. Your loyalty to Nadigh has been rewarded several times over. You were awarded membership into the Inner Circle."

The voice was male, ruling out the Heir. Nor was it the voice of the Emperor himself; Masákh had met him in person no fewer than three times. The information was straightforward, factual, non-threatening, but Masákh knew better. Membership in the Inner Circle was not open knowledge; this was someone with highest-level access. "Yes."

"I am your Circle liaison. You have not been given directive."

"No."

"Then obey my words. General Tokh is prying where he has no business. He is currently conducting a personal investigation not related to his duties. You are ordered to block and disrupt said investigation by any means necessary. Tokh has been warned. What lies down that path is out of his jurisdiction. He must be swayed to discontinue his investigation, or the consequences will not favor him."

Masákh thought fast. He was not privy to even a portion of Tokh's business. Tokh could be running a hundred investigations he didn't know about. "Do you mean the investigation into the attacks on his wife?"

"I do."

No further information came forth. "Do you have relative information I can use to distract him to another course? His wife's life has been threatened, and she fears for her child."

"The means is your responsibility. He seized the female at the point of his sword; he had no claim to her in the first place. He must not pursue his investigation further. So you are ordered."

"Are you the person he seeks?" It was a bold statement, out of line for a *whátaral*, but Masákh felt as if he were falling. To turn against Tokh, against the Lady Mímihn – it would take time for that to sink in. If he was to betray his commander, he needed all alternatives first.

Someone knew something they didn't want others to know; the figure turned, slow enough that the robes never let any footwear show. "No, I am not, and that is scannable truth. You have your orders, Major."

"How should I contact you when my work is complete?"

There was a faint snort under the veil, derisive but too small for a laugh. "You will either do or fail. If you do, you will be contacted again. Fail, and you will not like the consequences. Dismissed."

Masákh bowed before backing out. The figure could be anyone former *bhísroti* on down; it was not the time to fail on protocol.

He returned to the public area on the second floor and ducked into a restroom for privacy, where he was appalled to find himself shaking.

He'd received his first high-level orders from the Emperor: destroy the commander who gave him his life's success, or betray his Emperor.

Twenty-five

Zheníhda knocked at Tokh's home office door. "My apologies at the interruption, husband. A call for you came in on my comm."

"Your comm?" Tokh snatched it from her hand, but the call had ended. He checked the source, but it had been blocked. "Why yours?"

"Major Mátokhan wished to minimize the trace, and didn't wish to leave a message. He requested you meet him at the counter of the café Amaran in thirty *fasim*."

"Amaran? In the city proper? It will take me twenty *fasim* to get there." He stood and gave Zheníhda her comm. "You are absolutely certain it was Mátokhan on the comm? I sent him to Rochadapin."

"It was his voice and his face on the screen. I'm certain."

"Did he say why?"

"No, that was the entire message."

Tokh strapped on his belt, checked his weapon, and headed for the door, leaving Ghírandar in charge of the house.

The tables of the eatery were filled, but a few spaces remained at the standing bar by the kitchen. One was right next to his lead *aghát*. Tokh almost didn't recognize Mátokhan; he wore civilian clothing, conservative and bland for a *dihnarwharl*-privilege. A hat covered his forehead and dark shades covered his eyes, leaving just the paleness of his cheeks and the goatee to give him away as someone unusual. He wore his caste-pin but no military marks at all.

"Is this space taken, Good Citizen?" Tokh said.

"Not at all, Officer," Mátokhan said. "Please stand with me. Taking a *raffin* break?"

Tokh ordered a cup of *raffin* and a small pastry. He eyed Mátokhan's hand pie and *muhr*. "Good food?"

"Decent enough," Mátokhan said. He wet a finger to pick up fallen crumbs and relay them to his mouth. Tokh's fare arrived. Mátokhan pushed two paper tubes of sweetener toward him. "Here, Lord. You will want these. The *raffin* here is sometimes a bit harsh."

Tokh didn't care for sweet *raffin*, but he played along. As he tore the paper, he saw the writing inside the packet. He dumped the sweetener, then slipped the wrappers into his pocket. They kept up a light conversation, no more than two people passing each other on a busy day. Tokh finished his pastry and half the overly sweet *raffin*, bid Mátokhan a pleasant day, and left as if he had somewhere to be.

Tokh's heart raced to know what was on the paper, but he didn't dare read it before he got home. Obviously it was something Mátokhan didn't want traced, which meant high secrecy, and he wasn't trusting anything. Clever, with the sweetener. Even when he got home, Tokh decided not to open them in his office but went upstairs, locked himself in his own bathroom, closed the windows, and read them sitting at his wives' dressing table.

It was written in tiny Union letters, not because it was a Union issue but because any average citizen who found it wouldn't be able to read it, would think it was local gibberish from a traveler, and dispose of it without second thought. Another win for Mátokhan.

Source valid; ancestor: Tavern Ghar Rhal, Ganjamir City.

Tokh's eyes went wide. A chill crinkled its way up his spine, and he felt hope soar. General Engmar had been located, by a trustworthy source. Realization hit him like a correction stick: Mátokhan was Inner Circle. Trannor could give information to the Emperor, who could pass it to Mátokhan, and no one would know. It had to be from Trannor. Engmar wasn't a direct link; two generals meeting was so common it would be ignored. *Ganjamir, Ganjamir...* Ganjamir was thirty *nalis* outside Kerahnihn; close enough to keep contacts, far enough away to remain hidden. He clicked open his line, and sent a message to Khaním at the securities office.

By the next day, Tokh had his own confirmation. Khaním's man brought back photo evidence Engmar was indeed keeping quiet at the Tavern, and the computer agreed. He called his team together.

"We fly in, take care of our various business in Keranihn, then say we're meeting for lunch and head out there. Best case, we have a friendly chat, he tells me what I want to know, and we head back to the building to proceed further."

Tótoghar loaded up his jacket with his weapon, his ID, his comm, and checked the myriad other items *aghát* carried. "Worst case?"

Tokh sighed. "Worst case, I have to arrest him on a false charge, remove him, and bring him back to Keranihn, and it turns into a shootout. I'll try to avoid that. Engmar is no fool. He's a good officer. Mímihn doesn't fear him; that tells me he'll listen to reason. Be alert."

"I expect to return before dinner," Tokh told Zheníhda. "I'll message you when we leave."

"Wait – what do you mean, 'we'?" Mímihn said with a frown. "Tokh, you can't take everyone. We'll be unprotected."

Tokh kissed her jaw. "You'll be fine. Perimeter security will be on. I'm leaving Lieutenants Unav and Drazis from my office as guards, swapping off. They'll work from the empty apartment over the vehicle shed, so you need not have them in the house. They'll patrol the grounds and monitor communications."

"And you trust them?"

Tokh smiled at her, chucked her under her chin. "They are my own officers from Keranihn. I wouldn't leave them in charge of you if I didn't think them capable. You'll be safe. Both Lanag and Jora are good with weapons, and will be home from school later."

"They're children, Tokh. You couldn't leave Khaním?"

"If it'll make you happier, next time I'll request Khaním to cover for me."

Aila counted heads around the room. Zheníhda, Mímihn, Dalo, Fahni, Shanohr, two young girls, and herself. Eight unprotected females, a toddler, and an infant. And tottering old Thrit out in the shed. On Kerasím, a disaster waiting to happen. Thrit was *ghinadin*, lowest of all the castes. He was forbidden by law from having a weapon, and it would mean his life if he touched, let alone killed, anyone above *ghinadin* caste. Thrit was useless as protection.

"I'd feel better about the whole thing if you left me a weapon," Aila said.

Ráhnif gave a snort of amusement. Masákh turned his head slowly and gave the junior *aghát* a cold stare that Aila knew well.

"She has killed accurately and fearlessly before," he reminded Ráhnif. "The request is not inappropriate."

Ráhnif bowed his head. "Forgiveness, Masákh. It's odd, a wife asking for a weapon."

Zheníhda gave Tokh a brief kiss on his neck. "I will keep them in line."

"I know you will, my Little General." He gave Mímihn another kiss. She held her head up like a good Kerasi wife, but she couldn't erase the fear on it.

"Be safe," she whispered. "Don't be long."

Masákh put his hands on Aila's shoulders, but it wasn't enough for her. "Is it wrong to give you a hug?"

He shook his head. "No, but not lingering." She circled her arms around him, buried her face in his neck, and squeezed. He held her head long enough to whisper: *"If there is danger, the peace you seek can be found in my luggage, but don't make a mistake."*

Aila nodded. "Hurry back."

Masákh smiled at her, and it wasn't smarmy. He chucked her under her chin. "As if I had wings."

Twenty-six

The noise of the helicraft drifted fainter and fainter up the inlet, until silence remained. The females stood in place, looking at each other.

Zheníhda headed for the kitchen, waving her arms. "Go! Everyone, go about their business. It's just another day. They leave home all the time. They'll return later, just as always. Today's no different." She took a *raffin* cup from the cabinet.

"We don't have any business," Dalo said. "I'm stuck here to protect the children. We should at least be allowed to go to the markets."

Fahni rubbed her arms. "I've never been under guard before. Is there really that much danger to us?"

"Of course not." Zheníhda blew on her *raffin,* then sipped it. "Tokh's being overly cautious."

"Well, then I guess you don't mind Kesseh and Faelihn playing outside," Aila said. "Go on, girls. There's no need for you to be stuck in here."

Zheníhda glanced up sharply.

"Ka!" Mímihn barked. "I don't want her out there until Tokh returns. I can't see every danger, even if I go out there with her, and I don't trust officers I've just met. Kesseh will stay inside with me."

"I don't want Faelihn outside, either," Dalo said. "They can study lessons, just as if they were in class today. We can practice our Union with Aila."

"Look," Aila said, "let's just admit we're all frightened at being left alone, with none of our soldiers here. There are enough of us. We can make our own soldier squad, so we feel better."

"This is Kerasím, not the Union," Zheníhda sniffed. "Females are not soldiers."

"You don't need training to keep a watch. There are what, six of us? How long do you think they'll be gone? If we each take an hour watching out the windows, we'll feel like we're doing something to help ourselves. If you see something strange, yell out. If we think it's a problem, we page the officers, or Tokh himself."

Dalo nodded. "I can do that. Kitras has taught me how to look for trouble."

"I'll be no help," Mímihn said.

"You have a baby," Aila said. "Keep your eyes on him. Play a game. Make a cake. Watch the ComNet. We'll do the rest."

"I can do that," Mímihn agreed.

Having a watch helped. Fahni took the first hour, Zheníhda the second, and Dalo the third. Mímihn played with Niboh and Thoren, and Dalo and Aila practiced conversing with the girls in Union Standard. It was Dalo that broke the peace.

"I haven't seen a guard walk the courtyard. When was the last time someone checked in?"

Tokh had introduced Unav and Drazis to the ladies, set them up in the vehicle shed so they wouldn't bother them, and gave the officers their orders. Twice an hour one of them would make a patrol lap around the grounds, while the other called in to Zheníhda's com to make sure everyone was okay.

The room paused. "I don't know," Zheníhda said. She checked the time the last call had come through. She stared at Aila as if she held all the answers. "More than an hour ago."

Aila flew over to see the screen; the other women followed. "Call them. Ask what's wrong. Maybe they fell asleep."

Zheníhda gave a much more normal scowl as she hit the icon and held the com to her ear. "Tokh will kill them if he finds out." She waited, then ended the call and tried again. The scowl slid back to worry. "No response. They can't both be asleep."

Aila pulled hers out of her pocket. "I'm calling Masákh."

"A wife never bothers a husband on duty!" Zheníhda hissed.

Aila tried, tried again, and every hair began to stand at attention. One oddity was curious. Two oddities could be coincidence. Three was deep trouble. "I'm not. My com's not working. There's no signal."

Coms came flying out of pockets. "Neither's mine!" Fahni said.

192

Dalo ran through different commands and settings. "Dead."

"That's why," Zeníhda said.

"Shit!" Aila shoved her com into her pocket. "Shit shit shit shit! *Aaka!*" she said when the room gave her a blank stare. She ran to the window, but there was nothing in sight but empty courtyard. Aila double-checked the lock on the door as if the handle would melt in her hand.

"Shanohr! Make certain every door and window is fully locked! Every one!" The maid dashed off. "Zeníhda, do you know how to check the security system?"

Zeníhda dashed for Tokh's office. "Yes, the house, at least. I don't know the bigger settings." She searched the console for the proper controls while the others looked on.

"Ai-lah, what's happening?" Mímihn clutched Thoren to her chest as if she could hide him inside her ribcage. "Tell us what you know!"

"I don't know anything," Aila insisted. "But everyone's com not working is a very bad sign. Someone must know we're alone. I'm praying the guards haven't changed sides."

Shanohr ran up breathlessly. "All windows and doors down here are locked, Great Lady. There are many windows."

"Okay. Everyone upstairs, then," Aila decided. "You too, Shanohr. You stay with us now."

Zeníhda gave a soft growl. "Hired help does not join with the Lord's family."

Aila stared right back. "I don't care. This isn't a party. No one is getting hurt on my watch. Make sure all the upstairs doors and windows are locked, too."

Dalo shooed the girls up the stairs while lugging Niboh. "Here girls, take him with you. Go play in your room. Maybe he'll take a nap on your bed. Let us ladies have some quiet."

Faelihn clung to her. "I don't want to play. I'm scared."

Dalo pulled her off. "You're not a baby. Go. I'll be right here upstairs. I'll call you when it's time for lunch."

Aila ran to the end of the upstairs hall. At the front of the house, next to the *dhastal* head over the main entrance, were glass doors and a balcony. It felt more dangerous, more exposed before all that glass, but she could see most of the courtyard, the landing pad, the front edge of the gates, and out over the water without taking a step. From here, she could see over the hall railing to the dining room below. It was only a dash through Mímihn's room to survey the side yard. This should be their vantage point.

"What now?" Fahni asked. "What do we do?"

"I don't know," Aila said with a shrug. "Sit on Tokh's bed until we figure something out. Can you open a window and call up the hill, see if their system is out up above?"

"That's not how things are done in Imahlva," Zheníhda said with authority. "A *dahneg* does not yell out a window at a *fáhganid* and expect a reply."

"They're *dahneg* now, too," Kesseh reminded her.

"Well, you could always just run up the hill and ask..." Aila trailed off as a shadow caught her eye. Just to the right of her view, hugging close to the house, someone was moving. She shifted left and right, but couldn't get a better view without opening the balcony door. "There's someone moving out there."

"A guard?" Dalo said. The women ran forward in a herd. "Where?"

"I can't see. They're too close to the building. They don't move like a guard. They move... dishonorably."

Mímihn began to gasp and shake. "They're here for me. They'll take me back. Tokh, why aren't you here to stop them!"

From over the railing, they could see a figure in black check, then dart quickly below the window behind the dining table. A moment later, the front door gave a soft rattle, but it remained locked.

"We're going to die, and it's my fault!" Mímihn wailed in a panic. "Hide Thoren! Hide him! I can't bear to see him die!"

"No one is going to die," Aila said, but her voice wasn't as sure. The second floor had given them a slight advantage, but escape was impossible. There was no way to get two infants, two children, and six women in skirts over a balcony and down a makeshift rope without being caught, especially if there was a second or third person out there. "Grab the girls."

The door below continued to rattle; someone was trying to pick or disable it.

Think! Think! A locked bedroom would be a giveaway, even if they piled all the furniture in front of it. A locked bathroom would be even more suspicious in an empty house. Aila's eyes scanned the

194

hallway again, desperate for guidance, and they landed on the one shut door.

"The closet!" she ordered. "Everyone! Shanohr, unlock the door. No one will think a locked closet strange. Hurry!"

Aila counted heads to make sure everyone squeezed in. Thankfully it was a large linen closet that Shanohr kept impeccably organized, with wide shelves of sheets and extra bed covers, cleaners, brushes, pails, and anything else a cleaning woman might need. If only they had a weapon!

The peace you seek can be found in my luggage. Masákh's spare weapon. Aila turned to dash to her room, but the downstairs door clicked open. She glanced at her room in panic, but no magic weapon came floating down the hall at her command. Aila slipped into the closet and pulled the door shut as quietly as possible. She faced the ladies and placed a hand over her own mouth, silencing everyone.

Twenty-seven

They waited, afraid to breathe, the linens seeming to insulate and soak up every possible sound. Niboh, however, proved difficult to quiet.

"Down. *Ama*, down. Want down!"

"Niboh! Hush!" Dalo whispered. "We're playing a game and you must be quiet. *Shu shu shu.*" She tried rocking him, bouncing him, making faces for him, nursing him, but nothing lasted more than a minute. Mímihn handed him a scrub brush, but he banged it against a shelf.

"Niboh! Don't make me spank you!" Zheníhda whispered.

Shanohr motioned to Fahni to hand her a small cup on the shelf behind her. From it she held up a candy the size of a button. "Do you like *wahnah*? I'll give you some, but only if you don't talk. If you want one, you have to touch your nose." She wiggled the tip of her nose with her finger. Niboh smiled and wiggled his nose in reply.

Footsteps whispered on the hall carpet, back and forth, searching. The handle to the closet door gave a firm rattle. Only Niboh dared breathe, sucking the flavor out of his current piece of *wahnah*. It gave a second shake but held firm, and the footsteps hushed down the hall. The entire closet seemed to sag with everyone's exhalation.

Minutes passed in agony as they waited for the footsteps to descend the stairs once more. The rattling of the handle jolted them out of their relief. Something was jammed into the doorframe, and the lock popped. Aila hung on the handle, but it ripped from her hands as the door jerked open. She stepped back, blocking the women behind her.

A male Kerasi with several large weapons, a cargo belt, and a foul expression stood before them. His grin was more frightening than his weapons. "Well look what I found here. Winner's pocket. I want the lady of the house."

The closet stared back, too frightened to speak.

He repeated himself with less patience. "I want the lady of the house!"

Zhenihda unfolded herself in the back. "I am Great Lady Tokh daras Gilahn, and you will leave my house if you wish to remain alive."

His eyebrow sank over his eyes as he studied her. "You're too old. I want a younger one."

Zhenihda gave a horrible snort. Her voice could have cut glass. "Do not offend me or you will regret your words."

Thoren had fallen asleep in Mímihn's arms; she had placed him on a shelf, cradled in the folds of sheets. The stranger pointed to him. "Whose baby is that?"

"Mine!" Dalo said quickly, picking him up. "He's mine. You may check his blood; he'll show the same as my husband." That was truth; both Thoren and Kitras had the same father.

"I want to see milk," he sneered. "No milk, and that one dies." The plasma rifle in his hand pointed at Kesseh.

Kesseh grabbed onto Mímihn with a gasp; Mímihn moved in front of her. Faelihn grabbed onto Zhenihda with a shriek.

Dalo unbuttoned her blouse and removed a richly tanned breast. She'd been very lazy on weaning Niboh, and still nursed him twice a day. She twisted her breast and shot a strong enough stream to impress him.

The man nodded. "Okay. So who's is that?" He pointed at Niboh.

"Mine!" Fahni said in an instant. She swung him up and tickled his belly with her nose. Niboh broke into rolling giggles. "He's my son."

"Who are you?" he asked Aila.

Aila pulled herself up tall and channeled every bit of Masákh she could, cold, calculating, and unquestionably in charge, as she'd done against Tokh, and suicidal *fáhganids*, and even her own government at times, more arrogant than Zhenihda. "I am Great Lady Masákh ghas Lil, a member of the Union Council of Kerasi Affairs and acting Ambassador for the Planetary Union. I carry *dahneg* status and am under direct protection of the Emperor. Any offense to me and it will be treated as an interstellar incident, and your master punished by the Emperor himself."

The man laughed. "My sender doesn't fear the Emperor. So you're the one I want then." His head motioned to Mímihn.

197

Mímihn had gone so pale her golden skin was as tan as a bleached *aghát*. Aila leaned into his face with a snarl. "I guess your master didn't prepare you as well as you thought if you can't recognize the elder daughter of General Four Tokh dar-Gilahn."

The confusion in his frown said it was not the answer he expected. "Where's his other wife?"

"With him."

He kept his rifle trained on the females, but pulled out his com. With his finger he tapped and flipped through several photos. It wasn't difficult to recognize Mímihn.

"Liar!" he shouted at Aila. With a twist, he flipped the weapon around and hammered Aila in the side of her head with the butt. The ladies screamed.

Aila's head exploded with a blinding pain. Any stars she might have seen had gone supernova, and all that remained was a wall of screaming white. Her head, her teeth, even her neck hurt from the punch. She couldn't think a thought; all she could do was cling to a shelf and wait for her vision to clear. Something warm trickled down the side of her face, making her itch.

The man waved the rifle. "Come on. Come with me quiet and I'll let the others live."

"Touch her and you won't make it to the gate alive," Aila rasped.

He grabbed her arm and spun her around, adding dizziness to her woes. The weapon barrel jammed up under her chin. "One more word and it will be your last, *trixahg*."

Mímihn held up her hands. Her voice was calm, too calm. "It's okay, ladies. I'll go. I won't have anyone hurt worse. It's nothing I haven't dealt with before. I know what I'm doing. Everyone stay safe."

"Mimi!" Aila hissed.

"*Ama,* no!" Dalo said.

"*Ama!*" Kesseh cried. She tried to hold Mímihn back, but Zheníhda grabbed her.

Mímihn stepped forward and he seized her roughly by the arm. Before their eyes, Mímihn seemed to morph into a different person, as if she'd zipped on another skin. Her head tipped, a tart smile broke out, her body movements changed, even her voice softened until she was no longer Mímihn. She turned around and picked at his shirt, breathing on him.

"You know what's going to happen to me," she purred. "Wouldn't you like to have a run at unbruised meat first? I can make you a very, very happy man. What better insult than to take a Lord's wife in his own bed? Let them go, and I promise I'll do anything you want." Mímihn tapped her fingernail on the end of his nose and lips with each syllable. "Maybe even something you've never thought of."

He smiled at Mímihn, the cruelest, coldest smile Aila had ever seen, even on her arch-enemy Colonel Kassán. She felt dirty just for seeing it. He swayed a little with Mímihn. "Oh, we're going to have some fun, you and me, but not here. Oh no. I don't trust you here." He snaked his arm around her throat and pulled her forward. "I got what I need. I didn't come for them. Tell them to stay put, shut the door nice and easy, and I'll let them live as long as you come quiet."

Mímihn wasn't struggling. "I can do that. Ladies, please stay where you are. I'll be fine. Don't make this worse on me by getting hurt. Don't make it worse on the girls. Do as he says. I love you, each and every one." Her smile was as bright as ever, but Aila saw the look in her eyes. Mímihn considered herself dead already.

The man stepped backwards and leaned to close the door, one powerful arm still holding Mímihn. He arched backward with a loud grunt and released her. His weapon fired once into the ceiling and fell to the floor.

Mímihn whirled around. Her hands clapped over her mouth, but it didn't stop her scream. The ladies burst forth from the closet.

A large piece of metal stuck through the man's chest, and his face said he hadn't expected it. Then he gave a horrible gurgling sigh and the light faded in his eyes. It must have gone through at least a portion of his heart, for blood soaked his shirt in great waves. With a grotesque sucking noise, the metal slid backward as the intruder fell forward with a heavy thud.

Standing in the hall was the *ghinadín* servant Thrit, a long, sword-shaped metal tool in his hand. Tiny little wizened old Thrit, who might have been forty or might have been ninety.

"General hire T'rit t' look after young Lady Tokh. Say it T'rit's only duty. Protect her. No one allowed to touch her wit'out his permission. T'rit do t'at. Nobody t'reaten t'Lord's wife."

Mímihn grabbed and hugged him, castes be damned. She kissed him on his wrinkly cheek. "Thrit! Dear sweet Thrit! Thank you! Thank you! May the Fortunes bless your name in every temple!"

The ladies and girls rushed to hug Mímihn, Dalo holding Thoren.

Aila knelt before Thrit. A *ghinadín* who killed anyone but another *ghinadín* was put to death. No trial. No lawyer. No alternative outcome. That was Kerasi law, and Tokh would be required to do it. "You have the heart of a *dahneg*. I promise, I will find a way around the law."

"T'rit not worry. Lady Tokh safe. T'rit take care of body now."

"No!" Aila put her hand out to stop him. "Leave it. Go back to your rooms. Clean yourself. Be absolutely clean. Watch the road for us. You were never inside the house. The law can't touch me. I did this. I killed him. I've killed before and walked away. I, *dahneg*, order you to agree with me if questioned. Understood? You don't know what happened. You weren't here."

Thrit glared and gave an unhappy growl. "T'rit not lie to General Tokh!"

"I'll deal with General Tokh. You didn't come into the house today."

Thrit glared darker, then turned his head in anger he wasn't allowed to set loose. "T'rit not come inside house today."

Aila laid a hand on his shoulder – a bare hand, nonetheless. "Thank you, Thrit. Go. Take your tool. Make sure it's absolutely clean, too."

Thrit made his way past the ladies still hugging each other and thumped down the stairs. Aila wasn't going to be caught short again. She ran to her room, ransacked Masákh's precisely arranged luggage, and grabbed his spare plasma pistol and an extra power cell. She took his extra knife for good measure, and ran back down the hall.

"Enough! Enough fear. It's time to take back this house. Get the girls out of here. They don't need to see this. Shanohr, give me a sheet. Cover him up."

Shanohr rifled through the linens and came away with the very oldest and worn sheets, and she and Aila spread them over the body. It gave a faint wheeze as the sheet touched it. The girls screamed, and the ladies jumped away.

Aila seized the rifle from the floor and cracked the body over the head as hard as she could. "Fair's fair." It didn't move again.

"What do we do?" Zheníhda said. "It can't stay here. It will ruin the carpeting."

"We'll move it," Aila decided. "First, we make an army. Dalo, do you know how to use a weapon?"

Dalo nodded, perhaps the most serious Aila had ever seen her. "*Sukh*. Kitras taught me. I can hit the heart at ten paces if I don't have to think about the wind."

Aila handed her Masákh's pistol. "Here. Don't forget the safety. Zheníhda, where are Tokh's spare weapons?"

"I only know his swords and knives."

"Then get them. Now." Zheníhda spun in a swirl of skirts and rushed to Tokh's room.

"I have a dagger," Mímihn said.

"Then get it. Keep it on you at all times now. We won't come so close to disaster again."

Zheníhda brought two knives, wicked-looking things meant for nothing but the peeling of life from a body. Aila gave one to Fahni. That left everyone armed except Shanohr. Aila reached into her waistband and handed her Masákh's knife. Shanohr cooked; she would know how to use a knife. Aila studied her impromptu army.

"From now on, anyone comes through a door, you run and attack. Immediately. Question later. Don't wait. The only thing we have going for us is numbers and surprise. They think we're all sitting here shivering in our skirts, not waiting to take their heads. Got it? If you don't want to die, if you don't want the children to die, you stab anything coming through that door as if you're chopping meat for dinner, and you don't stop until the chunks fit in the pot. Everyone at once. Understand?"

Amazingly, Zheníhda looked the calmest – and most vicious – of the group as they agreed.

"I skinned a *ritidu* once," Dalo said. "Kitras killed it, but he wanted me to practice using a knife so he made me skin it, and he said I did an excellent job. I didn't tear the skin once. It's hardest by the feet, because they have such tiny ankles, but he …"

"We don't need to skin him, Dalo. We just need him dead, and if we do it right, there won't be enough skin left to bother, but I'm glad you can use a knife." Aila studied the group once more. Fahni was by far the strongest-looking, though Dalo was no weakling. Dalo was daring enough, but how strong was Fahni's nerve?

Aila hung the rifle from her shoulder. "Fahni, grab a foot. Dalo, take the other. Help me get him to the vehicle shed. Once we get him down the stairs, we'll wrap him and drag him on a sheet." Aila expected some sort of objection, at least from Zheníhda, but to her amazement Fahni didn't hesitate. She stuffed the knife in her waistband and hiked her skirt up. She was going to make an excellent wife for an *aghát*.

Shanohr put a hand on the sheet. "*Ka!* There's less blood in the feet than the head. To go down the stairs, you drag by the arms. Keep the blood below the wound. Less mess."

Every head turned. Shanohr was the silent one in the house. She spoke less than Thrit, just an occasional *Yes Lady*, murmured softly so as not to disturb anyone. Even Mímihn, who roomed with her before she became Tokh's wife, didn't know very much about her. She had a son and a daughter, and her husband had been dead five years. She was *tághinet*, the no-man's land of neither low nor middle caste. But Shanohr knew how to dispose of bodies.

Shanohr grabbed two scrub pads from the closet, small and absorbent. She lifted the sheet, stuffed one in the back wound, then rolled the body and tucked one into the front wound. "There. Now you won't leave so much."

Aila tipped her head in thanks while a chill shivered her spine. She was feeling flaky enough about touching a dead man's clothing but was trying to be strong for the ladies, and here Shanohr was sticking her hands inside him like she was stuffing a *hyrak*. "*Soyavoh*, Shanohr."

Aila took one warm arm, Fahni took the other, Dalo grabbed him by his belt, and they gave a mighty heave. At first his arms seemed to stretch until they would come off, but inch by inch the body began to slide on the carpet. It wasn't bad in the hall, but the feet bounced down the stairs with a sickening thud at each step. He was heavier than he looked, and they were winded by the time they got to the bottom. Once down, Shanohr helped them wrap the body in sheets and then roll it on top of another, so all they had to do was drag it behind them.

There was a back door from the hall by the maid's room to the alley between the house and the overhead cliff wall upwards. They hauled the body through the kitchen, through the narrow hall and onto the walkway. From there it was a straight private highway to the vehicle shed, two hundred feet away.

Almost. Aila almost lost her nerve when there between the vehicle shed and the house lay the body of one of Tokh's guards. They were three females out in the open, helpless prey to anyone with a weapon.

"Is he alive?" Fahni whispered.

"We're not taking time to find out," Aila whispered back. "Let Tokh deal with him. Sorry, Officer." Touching one dead man was enough for a day.

They thumped the body over the shed's doorway and shoved it tight against a wall. Dalo tucked the sheets in, Aila covered it with a stack of tarps, and Fahni parked a tub of walkway repair on top of it. As a final detail they leaned a ladder over it, as if the tools had been there a while and nothing unusual was going on, at least at first glance. They closed the door and retraced their steps, but they couldn't find spilled blood past the bottom of the stairs. The upstairs carpet, however, was soggy with it, and Shanohr was already hard at work getting it up before stains set in. Of all people, *dahneg*-privileged Zheníhda herself was helping her; it must have been a very expensive carpet indeed for Zheníhda to work alongside a maid.

Mímihn pulled at Aila's elbow. "You are too brave, Aila. Come, sit, put cold on your face."

Aila waved her away. "I'll regret it tomorrow, but I want everyone to see I was hit. Let's go over our story of what just happened. We all need to say the exact same thing, or Thrit will die for having saved us."

"I won't allow that," Mímihn said. "Tokh will break the rules this time. He must."

"I agree, so let's go over this," and Aila walked them through the death of the intruder over and over until everyone was perfect.

"Okay. We're halfway through the day; the men will return in just a few hours, and we are all alive and well. Everyone take a deep breath. We have already taken care of the worst. We'll keep taking turns watching. Make the children lunch. Help Shanohr scrub the carpet. Play with the babies. Watch your dramas. Don't be cold with fear. Each minute that goes is one closer to Tokh's return. Every minute gone, we're safer. Remember that." She scattered them away with a wave of her fingers.

Aila took the first watch, upstairs by the balcony doors. The ladies were quiet below but they made a good effort, making lunch, calming the girls' fears, and hushing Niboh so he would nap.

Aila's head throbbed until she couldn't always see straight, but she refused to give in. She'd always known there was more to Kerasi women than being the paint on a wall, fearful little illiterate dishrags who couldn't cross a street without a man's help. Mímihn's strength she had no doubt of: the fact Mímihn rose from bed every morning and carried on conversations was proof she was far stronger than Aila. But Dalo, Shanohr, Fahni – even prissy proper Zheníhda – when push came to shove, they had no trouble pulling themselves together and doing what had to be done, despite their terror, despite their caste. Kerasi women unleashed would be unstoppable.

Mímihn came up the stairs with a cup of *raffin* for her; Aila watched her from the third step upward. She handed Aila the cup, then turned her face to look at her wound. The side of Aila's head and her hair were still matted with blood.

"Let me wash that for you, before the husbands return."

A proper wife would have made herself look as if she'd been lounging all day and a home invasion and attempted kidnapping were a minor inconvenience, but Aila wasn't Kerasi. "No. I want them to see it. I want them to know how hard we fought. It's my badge of honor at the moment."

"It's stopped bleeding, at least." Mímihn kissed the wound. "It will be worse tomorrow." She fell silent, squirming a bit, before speaking so softly Aila could just hear her over the noises from below.

"Thank you. That was a foolish thing to do, but it was very brave. You're lucky he didn't kill you. I should have gone right away, not put everyone in danger. It was very selfish of me."

"You don't know if that would have helped. He could have killed everyone right there, killed Thoren to anger Tokh. It was my fault. I should've gotten Masákh's weapon when he left. I won't be caught that way again. I had just a little taste of your pain last year. I won't let that happen to anyone."

"What was it like, being in battle?"

Aila scanned the yard and the cliff through the glass again. "Very loud. Everything happened very fast. There was much smoke. Then the guards were shot and there were bodies on the floor, all burnt and smoking. I was too afraid to run. Then they attacked Masákh, and I stopped thinking. I grabbed his gun and shot his attacker and saved everyone. Now I'm not as scared. Now I know what to do. I'm very angry now. We should have done this in the morning, and we would all be happier. We're braver than we knew, aren't we."

Mímihn smiled. "Yes. Even Zheníhda surprised me. I didn't know she was that fearless."

Aila squeezed her hand. "We'll be safe now. You'll see."

Twenty-eight

The café was smoky with a wood-fired grill and half-full with diners extending their lunches as late as they could. "I'm meeting General Engmar," Tokh said to the pourmaster. "Is he here?"

"He doesn't leave," the man said, and tipped his chin to a table in an isolated alcove in the back of the room. Tokh threaded his way through the tables, followed by his team of *aghát*, their eyes noting every patron, every window, every exit, every possible weapon, six times.

The rheumy eyes caught sight of them, grew wide as if seeing a phantom, stayed that way for several breaths before the surprise faded, and Engmar let his head fall downward again. He sucked long and hard from his glass. Tokh slid onto the opposite bench; the *aghát* formed a wall before the alcove shoulder to shoulder facing outward, blocking it from public view.

Engmar didn't look up. He was nearly unrecognizable, grizzled and sweaty, his chin hank bushed out unattended and his jaw speckled with so much hair he had a disgraceful shadow-beard. He gazed into his cup as if waiting for a blow. Little waves sloshed up the sides of the glass as his hand shook. "You can't kill me, Tokh. I'm dead already."

"On the inside, for certain. Good. A dead man has nothing to hide."

"A dead man answers nothing."

"True enough." Tokh swallowed his anger. Engmar was so deep in his cup – and had been that way for some time, it was obvious – that he could barely form words, yet fear held him up. Engmar was a General with a good career, a full *dahneg* General, and he deserved respect. Outside of siring a bad seed, Engmar had done nothing to warrant the loss of that respect. If Engmar considered himself dead, he would never give up anything. Tokh needed to find the last little piece of him that was still alive.

"You're still a General, so speak to me General to General, if not as male to male. Tell me your story, so I don't have to escort you back to my office."

Engmar gave a grunt of amusement. "I'd welcome it. You won't treat me half as badly, but it wouldn't work. I'm dead."

Tokh blinked. The threat of a mind scan was enough to send most people running, begging cooperation from their knees in a cold sweat. Truly, Engmar was dead inside. Tokh's anger gave way to pity. He couldn't reach Engmar's shoulder, but he grasped him above his elbow in a gesture of friendship. "Then explain it to me here, and our business will be done. I owe you favor for giving her to me – I freed her from consort, and she is now my second-wife. With medical care, she's now the happy mother of my son. She's the joy of my days, and despite her fear she speaks only kind words of you. Why start this now?"

The General cackled. He looked Tokh in the eye, but Tokh couldn't tell if he was trying to pick a fight or make him leave. "I've *pushed* your wife. More than once. She was one hot brown *lihx*." He grinned triumphantly – drunkenly – and took a large swallow from his glass.

"I'm aware of that. It was before I knew her, and nothing I can hold against her. It's not as if she had a choice. Why start this now?"

"You have no idea, Tokh. No idea. But now I'm dead. You signed my death warrant the moment you walked in here. He's never forgiven you. He's done nothing but scream and throw things for six years. He hasn't forgiven me for bringing you to the game, and insists I helped you cheat him. He tried to take her back then, but you went off-world. He choked his wife to death. Claimed it was an accident while *pushing* her; the *fáhganid* let him off. His second wife took her own life in fear. I'm sorry, Tokh. He'll seize her, and torture her, and *push* her, and then he will kill her, perhaps all at once. And there's nothing we can do. He runs with a lawless crowd now." Engmar lifted the bottle of *dhurwah* with a shaky hand and filled his glass to the brim. A dribble spilled over the side so that when he tried to raise it, the glass slid down his fingers to thump on the table. He bent over to drain away the first half-inch.

"You're a Level Three General. A decorated *dahneg* General. You have power. I was unaware of enmity between us; a simple warning would have been appreciated."

Engmar remained hunched over the table, but the yellowed eyes rolled upward. Flames swelled up in them, a deadly fire that sparked and bit under the heavy silver brow, and for a moment the commander that had been glared back with intimidation, galled at the accusations. Then the blaze died out and the empty shell slumped back over the glass.

"Three. The slaughter pen of Generals, waiting and hoping we get picked for work in the government, which is the only way to Four. We both know why I couldn't move up. He twisted my ankle until it broke, Tokh. Three bones. That was his warning to keep my mouth shut, or he'd break the other. He threatened to have my pension revoked. He has the contacts to do it. He knows the unhappy ones like himself, the ones angry with the Emperor, the ones angry with you. You skipped clear over General Three, you have a home valued above your caste, a Senate seat, enough inroads to the Emperor that he showed up at your home. That shits on a lot of festering egos."

"His visit was a surprise to me; I had no preparations. I had no input on my fortunes, either."

"It doesn't matter. It happened. I'm seventy-one years old, Tokh. I can't fight him."

"Come, then. Come back with me, and we'll sort things right. It can be done. We'll see it through together; you have my word. I'll arrange guards for you, if you wish," Tokh said. He gripped the hand that wasn't holding the glass.

Engmar's gaze was lost to the thoughts inside. "It's wrong, Tokh. A father should not outlive his sons."

"I won't ask for his head. I will demand his *hihvat*, as I promised my wife for justice toward her. I'll allow it to be done medically. The rest he can be imprisoned for."

"Two daughters and a son," Engmar mourned to his cup. A sob cracked his trembling voice, but his spirit didn't leak. "I was so proud when he was born. I don't know what happened to him, where I went wrong. He was headstrong even as an infant."

"Some are just born that way, and there's little we can do to sway them. My first was like that, independent. I wasn't home enough when he was young, and my wife wasn't strong enough."

Engmar nodded, lost in a cloud. "Very well. I'll come, Tokh, if for nothing but to beg mercy for him."

Engmar tried to stand but rose only a few inches before falling back onto the bench. He tried twice more before Tokh took the glass from his hand and placed it on the table. Engmar put his hands flat and pushed himself to stand, but his steps were slow and tottering. The *aghát* broke their privacy wall, falling back to let the Generals pass.

Engmar was unsteady. The weak ankle didn't help, but the *dhurwah* was deep in his blood and several times he reached out to the backs of empty chairs to steady himself. Tokh walked beside him with mincing steps; the *aghát* took a step, waited, then took another when there was sufficient space.

The door to the café was before them when Ghírandar saw the hand move. "General!"

Tokh's hand flashed to his weapon and started to draw, as did six *aghát*, but Engmar was quicker. He jammed his plasma pistol under his own chin and pulled the trigger. A sickening stench of burnt blood and roasted flesh roiled through the air, and Engmar collapsed to the floor.

Tokh turned his head while he composed himself and resecured his weapon. The *aghát* formed an honor wall around General Engmar until the authorities arrived.

Twenty-nine

The returning aircraft thrupped its way past the house, hovered, then settled on the landing pad an hour before the boys were due back from school. Dalo, at post upstairs, gave a low shout. "They're back!"

"Don't! Don't you open that door!" Aila ordered. "Let Tokh open it. Make sure it's him." She flew up the stairs, weapon in hand, charged down the hall into Zhenîhda's room, tore open the balcony doors and pointed her weapon at the first person she saw. Her head pounded with the motion, making her stomach flop. Inside, she heard the others rushing up the stairs to their designated safe places. Her eyes didn't want to focus, but what looked like blue uniforms were spreading out across the courtyard, weapons ready, searching.

"Nihda?" bellowed a cautious familiar voice.

Aila raised the rifle and squinted at the sight. "*Hoxt!* One step and you die. Say your name!" she ordered with as much force and threat as she could squeeze out. The outdoor light hurt her eyes and made her head ache worse, and the tip of the rifle trembled.

Tokh's weapon was already in his hand; Aila knew she didn't stand a chance against him. He could no doubt shoot the rifle from her hands and not even get dust on her, but it was all or nothing.

He looked up, saw her, or at least saw the weapon pointed at him, and raised his hands outward, though he didn't drop his weapon. "General Four Tokh dar-Gilahn, and you are standing in my house."

"Where's Masákh?" There were now at least four weapons drawn and aimed at her. One wrong move and she was toast. *Keep it steady.*

Down below, Masákh eased forward, arms out but weapon in hand. He wasn't a sniper like Tokh's son Kitras, but he had more than one marksmanship award. His voice was cautious, not angry or accusatory. "Aila? I am here. Lower the weapon. What's wrong? Why were the gates open? Why did no one answer our calls? Where are the guards? Where did you get a rifle?"

"Answer me, Masákh! Is it truth? How many of you are there?" She didn't lower the weapon to look at him.

"General Tokh, six *aghát*, and two *bhántanok* officers, the same as left this morning."

"You're sure? No one behind you? No one not accounted for?"

"With certainty."

Aila lowered the weapon; the men lowered theirs. "Hurry, then!"

The females rushed down the stairs. Zheníhda whipped open the front door but Mímihn seized Tokh first, unwifely and unladylike. Fahni seized Haghíde; at first he seemed afraid to touch her, then remembered she was his wife and it was allowed. Aila ran to Masákh with the rifle slung down her back, hugged him, and wouldn't let go. He gave her a brief embrace, felt the crustiness of her hair, and noticed the blood and the marks on her swollen face. Once again he became the terrible dark authority that frightened her.

His face went blank, his words bitten off with unmistakable precision. Aila backed up a step, but he closed the distance. "You will hand me your weapon. You will tell me how you were injured without missing a detail, and do not tell me you walked into a wall or tripped on a child. I will know the truth."

Aila surrendered the rifle. Tokh strode over and examined her head. He took the rifle from Masákh.

"I won it fair and square," Aila said with a scowl.

"Kh-J-T 1148, military issue only, twelve pulses per second," Tokh said. He pulled the powerpack, then placed it on the dining table. "Weapons. Any females with weapons, I want them on the table, now."

The women shuffled forward. Aila put down Masákh's dagger. Dalo put down Masákh's plasma gun, a dagger, and a sword she'd taken from the wall; it was a decorative item, but had a sharp tip and could have done serious damage skewering someone. Tokh's wives and Fahni dispersed a small arsenal of daggers and knives in an avalanche of clinking metal; Shanohr added two lethal butcher knives from the kitchen. Last, looking very guilty because they'd done it in secret, Faelihn and Kesseh stepped forward and added a meat-knife each that they taken from the kitchen, and Kesseh placed Joralan's razor-sharp training sword on the top of the pile. Zheníhda frowned, but no reprimand came forth.

The men stared at the pile. Aila snatched Masákh's spare plasma gun and danced out of reach. She stuck it in the waistband of her skirt. "Uh uh. No way. You can have this back when you're screwing a rat's ass in Hell." The room stared back at her; even Masákh couldn't connect the image. Aila rolled her eyes and sighed. "I'm not explaining it right now. I'm not giving this up. If I'd had it in the first place, my face wouldn't look like this."

Tokh pulled a chair from the table. "Sit. All of you. I will have answers. Nihda, I left you with strict instructions. Why was the gate open? Where are Unav and Drazis? Why did you not respond to my calls?"

Zheníhda acted as if nothing worse had happened than she'd dropped a tray of dinner rolls. She knew exactly what Tokh wanted to know and how to tell him. Aila understood why he called her his Little General. "Something is blocking out communications. They went out about three hours after you left. I checked the system as much as I know how. Aila and Fahni found one of the guards dead; we assume the other is as well. We didn't look for him, but we haven't seen him. We tried to barricade the house, but we couldn't keep out the intruder. We hid, but he did find us. It wasn't your guard. He wasn't wearing a uniform."

Tokh paled. "An intruder made it into the house? What did he do? What did he take? Was anyone hurt?"

"He wanted me," Mímihn said, shaking again. "Aila saved us. She spoke to him like a *bhísroti*. She lied to save me, and when he realized she lied, that's when he hit her. He was trying to drag me away when Aila killed him."

Tokh had been pacing before the table. He spun on his heel. "You what? Who? Where?"

"I don't know who," Aila said. "We didn't touch him beyond moving him. Fahni, Dalo, and I dragged him to the vehicle shed. He's under the tarps."

Haghíde stared at his new wife as if she'd appeared out of thin air. "You moved a body?"

Fahni nodded. Her excitement over the day sounded just like Haghíde. "I learned many useful things today, though you probably already know how to do them."

"Haghíde, Ráhnif – secure the gate. Make sure you wear gloves; you'll scan it for prints later. Then search for whatever is jamming communications and disable it. Masákh, Tótoghar, find the guards and tell me how they died. Mátokhan, Ghírandar, females, come with me."

"Kesseh, Faelihn, stay with the babies," Zheníhda ordered.

Tokh unwrapped the body and examined it. He pulled out the cloths, examined the wounds, photographed them with his com, then took photos of the man's face. It was hard to miss the head wound; the skin hadn't broken, but there was a small dent in the skull.

"Which came first?" Tokh asked.

Everything was still surreal, not registering as abnormal at all. There was an excitement among the ladies that belied the seriousness of what had happened, an eagerness to tell their story and a desire for praise for coming out alive. The feeling blocked any horror Aila should have felt, expected to feel, standing around a dead body as if it were a water cooler. Kerasím did strange things to people. "That was later. He was still moving a little, so I hit him with the rifle. I owed him one." She motioned smashing the weapon down as hard as she could. Tokh eyed her strangely, but nodded. He walked to the stairs at the back of the shed and called up them.

"Thrit!"

The *ghinadín* rushed down from his rooms. "*Sukh*, Lord General."

"Do you know anything about this body?"

Thrit's surprise was real, and Tokh saw it. "T'rit put no body t'ere, General. T'rit be upstairs. Guards no like T'rit."

"Did you know the guards are dead?"

Panic flashed over Thrit for just a second. He had no lie for the question. "T'rit see one on ground. T'rit not t'ink he supposed to be t'ere, so T'rit go back upstairs and close door, stay quiet." That was truth; he just didn't mention what happened between the two actions.

Masákh and Tótoghar entered. "Both shot in the chest, General," Masákh reported. "Wounds consistent with a plasma rifle. Unav is across the yard in the gardens."

"Get them in here. I don't want the neighbors spotting them." Tokh's com signaled from his hip, and he hit receive.

"Situation normal," Haghíde said. "Following protocol."

"Good. Aid Masákh and Tótoghar, meet inside."

Inside the house, Tokh transferred the photos to his computer. While the database searched for a facial match, he enlarged the photos of the wounds, measured them, stared hard at them. He had the ladies re-enact their hiding, the stabbing, how they dragged the body. The carpet looked clean but was still wet. He listened without comment, but he didn't seem happy.

He questioned Aila. "Tell me again how you killed him."

Aila shrugged. "I ran down the hall, grabbed a knife from my room, and came at him full force from behind."

"Show me." Tokh handed her a writing stylus and turned Dalo's back to her. Aila mimicked a vicious stab upwards, between the shoulderblade and spine.

Tokh wasn't buying it. "The wound is too wide for that."

"Of course it is," Aila said. "I shifted it back and forth to do the most damage. It sliced it wider."

"Which knife?"

Aila snorted and rolled her eyes. "I don't know! A metal one. You made us pile them all on the table. I couldn't tell you. I wasn't looking at it when I did it. I was kind of panicking."

Tokh nodded, and let her go.

Shanohr was trying to put food on the table when Tokh emerged from his office. "Everyone in the house was in that closet?"

"Yes, Tokh. Everyone but Thrit and your guards," Zheníhda said with annoyance.

Tokh pulled out a chair and sat. He drew his incentive stick, extended it, and called Faelihn and Kesseh before him.

"Faelihn, has your *bo* ever hit you with an incentive stick?" The girl nodded. "It hurts, doesn't it. It hurts very much. It can even make you bleed. I'm going to ask Kesseh a question, and if she lies to me, I'm going to hit you with mine. Each time she lies, I will hit you. I don't want to hit you; what I want is the truth. If she tells the truth, I don't need to hit you. Understood?"

Mímihn pulled on the girl. "You can't hit Faelihn! That's absurd! Why would you do that?" Tokh reeled Faelihn back.

Faelihn was horrified. "Why are you going to hit me if Kesseh lies? That's not fair! I didn't do anything wrong! Hit her!"

"That's the way the world works. Answer me, Kesseh: Who killed the man taking your *ama*? Someone else was in that hallway. Who was it?"

Kesseh's eyes went wide. She spun around to Zhenîhda, desperate for help.

Zhenîhda gave her husband an evil eye. "Stick to your officers, Tokh. You can't pick on young girls. You were given the answers how many times now. You're holding up dinner with your conspiracy games. Beat Faelihn and I will set Kitras against you."

"Please, *bo*-Tokh, don't hit her!" Dalo pleaded. "She's a good girl who's done nothing wrong! Why would Kesseh have any reason to lie to you? They're terrified by what happened today."

"I didn't see, *Bobo*!" Kesseh pleaded. "The door was in the way. That's the truth!"

Tokh was calm and patient, far beyond anything Aila had ever seen from him. This was a test, and he was willing to sacrifice his own smalldaughter for it, but was it better to give in or stay strong? She was sacrificing the child just as much as he was. The ladies would hate her, but they weren't giving in, either, even the child's mother.

"I didn't ask if you saw it. I know Great Lady Masákh didn't kill the bad man. Who else was in the hall? I need the truth, Kesseh." Tokh pulled Faelihn to his knees. Faelihn screeched and yanked on her wrist. "Veh... Moh..."

Kesseh burst into tears. She hung on the incentive stick. "Thrit! Thrit was upstairs, and he had the big long trimmer and it was sticking out of the man's belly. Please don't kill him, *Bobo*! Please don't kill him!"

The light went on over Tokh's head. "Thank you, Kesseh. A good lady always tells the truth." He kissed her on the top of her head. He kissed Faelihn and released her. "See? I told you I didn't want to hurt you."

Faelihn ran straight to her mother and buried her face in Dalo's side. "Stop it," Dalo said crossly, and made her stand. "You weren't hit, so why are you crying? Ladies of nine do not cry without reason."

"Ráhnif, tell Thrit to bring me the hedge trimmer." Tokh stood up and slipped the collapsed incentive rod into its holder. He faced Aila nose to nose. She stared right back, unflinching.

215

"You lied to me. I needed facts, not lies. I expect nothing less than truth. I should demand you be punished."

"I will not allow an honorable man to be put to death based solely on some bullshit caste label," Aila replied. "I have a small amount of leeway through diplomacy and caste. I insist on taking the charge."

Ráhnif entered, followed by Thrit carrying his weapon. He handed it over with a bow. There was a long metal blade leading to an insulated grip. When activated, a laser flowed around the edge of the blade, making trimming of garden plantings almost effortless. The width of the blade, the shape, matched the tearing and wound size on the dead man.

Tokh examined every inch. "Excellent job cleaning it, Thrit. I can't find a trace of blood or tissue. Yes, I know you were the one who killed the intruder. I want you to know something: look at these females. Outside of Shanohr, the lowest-caste female here is *whátaral* by marriage. The rest are all *dahneg* by privilege, currently the highest caste there is below Emperor. Not one would not break her lie to protect you. That's impressive, and you'd be hard-pressed to find that loyalty to a *ghinadín* servant anywhere else."

Thrit bowed. "It been a great honor to serve t'e General."

Tokh handed the trimmer back to Thrit. "There's one thing everyone here has forgotten. Dead men tell no tales. They can't deny a story. There are two dead brownshirts in my vehicle shed, left by me to protect my property. Any one of you could have told me the guard killed the intruder, and no one would ever have been the wiser."

The women all sagged with relief at the unseen solution, except Aila. She frowned. "That doesn't make any sense. How could the guard kill the intruder if the intruder killed the guard? He turned around with metal through his chest and fired? Or was the guard so caught in remorse he grabbed the weapon and shot himself clear across the yard?"

Tokh wasn't used to being questioned. His face darkened and he puffed himself up. "Do you know for a fact there was not a second intruder waiting outside? One that shot the guard as he walked outside but was scared off by something else, or recalled? Plasma fire is untraceable to a specific weapon; only intensity differs."

"No, I don't."

"Then it's settled. Drazis killed the guard, but was killed when he returned outside to speak with Unav, who was already dead. Two Captains died with honor in the course of duty and will be rewarded posthumously. I will contact their families later and explain their heroism. Thrit, please return the tool to its place. Thank you for your attention to detail. There will be a team here in an hour to remove the bodies. Nihda, my men and I will eat now."

Investigators came, but quietly, along with General-Four Asvarihn, a former-*fáhganid* justice officer for the Imahlva region. The generals sat in Tokh's home office behind closed doors, drinking *dhurwah*.

"This is dangerous, Tokh," Asvarihn said. "You should consider moving your family out of here. If they can breach your home, you aren't safe."

"To where?" Tokh shook his glass just a little, watching the black liquid swirl, going through the motions but not drinking much. He wasn't in the mood. "A hotel? How is that safe, with servants going in and out, never knowing who has touched the food? The palace? They assassinated the Emperor and several diplomats there, remember? Where is there adequate housing on a military base for ten people? I can't think of a place any safer than here. I know the layout of the grounds and building. I know the security system. I know where I failed, and what I'll fix tomorrow. There're seven fully trained *bhantim* officers here, and a crazy diplomat who sees herself as one of them and has a kill to her name. I won't be drawn out again until this is resolved."

"There's an idea," General Asvarihn said. "Send the Emissary back to the Embassy for safety, have her take your wife and child with her. No one can touch the Embassy. They have their own security; even we don't know what kind."

The more Tokh considered it, the more he liked the idea. "Will they allow it, or is that improper interference? Can she be a guest, or must she seek asylum to stay there? I can inquire, if need be. I'll keep it in reserve if all else fails. The danger lies in transportation."

Asvarihn pulled out his com, thumbed a setting, then handed it to Tokh. "We identified your intruder. Ozrahl Trangmun, age thirty-eight, a *nhásarwharl* mercenary from Soras Utep. He's done three turns in Thanas Kril regional prison for illegal activity. He made it as far as cadet before being dishonorably discharged from the military for being intoxicated on duty and firing a rifle into a crowd. Learned the rest of his training underground, a lot of activity in Kanok Sohr and other spots of unrest. He'd work for almost any cause, if the price was right; kidnapping females didn't even count as work. He's wanted for questioning in at least fifteen jurisdictions. Your guard would have received a substantial reward for taking him out, had he lived."

"Perhaps the reward could go to his family," Tokh suggested. "I lost two men; perhaps it could be split between them, as they were both on duty. They're lieutenants; no doubt their families can use the money."

"I can see to it."

"So who put out the contract?"

"They're tracking that now. Since we have your person under suspicion, it shouldn't take much to show a trail of payoffs. The problem," General Asvahrin said with a sigh, "is what we do with the information we find. Poking a nest like that can get you stung. You're high up now, Tokh, but maybe you haven't been there long enough. You're a top-level interrogator. You know a lot of secrets. Nághtas is dead, but there are a lot of people who hate Nadigh even more. Nadigh's cagey. He knows that, and his security is probably the tightest of any Emperor, ever. He's got databases you've never dreamed of. You're part of his Senate; don't be surprised if he knows the date you shot your first fluid. Nadigh's made tremendous changes which have proved good for the most part, but he's made enemies in the process, and some of them are very powerful. He knocked the *bhísroti* down but he didn't neutralize them. He left them their positions and their wealth, hoping to appease them, and for the majority it did. Those that took offense are moving their money and gaining power feeding insurrections and anarchy, fueling hatred."

Tokh stroked his chin hank, twirling it around his finger. "Kanok Sohr."

Asvarihn shook his head. "Not necessarily. Kanok Sohr and the whole Yomebor region is more about civil war among itself. Saying it wants autonomy from the Emperor brings money and weapons into the area, but it will never happen. It's the various local *bhísroti* and *fáhganid* families infighting for control more than anything, and getting the populace to fight for them without knowing it. It's a training

218

ground, yes, but then the real enemies leave and move out on their own, looking for chaos and greed to feed off elsewhere. If Engmar's son is involved as you think, that's a network you don't want to mess with. They have no rules of engagement, collateral damage means nothing, and the Emperor will cut you off to keep them from tainting him. If you go after him yourself, you risk losing everything."

Tokh swallowed his drink, waited for the burn to pass. "That's what annoys me, I think. Nadigh has the power to stop him cold. Look him up, share the information, and I will end this, but I've been told it's a personal matter and the palace doesn't interfere on personal matters. So unless it directly affects the palace, I'm on my own. I need locations, routines, personal data. I'll take care of the rest."

"I don't have a lot of contacts in those areas," Asvarihn said before draining his glass, "but let me see what I can do."

Thirty

Reality hit the ladies that evening. Neither of the girls could sleep; Dalo went in to sleep with them. Mímihn refused to sleep anywhere but next to Tokh, even if he insisted on *pushing* her, and she wouldn't sleep unless her dagger was under her pillow. Zheníhda waited an hour, then appeared in their room.

"Tokh, if you are done with your business, I would ask to sleep next to you as well. I don't trust the balcony doors." Never, not once, had Zheníhda voluntarily come to his room if another wife was there, even if all they were doing was talking.

"Of course, Firstwife," Mímihn said before Tokh could say a word. She slid over in the large bed to make room. "Thoren only wakes up once, and I'll be quick to quiet him so you can rest."

Tokh made room for her on his other side.

The day hit Aila all at once. Masákh had already removed his jacket and shirts and loosened his pants. He slid behind her where she sat staring into space on the lounging sofa, pulled her hair to the side, and nibbled slow kisses across the back of her neck.

"I have heard incredible tales of your bravery," he said against her skin. "You raised an entire army from a group of upper-caste females and children, armed them with forks and knives, incited them to follow you into death, killed a prisoner, locked down your fortress, and then threatened a Level-Four General, all without leaving your home. You even took responsibility for the actions of your troops to protect them. You are a fierce and able warrior. I pledge you my loyalty." He licked behind her ear, then sucked at her lobe.

Aila pulled away. "It's not funny, Masákh. You have no idea. Those women would have been dead or assaulted if I hadn't done something. They haven't been trained in paranoia like I have." She stood up and paced the room, fighting to keep her tears inside.

Masákh seemed hurt. "I was not making humor. I meant my words. Upper caste females aren't known for bravery and do not engage in violence. You had them armed and hiding bodies in a matter of hours. That's an impressive feat."

"I didn't make them anything," Aila argued. "I merely gave them permission to defend themselves by setting an example for them to follow. I wasn't going to be taken hostage again, and I wasn't going to let them get Mímihn. I tried, but I wasn't fast enough or smart enough. I should've gotten your weapon right away and I never would have gotten hurt. He never would have made it to the stairs. Kitras has taught Dalo some skills, maybe more than me, but Fahni was the real surprise. She was such a help – she knew exactly when to lie, and how, and she jumped right in. She's amazing. Haghíde knew right away he shouldn't let her get away from him, and he was right. She's the perfect wife for him."

He rose and wrapped her in his arms. "She isn't half as amazing as you. When I think I can't be more proud of you, you do something even greater. You're so much more than I could have imagined."

All day, Aila had wanted only one thing: Masákh's arms around her, holding her, protecting her. His skin was warm beneath her cheek, his chest hairless and so lovely to look at. The scent of his cologne was enough to induce relief; it was a part of him. Way back when, she knew he'd entered her cell by his scent alone; in the presence of that scent she knew nothing bad would happen to her. That feeling had intensified over the years. She depended on it. This moment, this very ten seconds of her life, was utter perfection, and she didn't want it to end.

Masákh broke the spell. He kissed her, gentle movements on her neck and face, but they invariably became stronger, and his hands started to undress her.

She pushed him away. "No, Masákh. Not tonight. The whole side of my head is killing me."

"This is Kerasím. By your own words, we follow Kerasi rules."

Aila turned to glare at him. "Your need to get off twelve times a day is more important to you than my well-being? Than my level of pain? I took a rifle-punch to the head. That doesn't make me feel like *pushing*. It's not like you didn't *push* me last night, or the night before. I'm very upset by today's events. *Pushing* is not in my thoughts right now."

Aila couldn't tell if he was disappointed or contrite. "You are correct. Your health should be more important than my desires. I'm distressed at your injuries, and that you feel poorly."

She returned to his arms. "Just hold me. I want you to hold me, and not let go."

To her relief, he did. Aila slept better than she expected, curled in Masákh's arms, his leg over hers, *hihvat* hot against her hip, the safest place in the universe.

And his blaster tucked between the mattress and headboard, just in case.

Tokh refused to leave the house. He had nothing pressing in Keranihn. He shuffled men about, called in his electronics team to revamp his security system, brought in four higher-ranking security guards with special weapons experience, and set four of the *aghát* to scanning the property foot by foot, searching for spy equipment.

Mímihn and Dalo missed breakfast altogether, coming down the stairs as Shanohr was putting away the last of the dishes. The room did a double-take.

Mímihn was unrecognizable. Her rich black hair was yellow against her golden-tan skin.

Daffodil yellow.

Daffodil, a foot shorter, and pulled up and flipped over the side of her head, to cascade down to her right shoulder in a fall of curls. Her shirt was high-necked but sleeveless, her skirt striped and angled and layered with black lace and twisted sideways, so the ruffles that should have spilled down the back now poured over her left hip, balancing the pull of her hair. Her makeup was different, accenting different parts of her eyes to give them a different shape. She looked strange and stunning and half-dressed and ultra-modern.

"Do you like it?" Mímihn posed several ways to show off her hair. "Dalo did it for me. She's right: all they had to do was look at a picture to find me. I need to hide myself in plain sight. Now I don't look like me." She spun a pirouette and ended with a flourish. "What do you think?"

The room pulsed with silence.

"It's very different," Aila said. "You're bright and shining and look like you just came from Keranihn."

"I would've gone really short on her hair," Dalo said, "but she didn't want to cut it all off."

"Thank you for that." Tokh stared, just stared, his face reflecting no emotion at all.

Mímihn whirled over and kissed him. "Do you like it?"

Tokh could have been staring through her for the blankness he showed. "I don't know yet. You're not you. If it helps, it's for the better."

She let go of him and went to the kitchen. Zheníhda watched her pass, not quite sneering but with a lowering of her eyebrow somewhere between disbelief and horror. "I don't know whether to plant you in the ground or pluck you and put you in water."

Mímihn laughed her sweet laugh, something they hadn't heard in days. Either she was pleased, or she'd lost her mind. "Oh, Nihda! I do feel like a sun-flower! Better pluck me and put me in water; I don't think it's safe to stand outside yet."

Thirty-one

Aila woke as Masákh climbed out of bed. She rolled over and grabbed for her com. No messages.

"Dammit!" She shook it with futility, as if the message were just misplaced inside her com and she could dislodge it into the text feed. "How many days has it been?" she said to Masákh in the lavatory. "I should've heard back about an extension or a ship long before this. Why haven't they answered my request?"

Masákh exited the lavatory and began to dress. "Are you sure they received it?"

Aila checked her queue. "Yes. It was received and opened on the day I sent it."

"Then I don't know. I suggest you call the liaison in charge of visitation. If you wish, I'll speak to Ráhnif about it. He may know a different person to contact. Lady Tokh's menace has threatened you indirectly and wounded you once. It may be best if we were to leave as soon as possible."

"It takes a week to get a ship out here, and they can't cross into Kerasi space without permission. You think they'd be sending me reminders that my time was up, and what flight was I taking out, and stuff like that."

"I'll work on it, if possible. I can sense your mother's anxiety increasing from here."

Aila bounced from the bed and kissed him on her way to the bathroom. "Don't you know it! Thank you, darling."

Masákh finished dressing, then checked his comm. The single message bore a sending ID of the palace. He made sure Aila was still in the other room and clicked it.

Pay attention to your assignment, Major. You were warned.

Masákh's heart rate sped up, and he felt his innards tighten. He slid the message out of the main feed and into a secure file before slipping the com into his jacket.

Breakfast and interacting with the household took Masákh's mind off the issue, but by the end his stomach was so knotted by impossibility he couldn't bear the thought of having to work alongside General Tokh all day, bear his hospitality, keep a friendly smile while being forced to destroy him, and send Lady Tokh, younger, to a violent and painful death. Tokh would kill him if he knew, and his teammates would piss on his corpse. Aila would kill him – at the very least leave him, which she could very legally do inside the Union. And by loyalty to the General, he was also bound to protect his wives. Did he not spend yesterday helping interview General Engmar, and investigating the death of a kidnapper? His wife had helped thwart the attack; his wife's actions reflected on him. Even with threats of violence – which Masákh swore many oaths he would never do – Aila would never allow Lady Tokh, Younger to be harmed.

General Engmar knew the trap. There was no escape. Aila needed to leave Kerasím. This day. And Masákh needed to accompany her. Leaving was the only chance to avoid the trap, but permission to leave had to come from the palace, the palace that wanted him to finish his assignment. They would never be allowed to leave until the task was done, but how did he explain to Aila her permission was probably not coming until Lady Tokh had been sacrificed?

There was only one person he might trust for advice, though he hated doing it. The last thing he needed was to appear weak, and he could feel the disdain sting him in advance. Masákh waited for his moment, then slipped into the lavatory so quickly Mátokhan nearly closed him in the door.

"I didn't know you liked watching other people take a piss," Mátokhan said. "It's not like you haven't seen my *hihvat* before. If you wanted a viewing, you could've asked. It's rather spectacular, I must admit." He proceeded to urinate as if Masákh wasn't there.

"I needed to speak with you privately."

Mátokhan finished, adjusted his trousers, and stepped around Masákh to wash his hands. "I see no one but the two of us. Your

225

breathing is giving away your mind. You must regain control, or others will be controlling you."

Masákh still bore his composure, but to anyone who knew him he was twitching like a leaf in a sudden breeze. "You're the only one I can speak with. You've been in the Circle for many years. I'm having difficulty with an order…"

Up snapped Mátokhan's finger. "Never! Never discuss an order with another. Your orders are yours alone. You must never discuss them except with the one who gave them to you. Orders do not exist."

"That's not the issue. You have orders, I have orders; that is assumed fact. What am I to do when there are conflicting orders? Which do I follow?"

"Conflicting with who?"

"When my Circle orders are conflicting with the oaths I swore as an *aghát*. I have not been released from the *aghát*. I took those vows years ago and I have never yet in my right mind violated them. If I'm given an order that compromises my oath, which am I to follow?"

Mátokhan pulled back, such a slight movement it wouldn't have been noticeable to anyone but Masákh. "You trust me too much, Masákh. We're Brother *aghát*, but Inner Circle has no brotherhood. You must never trust anyone. You've said too much already."

Masákh took a step forward, not giving Mátokhan escape. If he didn't resolve his issues, he would break more than one trust. "I didn't ask for this. I never wanted this. I'm *whátaral*; I should never have been given it, but we both know why it was done. All rules can be broken, when those in power wish a longer reach. I haven't acted on the conflict yet, but I see where the path leads. I need to know what I'm supposed to do when I hit that crossroad. Have you ever had such a crossroad?"

Mátokhan sighed. His lips pressed down with resignation, but his gaze was inward for a long pause. At long last he nodded. "Yes, but it resolved itself before it became critical. Once you're Inner Circle, it supersedes all other orders."

"That's unacceptable. I've never been asked to take any oath for the Circle. I've declared no loyalty. I haven't renounced my *aghát* position," Masákh insisted. "I was handed a badge on a ribbon without warning, congratulated, and told I was a member. That's it. No one has ever asked a thing of me."

Mátokhan laughed to himself, his arrogant amusement bubbling up. "Only you. Only you, Masákh. So uptight and indoctrinated that you can't deviate from the path they taught you. You were caught too young, my brother. They kept you moving down a corridor, never letting you see to the sides. You only know the straight path. You're a General's pleasure-dream. Why did they Inner Circle you? *Because* you're a General's pleasure-dream," he answered himself. "They know you'll carry out an order if it kills you. A few tests to prove it, and they know you won't fail. They have their puppet."

Mátokhan put his hands on Masákh's shoulders. "We are Tokh's *aghát*, One and Two. I haven't worked alongside you as much as the others because of that. You're excellent at what you do, that's not disputed, and when I'm a colonel assembling a team you will be one of my top choices, if I can sway you. I admit it, so bask in that praise. As Inner Circle, I can't speak to you on anything. Even a nod in recognition could be too much. But as your brother *aghát*, I will say this: look to the sides, Masákh. Look to the sides. Get your vision off the path before you and look to the sides. Look for the forces at work, see where they go, see how they affect the Emperor. You're a Major in the Kerasi army, an *aghát*; you know there are many truths. Find your truth and hold to it. Even under a scanner, if your narrow truth is true they can't break you. If you truly can't hold to it, then you need to make a choice. I don't know what will happen if you hand back your honor. You swore an oath to the Emperor at your commission, to protect and serve without regard to self and give your life to the Emperor should he request it. 'Loyalty, duty, honor to the Emperor.' Not your commander. Not your brethren *aghát*. *The Emperor*. Not Nághtas, not Nadigh, not even Rimas, should it come to pass. Just 'the Emperor,' whosoever holds the title. It was the Emperor who raised your caste, who raised your rank, who chose you for Inner Circle. If you hand that back, you break that oath. If you officially resign before an issue is public, then you may be safe. You'll be probed, lose your career and any chance at pension, but you may live, probably with infamy, possibly with exile. Make sure you weigh that into your decision."

Masákh's sigh was laced with audible pain. "You're correct. It doesn't help, but you're correct. So answer me this: at what point are we part of the problem, not the solution? And what then have we been working for, for the last *twenty years*, if not the solution?"

Mátokhan, so smug, so quick with sarcasm, so full of disdain, blinked in silence. The thought turned over and over in his head, but no witty answer came forth. There was almost melancholy in his voice when he said, "I think you've hit on a deeper truth than I ever realized. I must think on that. I don't know."

Masákh nodded, and opened the lavatory door. Mátokhan touched his elbow.

"Don't resign, Masákh. I meant my praise."

Masákh bowed his head. "I'm deeply honored, Brother *Aghát*. But what's the point, if the Emperor can tell me to refuse you?"

The more Masákh thought about it, the more he realized the two orders were not mutually exclusive. *Look to the sides*, Mátokhan said. *Find your narrow truth, and you will be unbreakable.* Sides. What would the palace – the mighty Emperor Nadigh the most powerful, ruler of all Kerasím, care about the wife of a senate member? Did she bear secrets they feared? Did he know her from her before-times? Was she a pawn to control Tokh? Did Tokh's investigation step on a sore toe, and by controlling his wife, they could control him? The scope began to unfold before his eyes, and he found a cowardly solution, breaking neither vow. He sought out Tokh.

"Speak, freely," Tokh invited. "If it's not solid information, I'm open to the smallest of possibilities."

Masákh bowed. "Lord General, I fear that we have reached an impasse in the current investigation. Without resorting to risky illegal means, there is little more we can do until the perpetrator makes a fatal mistake. While my time here belongs to you, it is only a matter of days before a ship will arrive to return us to our Union duties, jobs we're in jeopardy of losing from the length of time we've been away. In the days remaining, I have a line of insight I wish to investigate that pertains to your issue. It may prove to be blocked, but I would like to explore it as long as I can. However, it would mean starting out in Ganjamir City and pursuing leads from there. It will be necessary to be away for as much as a week, working leads around the clock and wherever they take me. I don't trust communications, but could meet with others to relay new information. I would like your permission to pursue my leads."

"Elaborate."

"I would rather not, General. My ideas are no more than possible tangents to follow. With luck, it will circle around to meet the goal."

Tokh sat back and gave him an amused stare. "Your wife is disagreeing with you already?"

Thank you, General, for the easy out. Masákh gave a chuckle and spoke a narrow truth. "She's growing restless with the wait for permission to travel. I'm sure you're aware it's difficult to carry out investigations with females making demands of your time. I merely wish to work a few days uninterrupted. I have faith my wife will be safe here, and that she'll prefer the female companionship to watching me work."

Tokh spread his hands. "Of course. Very well. Keep me informed as to your investigation. I have no contacts in Ganjamir, but General Narrah is in nearby Jabarani. I'll ask him to lodge you with his men."

"You are most gracious, my Lord."

Aila watched Masákh pack in horror. It never took him more than five minutes to pack to leave anywhere; the trained soldier wore mostly uniforms, and knew how to flee in an instant. Some emergency rations, his electronics, his grooming kit, and he was ready for anything from a trip to the palace to acting as advisor and translator in hostile alien territory.

"What do you mean, you're leaving on a mission?" Aila said. "You're leaving me here like a suitcase you'll come back for at some point? Where are you going? What are you doing? Why aren't you taking me with you?"

Masákh smiled, but Aila wasn't sure what to make of it. It wasn't one of his tell-tale expressions. He stopped moving and took her by her shoulders. "This, now. You're married to a Kerasi officer. This is what we do. We leave to perform tasks, then return home. Ask your wife-friends. You know I can't discuss my work with you. I expect to remain here in Gada – you would probably call it a country; we call it a region or section – and I will cut short my tasks and return as soon as you receive permission to travel. Officers do not bring wives on missions."

Aila stared, hurt and fear accusing him of deliberate abandonment. "Every time you leave me, something bad happens. I let you go for your training; that's enough. Look what happened the other day!"

"And you handled it perfectly. I cannot have more pride for you. Your thinking and strategies saved a houseful of females. If it will ease your distress, I'll trust you with my spare weapon, as long as you agree to keep it hidden and not announce the fact. You've stayed at Tokh's before without incident. I trust the General."

"Without incident? Your sorry wounded ass wasn't here when Vanora tried to kill me, if you'll recall. Tokh had to save me."

Masákh paused. "I did forget that portion." He closed his bag and hefted it. "Either way, I must leave. I'll call you if and when I'm able. Please do not call me unless it's a dire emergency." He moved toward the door; Aila followed him.

"Don't call me, I'll call you. In the Union, that's the moment women become suspicious there's another wife somewhere, and you're two-timing them. We've been married two whole weeks. That's just lovely. What's her name?"

Masákh was already to the stairs, but he spun around and stroked her face. "On the honor of the Emperor, I'm keeping nothing from you. I have no other wife, nor interest in one. If I could take you with me, I would. I enjoy our conversation and I rely on your insight and I most certainly will miss your warmth against me when I'm alone in the dark. You spend your time as a diplomat trying to understand the issues faced by Kerasi women; you are now a Kerasi wife, on Kerasím. Learn how to be one."

Aila watched his back descend. "I will never become your mother!"

Thirty-two

Aila watched Masákh leave. Her head whirled in confusion. Why would he do this? Old fears came flooding back. No matter what her fears, no matter how afraid she was, good things happened when Masákh was with her, bad things happened when he wasn't around. Sure, all the psychotherapists her parents had forced on her – every one – had pointed out it was a standard tactic to make a victim dependent on a person, a simple act of conditioning, and it had nothing to do with reality. Aila did many things during a day for years without Masákh, and nothing bad had happened. Aila's head understood that. But experience was a separate fact from logic. Here she was, six years later, no longer a prisoner, and Masákh had left her side for just a day – and she hadn't been overly upset – and the house had been broken into, people died, and she'd been threatened and clobbered in the head. That wasn't a planned manipulation tactic. Last year, when Masákh was injured rescuing her and in a hospital for a week, her own people – both Secretary Kel, and then Vanora Aikerman, made every effort to kill her off. That wasn't a plot by the Kerasi people, nor any mental manipulation on Masákh's part. That was reality, pure and simple.

And now he'd left her, by his own design, without telling her his destination, and she was all alone without him.

There was no other explanation. He had a secret wife. She was actually his second-wife, and he had to attend to the first.

Maybe he even had children she never knew about.

Mímihn caught her crying silently at the window.

"Ai-lah! Why do you cry?"

Aila sniffed and wiped her eyes on her fists. "He left me, and wouldn't even tell me why. Just, 'a mission.'"

Mímihn stared at her blankly, but Aila continued to weep. "He's an officer. That's what they do. They go, they work, they come back. It's

231

not your place to know what they do. If he's able, he'll discuss it when he returns."

"What if he's lying? In the Union, when a male leaves his wife and won't tell why or where, it means he's doing something wrong. He might be seeing another female, or already have a wife and family he didn't tell you about. What if he lies?"

Mímihn still studied her as if Aila had three heads and Mímihn wasn't sure which one she was supposed to talk to. She shrugged in confusion. "That's what soldiers do. They don't lie, because lies will be discovered and they'll be punished. If Masákh had another wife, Tokh would know about it. What did he tell you?"

Aila sniffed again. "That my job is supposed to be to learn about Kerasím. I'm now a Kerasi wife, and I should learn what it is to be one. Every time I've been here, it's been a holiday, or a party, or a crisis, and those aren't normal days. Even now, you're under threat. I spent one whole day alone with his mother, and it was one of the most unbearable days I have ever spent on Kerasím."

"That's true," Mímihn said with a tinge of sadness. "But come. Sit on the patio and I'll get the wives. We'll drink *raffin* and tell you about our days."

Dalo and Fahni joined them on the patio, and with a little effort Mímihn coaxed Zheníhda as well. Fahni hugged Aila before she sat.

"You're not alone," she confessed. "I cry every time Haghíde leaves me, but I don't let him know. I'm once a widow; I don't wish to be one twice. I like him so much, I don't want to lose him."

"You get used to it," Dalo said. She kept a sharp eye on Niboh, running between the gardens on the stone paths, playing with a *rahl*-ball. "Kitras and I are married twelve years. He's involved in all kinds of dangers. Snipers and secret operatives don't patrol street corners. I had to make myself stop worrying, or I'd be forever in the clouds. It's easier when you have children. You miss your husband, but the baby demands all your thoughts, so there's no time left to worry and you have someone to talk to. I don't think about bad things."

"In twelve years, Vihren will be seventeen, and I won't have to worry so much," Fahni said. "My first marriage lasted six years; I can only ask the Fortunes that my second will be much longer."

"Niboh! Do not pull my flowers!" Zheníhda said. She stared sourly into her *raffin* cup. "I knew I shouldn't come out here. You're all new

232

wives, every one of you. You make me feel as old as the empire. Wait. Wait and see what your worship does when it's twenty-five years later and he brings home a second-wife. Or a third. Or he's gone for more than a year at a time with no word, and then he comes home thinking he rules the house, even though he's never there. Wait until he's wounded, but they won't tell you how bad, or how many months you'll have to nurse him back to health on top of caring for your children. You'll be bitter at the army as well. Back in Ierot Thoran, there was a wife whose husband took shrapnel to his head. He was unable to walk, could barely feed himself, and he was only twenty-eight. She would have to care for him like a baby to the end of his days."

"What did you do, then?" Aila asked. "How did you fill your days? In the Union, women at home read and discuss books with others, or work, or volunteer, fill their days with meaning. You can't do most of that."

The look Aila received wasn't comfortable, but Zheníhda remained civil. "You find a routine. You keep a clean house. You shop. You take your children out to play. You can watch the ComNet or listen to books. You make friends with the people in your building, or your neighbors, and then all the wives go out for entertainment together. Some females run little businesses out of their apartments, whether making clothing, or jewelry, or painting dishes, or cutting hair or such, and the women of the building visit them for services and gossip. You can have a very full life without your husband around. But that's in the shelter of apartments. Imahlva is too high-caste. Everyone is spread out."

She stood and took her cup before looking down her thin nose at Aila. "We're not as dull as you think we are. When you visit they blow up my yard, invade my home, leave bodies in my gardens, and threaten my smallchildren. Not one other person in this town has those issues. Nothing's normal when you're here."

As she turned to the house, a female's distant screech sounded thin through the peace of the neighborhood. Zheníhda's head snapped up, the rest of the ladies all spun around, but the house blocked the view of the far end of the yard.

"That wasn't me," Aila said.

A male's voice followed it, shouting, but the words were indistinct.

"Who is it?" Mímihn said. "I can't see that far."

The female screeched again.

"I don't know," Zhenihda said, listening hard. She put the cup down.

Strained whisper-shouts rained down from above. "Nihda! Nihda! Open your gates for us! We want to see as well!"

Something was happening. "Hurry!" Zhenihda answered, even though it meant shouting up a hill to a formerly-*fáhganid* house in Imahlva and expecting a reply. She ran inside to hit the switch for the gate. Mímihn hefted Thoren onto a hip, and Dalo snatched Niboh before they all rushed to the other end of the property. Ghírandar and Haghíde ran out behind Zhenihda, weapons drawn.

Here by the street, the shouting was much louder, but still no one was visible. Over and one up, the *dahneg* neighbor Gilmaneg was out on his balcony with his two wives and his beastly fat consort, watching the neighborhood with spyglasses to his eyes. He had pinpointed a house on his side of the street, far below.

Haghíde stood in the road, taking in every detail and looking for trouble. "Stand back! You shouldn't be near the street. What's happening?"

"We don't know yet," Fahni said, peeking around the gate, "but it's that way."

"Decoy?" Ghírandar said.

"Possibly," Haghíde replied.

"Don't be silly," Mímihn said. "It's not about us. Go back inside. Leave the females to female things."

Down the side of the street hustled *fáhganid* Judge Wahtegahn's two wives, Arshmuhn and Gahna, and their housemaid Darain, along with the young once-*bhísroti* wife Jália from the house once more up the hillside, escorted by her *nhásarwharl* servant. They dove inside the gate, Arshmuhn ten years older than Zhenihda, eighty pounds heavier, and winded from rushing.

She fanned air toward her face. "Uh! Uh! Fortunes give me breath! I'm too old to run like that. I knew it couldn't last. Rakhnar must have found out."

Ladies whose husbands were home stood on their balconies, trying to see over rooftops and through the landscapings, pocket coms in hand. Those whose husbands weren't home scurried down the street like stalking cats, gate to gate, with or without servants to escort them.

The noises continued. Sometimes words could be heard; from the gate it sounded like two men arguing, a female crying, punctuated now and then by screams and pleading. From the top of the hillside came the piercing klaxon of an emergency vehicle, a second, then a third, their orange lights flashing in sets of three. They skirted slowly down the steep street as far as they could, making wives dodge to the sides. When they reached the level where the cliff dropped and the street turned to stairs, they parked and moved en masse down the walking lane to the house three down and second-row back.

Zheníhda leaned out the gates, standing on her toes for a better view. "Pehris," she confirmed. "Having the law here doesn't bode well. Who called it in?"

"I don't know," Arshmuhn said.

"How far is she?" Mímihn asked quietly.

"Mmm, I'm not sure," Gahna said. "She's definitely showing."

Mímihn said nothing, but pressed her lips together and looked upset.

"What's going on?" Aila whispered.

The lowest row was *dahneg*, tiny homes clinging to the cliffs. Jália gazed across the houses. She was beautiful, perhaps the most beautiful *bhísroti* Aila had ever seen, in her early twenties with light bronze skin, high cheeks, and lovely dark eyes brushed with a perfected hint of makeup. She wore a blue veil over her hair and under her chin in a gorget. A jeweled net of silver chain sat over it, studded with dark blue stones and a large cabochon that hung in the center of her forehead. She moved with the air of a goddess.

"Pehris has been having an affair for the last two years. Her husband Rakhnar had suspected so, but couldn't prove it. It sounds like he caught them."

Gahna pressed her hands to her face. "He's going to kill her. She's such a sweet girl."

Zheníhda pulled out her hand unit and tapped the images. "What's going on?" she asked. She nodded several times before cutting the call. "Tanoor says we can stand with her."

"Stay here," Haghíde said, pistol ready. "Let us assess the situation first."

"You will not," Zheníhda said with authority, and pushed him aside. "This is the business of females. We're going, but you may accompany us."

They moved together as a cluster, peering out the gate, then running on tiptoes across the street and down two houses. Thrit appeared at Mímihn's elbow as they hit the street; he hadn't been in sight a second before. He caught the eye of Jália's servant and opened his mouth in a mocking noise that was half-laugh and half screeching animal. The servant glared at him and curled his nose and lip in a sneer that made him look like a rabbit about to attack, and he gave a deep, angry growl. Aila gave them a brief glance, but didn't have time to inquire.

They picked up several lone females as they scurried, Haghíde walking behind Zheníhda and Ghírandar covering rear. The cluster turned at the first house at the bottom with the instinctive grace of birds in flight, rushing across the house's yard to where more than a dozen neighbor ladies had gathered. From over the dividing wall they could see most of the action in the small courtyard of the next house. One male was on his knees, hands bound; another argued loudly with six armed city officers. A pregnant female knelt on the ground, wailing. Her hair was a mess, her veil on the ground, and the sleeve of her blouse torn.

Dammar, of across-the-street-and-back-one, waved Zheníhda forward. "Hurry. They're nearly done."

"Did he catch them together?" Zheníhda asked in a whisper.

"Worse," Dammar said. "Rakhnar had them run a test on the baby. It's not his."

The group, minus Aila, gave a collective gasp.

"Poor Pehris!" someone mumbled.

"She's still alive and kicking," Jália said. "That's something."

"He must truly love her," Mímihn said. "Or he wishes to make her suffer. It's too soon to know."

The gathering gave a mournful hum of agreement. Two officers took the bound man and walked him to a vehicle; two escorted the wife to another, while Rakhnar, perhaps in his forties, his face an apoplectic brown, stalked behind them to the third vehicle. He wore a cape despite the heat, intimidating his targets and announcing his status to the city officers. His head turned to glare at the wives as they crunched closer together.

"Go ahead! Go ahead and stare!" he shouted at them. His finger accused them, then waved wide to include all the watching eyes above them. "Every one of you who knew this was happening is just as guilty! Don't be surprised if your husbands root you out as well! A curse on every one of your *lihxu*!"

"*Gah!* Like he knows what goes on," Arshmuhn sniffed. "I know more than he dreams of. If he cared about her at all, it wouldn't have happened." The crowd gossiped for a bit, then broke up so they could disperse as a group.

"What will happen to her?" Aila whispered to Mímihn as they trudged up the hill. They swapped the baby back and forth when their arms tired. "Will he order her put to death?"

"The Emperor has forbidden that without proper reason," Mímihn reminded her. "I don't know if that counts. It remains up to her husband. She can't be held accountable for the affair; that's entirely on her lover. He can be publicly shamed, beaten, fined, or castrated if Rakhnar wishes. He can divorce Pehris, force her lover to marry her, he can keep the child or order it terminated, or any combination. We will have to wish for the best. He didn't seem to be in a forgiving mood right now."

"No, he didn't," Aila agreed. They reached the gate and turned in. Thrit hung back and gave Jália's escort a final mocking noise, accompanied by several obscene gestures before following the ladies and closing up the gates.

Dalo burst into laughter as they crossed the yard. "Well, we don't have to watch the ComNet programs today. We had a theater performance live, all to ourselves. That's something. Perhaps they should write a story in Imahlva."

"Does that happen often?" Aila asked.

"Of course not!" Fahni said. "If it did, we wouldn't be so interested. Actually, that is the first female I've ever known where that happened." She caught Haghíde's eye and gave a blushing smile. "Some of us have no need."

The discussion went on all day, and Aila learned many things about the seemingly sheltered lives of Kerasi housewives. It was difficult to tell what was "normal" and what was caste-dependent, as they were in an exclusive neighborhood. Dalo had been born *dahneg,* married down to *dihnarwharl,* and now had *dahneg* privilege again, but Mímihn had been born *rhibani* and married her way up, Zheníhda had been born *nhásarwharl* and married a *dihnarwharl,* and Fahni was born *dihnarwharl* and was now married to a *whátaral.* Everything here seemed another world entirely from Masákh's *rhibani* mother's dull, almost bitter life. Somehow, Aila couldn't see his mother having empathy for a female pregnant with another man's child, even if she'd been married against her will.

Aila slipped outside to find Thrit as the sun was setting. He sat on a small plastic chair outside the vehicle shed, watching the sky roll through its kaleidoscope of colors over the water, puffing on a fat roll of whatever dried leaves the Kerasi used for tobacco. Aila's nose twitched at the heavy smell. Smoking was frowned upon in the upper castes; Tokh didn't tolerate it anywhere in his presence. Smoking in the trenches could give away a soldier's position; smoking in barracks made everyone stink and was bad for the lungs, cutting down on fitness. Smoking could start fires. Anyone on his payroll kept their habits hidden.

Thrit noticed her and stood up quickly, hiding his hand.

"Sit! Sit, please." Aila knelt on the ground a polite distance away "Continue. I'm not here as *dahneg.* I'm here as Human. I have much to learn. Please, may I ask you questions?"

Thrit squatted; sitting on a chair when a superior knelt was not permissible. He took a puff of his roll. "T'rit not know much. T'rit know Great Lady doan make talk with *ghinadin.* T'rit know Great Lady take too many risks. See t'at on t'ComNet."

"*Gah.* There are no risks to being friendly except that you might make a friend. I like talking with you, Thrit. I'm Union; we don't recognize caste, you know many things, and I'm here to learn. This morning, what were you doing to the *bhísroti* servant? You made noises to each other. Is that a greeting between servants, or was it rude?"

Thrit gave a deep chuckle and sucked on his tobacco. It took well over a minute for him to answer, never looking at her, just the sky colors.

"He *trixorihn*, t'at one." He paused to spit on the ground. "T'ink he *bhísroti* working in t'at house, but he just *nhásarwharl*. T'rit see many *nhásarwharl* come and go. Great men, much honor. Some of t'e General's men, many ribbons. Not one servant." Thrit spat again. "Anyone can wipe *aaka*. *Aaka* smell t'same from *bhísroti* or *ghinadín*."

Thrit pulled on his roll and gave another distant, disturbing laugh. "T'rit know T'rit *ghinadín*. T'rit remember living in t'Mounds. T'rit not pretend. But T'rit do t'job, stay clean, make no trouble. Move to better job. Move to better job. General hire T'rit to protect Consort. T'rit 'spect wild female wit' jealous owner, make trouble, but she just baby, very frightened, no eyes already. T'rit feel bad. She tough one, though. Big *khatas*. She too nice to T'rit, say we equal, both servants, treat T'rit like *tápatihn*. General not jealous kind. Very kind to consort. T'rit see it. Kind to T'rit. Never talk bad. Never hit. No one ever t'at kind to T'rit. T'rit work very best for General. An' he take T'rit places... Places *nhásarwharl* fool never dream."

Thrit laughed again, remembering. "T'is *ghinadín* not soldier, but been on soldier ships, wearing fancy uniform. T'is *ghinadín* sail between t'e stars, like Fortunes of Night. T'is *ghinadín* walk streets on Union world like spy, no one know it. No one spit on T'rit. All people say Bright Morning. Doan know words t'ey say, but know voice, see happy faces. T'rit gain trust of General; he break laws, trust so much. T'rit make sure to keep trust. He marry consort, give her eyes, no need T'rit now, but still he keep T'rit, pay too well. T'rit serve house, clean yard, do best work. Give T'rit rooms like *rhibani*. Know too much of General's business, an' he still trust T'rit more.

"T'at *nhásarwharl*, he got none o' t'at. He have caste to do anyt'ing, but he just servant. T'rit just *ghinadín* castrate, but T'rit have more respec'. He t'ink he everyt'ing because he servant to *bhísroti,* one step below Emperor. He forget he doin' T'rit's work. He forget *bhísroti* now *dahneg*, and General is *dahneg*. We bot' on same street, look at same sunset. T'rit not take *aaka* from *nhásarwharl*. T'rit see Emperor with own eyes, right here in General's yard. *Nhásarwharl* never see t'at. Yes, General or Little General notice, get complaint, T'rit get trouble, but General unnerstan'."

Aila gave a soft laugh. "Little General? You mean First-wife Zheníhda, don't you."

239

"Gaaah. Not say not'ing. Not give names. Many Generals here, giving orders." Thrit stuffed his roll in his mouth to plug it.

Aila still smiled. "I've heard the General say it. Don't worry. Thank you, Thrit. Thank you again for saving everyone the other day. General Tokh knows many things, and he knew you were the best servant anywhere. He must be so relieved to have you here."

Thrit dragged on his roll, then waved a hand at her. "Go! Go back to house, before someone see you speaking wit' *ghinadín.* Make husband mad, he see you. Soldiers tell him what you do, make big trouble for T'rit. Go!"

Aila stood and bowed anyway. "Pleasant evening, Thrit."

Thrit watched her leave, drawing a puff with a dangerous glimmer of self-satisfaction.

Thirty-three

Masákh never saw General Narrah; he was told to report to an address that wasn't so much a safe-house as a dormitory-on-the-fly. Officers and soldiers on their way to other places, awaiting reassignment, or perhaps recovering from medical treatment but not yet ready for duty would be given a bed in the house, which held up to ten soldiers at once. Five others were currently in residence, giving him a fair amount of privacy. The other men were friendly and pleasant, prodding him with endless questions about the *aghát* program, did the surgery hurt, how could they join it, what was the Union like. They were decent men; though he didn't know their specialties or their training, Masákh didn't have the heart to tell them they were likely too old and didn't have a *nunu*'s chance of getting accepted.

He had full access to the ComNet and military databases, but Masákh didn't know General Narrah beyond what he gleaned off his handcom on his ride to Jabarani. Public information often belied private concerns, and thus there was no basis for trust. Instead, he hired a vehicle to take him on the forty-five minute ride to the military base at the spaceport and use their computers. Being in the Kerasi military had its perks: anyone could hop a military flight going anywhere free of charge just by showing ID and turning up; the plane was going that way anyway. Next flight won't leave until morning? Show your ID to the person in charge, and they would see if an empty bed was available on base, and chances were you had a bed and a meal for the night. Having a Major's rank, *aghát* clearance, and Inner Circle pull? Masákh might sweet-talk his way into anything, including the palace if he dared.

He sat outside at the Emperor Kumroh Spaceport in the memorial courtyard dedicated to those who had lost their lives in space. It was beautiful and secluded, with flowers, shrubs, and a tall cement fountain blasting upwards like a vapor trail, then falling back to ground. He needed a direction to start in, but what? What did he know? What had

241

he overheard? General Engmar feared his son, claimed he had fallen in with a violent crowd. Violence usually carried some type of detention record. Military crimes would be listed in the military records, but Engmar's son was not military. One: Engmar's son wanted to reclaim Mímihn, as vengeance to Tokh. Two: the son had enough contacts to find out where Tokh lived – and gain access to a high-caste neighborhood. Three: Tokh's attempt to locate Engmar's son was treading on something no one wanted disturbed. Four: large amounts of money were needed for that much surveillance and attempted kidnapping. Tokh feared the money came from illegal sources. Which ones, and why would the palace be so upset about Tokh finding out that they would sacrifice Tokh's wife? What was really going on? Someone had a very long reach.

Engmar was the link to all of it. He would start there.

Five hours later, Masákh was a virtual expert on the life of the late General Three Engmar, thrice decorated for bravery, a man so afraid of his only son he took his own life rather than face him again. The son was mentioned in the various biographies as having a difficult past, but Masákh was unable to pull up Engmar's financial records beyond a few public investments; not with a *whátaral* Major's rank. *What next?* He called Ghírandar. They were a team, each with special abilities. Ghírandar had law access.

"You've no doubt already pulled the records for the General. Can you send me the court records for Engmar's son?"

"I can do that," Ghírandar said. "Each charge was public, so there shouldn't be a problem with a list of public information on a private individual. I can have it for you in three or four hours when I'm able to access it. Just keep it secure in case."

"It will be done," Masákh promised. He called Tótoghar. Tótoghar was an avid reader of biographies, able to pull comparative conclusions across reams of life stories, and thus interpret motivations and failures in history.

"So what now, Togha? I have every scrap of information I can gather, but it's not helping. Ghírandar's information might help me, but it won't necessarily solve it."

Tótoghar laughed. "I take it you're not one to read the indexes at the back of the book. Primary sources, my friend. Time to get your boots dirty. Start at the source and knock on doors. Interview people. Press for the information no one has mentioned. It's out there. Ten investigators may have spoken to them already, but there's always something they forgot to mention. Get that bonus, and you've got your lead."

Masákh hopped a transport to the son's last known address while he waited for Ghírandar's information.

It was an odd place to see a *dahneg* sitting with a former *fáhganid*, a little picnic area near the side of a road between the villages, where the hillside fell steep and created a natural viewing spot over the water in the distance. Persons of that caliber didn't sit by a road; they sat in taverns and private little clubs where they wouldn't be defiled by the lower castes. Tokh and Trannor sat there anyway with bottles of *muhr*, just two travelers pausing for a rest. In reality, it was the safest place for them to speak to each other. There were no trees nearby to hide listening equipment and no reason for them to be there, they could see both the street and the air, and any other travelers who wanted to stop would be intimidated by them and keep a wide berth. Here, they could speak with perfect privacy.

The silence lasted several minutes before Trannor spoke. "Have you made progress on your 'issue'?"

Tokh let the words float on the air before answering. "I'm still waiting for the needed assistance from your department. Each passing day increases the likelihood something dangerous will happen to my family, and if it does, I may have to take matters into my own hands, and I won't care about the damage I create."

Trannor's face clouded over, and he gripped the bottle of *muhr* as if he planned to use it as weapon. "I've explained to you quite clearly, Tokh, why I cannot get involved. The issue is closed."

Tokh rolled his lips around. "No, you've explained why you fear getting involved. *Fáhganid* fear little. Perhaps we should discuss your fear instead."

"I don't fear you, Tokh. It's you who should know to fear me."

Tokh's eyebrow raised in disapproval as he pulled his noose. "How old were you when you found out the truth about your biological father?"

Tokh dangled from a dangerous limb. It was a vague, open question, said on speculation, with no proof. The flicker of terror in Trannor's eyes told him all he needed to know.

The light darkened over Trannor, and the *fáhganid* privilege rose stormy and true. Tokh had never seen him so angry, a towering, smoking rage that would have sent greater men running. His voice rose with it.

"You dare call me a bastard? Desecrate the name of my father, *Fáhganid* Royal Justice Rusitahn?"

The fact Trannor jumped to that conclusion almost insured the guess was truth. Tokh pretended this was a simple interrogation and the rantings were the distraction of a guilty man, not someone who could take his head before he could flinch. His face stayed cold as stone, his voice factual.

"There's an 83% correlation of facial features between you and the current Emperor, 69% with Advisor Moragh. There is a 66% correlation with your brother Kursan, but a 32% correlation in features between you and Royal Justice Rusitahn Shill, by our own security software. Your parents of record both worked for the palace. How old were you when you learned the truth?"

Trannor's glare could have melted titanium. "You can be imprisoned for making that claim. Before you even think to stand up."

Tokh dared to meet the burning eyes. "Imprisoning me will not change the truth, only insure that the information does not remain private."

"You can't win at your folly, Tokh dar-Gilahn. I can erase your career with one call."

"You either trust me or you don't, General Trannor. The choice is yours. I'm unaware of anything I have done to lose your trust."

Trannor's shoulders eased, and the storm cloud thinned. He sat back unhappily, daring himself to trust truth. "What were you after? What made you run a feature ID?"

"In truth, nothing," Tokh said, blinking at last. "I saw a photo of you and the Emperor standing next to each other at an event. It struck me how similar you were in structure, your height, your shoulders, the way you stood. You said you had grown up as friends with the Heir. I made a wild guess, and ran the comparison."

"Who else knows?"

"No one I'm aware of. So I'm correct in my assumption?"

"Tokh, if that speculation leaves this table, it is fact that I will kill you, your wives, see that your son is dishonorably discharged, and ensure that your other sons will never be accepted to any Academy on this planet. I'll marry your daughter myself if I must. You fear your family is in jeopardy; that information loosed will most certainly jeopardize mine, and I won't allow that risk to move beyond this table."

Tokh bent his head in honor. "Then you understand my plight. I apologize for my troublesome weak memory."

Trannor sighed. He gazed over Tokh's head at the skyline in the distance, a picturesque view of clouds and water and reflected sunbeams framed by red-leafed trees. "Nothing I've said is false. My father was a Royal Justice, my mother a Lady Servant to Naghtas's daughters. I was allowed to be a playmate for the Heir at the age of five onward, and we are the closest of friends. I was twenty-two when I learned we are also brothers."

"Illegitimate."

"Among countless others, but because I was born at the palace, they knew. No one can refuse the Emperor. If he *pushes* your wife, you thank him for the honor. My father knew. He was paid quite handsomely to remain quiet. Nadigh is born of Naghtas and Erillori, his second wife. Moragh is born of Naghtas and Merilar, his third wife. Turweg was born of Naghtas and Trenahra, his eighth wife, and Naghtas the Younger by his twelfth wife Lassehne. I have the same amount of brotherhood and royal line to Nadigh as do Moragh, Turweg, and Naghtas the Younger, but I was not born of a Royal Wife."

Tokh frowned. "So that leaves you in line for the throne, should Nadigh, Moragh, and the infant all die."

Trannor swallowed a mouthful of the *muhr* and shook his head. "No. I'm not acknowledged. Even if I present blood evidence, I was not acknowledged by Naghtas. His infant son Naghtas was born after his death, thus he is also not acknowledged nor able to take the throne. The Palace knew, hence I was allowed to play with the Heir and given great privileges, but I don't wish the throne, have signed that I'll never accept it. Should both sons die, and assuming Rimas died as well, the line could either shift sideways to Naghtas's brother Durghid, or skip down to Rimas's son Targha. That would depend on Senate vote. I would remain on the sidelines, perhaps as advisor, but that's as close as

I wish to come. A *fáhganid* can never take the throne. Nadigh knows the truth, as does Durghid.

"That, Tokh, is why I can't get involved. Anything I do can be seen as coming from Nadigh, and that's a disruption of power he doesn't need at the moment. I want to help you – I understand your pain, and I do fear for your family, that is truth – but because of my ties I can't move a finger that might be seen as having palace approval. With palace scrutiny on me I can't even send guards to patrol your street. I can send a flyover twice a day, but that won't help."

It couldn't have been an easy childhood, watching the privilege your friends received and knowing you could never achieve the same, and then after all that time finding out your lineage was exactly the same, but not only could you not share the information, you couldn't receive even the acknowledgement of the Emperor that you were indeed every bit a son as his others. Yet Trannor had prevailed, put any bitterness behind him, and remained a loyal servant to his brother-in-secret. That explained many decisions he'd made over the years, and how fast he'd been able to pull strings when needed. But Tokh wasn't looking for excuses.

He nodded as if accepting the explanation. "So what you're telling me is that despite having access to every database there is, you won't assign the lowliest grunt to search for a simple name, or address, or com address, and give the information to an anonymous source who can then transfer the information to someone who can transfer the information to me, without ever knowing what it is or what it is about? I'm not asking for guards. I'm not asking to hire a Silencer. I'm not asking for upgraded security or weapons beyond my reach. All I need is a location. I will take care of the rest. If you can't do that simple task, then please explain why. You owe me that much."

Tokh crossed the final line, and Trannor shut down faster than an emergency door. The General stood up and tipped his head in dismissal, cold as a worm in a snowbank. "I owe you nothing, *dihnarwharl.* Don't reach beyond your place, or you may very well lose the hand that feeds you." He turned and left Tokh sitting alone in the sunlight.

Aila gave a frustrated growl and slammed her finger onto the comm screen. She seemed as if she were about to throw it, but stuffed it into her pocket instead. She stalked to the dining room window and stared out over the courtyard to the hazy faint line of the far shore. "Is there a blackout on communications in this house, or is it just my comm that's not receiving?" she asked the air.

Mátokhan was Tokh's officer of the day, monitoring his office, taking his calls, and keeping the house secure while Tokh was elsewhere. He had just begged a large sandwich and cold *raffin* from Shanohr, and stood by the kitchen wolfing at it. Watching him, Aila was glad his *aghát* teeth had been filed Human-flat; seeing him tear into meat with those yellowy Kerasi points would have been too close to a horror video. *Guest sees Host tear into food with pointed teeth; Guest later finds Host tearing into victims.* It was too easy to imagine Mátokhan as a were-beast or something.

"What's your issue now? No message from husband in the last hour? Could it be he's working on his tasks and can't answer every lonely howl you make?"

Aila turned to glare at him. If Mátokhan could be a were-beast, why couldn't she shoot lightning from her eyes and zap him in return? She'd chase him around the yard until she was too exhausted to move, and he was so sore he'd surrender. A sneer curled the corner of her lip all on its own. "No! You think I'd bother him at work? I've been waiting forever for the palace to get back to me on travel permission. I need the date and identification of the ship we'll be on, so that our ship can meet them. I sent the request six days ago. *Six.* I should have heard back in a day at most. It's not like it's a surprise I'm leaving; that was arranged before I arrived and confirmed on my arrival, not once, but twice. My government is screaming at me to return. Did they run out of ships or something?"

"Are you sure you're messaging the correct address?"

"*Yes*, I'm sure. You may be the only one who doesn't think so, but I'm not that stupid. You have it easy; you're back home, free to visit friends and family and soak up the luxury living here on the oceanfront. I've got classes and work that I've been away from far too long. I'll have to start my classes over at this rate; I won't get credit for the work I've already completed. I don't think they can fire me from my job, as long as I bring back enough reports. And holding me here is not helping the issue. I need to get home!"

Mátokhan gave a scornful snort. He placed his cup on the table, wiped his mouth, and came to the window, not quite close enough to touch her. "Do you ever listen to yourself? Whining like a lazy *solahrin* that the Fortunes haven't put you at the front of the line for favor? I have a job in the Union as well. As does Masákh. As does Haghíde. We also are now overdue at our jobs, which doesn't look favorable on our word. Because we're Kerasi, we're suspect of bad intentions, so we must be twice as reliable as you. We can't leave until you do. You stomp your feet that you're inconvenienced, when in truth, everyone in this house is inconvenienced, and you're at the root of it. If you weren't here, we would've returned weeks ago, on schedule. Tokh invited you as a holiday guest for two weeks; you are now three weeks past that, living off his hospitality, which, I'm sure, is wearing thin. He's in the middle of a grave personal crisis that has threatened his wives, children, and smallchildren – brought on, of course, because of your wedding and its resultant political publicity. While Tokh is thankful to have the extra assistance of the three of us, you are a chain around his ankle on top of his crisis. He must also think of your protection as well. He must think of how the crisis, of how his actions, will be seen on an interstellar level, and how that may affect the Emperor's business. Every day you're here, you complicate his life. Yet he remains a welcoming host, because he is no less than General Tokh."

Aila smarted as if he'd whipped her with an incentive stick. She couldn't think of a single thing to reply, let alone a stinging one. Her wind deflated until she had hardly any voice at all. "It wasn't my choice to get married. It's not my choice to still be here."

Mátokhan had clamped down, any trace of friendliness gone, and the cold remaining emptiness made her want to run. "Save your cries of pity for the Union. No one here has time for them."

Thirty-four

One of the first things Tokh had done was track the communication sources: they were encrypted; hard to break but not impossible. The problem was they were sent on a dispersed beam: the signal was broken up and sent through an array of satellite transfers, traceable only by the most painstaking methods. To repeat the attempts would be a waste of time.

Tokh had not received clearance to access bank or tax records. Those things were private, and not even Justice Wahtegahn had been able to grant Tokh permission. The information would make all the difference, but if Tokh couldn't gain access, a *dahneg*-privilege General-Four Senator, how could a lowly *nhásarwharl*-privilege Major hope to succeed?

The thought rolled around Masákh's head. If all legal channels had been pursued, then only illegal ones remained. Tokh wouldn't risk that – not yet. He had too much to lose. Masákh had been working inside the Union for the last six years; he'd lost most of his Kerasi contacts. The truly unsuspected approach would be to ask Ross Halian if the Union, using their resources, could find the information for him, but that would mean the Union would have to admit to their own spy capabilities, and that was not likely to happen. Masákh could try soliciting help from random, less than law-abiding individuals, but *aghát* stood out where ever they went, thanks to their facial surgery. It not only scared off those trying to stay under the radar, but left *aghát* too open to extortion, hence the unfailing need to be honest. He needed a method he could perform by himself, a way underground without being recognized.

With a start, he realized the solution.

Underground.

The Undernet.

The Kerasím Global Communications Network linked the entire planet, providing unlimited communication, entertainment, and informational resources. It was available to every home and business, paid for through taxes and commercial waves. Cities sometimes relied on cabling for heavily populated areas, but suburbs and remote areas relied on satellite delivery, thus any *ghinadín* slum, most of which lacked electrical wiring or plumbing from vandalism, could pick up the ComNet if they had a solar battery and something to receive it on. The Global ComNet linked an entire planet as one common people, with four hundred wave channels of entertainment and educational programming, and thirty regions of local communication services. The military operated on another twelve channels unavailable to the rest of ComNet users.

But that didn't cover all available signals.

There were still thousands of empty waves waiting to be pulled into use when needed. And that was where the Undernet entered. The unused waves were supposed to be blocked out, inaccessible to anyone without Imperial license, but hackers found ways in, and those that could tapped the undernet as their own private communication network, a place as large as space itself with occasional random meteors of messages flashing across it. Here was where encrypted data was stored in deep wells, safe from hackers using traditional methods. Here was where criminal deals were arranged without anyone knowing, unless ComNet police discovered them. No doubt the palace used several waves for its own private communications, but here, in the ectoplasm of anonymity, anything could be found if the operator was smart enough, and patient enough. Surely the information Masákh needed could be pulled up from Undernet files.

The problem was getting to them. If he used a public com center, his actions would be traced and could identify him. To use a military computer he would have to input his ID, which would expose him. Using his personal com would also incriminate himself. He needed a blank device, something without an identification number.

Like the kind used to fix computer and electronic equipment.

He grabbed his com.

It didn't seem like Masákh had been home not three weeks ago. The heat of Kinas Dagh, the faintly metallic smell of the sand, the stink of refuse baking in the desert made it seem as if he'd never been used to any of it. His brother Narukh met him at the *eel* stop, and they clapped shoulders.

"Come. I told Dinati I had to work late at the store. We're the only ones here." They walked to the alley behind *Vinbayez Shugal So,* the name of their father's electronics store, which, in Union Standard, translated to *Current Potential,* and entered through the back. "You're not too popular with *Ama* right now."

"I can imagine why. Nothing changes out here in the desert. They might as well be living in the time of the Giant Marmu, when this was all lake bottom."

Narukh turned on the lights in the back room. He was five years younger than Masákh, and Masákh's early fortune meant they had grown up knowing about each other, but never having the chance to be brothers. "Yeah, well, I try my best. That's why this store earns more money than *Bo's*. I know what's new and in demand with the younger crowd, while *Bo* is still catering to repairing outdated *aaka* for old people. He goes to the trade shows with me, but thinks new tech is a waste of money and no one will want that. What can I help you with?"

"I need a blank tester. I know *Bo* uses them to check repaired equipment. I need to get into the Undernet, undetected."

Narukh leaned away and eyed him with amusement. "Mr. Perfect Son Prissy-Pants wants to do something illegal? *Ama* would never believe it."

Masákh glared back. "Of course she would. But she would blame my wife for it."

Narukh laughed. "Yeah, probably. I hear about your visit every time I see her. What do you need the Undernet for?"

"I need to locate information that's being blocked by other sources."

"Legal stuff? Or spy work?"

"Both," Masákh said. "I'm trying to track down information on a criminal that no one has been able to obtain. You may help me in my search, but be aware, if anyone finds out, it could mean great trouble."

"Is there a pretty female involved?"

It didn't take Masákh long to answer. Great Lady Tokh, younger, was one of the most attractive females Masákh had met from any caste, and not just on the outside. It was her spirit alone that pulled attention before anyone could notice her face. "Prettier by far than the Crowned Beauty of Daghnahn, but she remains only the wife of a friend."

"Good enough. As long as there's a female involved." Narukh reached across a stack of spare keyboards to slide an operating chip off a shelf. He searched the shelves to the side, retrieved a working interface, blew some dust off it. With the proper tool, he slid a cover off the back in seconds, inserted the chip, replaced the cover, flipped it over, and turned it on.

"Okay. Up and running, no tracing ID. Now to slip into the Undernet." Narukh tapped a series of controls, then shut off the operating system, leaving the monitor blank. He booted new root menus, then tapped in a long string of commands. After several flashes on the blank screen, a disappointing blinking cursor appeared. No *do not enter* signs, no dire warnings, no screeching alarms to instill terror and make the heart race, just a black screen and an orange dot.

"And we're in," Narukh said. "The entire world is available to you, if you know how to look." He looked similar to what Masákh looked like before he became *aghát*, a little heavier, a little beefier, perhaps a tad shorter. He looked like a Kerasi every-man, whereas Masákh's *aghát* features set him apart from all but a handful of Kerasi. "Why did you think I knew how to scale the undernet?"

"We do have the same *bo*, don't we? I was helping in the store since I was six. I come back to check his books even though you're perfectly capable, because the law says I must. Perhaps thirty percent of his business is fixing computers that have been targeted with destruct codes while trying to access illegal content on the undernet. If he knows how to resolve the issues, he knows perfectly well how they got there, and that means you do, too."

Narukh gave a soft snort. "Correct as always. Well, I'm happy to help. Something exciting instead of the land of fried fuses and endless sand. What are we doing?"

"I need a comm address, an actual address, and the prize pocket would be accessing a bank account. Not to take anything, just to copy the transactions."

"Shouldn't be that hard," Narukh said, and his fingers flew over the command board.

The comm address came easily; tracing the calls to a location proved difficult, so they moved on. Using the name and the business brought up many leads. "He's heavily into consort content," Narukh said, pointing out links. He used a different interface to cross-reference some comm addresses. "A lot of these are places that deal in underage and kidnapped females. You said he runs a bakery-supply business. Why are there... one, two, three, four... twenty-seven transfers to a landscaper in one day?"

"A landscaper? Perhaps he has a relative that works there?"

Narukh frowned. "A *dahneg*? Be serious. Unless they own it. It doesn't make sense. That tallies up to 25,000 *dakra*. That's crazy. Not even the Governor pays that much for gardening. Here's another one. Deposits made in one month – that's more than a bakery should hope to make in a year. Not right. Worse, the numbers match. If you tally everything coming in from here, it matches up with the withdrawals over here. It's like a river of money, just passing through."

"That's why I needed the information," Masákh said, pointing to the screen. "Follow the trail. Start with that number."

They worked deep into the night, Narukh running three screens and Masákh working off his hand com, cross referencing information until a picture began to form.

"Aaka!" Narukh grunted, and slammed a finger on the control board. He tapped back, tapped back, then shut the machine off, disconnecting. "Sorry. I set off a tracer alarm. Someone truly doesn't want to be disturbed at any angle. That's really high-up, if they're worried about being tapped from underneath."

"It can't leave a marker, can it?" Masákh said. "I don't want anyone in danger."

"Nah. I have no ID, and I was working off a mirror dummy anyway. It should reflect their own data back at them."

"Be certain. What number were you tapping?"

"That would be..." Narukh flipped through the scraps of notes they'd made. "Hozar, former *bhísroti*, formerly on the late Nághtas's Emperor's Council for Urban Development. Nadigh let him go last year and replaced him with former *bhísroti* Algardihn "

Masákh gave a soft grunt. The information he'd gathered was extremely dangerous, and he wasn't sure what to do with it. One didn't walk up to the Emperor and say, "Your Majesty, my illegal searches have turned up a potentially treasonous plot in your cabinet," even with proof. Not a *nhásarwharl* by privilege who was told by the palace not to let anyone dig deeper and find such information. But why? Why would the palace not want to know about weapon smuggling and underground money trails? Unless the palace was running the scheme. But that still didn't make sense. Unless someone in the Senate was running it under the Emperor's nose, and the Emperor was unaware. If the Emperor was unaware, why would he give Masákh an ultimatum to keep the information hidden? Unless the liaison knew but not the Emperor, and he was feeding the Emperor false information. The deeper Masákh dug, the more questions were raised, with fewer answers.

"They created a transport system for banned weapons. I've been to some of those places, trying to drive out rebels. Now I'm not certain if they're rebels or not. They lose their homes, the *dihnarwharl* owners of the buildings lose their income and cry to the governors, and who comes in to rebuild? The development companies Hozar and his fellow investors have stake in. The more weapons supplied, the more destruction, the greater the need for rebuilding. They sell weapons for profit that destroy buildings, so they can make money from fixing them. Meanwhile, the people yell at the Emperor for not stopping the conflicts. And Tokh's target is making a fortune far above his caste transporting the weapons in his bakery trucks. That's the only answer. Run me one more thing." Masákh motioned to Narukh's anonymous computer. "Tap me into General Tokh's communications. I need to see what it's attached to."

The sky had a faint line of light at the eastern horizon when Masákh bid Narukh goodbye in the alley behind the store. In a special pocket of his jacket, hidden behind his ribbons, sat a data chip with every name, every link, every bit of treason on it. His death sentence. "Take care, my brother, in case I don't see you again. I can't allow the information not to be told, but when I do, my life will be forfeit. Those whose power we've uncovered won't take lightly to being questioned, and they'll want my head."

"Then stay safe, my brother. I enjoyed every minute of our search. Thank you for letting me share in your excitement. I wish you would do it more often. There is so much more of the world than wiping viruses and soldering wires. I wanted to follow you to the Academy. I wanted your glory. *Ama* wouldn't let me. She said the army took her greatest son, they weren't going to get the other, and someone had to take the business from *Bo*."

Masákh clapped his brother on the shoulder. "You're by far the braver for staying here, but it's also much safer. Keep the family well."

Thirty-five

Masákh saw him coming from where he sat by the central fountain in the Turmayaan district of Keranihn, a middle-caste village. He stood up as Mátokhan crossed the busy street. Matokhan wore common clothing, and both wore dark shades, drawing less attention despite their washed-out skin and lack of chin hank.

"What news, Brother?" Mátokhan said.

Masákh gave no greeting, just aimed his comm at his fellow *aghát*, tapped it, and held his hand out. "Give me your comm."

Mátokhan made a face, but he handed it over. Masákh turned it off, then put it in his own pocket. "Now we're free to talk. You may have it back when we are done."

"You don't trust your own team member?"

"I trust no one right now," Masákh said, monitoring the tiny electronic readouts on the inside of his eye shades as the electronics scanned and rescanned the immediate vicinity for tails or suspicious activity. "Come. Walk with me." They picked their way across the square, through the arches of the village center, and down the sidewalk of a less congested street.

"Something's spooked you. What did you discover?"

They walked two blocks in silence. Masákh stopped at a window café and purchased two bottles of *lipuhr*, a common drink in the far east of Fash Noor but available in Keranihn, like everything else. He pointed to a small playground, empty from school and the lunch hour. Masákh sat on a bench, checked the scanning feature on his pocket comm, and put it back. No listening devices in range. He handed a *lipuhr* to Mátokhan.

"Speak, Brother." Mátokhan opened the bottle and took a sizeable chug.

Masákh copied him. "You said you never hit a point where your orders conflicted. I did. I did as you counseled: I found a narrow truth and I stuck to it, but I fear it won't be enough to save me. I did the research the General is forbidden from doing – don't worry, that was no one's order but my own. I break no oath saying it. I've put in many hours of travel, spoken to reluctant sources, spent sleepless nights tracking information. Now I have information. Serious information. Information far beyond what I ever meant to find, and I see why the General was forbidden from openly seeking it."

Mátokhan waited, but at last had to prompt, "And?"

"And now I will pass it on to General Tokh. When I do, my life is forfeit. The moment Tokh receives it, the palace will have a price on my head. When Tokh finds out why I left, he will have a price on my head. Either way, I don't come out of this alive, but I will have fulfilled my narrow truth and carried out both of my orders. I will die knowing I did the right thing."

Masákh gazed off into space, blank and silent. Mátokhan bent forward, studying him, but couldn't see through the dark shades. "May I know what the information contains?"

"It will be up to Tokh to give you details, but as leader of the *aghát* and near-colonel, I'm certain he will."

"But you will not tell me."

"If I do, you would have to kill me for failing two directives."

"So what will you do after you give him the information?"

Melancholy coated Masákh's face, but he seemed to have accepted his fate. "Drop out of sight for as long as I can, until they catch up with me. There are two possibly truths: either my orders did not come from the Emperor and I am as much a victim as Tokh, or if true, I have lost my faith in the future of Kerasím. I would beg you, as Brother *Aghát*, to see that Aila makes it safely aboard the Union ship to return to our home. Her parents will be pleased by my absence. Give this to her." He pulled a very thick envelope from an inside pocket, sealed with reinforced adhesive straps. "It's all my accounts. When it's learned Tokh has the information, they will seize my finances, and she would receive nothing. This way, she'll have a dowry."

Mátokhan pulled off his eye shades and stared hard. He put down his empty bottle of *lipuhr*. "Keep it. You'll need it. Think, Masákh! Think! Don't look at the straight path; look to the sides. You're the husband of a Union Emissary. You have friends in high places."

It took a moment for Masákh to understand. He slid the envelope back into his jacket. "I do, don't I. Perhaps I should find out just how strong that friendship is. If it's poor, I'm no worse off, and they will make sure Aila receives this. I won't risk giving away my location by answering communications. When I'm certain the situation is secure, I'll be in contact. Three days, I hope."

He removed Mátokhan's comm unit and handed it back. "Please give my respects to General Tokh, with my loyalty, duty, and supreme honor."

Masákh stood up. He half-expected a plasma shot to his back as he walked, never looking behind. Mátokhan wouldn't fail a rule, but he played it to the letter, as expected; he didn't know Masákh's orders, he didn't know the information on the chip, therefore he didn't yet have cause. Masákh turned the corner, out of sight, and disappeared into the city.

Masákh presented his Union ID to the guards at the gates, and again inside the waiting area of the Union Embassy of Keranihn. It was a stately building just two miles out of the center of the city, seven stories and sixty-three rooms, bright yellow bricks with pink and white trim, a high, sturdy wall surrounding the yard, and a heavy metal gate. Forty-eight staff were assigned there, though a few had their own apartments scattered nearby.

"I wish to speak with Ambassador Major Ross Halian. I don't have an appointment, but if you tell him Masákh gha Lil wishes urgently to speak with him in person, I'm sure he will agree."

The greeter matched him in the computer, confirmed his Union ties, and immediately paged Halian, who appeared out of a back hall.

Halian bowed. "Major Masákh! *Morae! Morae!* Come in, friend! How is married life treating you?"

Masákh bowed in return. "My marriage is most pleasant. Thank you for asking." He removed his plasma pistol and service knife and handed them to the house greeter, then placed his hands upon his head to be searched. The greeter glanced at Halian; Halian gave the slightest nod to proceed. No one believed it necessary, but caution was never a wrong move.

"As husband of a Union citizen, I respectfully ask the Planetary Union for political asylum. If I step outside your grounds, my life is forfeit. I'm willing to exchange limited information for the courtesy. I'm willing to pay any incurred costs, and respectfully ask to apply for full citizenship, renouncing all ties to the Kerasi Coalition."

A stunned expression took over Ross's face, then grew serious as he thought further. "Masákh, where's Aila?"

"It's my sincere belief she is in good health at General Tokh's in Imahlva. That's where I left her."

"Does she know you're here, seeking asylum?"

"No. She does not."

Halian took a deep breath and blew it out. He motioned for Masákh to follow. "All right. Let's talk."

Halian offered him a seat in a private sitting room, fit for a Kerasi male in heavy dark wood and red upholstery. "Would you like a drink?"

Masákh bowed his head. "Water, please." This wasn't the time for a loose tongue. Every word had to be examined in minute detail, on both sides.

Halian handed him a glass, then sat nearby with a popular brand of *muhr*. "I've known you five years, Masákh. I've seen you interrogated, imprisoned, angry. I've wrestled you for weapons, and I've learned to respect you as a diplomat. I've heard nothing but praise for your work inside the Union. I had reservations about your marriage, still do, but I put my faith in my respect for you. Time for truth: what's going on, how much danger is Aila in, how much danger are you in?"

Masákh bowed again. "On my oath: I was given conflicting orders from my commander and the palace. I found a narrow truth that allowed me to carry out both, but in doing so I also failed both orders. I firmly believe there will be a price on my head from both sides. I can attempt to hide on Kerasím, but the army is large and *aghát* are difficult to conceal. My only chance at safety is to return to the Union. My death will leave Aila in a very dangerous position while she is on Kerasím."

"Were your orders detrimental to the Union?"

"No. They involved a local investigation. I do not believe the Union is involved, at least from my data. That is truth."

"Okay." Halian sighed again as his threat level slid downward another notch. "How much does Aila know?"

"Only that I was leaving for several days on a mission. Do you know if she has been able to contact the return ship yet? She was most anxious at the lack of response. I was hoping to find it already en route, so that the wait would be minimal."

Ross Halian frowned. "I've not been informed of any incoming ships. Any inbound Union ship contacts us to make sure we are not in need of supplies or evacuation of personnel."

It was Masákh's turn to look confused. "She has been attempting to get permission to leave Kerasím for several days. If she hasn't yet had contact, that makes it almost a week. Why wouldn't she have had a response in that time?"

Masákh was not prone to anxiety. Most questions could be thought out and reasoned, but when Aila was involved, his patience for introspection had limits. Something wasn't right, and the three hundred miles between Keranihn and Imahlva now seemed like three billion. Aila's warning echoed in the back of his head.

"I don't know," Halian said. "It's a simple process – call the Kerasi-Union relations office, request permission for a ship to enter their space, you get approval, contact the outpost on Meram or Kye, get the registry of the ship, then send it back to the K-U office so they know which ship to approve. We've never had an issue yet. Did she contact the right office?"

"That's not something she would mistake. Being unable to leave Kerasím at will was one of her greatest concerns if she married here."

Halian wasn't as adept at hiding his concern. He went to the room's ComNet interface and tapped the controls. Masákh followed, but stood out of camera range.

"Pleasant day," Halian said to the secretary. "Can you tell me if a Union ship is inbound for Kerasím? We're running low on a few health items and I want to be sure they'll have enough on board."

The *nhásarwharl* on the other end tapped his computer screen. "There are no Union ships currently headed for Kerasím."

"Do you know if one has been requested?"

There was another pause. "No. No requests have been made through this office."

"Is there any other office it might have gone through?"

The *nhásarwharl* gave a deadly glare. "All requests must go through this office. No one else has authority."

Halian gave a chuckle. "Then I shall have to have a word with my secretary. Can you tell me if Union Councilor Perrin is still on Kerasím? Perhaps I can coordinate things with her."

"Councilor Perrin has not requested permission to leave and is currently in violation of her letter of visitation."

"That's a problem I will address immediately. I'll contact her right now. Thank you."

Halian cut the call and turned to Masákh.

"Impossible," Masákh said. "I was in the room when she placed one of the requests."

"Something's not right," Halian agreed. "You're off the grid; let me handle this. She needs to come in. I can send someone to fetch her."

"I don't wish to alarm her if there's no cause. She will want to know why. Aila's com unit runs off General Tokh's household communications; if they are compromised, my location could be uncovered," Masákh warned. "I would ask you to delay just a few days. The *aghát* will ensure her safety. Perhaps you could request the evacuation ship. Once you are certain it is on its way, you would have a viable, expected excuse to call her in for a discharge visit, and we will be able to leave in peace."

Halian's mouth pinched up as he considered it. "I don't like it. I'd rather she was here, even if I have to send her the invitation by courier, but I'll trust your instinct. I don't need a public battle over personnel. Three days. The moment that ship hits the border, I want her here, in person, under my protection."

Masákh bowed. "Thank you, Ambassador."

Thirty-six

Tokh stared at Ráhnif in puzzlement as Zheníhda bowed him into Tokh's home office. She shut the door and left them alone, as a good wife should, though Tokh was never quite sure how often her ear was pressed to the door.

"I sent you back to the palace," Tokh said.

"I was given order to return for one week," Ráhnif said with a bow. "I wasn't informed if it was a Palace request or yours."

"It wasn't my request, and I wasn't informed."

Ráhnif removed a small envelope from inside his blue suit jacket and handed it to Tokh. It bore a palace seal, and was marked as strictest confidentiality. "I was also instructed to give you this, General. I would suspect it's the answer."

Tokh took the envelope, held it up to a light, then opened it with his knife. Nothing exploded, which was always a good sign. Inside was a small strip of paper with grid coordinates machine-printed on it, anonymous and untraceable.

Tokh's heart soared as the picture fell into place. Trannor sent Tokh's own man back, something so ordinary it wouldn't be questioned. It was all he could do not to kiss Ráhnif in gratitude.

"Surveillance only," Tokh warned Khaním over his handcom. "Take no action, no matter what you see. Observe, record only. They'll already be on alert, so use extreme caution." He didn't trust his house system for something this important, and used a separate private line with a security level available only to those in the Imperial Senate. With an additional scramble and a satellite scatter, it was as untraceable as Tokh had ever been taught.

"I've got a four-man detail setting up on each point, and a mobile comm station set up a *nali* away," Colonel Khaním said on the comm. "Instructions are clear."

"Record everything and put it on an encrypted chip. Don't trust that over the comm. I want it in my hands by dinner, and I'll make my decisions."

"It will be done, General," Khaním promised.

He'd been told repeatedly this was a personal issue; Tokh had the power to deal with it himself. Khanim's surveillance had been thorough; the plan was set. He pulled four of his *aghát*: Tótoghar, to move everyone into position quickly and monitor the action from the air; Ghírandar, to make sure everything stayed this side of the law and there were no outs; Haghíde, as leader, and Ráhnif, for the experience. He pulled twenty-five of his most seasoned troops, including five specialists who could track and locate using stealth equipment. Mistakes were not an option; there wouldn't be a second chance.

All along, Tokh had spoken with his neighbor one-above, Justice Wahtegahn. Wahtegahn wrote the warrants and signed the orders that gave Tokh power to act, relieving General Trannor of any possible connection. Tokh was *dihnarwharl* with *dahneg* privilege, but had no power over full *dahneg*. *Dahneg,* however, could not trump a Justice order.

Their target was in the city of Narinth, half an hour from the Keranihn Space Port. The walled villa was rather expensive for a mere *dahneg*, but considering his foe would have inherited any property from his father's death, and perhaps any insurance payments on the deaths of his wives in the past six years, it was possible. Tokh's surveillance team watched from a distance using the latest in tech. Five tiny flying night-spy cameras disguised as lace-winged hover-flies sent back information from inside the grounds and the villa itself, giving a good idea of the rooms and personnel inside. Their target seemed to have a group of nine or so other males, three patrolling the small grounds at all times and the rest inside. Also inside were three females, assumed to be consorts, and all three were being treated poorly. Three microphones were dispatched inside the walls as well; as the garden contained several *bilfon* trees, they were set inside three large tree-nuts and dropped over the wall at night by a spy-fly, innocuous as fallen leaves.

Colonel Khaním helped with coordination. They waited until almost midnight, with eight men accounted for inside the villa's grounds. Seven men in Tokh's group wore devices that made them invisible to scanners. They crept up to the gates, hit the electronic gate-locks with pulse-interrupters, and burst into the yard. Three guards were taken down with barely a sound. The second wave advanced into the yard, while the first wave turned their attention to the doors. They zapped the locks free and waited. At the back of the house, two officers fired grenades through the windows.

Breaking glass alerted the people within, but the unexpected flash of grenades caused panic. The screams of females rose high and loud over the shouts of the men; after a count of two, twenty of Tokh's men stormed the doors. There was a brief round of fire: four males had been involved with the three females and wore no clothing or weapons; Tokh's officers wore armor. One suspect had been killed by the grenades. Three had been drinking and playing Tabs; they'd been caught by surprise and though they were well-armed, had no chance against ten of Tokh's best. The third dropped his weapon and surrendered before the first victims could hit the floor. The survivors were secured by the wrists and ankles by the time Tokh strode through the house.

"Three casualties," Haghíde informed him, stepping over a body. "Six rooms secured; scanners find no hidden rooms or persons."

"Excellent."

"What should be done with the females?"

Tokh glanced over. The three naked females huddled together crying in a single terrified mass. Bruises were visible on all of them; at least one of them was bleeding. "Treat them as rescued prisoners of unknown origin. Cover them, or allow them to dress if they have clothing. They're to be taken to a female hospital for treatment, then if they're able they can be returned where they came from or I'll ask the palace if they can be assigned there as servants. Any officer who touches them will face my sword."

"Understood." Haghíde moved to obey.

"Tokh dar Giláhn," drawled one of the naked men on the floor. "I'm impressed. You found me. Did you do that yourself, or did you have help? It's going to cost you quite a pretty *harím* to fix the damage to my estate."

Even without having seen surveillance videos and identification photos, Tokh would have recognized him. Six years hadn't aged him at all. He rolled on the floor naked, the curves of his buttocks clenched with the effort of lifting his shoulders off the floor with his hands bound behind.

"That's up to the court, when they sell the property," Tokh said. Though his instinct was to beat him to a bloody pulp, crush the scum's head under his bootheel, shove a control stick up the bastard's ass and fire it at five-second intervals until it reached the base of the tongue, Tokh was a professional, and he needed to be nothing less than professional about this if he was to get maximum penalty from it. Everything had to be exactly from the book.

"Emrehl kasihn Garsuuhl, only son of Engmar kasihn Garsuuhl, you are under arrest for unlawful surveillance, stalking, harassment, threatening, acts of terror, and attempted murder."

Emrehl, the name that so terrified Mímihn she couldn't bear to say it under any circumstances.

He laughed with ease. "Untie me, Tokh, and leave my premises, and I won't press charges against you. *Dihnarwharl*, even a privileged *dihnarwharl*, can't order *dahneg* about, nor arrest us, nor detain us or even touch us, for that matter. Now release me." The humor disappeared, and the final order aired itself cold and short-tempered.

Tokh removed the printed orders from his pocket and unfolded them. "'It is to be known that General Tokh dar Gilahn of Imahlva, Gada, is hereby ordered to seize and detain *dahneg* Emrehl kasihn Garsuuhl of Narinth, Gada, for wanted crimes and injuries detailed below, as well as any who have aided him, by order of Wahtegahn Urdihn, *dahneg* Justice for the region of Gada. By the powers given me by the Region of Gada, these orders will not be superseded without my name and stamp.' Shall I repeat the charges for you?"

The laugh this time was annoyed. "It's bogus, Tokh. My lawyer will be back soon, and he's also *dahneg*. Give me pants, take me to court, and I'll be back here by sunbreak, with you in chains and charged. Must we play this game? Return my property to me and I'll graciously forget this incident."

It was so hard to hold back his boot. *One good stomp.* Tokh squatted down almost on top of Emrehl's head; if he'd also been naked, he could have slapped Emrehl's face with his *hihvat*, which in some ways would also have been satisfying. "Not this time, I'm afraid. You're not going to civil court. You threatened the life of a General and took action against a General's property and family. You will be held in military holding, in a high-security area, under a false name. Not even the manager of the building will know you're there."

The next laugh was for show, hiding uncertainty from his cohorts. "I'm not military. They can't prosecute me."

"You're right." Tokh's years of interrogation took over. His voice was clear and calm as a text book. "But there is one who stands in front of me in the line to charge you with crimes, and she is not military. She'll have first say with a Justice. Only then will I have right to seek damages from what's left. We'll settle it there."

He stood up. Tokh was Kerasi, he was getting old, he was far overweight and it took a lot of force to shove himself to his feet again without pulling on something. It wasn't his fault that the motion was accompanied by a strong blasting fart, inches from Emrehl's head. Those things happened, and they didn't leave marks. Emrehl made a gagging show of protest before cursing Tokh and his next six generations.

"Take them out," Tokh said to Khaním. "Take them to S&I and put them in basement holding, under my name only." The Securities and Informations building was where Tokh and Khaním worked. The basement level was for prisoners awaiting mind scan. Just being held on the same floor was often enough to crack the hardest of criminals.

Tokh stepped aside and placed a call home. "It's done. I have him in custody, bound and loaded on his way to my building."

There was a silence. "No mistake?" said Mímihn's whisper.

"No mistake. You may sleep now, my *falahndi*. You're all safe."

There was nothing in the earpiece but the weeping of relief.

266

Thirty-seven

Tokh remained in Keranihn overnight, as the real work snowballed before him with identifications, legal proceedings, and investigations to be undertaken. Breakfast was a celebration.

"I told you it was only a matter of time," Zhenihda sniffed over her *raffin*. "Tokh does not fail."

"I can go home at last," Dalo said. "Kitras will return in two weeks. I'll be so happy to be away from stairs," and she ran from the table to pick Niboh off the staircase for the fifth time that morning.

"You can return to classes again," Mímihn said to Kesseh, who wrinkled her nose. "You'll have much work to catch up on."

Kesseh's eyes rolled to the ceiling, but it was in thought. She switched to her best Union. *"Yes, but I did much prrractiss speaking with Laydy Aila, and now I will speak best in school".*

"I can speak vehrry good now, too," Faelihn echoed.

Fahni laughed, not understanding a word. *"Allo. Goot bahy.* I should come to school with you. Haghíde received his permission for Vihren and me to come to the Union with him. I cannot believe I'll be living not only in another region, but another world. I'm so scared just to be on a spaceship."

Aila squeezed her hand. "You will love being there. I will teach you everything you need to know."

Now that Aila knew Mímihn was safe, it was past time to go home. She would miss her friends dreadfully, but Aila had stayed far longer than she'd ever meant, enough for three visits. She missed her Human family, too, and her coworkers, and even the doorman to their apartment building.

Yet again she sent a text to the palace, asking for clearance for a Union ship to enter Kerasi space. Her next message was to Masákh, though she knew he wouldn't answer right away. The man was caught;

Masákh could just get his ass back to Imahlva and get ready to leave. She wanted a ship *today*, not five days from now.

Masákh sent her a brief message that he was wrapping up and they would be together quite soon, but not a goddamned word from the palace. By dinner, she sent a message to Kye.

"Look, I've tried contacting the palace directly seven times," she said to the coordinator, "but I'm not getting anywhere. Can you please send a ship before my mother starts a war? Maybe if it's sitting at the border flashing lights toward Kerasím the palace will get off its ass and hit the approval button."

The flight coordinator shook her head. "That's not the protocol, but I'll see what I can do."

Nothing.

It wasn't until the next morning, after Tokh had returned, that Aila's hand comm beeped a call in the middle of breakfast. Mímihn looked up in terror, the rest of the table paused in alarm, but Aila expected it was the palace with her answer. She read the message through three times, frowning, then closed it out. It was the palace, but not the message she'd been hoping for.

"General, will you be going to Keranihn today? I've been requested for an interview at the palace. Since Masákh isn't here yet, I'll need someone to accompany me."

Tokh shoveled in another mouthful of breakfast cake and gravy, and thus took a moment to answer. "Who's doing the interview? What is it for?"

She showed him the message. "I don't know. It just says an interview with the Emperor's Ministers, and is signed by the Minister of the Interior. I started off this trip with an interview; perhaps it's an exit interview, since I requested permission to leave."

Tokh studied the message, and the coding behind it. "It was indeed sent by the palace. That's their signature. I don't know what the Interior department would want with you, but you've done strange interviews for promotions before. I'll send Ráhnif with you. He's palace-approved; he'll have access to information I won't. You'll message me at the conclusion and return immediately; no unapproved tours until my business has concluded."

"I understand. Thank you, General Tokh."

Mímihn primped Aila's hair for her, gave a strand one last twist, and pushed her thumbs against Aila's mouth to make her smile. "Don't lose your smile. Remember, more than anything, Kerasi males are mirror-lovers, and those who go before cameras even more so because of what they do. Every one of them thinks he is the strongest, the best-looking, the most powerful, the most charming, that his *khatas* don't smell. You must play to that. Make him feel that he is the most important person on Kerasím, and you'll win all the hearts. Ask them when the interview will air, and we'll all watch it together."

"I will shine like your hair," Aila promised, and they both laughed.

Tokh had too much to do to waste time lounging around. He grabbed a second cup of *raffin* from Shanohr and headed to his office. He had barely sat when Shanohr knocked at his door, and he allowed her to enter. She handed him an envelope with a bow.

"A courier just delivered this for you, General, of highest importance."

Tokh nodded his thanks, accepting the small envelope as if it might explode. As Shanohr closed the door, he held it up to the light; nothing showed, but it was padded, hiding something. Then he noticed the small symbol in the corner, sign of the *aghát*. He tore it open with less fear.

He pulled out a small paper, with a data card attached. The paper said nothing more than *With loyal regards, Masákh*. Tokh stuffed the card into his reader.

"General Tokh," Masákh said on the recording. *"Please understand there's a price on my head for giving you this information. I have been given opposing orders, but neither have I been released from either vow of loyalty. You ordered us to help you solve your wife's issue; the palace ordered me to stop you from investigating. My compromise was to investigate the issue myself and decide who had the greater truth, but what I discovered is much greater than expected and beyond my ability to direct, so I pass it back to you. My life will be forfeit either way, but for the honor of the Emperor, it must be addressed. General, your comm system has been corrupted. The calls on your main link are being re-routed through a third party. It is highly*

likely that calls in or out have been intercepted and falsified. This may be why the Palace has no record of Aila asking permission for a Union ship to retrieve her. Unless the palace is lying, her calls were received somewhere else. If you will examine the enclosed data, it should pinpoint exactly where some of the calls are going. I don't know if your security lines have also been infiltrated. Treat any incoming or outgoing calls as being monitored. You will also find every bit of evidence I have found of illegal smuggling operations involving your targeted individual, a trail that climbs well into the palace itself, though I don't know if it leads to the Emperor. I hope this information helps solve your difficulties. It has been an honor and the highest privilege to serve you, General, but my time is done. My regards to my team and to your family."

Tokh sat back in his chair, both stunned and relieved. It was too much information at once. How long had he been monitored? What secrets had been breached, and to where? He reached into a drawer, pulled out the General's Manual, and looked up the proper code. The note to Trannor, sent on his most secure line, said simply, "The Emperor is overboard. 521A active; responding. Depth unknown. Please confirm."

By the manual, Emperor overboard/521A meant communications had been compromised by a hostile source, and it was unknown how bad the leaks had been. Tokh glared at his black screen in disgust. No wonder he'd had such difficulty trying to track down information. What to do about Masákh... It wasn't like Masákh to commit suicide. He would go underground, into hiding, if he thought his life were in danger, until he found a way out of it. Especially now that he had a wife.

Wife.

Tokh's heart skipped a painful beat. Aila Perrin had been using his household comm waves all along, without added security. *Calls were being received elsewhere.* Her interview might not be real. Tokh didn't dare send out a recall from his equipment until it had been thoroughly scanned for parasites. He grabbed a paper and scribbled on it.

"Thrit!" He shouted into the intercom to the vehicle shed. Thrit appeared at the door to his office no more than a *fasím* later.

"Take this note to the mail office. Go to the window for comm messaging. My name and office are at the top. Tell them to send it highest priority, no matter what the cost. Lives may depend on it – Great Lady Masákh's, to be exact. As fast as you can get it there. Make sure you bring the paper back, don't let them keep it."

Thrit accepted the paper, folded it and bowed. "T'rit know where to go. T'rit move like t'e clouds." And despite his brittle appearance and presumed age, he was gone in blink.

Thirty-eight

The palace of Derahl Nor never ceased to impress, but Aila had grown used to the security and now took it into consideration. She wore Kerasi-conservative for a *dahneg*; a sleek embroidered white dress with a large brightly-colored scarf wrapped around her head and shoulders, and simple beaded black wedge slippers. Down, the scarf was a fashion statement, but it was thin and light and could be pulled over her face like a proper veil if needed. Under it, she wore the necklace Masákh had given her, stating her position as a married female. She carried nothing extraneous beyond ID; Ráhnif carried her cash-card and com unit for her. It made getting through security a snap. Ráhnif had his credentials, but even as a palace *aghát* he wasn't allowed weapons inside the building. Because of his clearance, they didn't need a special *aghát* to accompany them; Ráhnif was already that *aghát*.

Aila accompanied him with ease, but on a more reserved basis. Ráhnif hadn't been one of Tokh's *aghát* during her captivity; she didn't have that long-term trusted rapport with him.

"Are you nervous about your interview?" Ráhnif asked as they walked the interminably long halls.

"No," Aila said. "I have no idea what it's about, but I've done eight televised interviews for Kerasi ComNet, been grilled by ministers and panels when I arrived, been interrogated by that General Trannor. I've had interviews with Heir Rimas and with the Emperor himself; I even had one with Emperor Nághtas before he died, so I'm sure this is just one more minister who wants to get points scored. Knowing how the chains of command work, I'm certain it had to be approved by Trannor or His Majesty first."

"That is most likely truth," Ráhnif agreed. "Tokh would have been informed to make sure you were sent; Masákh would have been notified as you are his wife and he would have to give permission."

"Not necessarily. I'm also a Union citizen, and I can and do act independently. I haven't spoken to Masákh today, so I don't know if he was informed."

"That is possible as well."

He located the correct room, a conference room on the second floor. "I will wait here in the hall for you. Just step outside when your interview is complete." Ráhnif knocked on the door and opened it to a tiny reception area.

"Aila Perrin, as requested." Anything further was not his concern, so he left her there and returned to the hallway. The *nhásarwharl* at the desk buzzed her into the inner room.

And immediately Aila wanted to turn and leave. It didn't look right. It didn't feel right. It was an inner conference room with no windows, just a large table and perhaps fifteen or twenty chairs. A *dahneg* stood up, wearing the badges of the Senate Council; he was indeed a cabinet minister, and almost guaranteed to be a former *bhísroti*, the old highest caste under Emperor. Two guards stood at opposite walls, tall metal poles in their hands as if they were marching in a parade immediately after.

That was it.

No cameras. No interview couch. No members of the councils concerned with Union or foreign affairs, no ambassadors, not even General Trannor, who was almost always present somewhere in the background whenever she was interviewed, being directly responsible for overseeing Union-Kerasi relations. Not even a palace *aghát* for translation. A single minister wishing to make himself known wouldn't use a private conference room; he'd meet in the open on the main floor, where anyone and everyone would see him speaking to the Union delegate as if they were great friends, flaunting his power and contacts. This was something hidden and unapproved.

Aila didn't try the door, but she gave it only a 50-50 chance of being unlocked.

She summoned up her best *aghát* manners and bowed. "*Do you speak Union?*"

"*Ka.*"

"*Then may I request my translator from the hallway, so we will not mistake each other.*"

"*Ka*," he said again. "You speak enough Emperor to be understood. I will speak slow. Sit. *Koormaht*." He pointed to a chair, and Aila complied. He didn't sit, but lectured her as if she were a young child in trouble.

"I am Sihn Ran, Grand Senator of his Majesty's Imperial Cabinet. You are the wife of Major Masákh gha Lil, of the Inner Circle, correct?"

Aila gave a bow of her head. *"Sukh."*

"Does your husband share information with you, share his orders or commands with you, Inner Circle or other?"

Aila let her head drop. Again, those questions. She must have answered them fifteen times over. Every person she met asked her the same thing.

"*Ka*. No. He does not. Not only is he forbidden from telling me such information, I would not listen, because I don't wish him trouble. And I don't care what his orders are. I know he has a liaison to the Emperor, but I don't know who."

"But you should. Major Masákh is Inner Circle. That's a rare and powerful distinction. Even I don't have that. It carries great responsibility. And when problems occur, people outside the circle can become involved. Such as now."

Aila frowned. "What do you mean? What problems?"

The *bhísroti* sighed and parked a hip on the edge of the table. His clothing was beautiful, blues and blacks in blocked sections with gold trims at the edges of his shirt, and he wore black trousers. The gold edging stuck in Aila's head for no reason at all: perhaps an inch wide, a woven trim with a teeny gold edge, a teeny black band, then a field of gold, and inset in the middle gold ribbon every inch or so was a tiny blue crest woven into the design, a pointed thing that reminded her of the spade in a deck of cards. The design imprinted itself on her brain, an inconsequential clothing motif that shouldn't even have been noticed, but the stranger the interview became, the more it held her attention.

"Major Masákh was given orders. He was ordered to interfere, disrupt, distract, interrupt, and if necessary outright block certain ongoing investigations. He did none of that, or so little that the investigation ended with disastrous results. This is a grievous error on his part. It shows a distinct lack of professionalism and loyalty, both of which lead to punishment."

Aila pinched her mouth tight to control her words, but let her anger explode from her eyes. "Major Masákh's loyalty is to the Emperor, truth that has been scanned and confirmed. Even I know that as unbreakable fact. He volunteered his head to Nághtas, with Nadigh as witness. Prove your words, or I will call them false." The words sounded stuffy, but Aila's Kerasi vocabulary wasn't always as great as she wished. Basic conversations were easy, but political arguing was a level she didn't yet have.

"I need not explain to a female. You hear my words; you follow my words."

Pieces weren't adding up. *What you think is going on at any given time may not be true.* No one discussed Inner Circle orders. No one. Orders were between the Emperor and Member, no one else. Everything was so hushy few members knew each other. So why was this guy telling her this information?

Aila's brow furrowed, and she tried to do as Masákh had taught her, pull out details and gossip that might be relevant. "Are you Masákh's liaison? If you aren't, what is your part in this? If you are, why are you discussing Inner Circle business? You're breaking vows telling me this. It's very possible you don't know all of his orders, and therefore he's well in his business. I will hear no more. This meeting is ended." She stood up and turned to the door.

"You were not dismissed," the *bhísroti* said, his voice commanding but not yet angered.

Aila turned back, an acid reply building on the back of her tongue.

"There is a message you will carry back to your husband."

Aila waited, but no words came forth. "And the message is…?"

"You are the message," the *bhísroti* said without blinking. "You will bend on the table."

Every hair on Aila's body stood up. "*Kho dag an fi*, I do not understand."

"This is the message you will bring to Major Masákh. He will do his duty, or greater humiliation will occur. You will bend."

A giant hand seemed to reach into Aila's chest and squeezed her heart until it stopped. Heat left with her circulation, and she felt frozen right through her center. "I am a Union diplomat. I bear the Emperor's

Protection. Any assault to me becomes an incident between our worlds and will damage the Emperor's peace with the Union. That is Emperor's law, and that is truth."

"You are married to a Kerasi, on Kerasím. You are a Kerasi wife. We have taken steps to minimize your humiliation in that no other audience was permitted. You will now bend." He stood there patiently, as if he did believe she would throw herself on the table at his command.

"*Ka*," Aila said with authority, and stepped backward to the door. He signaled the guards with a finger; they moved in and grabbed for her.

Damn the dress! Why hadn't she been bold enough to wear pants? The dress ended halfway between her knees and ankles, too long and too fitted to kick higher than the guards' boot-covered ankles, and her soft beaded slippers were worse than being barefoot. No matter how much self-defense training she'd had, Aila was no match for two Kerasi guards. Her fists were grabbed in mid-punch, and her arms brought under control. All she could do was scream and jump and pull while Senator Sihn Ran watched as if the whole thing was taking far too long and he was going to be late for his nail appointment.

"You can't do this!" she screeched as they dragged her to the table. "I'm Union! I'll demand your head from the Emperor! You can't do this, by Emperor's Law! NO! Ráhnif! RAHNIF!"

The guards secured her with their metal poles. One pole pressed against the back of her neck, locking her head, the other just under her shoulderblades, crushing her ribs. If she tried to lift upward, the hard metal dug under the bones and made any movement agony. Her hips were above the edge of the table; the weight of her dangling legs dug the corner into her thighs. Her kicking had no leverage to do damage, and the pole crushing against her ribs made breathing and screaming difficult.

The *bhisroti* stood by her hip where she couldn't kick him. He eased her dress up with respect, and Aila's disbelief became reality. One of the guards pulled her scarf over her head so she couldn't see. At least they made no comments.

"It is true," Sihn Ran said as he explored her Human parts. "They don't have a ring. Most strange."

And then he was in her. The pain of the rods pressing into her neck and back distracted Aila, but not enough. She was aware of what was happening, every word, every breath, every movement, yet somehow her brain continued to function as if she were separate from what was happening, her mind gone elsewhere, wondering about inconsequential trivia such as what Zhenihda might be making for dinner and if the spices were going to bother her stomach, and if Thorin would be napping when she returned and how long Mimihn would hover around her asking questions.

He ground himself against her one more time with a sigh of relief, pulling her hips and holding her, then backed away. She heard him adjust his clothing, and then his hands had the audacity to pull hers back into place as if nothing had ever happened. The rods were lifted, and for a moment she just lay there, blank and empty inside and out.

Senator Sihn Ran patted her bottom. "Up. That is the message to take back to Major Masákh. He will follow his orders, or else the warnings will escalate. That is all. You are dismissed."

Aila backed from the table until her feet touched the ground, then pushed herself to stand. Her ribs felt bruised if not possibly broken, her shoulders and neck strained, her hips bruised from his weight pressing her against the table edge. Everything seemed to hurt at once. She straightened her dress, adjusted the scarf back around her neck. At last she faced Sihn Ran with eyes as cold and dead as she wished him to be.

"You have just assaulted the house of gha Lil. You have just assaulted the house of dar-Gilahn. And you have made an act of war against the Union without the permission of the Emperor. By his hand or mine, you will die for this."

He patted her cheek. "I'm not worried, Little Sweet. Major Masákh knows his place."

Aila turned and left the room while her legs still worked. She breezed past the receptionist with her eyes locked forward. She burst from the door and gave a dreadful jump when Ráhnif snapped to attention to her left, and she almost, almost screamed.

"You look most upset," he said with concern. "Did the interview not go well?"

Aila managed a deep breath despite the pain and tucked herself into the part of her mind that hadn't been in the room. "No. I am extremely angry and extremely insulted. We will leave immediately, before I beat someone to death with my anger." She squeezed her eyes shut, hard, harder, forcing her turmoil behind a wall. She could not, under any circumstances, lose her cool anywhere Sin Rahn might see her. Her lungs drew a slow painful breath, and she opened her eyes.

Ráhnif frowned at her, but Aila began to walk with increasing speed down the hall. He hurried to catch up.

"How far are we from the Embassy?"

"Perhaps twenty *fasím*? Did you wish to stop there."

"I don't know." Aila's voice cracked. She stopped walking, fighting so hard for control. "I don't know. I probably should. I should discuss it with Mr. Halian, file a report, but I don't want to deal with it right now. I do and I don't. I need to think first. If I do, it's all going to go bad real quick." Halian would rain hellfire down on the Emperor. He would get her a ship immediately. He would keep her safe. But she would have to tell him what happened, and right now those words weren't ready to be released. Not to him. Then he'd demand she see the medic, and that wasn't about to happen. Not right now. And there was no way in hell she was telling them anything that could possibly get back to her mother. Oh no.

Masákh, I need you!

"You do look ill. Do you wish to discuss it? Perhaps I can clarify something for you. Do you wish me to arrange transportation to the Embassy?"

Aila paused, wanting and not wanting it, but Tokh would kill the bastard and Halian couldn't do more than stomp his feet. Tokh knew the laws. "No. Not yet. I don't wish to discuss it right now. Just get me back as fast as possible."

"That may be better. I received a special message from General Tokh just a moment ago. He wants us to return immediately, no matter what has been requested of you. Come."

* * *

Ráhnif hurried her back through security and to their air transport. Aila sat very still in her seat, her mind blanker than all her visits to Kassán and his mind scanners. Her back hurt, her hips hurt, and it hurt her ribs to breathe or move her arms. Tears were swelling, and she didn't want them unleashed. Not where she'd have to explain them.

278

The primary goal of the aghát is to keep you from harm. The primary goal of the aghát is to keep you from harm. The primary goal of the aghát is to keep you from harm.

The memory echoed in her empty head, a single thought and nothing more. Her eyes slid sideways. Ráhnif was the newest *aghát*. He had access to the palace. He had no history with her. He stood in the hall while she was assaulted in a most despicable manner. Coincidence or not?

"Forgive me, Ráhnif. I'm upset and I'm feeling suspicious about many things. Whom do you serve?"

He frowned. "I am sworn to the Emperor and all his laws, under the command of General Four Tokh."

"All his laws?"

"All his laws."

"And do you serve General Tokh's family?"

After a pause, he gave a nod. "I believe yes. I don't take commands from them, but I respect and defend them as I would my commanding officer and all his property."

Aila nodded slowly. "I'm not accusing you, Ráhnif. I have no reason to suspect you are disloyal, but if I discover you have been disloyal to General Tokh, I will take your head before he can."

Rahnif's anger at the insinuation, at being insulted by a female, seemed to match her own. His words were sharp and unforgiving. "Great Lady Masákh, if I ever dishonor General Tokh, I will hand you my own sword to take my head before he hears of it."

Aila exhaled with relief, and allowed herself a tiny smile. She patted his gloved hand. "Thank you, Ráhnif. Those are the most comforting words I've heard today."

Ráhnif requested permission to land; Tokh met them in the courtyard, Mímihn rushing out behind with Thorin in her arms. Good. Mímihn would be distracted.

Tokh wasted no time. "Excellent. You're back fast. What type of interview did they request? Who was involved? What kind of information did they request? Was it strictly government or was it also a ComNet interview?"

Not an ounce of warmth radiated from Aila, hostile and precise as her mother often was. "General, you dragged me into Kerasi politics the moment you kidnapped me on Fornax. If I've learned one truth about your politics, it's that nothing is discussed with anyone who is not immediately involved. Therefore, I would appreciate your respect for that rule. I'll tell you this: you will recall my husband immediately, and you will secure me permission and ability to leave Kerasím as soon as he arrives, as is my right by Emperor's Law. Know that I am supremely angry, and I have been most insulted by a political system I no longer wish to deal with. I respectfully ask you comply with my wishes; if I must take refuge at the Embassy, there will be war with the Union. That I can promise you as truth. If I find out Nadigh had involvement in today's disgrace, there will never be another peace treaty in our lifetimes."

Aila entered the house and went to her room, leaving Tokh, Mímihn, and Ráhnif with too many questions.

Aila stayed in her room. She skipped lunch, but did join the crowd for dinner, for appearances' sake. While her heart cried out for *lunahl* – and *bohjis*, and *gohr*, and *rhimahdia*, and anything else Tokh might have kept in his cabinets – she didn't dare let her guard down. She sat with water, smiling faintly whenever anyone laughed. Ráhnif didn't speak further of the morning, to her relief.

"Did you place my request for travel release?" she asked Tokh.

"I'm having difficulties with my outgoing communications," he said, "but I will place your request the moment they are functioning. This is truth."

Aila's stone-cold glare seemed as if she herself could scan his brain for confirmation. "The clock is ticking, General. Make it soon."

Aila returned upstairs, unable to socialize any longer. She didn't do anything; just sat on the lounge with her com in her hand, hoping beyond hope that any second Masákh would call her and make the world right again. He would know where the lies were, how to set things right, how to get revenge. A knock tapped at her door.

Mímihn slipped in the room. "Fahni is playing with Thoren, so I came to visit with you. You're never angry like this. Do you wish to talk about your day?"

Aila stood up, despite the pain. "No. I want Masákh to come back. He's been away from me too long, and I need him to hold me and tell

280

me he missed me, too. I was only supposed to stay here three weeks; it's now six weeks and I must get home to my other business. I'm falling behind in my job and my studies. My mother is screaming at me because I haven't left yet."

Mímihn's sweet smile lit up the room, brighter than her gleaming yellow hair. "I can't say how much your visit has meant to me. I'll have terrible loneliness when you leave."

She placed her hand on Aila's arm in the gentlest of motions; Aila gave an involuntary jump to the side and panic flashed in her eyes before she relaxed again. Just as fast, Mímihn's manner changed. The endless cheer faded, replaced by a storm cloud dark and threatening.

"Aila? Why did you move like that? That's not you. Aila, what happened at your meeting today?"

Aila replied with a Mímihn-like smile. "I told you, I won't discuss it. I spoke with a Senator whose words were less than pleasing."

And Mímihn, little joyous Mímihn, who always seemed so much smaller and delicate even though she was less than an inch shorter, seized Aila by the shoulders, shoved her backward against the wall and pinned her there with a forearm pressed hard across the base of Aila's throat. Aila gave a cry as pain radiated across her shoulderblades, and the pressure and trapped feeling brought terror flooding back.

"Don't lie to me!" Mímihn raged. "I know that jump! I know the fear behind it. I know what causes it. Even with my poor eyes, I see the fear in yours! Tell me what happened! There's pain in your movement that wasn't there at breakfast. If you don't tell me, I'll ask Ráhnif!"

"He wasn't there!" Aila's head spun. The day was trapped inside her, making her dizzy. She couldn't think, couldn't find the right words in the right order or even figure out what to say. "If I say anything about the day, I'll start crying and I won't stop. I didn't expect insults, and I couldn't find Kerasi words to reply to them. I'll wait for Masákh. I need him more than I need breath right now."

Mímihn softened back to herself. The arm came down, and she took Aila's hands in hers. "A good wife doesn't pour her sorrows on her husband. She pours them on her lady-friends, who will help her bear them. How many were there, Aila?"

Aila found that safe little corner of her mind that didn't seem to be in the same moment, and inside her mind she closed her eyes and stuck her fingers in her ears so she couldn't hear her real-self whisper, "One."

"Did he hurt you?"

Aila wouldn't look at Mímihn. "I don't think so. The guards hurt my shoulders."

Mímihn insisted on checking. "You're bruised across here," she said, trailing a finger across the mark, "but it's not too dark. You were lucky." She pulled out her com and tapped an icon. "I'll have Fahni sit with you if you wish. I'll inform Tokh."

"*Ka,* Mímihn! *Ka!* Don't tell him!" Aila grabbed for Mímihn's handcom, but Mímihn danced out of the way.

"I must. With everything going on? How do you know it's not tied up in everything else? You're his daughter, and without your husband here, he will handle it. Now it's not just me in danger but you, and you're special."

"I won't discuss it! Don't do it, Mímihn! It's my own business!"

But Mímihn did, even though Aila waved Fahni away. If Tokh knew, the whole house knew. Assault was not a shame on Kerasím; it was far too common, but Aila wasn't Kerasi. Her face flamed with every step she took down the stairs at Tokh's request, and she let the cold and nasty attitude take over, keeping everyone away.

Three *aghát* were currently at the house – Mátokhan, Ráhnif, and Haghíde, and of course they were in Tokh's office with him. No doubt Ráhnif was in trouble, deserved or not.

Aila cut them off. "I told you, I won't discuss the day's meeting."

Tokh waved permission for her to sit in the chair by his desk, but Aila meant what she said. "Mímihn has made a bold accusation of what occurred at your interview. Does she speak truth: you were assaulted?"

"I told you. It was a closed meeting. I won't discuss the proceedings. You should understand that. I answered no such question from Mímihn, and that is scannable truth, as you are so fond of saying."

"I demand to know!" Ráhnif stepped forward with a snarl. He'd lost his polite subservience as the lowest ranking *aghát*, as fiery and fearsome as any of his teammates. "I demand to know if I was deficient in my duties."

He did have gumption, after all. Aila stood under his nose and matched his scowl. "Did you or did you not lead me to that meeting with false intent? Did you know the business that would be carried on within? Did someone besides Tokh give you an order?"

Ráhnif seethed, but Aila saw the fear in his eyes as well. He thought he'd messed something up, and he was worried. His ass depended on her answer, too. "My orders came directly from General Tokh and Tokh only. I was to escort you to the palace, wait for your business to be concluded, and return you when you were finished. That was my only directive. I knew nothing more and that is truth, on the honor of the Emperor!"

Aila's eyes remained locked on his, intolerable arrogance from a female. "Then you weren't deficient, were you." She broke her gaze and turned to Mátokhan, standing serious and silent next to Haghíde. "You're the one I'll have words with when my tongue is ready to yell. I won't play your games anymore. I'm done. I'm not convinced you don't know something, buried in your layers of secrecy, but you'll never tell, so I'll never know."

Mátokhan started to swell with anger, but Tokh stopped it. "Enough!" He unlocked a drawer and took out a rolled case, which he opened across his desk. It looked like a medical kit; he removed three vials and one of several syringes and placed them on the desk.

"My primary job is that of acquiring information. I am a level five interrogator, one level from the top. I will ask you once more to disclose what occurred today. If you don't cooperate, I will have you held and medicated. The choice is yours. If you prefer a female presence, I will ask Mímihn or another female to witness."

"Yes, I want a female present." Aila eased down into the chair in defeat. A pained little giggle escaped her. "General, if I relate any words of today, I assure you I will cry, and I won't stop, and I won't be able to speak."

"Understood. You will comply anyway." Tokh sat at his desk and waited. Mímihn slipped into the room and knelt on the floor next to Aila. She didn't understand Aila's Union speech beyond a few words, but she was available for comfort.

"Begin," he ordered. "You received a message from the palace. I saw it. I verified it, even though it was vague. I sent you with Ráhnif as protection as he is most familiar with the palace."

Aila nodded. "And everything was normal until I walked into that room. I knew immediately it was wrong. I've done enough interviews. My mother warned me. You warned me. All the *aghát* warned me. Even Sóghar warned me. Because I didn't see the *aghát* as a threat, because my time here has been mostly civil, I never expected harm. I walk around Kerasím flaunting my protection, my diplomatic status, my *dahneg* status, and it's always worked. I had respect. Today my status failed me. And I was degraded, demeaned, insulted, and yes, assaulted in a most vile manner. I was treated like a... I don't know what. Less than an animal. Like dirty sheets. This is despicable. This is unbearable. This is unacceptable. I want to go home. Now. I want the next ship out, back to the Union. I won't wait. Put me on a ship tonight and I will wait at the border."

"Why?" Tokh demanded. "How many? Were you given names? Did you see any rank or identification? What room was it? What did it look like?"

"Room 2081," Ráhnif said.

Aila shook her head. She knew better than to expect sympathy, but even a single word would have been nice. "A conference room. Empty, with a table and chairs. A *bhísroti* with two guards. I know, all *bhísroti* are now *dahneg*, but he was still a *bhísroti*. He wore blue and black, and his chin had two braids. Each side had a bead near the top to hold it out, and they came together into another bead at the bottom so it made a circle. I don't remember any badges."

"Not a circle," Mátokhan said with disgust. "It is a vulgar suggestion of female anatomy. Common among certain former *bhísroti*."

"Did he give a name?"

"Senator Sihn Ran. He didn't say what he was Minister of."

"I'm on it," Haghíde said, and pushed around the room to one of the computers.

"Any other identification? Anything at all?" Tokh said. "Rings, buckles, button designs, patterns on the clothing, badges or ribbons. Cosmetics, scars, cut of the hair..."

The word pattern came back to her. "On his shirt he had gold ribbon around the collar, down the front, and around the hem. It had a pattern on it. You won't understand what a spade is." She motioned for paper and a writing instrument. "It looked like this. Like a heart lying down. That's the only thing I can tell you."

"*Hag chamar*," Tokh said with a glance. "An arrow with a rounded end. It enters easy, but leaves great destruction when removed. Connection?"

Mátokhan frowned. "Possibly. I must check something before confirming it. If so, it's something you may not want to be involved in, General."

"I've heard that before, from higher sources than you."

"There is no Senator listed by the name of Sihn Ran," Haghíde announced. "I have run four different spellings, including 'similar to.' Nothing comes close. Is it possible for a non-Senator to be granted use of a conference room?"

"Run it through a *bhísroti* database," Tokh said.

"Possible," Ráhnif said, "with the right connections. It was second floor, unguarded. It wouldn't be difficult. I'll make inquiries and see if I can learn who requested the room, and when. It had to be signed out by someone. Nadigh is very tight on security; there will have been cameras."

Tokh turned to Aila again. He was all business, the great General getting to the bottom of an issue, but he wasn't unsympathetic. "You do understand how the word 'assault' is used on Kerasím? What it implies?"

Faced with the word, Aila's bravery began to slip, and the reality of the day leaked from the dark corners of her mind. Her voice shivered, and Mímihn slipped her hand into Aila's. "Yes. I understand it. And that is exactly what happened to me. I will not describe the details. We both know what male Kerasi do to female."

"Did he grab you at the door without word, or give reason?"

Aila nodded, fast and shaky. "He knew Masákh was Inner Circle. He wouldn't say how he knew, but he did. He said Masákh wasn't following orders, and this was a warning to him. And that's where I blame Mátokhan."

"Me?" Mátokhan whirled around with affront.

"You! You knew Masákh was upset over something. I knew it. Haghíde knew it. Not what, but something. You're the lead *Aghát*. You're supposed to be his friend. Why wouldn't you help him!"

"Not that I would not, but I *could* not! I know the difference in those words. Do you think I want to see him fail? I did speak with him in vague terms, but we can't share orders. Ever. Even if we have the same order. That is law."

The tears brimmed in Aila's eyes. She rose from the chair to face Tokh. "You told me for the last six years you would protect me. You claimed me as your daughter, of the line of dar-Gilahn. Tell me, General: what would you do if it had been Kesseh instead of me? What would you do, even if he outcasted you?"

Tokh's face took on a yellow tinge. It was impossible to tell if it was arrogance or a father's wrath that spoke. "I would take his head. Legally, if possible, and if not, I would pursue other paths to the same end."

Aila nodded. "Then prove your promise, and do that for me. I want a head. I want his head, no matter who sent him, no matter what his name or caste, no matter what his ties to the throne. I'll hold my tongue for the moment, but you warn your Emperor: this counts as an act of war against the Union. I will bring more trouble to this world than your beloved Emperor thought possible. He wants progress? It starts with me. Now. I want restitution, or I will destroy you. I am that angry. And I want Masákh returned. Now. And I want off this planet. Today."

Tokh bent his head. "I can't speak to the Emperor directly, but I can to those who do. Your message will be relayed. I have tried to contact Masákh on a private line; he has yet to reply. I don't trust my equipment at the moment."

"I know for fact he was in Keranihn the other day," Mátokhan volunteered with a grim expression, "but I cannot swear to his present location."

"Then have someone else send the request! Don't tell him why," Aila warned. "Not until he's returned. I don't want to distress him more than necessary."

"It can be done."

"And you!" Aila turned again to Mátokhan as the tears fell at last. "Leader of *Aghát*! You told me – you *promised* me – that no matter how things seemed, the *aghát* had my back covered. I didn't realize that was how you meant it." Betrayal crushed Aila's resolve. Mímihn grabbed her as ten hours of tears exploded at once.

Mátokhan, conceit personified, hung his head. "I apologize with deepest shame at my failure."

Thirty-nine

Mímihn spent a hard night with Aila as she cried herself into exhaustion so deep she couldn't relax until Mímihn retrieved *gohr* from downstairs. It was mid-morning when Mátokhan knocked at Aila's door.

Mímihn answered it. "This is not a good time for conversation. I'm afraid the assault has left her a bit weak in her thoughts. She's rather violent and won't listen to sense."

"It's unavoidable," he replied, and she allowed him in. Aila sat on the bed, dressed in Union pants and a shirt. Around her waist she wore Masákh's dress uniform weapon belt and his extra plasma pistol. The glare from her red eyes could have melted steel.

Mátokhan bowed. "General Tokh wishes you to know that he is working on the issue of communication and that Masákh will be recalled as the first priority when he trusts the connection. To do so without proof of security could endanger Masákh and others. Truth: When I last spoke to Masákh, he planned to seek refuge until he felt a danger had passed. No, he did not specify the danger, nor did he tell me where he was going. He did tell me that when he felt secure, he would be in contact with you. He anticipated it would be just a few days. If he has gone where I hope, and been received, he is indeed safe at the moment. I don't know if that gives you comfort, but it is truth I have not shared with anyone else."

"Thank you." Aila bit the words off as if launching a lethal weapon. She drew the pistol and aimed it at him. "You may leave now. I've cried my tears of shame. Today I'm angry. I'm angry enough to massacre your entire senate and laugh as they run. That's what they deserve. I wish to see no males until my husband returns. I suggest you leave."

Mátokhan raised his hands and bowed his head. "Understood. But two days is a long lead for an enemy, and should not be wasted. You may shoot me, or you may accept my honest help, laws aside, but know that if you shoot me, I cannot help."

"Speak." The weapon didn't budge, but he lowered his hands.

"Tell me exactly what was said to you regarding Masákh. I will make it my honor to discover what is truly going on. Something has distressed him from the start, and I'm beginning share his suspicions. Masákh won't know to question but I will, and I have resources he doesn't yet possess. Yes, I have failed you. We have all failed you in that we didn't suspect deceit. We have failed Masákh's trust as well. We won't be caught again. If you'll permit me to investigate the matter, put the weapon away and tell me what you know. You will break your vows and I will break mine. It could very well save his life."

It was strange. Mátokhan was never contrite. Never. There was always some wiseass comment leaking out somewhere. Except now. Never had Aila seen him so earnest and focused away from a negotiating table.

She holstered the weapon. Mímihn slid next to her on the bed and rubbed her back, Thoren on the pillows behind her. "I've gone over it and over it in my head. I kept asking him if he was Masákh's liaison to the Emperor, but he wouldn't answer me. All he kept mentioning was that Masákh was failing at his assignment. He was ordered to do everything he could to interfere and block some investigation, and he wasn't doing it hard enough, or right enough, and hurting me was the message to him to straighten up and do his job, or else."

"He didn't specify the investigation?"

"No. I'm sure of that. Just 'an investigation.'"

Mátokhan took a deep breath. He didn't berate her for not having enough information. It seemed to make sense to him. He eyed Mímihn with distaste, as if he wanted her to leave but chose not to request it. Not that Mímihn understood that much Union Standard anyway. "I don't wish to distress you more, but here is my truth: that confirms my fears. There are no liaisons for Inner Circle. You respond to a data address. The address contacts you. No names are used. No identification beyond the encrypted code. When needed, you will meet with the Emperor at an assigned time and place. It might be daily for a week to work out a plan; it might be once a year to stay in contact. You are contacted only when needed. That's all.

"Second, the pattern you reported on the clothing is a known symbol of a semi-secret society: Hag Shinsuum, the Silent Arrow. Some members are known. Many are not. All are wealthy. Almost all are former *bhisroti* or *fáhganid*. All believe they come from some amount of royal blood, and that they should have a say in the government. They buy influence to control many things – manufacturing, markets, trade, even utility supply. They deal in many illegal activities as well – abduction of unmarried females for off-world sales, addictive substances, weapons dealing. Nághtas didn't pay them enough attention. Nadigh sees them as a threat and would like them suppressed, but they're powerful enough to cause him great grief. It's possible that someone has intercepted Masákh, given him false orders, and he's interfering in something he should not. There are very few members to the Inner Circle, but I do know this: members take their work seriously. If there's an issue, it's that member's alone. If it was so severe as to cause the removal of that member, his wife would be compensated and taken care of because he had been an honored member at one point. Never has a wife been threatened or harmed because of her husband's failure. This does not happen. That is not the purpose of the Circle."

Aila gave him a smarmy smile like she was used to getting from him. "You failed me. Don't fail him. If he dies, I'll seek your head as well."

Tokh steeled himself for the potential battle to come. He'd played the games, danced the dances, too many years. Yes, his fortune was due to luck rather than kissing *khatas*, but he'd also gotten the fortune by knowing when to throw his *khatas* around. This was one of those times.

He hit the comm switch on his system, a new separate line that was tightly encrypted and perfectly clean. Trannor's call went directly to message folder, but he left the message anyway. "General, you're the one in charge of Union-Kerasi relations. I will assume you already know about Emissary Perrin's assault at the palace yesterday morning. I want to know one thing and one thing only, General Trannor: Did you order the assault? If you did, I will assume I have full discretion to discuss it with the Union. If, by chance, you did not, please inform me if you want me to handle it as family business, or you as Union Director."

Tokh closed out. He'd never had doubts about Trannor, but Trannor's refusal to help him with Mímihn, and the stalemated threats between them, had left him with a bad taste.

He waited, two, three, four minutes, but the comm stayed quiet. Either Trannor was ignoring him from spite, or fact-checking.

Tokh's anger grew with the silence. Just as he was about to take matters into his own hands, the line beeped. Tokh watched the clock and waited a full fifteen seconds before accepting it.

"Tokh."

Trannor's face was dark liver, and his eyes said he would no longer be pushed around. "Tokh, explain yourself or I will have you demoted to Colonel before you can disconnect. You have exactly ten seconds."

Tokh took a deep breath. An interrogator did not fall for bait. Not one that lasted, at least. "Exactly as I said, General. At our last meeting you made mild threats toward me. Now Aila Perrin has been assaulted by a Senator at the palace. I want to know if the two actions are coincidental or not. You are in charge of Union-Kerasi relations. What's going on, General? I need to know."

Trannor's gaze lost its deadly intent. His skin tone fell from brown to pasty mud. "What are you saying?"

"That the Emissary was physically assaulted at the palace not one full day ago by a Senator Sihn Ran and two of his guards."

Trannor blinked at last. "That name's not familiar."

"Probably because there is no senator on record by that name."

"Tokh, I understand the situation looks poor from your viewpoint, but I swear on the name of my father I neither ordered an assault nor knew about it. In truth, I'm ashamed that even in anger you would think I would do such a thing. I have never, in my entire career, ordered a female assaulted. It goes against everything we've worked for, everything we're trying to do."

It was Tokh's turn to be cold and unyielding. "General, my wife has been threatened, my house invaded, my daughter by law assaulted, and my communications compromised. I believe nothing anymore. This is my last patience. The Emissary has forbidden me from contacting the Union, but if I cannot get to the bottom of this here and now, they are my next call."

Trannor's blustering disappeared. "I beg you, Tokh, don't inform them just yet. Give me an hour or two to see what information I can gather. I don't want to go before them empty-handed. Showing that we've already been working to correct the situation is a much more favorable position. Please, give me just a little time. Hours. If you don't hear from me by the dinner hour, you may act as you choose. "

"Do what you will," Tokh said with his head high, "but she is not of a mind to wait long for revenge."

Fahni brought Aila's lunch to her, relieving Mímihn. Mímihn knew what to do and what to say; Fahni acted as if she were afraid of Aila. Perhaps it was the weapon.

"My husband is most deeply troubled by your incident," she said at last. "He thinks most highly of you. He wouldn't even *push* me last night. He feels he has failed you and that he has lost your trust, and that of his greatest friend Masákh. He's afraid of what Masákh will say to him. His heart is dying."

"I don't blame Haghíde. Please tell him so. He was not at fault. I don't trust anyone right now, but tell him when I'm ready, he will be the first person I'll trust again. I'll make sure Masákh understands."

Fahni squeezed her hand. "You truly are as great a lady as he claims. I'm sorry I don't know what to say to you. I know Mímihn's secrets, but I'm one of the lucky females who has never been assaulted. If I can do anything for you to ease your pain, please tell me. I don't know what to do."

Aila still had trouble looking anyone in the eye. "I was you yesterday, Fahni. *Yet.* You've just not become one of me *yet.* And that's why I will stay angry enough to rip the stars from the sky: so you never will be."

By mid-afternoon Tokh decided to take a break, get some air, and clear out his head. Walking around the gardens put his mind at ease and let his thoughts flow, leading him to insights he never found while sitting at his desk. He was about to switch the system over to automatic when a light flashed on his security monitor. Someone was at the gate requesting admittance. He hit the com switch. A dark vehicle waited at the gate, small, average, undistinguished. "Yes?"

"Trannor, General Five, requesting entrance."

Tokh's hair stood up. *Trannor? Here? Unannounced? Why would he not fly in?* He jumped to his feet, hit the switch for the gates, and ran out of the office so fast he was dark in the face and winded by the time he reached the door.

"Nihda! We have guests; General Trannor at the very least. I don't know why he's here, so be prepared for anything." It would have taken Trannor four hours to navigate the distance from Derahl Nor, providing there were no slow-downs on the massive bridge over the Satekor River. Trannor had all types of aircraft at his disposal; no one bothered with the lengthy road journey.

Zheníhda rushed to the kitchen to ready refreshments, desired or not. She sent a voice message upstairs to Mímihn to assist her and Shanohr.

Tokh opened the door as Trannor strode up to it. He bowed low. "General! I apologize. I was not informed of your impending arrival."

"Of course not. I told no one. Is there room in your shed for my vehicle? I wish it out of sight immediately."

"By all means. Thrit will see it is stored and cleaned for you." Ráhnif was at his elbow; Tokh waved a single finger, and Ráhnif ran to inform the servant. "He will see your driver is also properly treated."

Trannor's eyes took in every detail of the rooms, lingering long at the glass eyes of the stuffed *dhastal* head high over the door. He counted the heads: Tokh, Zheníhda, Ráhnif, Mátokhan, Shanohr, and Mímihn stepping silently down the stairs to stand by Zheníhda. "I came alone. If you're running security, I request it be turned off for now."

"The house is clean," Tokh insisted. "Will you honor us by taking a seat?"

Everything about Trannor said he was rushed and nervous, checking behind doors to see who might be listening. He darted here and there, checking out the windows toward the cliff, as if he wasn't sure what might be lurking there. It was a former-*fáhganid* house, and Trannor was former-*fáhganid*, so he shouldn't have been insulted by it. "Perhaps after. I've come to speak to the Emissary."

Tokh glanced at Mímihn. Mímihn kept her head down and bowed. "Revered Lord, she refuses to leave her room until her husband returns."

"Then you will inform her General Trannor wishes to speak with her, and if she won't come to me I'll come to her." Mímihn bowed and ran up the stairs.

She glided down a few minutes later, Aila trudging behind, each footfall slamming its landing with the grace of a cement block. Haghíde followed behind, a self-imposed bodyguard.

Aila stopped three steps from the bottom. Her face was a fearsome mix of tears and an anger that double-dared anyone to cross her path. She didn't bow, didn't even bend her head but stared at him in a heartless manner, Masákh's pistol still at her hip. "I'm not listening to a word of your bullshit. Unless your words are 'Your husband has arrived and your ship is here to take you home,' I have nothing to say to you or any of your kind."

Trannor moved toward her. Aila snatched her weapon and pointed it directly at him, a high crime for anyone, let alone a female. Behind her, Haghíde reached out a hand in panic but stopped short of seizing the weapon, lest she fire.

"DON'T come near me, or I'll drop you right here."

Trannor – General Trannor, General *Five* Trannor, former *fáhganid*, member of the Emperor's Elite, Director of Union-Kerasi Relations for the Kerasi Coalition, Commander of Lord Tokh, dropped to his knees before her, head bowed. "In the name of Kerasím, I wish to offer my sincerest apologies for the behavior of my people, and ask what I can do to protect you further."

"You expect me to believe that for a second?" Aila sighted the weapon on the back of Trannor's head. "I ought to blow you away right now just for being on the High Council."

Trannor didn't look up. He spread his arms out from his sides. "As you see fit, Councilor, though I come to offer my considerable services at great personal cost. Perhaps you would choose to hear me out before you execute me for my bravery."

Aila thumped down the remaining stairs, holstered the weapon, and sat on a chair at the edge of the room. Haghíde stood next to Aila; Mátokhan paused, then stood at her other side, his failures still stinging. Tokh pulled over a heavier, more caste-appropriate chair for Trannor.

Trannor sat forward. "I would prefer to converse in private, but I sense you would not allow that. I'll speak anyway. What I say is truth. If you wish, I'll submit to scan; Tokh himself may run the interrogation."

Aila snorted. "We both know scans can be faked, as can interrogations. Been there, done that."

"The offer stands. How do you know this is truth? Because I'm not here. No person knows where I am outside of this building. I didn't even bring a communication device. I have no authorization to be here and if I'm discovered, I will be suspect. I have worked to build Union-Kerasi relations for twenty-eight years. I risked my life for it; had I been discovered in Union space, we both know what would have happened. The event that occurred went against every policy the Emperor is trying to change. The Inner Council discussed the issue and although we cannot change the event, we, as the ruling council below the Emperor, condemn the action and apologize for the government of Kerasím."

Aila looked a fright; her hair was uncombed and greasy, dark circles marred the skin under her eyes, the orbs were bloodshot and her eyelids puffy from sudden bouts of tears. It made her subsequent sneer that much more intimidating. "I'm done with your government. I don't believe in them anymore. You sing sweet songs of change, but you do nothing. Once upon a time I believed in your Emperor. I loved him like my own President. I don't anymore. You know his words have shown no substance, yet you still give him your loyalty. Would you dare criticize him in public for it?"

Trannor frowned. "Do you wish the incident made public?"

"No! Absolutely not. Too many know my business already."

Trannor made a face, sighed, then spoke. He reminded Aila of Mátokhan, but without the smarminess. Trannor's power was unlimited; he didn't need it. "Understand, my family has served the Emperors in one capacity or another for at least two hundred years. My father was a Royal Justice. I grew up at Derahl Nor. Being Heir is a difficult position for a child. There are no peers, because you are the only *Thosikh* child. When I was perhaps five, Heir Nadigh saw me playing on the grounds and demanded to be allowed to play with me. His siblings were all *bhisroti,* so I was only a step below that.

"Over time, we became strong friends. There was a group of us, perhaps five, if you counted Royal Son Moragh, approved by the palace and granted immense privilege. My firstwife is his direct cousin. Our trust springs from a lifetime spent together, bonded by blood and brotherhood, not politics or profit. That's where my loyalty is born from. And that is why I worry what the repercussions will be if I'm found in unapproved contact with you. I run my department and my department only; Nadigh may be counseled, but he can't be told what to do. I will not betray him; I'm afraid to approach the Union behind his back, even if it falls within my duties."

Aila threw herself forward, almost falling to the floor in the process. "I forbid it! You are not to contact the Union over this! Not the Embassy, not the Ambassador, not a council, not the Secretary. Do you understand me? I will handle the Union. If you spring that information on them while I remain here, you'll bring their anger down on your heads. I have worked too damned hard – Tokh has worked too damned hard – for the peace we've achieved, and I will not let your bullshit aristocracy think they can destroy that by attacking me. I will not be your pawn. At worst, I need that to be kept in strictest confidence as a counteroffensive. The message given me was meant for Masákh only; no one will expect me informing his superiors. I know that attitude, and they fully expect me to be a good little servant and do as I was told. That assumption will give you time to act; I warn you: my price for cooperation is a head. Don't waste that time."

Aila paused. She'd had hours to mull things over in her head, various scenarios and various solutions. "What was Her Lady Majesty the Heir's response?"

"I don't believe she is aware of it. She was unavailable at the time and didn't attend the meeting."

"Good. Keep it that way. It was my assault, it happened to me, it's business between my husband and myself; no one else was there, no one else should ever have been involved. Right now you've lost all my sympathy and all my grace. I hope your world explodes in civil war, and you all crash and burn."

Trannor nodded. His face was unreadable, but there was an air of sadness about him that seemed genuine, as far as Aila could tell. It wasn't what she expected. "Very well. Your argument is strong. I'll relay your wishes to those I trust most."

He stood up; Aila's feet slammed the ground a second later. "I am not done. I did not dismiss you."

Trannor turned slowly. No one ordered him to do anything, unless they were former *bhisroti* or *thósikh*. Certainly not a female.

"I want my husband out of the Inner Circle."

"The Inner Circle is entirely Nadigh's business. I don't know the members, I have no influence over them, nor do I know what they do. That's your husband's decision, not yours. I can't help you in that request."

Aila bored her eyes into Trannor's, fearless and tyrannical. "You know at least two. You were present when my husband was inducted. I was assaulted specifically to increase someone's control over him, to keep him from disobeying someone's orders, real or fake. I want him out, alive and unharmed. You admit you have the ear of the Emperor. You'll find a way."

Trannor's fish-eyed stare scared her, but Aila kept the fury in her eyes. "I don't control the Emperor, nor would I ever make an unsolicited suggestion to him. However, I understand your concern, and should an appropriate moment arise where the question would not be out of line, I will make an inquiry and inform you of what was said. That's the best I can offer."

Aila's fire withdrew. She broke her gaze and bowed her head. "That's acceptable for the moment. Thank you most graciously, Revered Lord."

Trannor gave her the reproving stare a parent gave a disrespectful child who had apologized, then turned away. "Come, Tokh. I have information we must discuss."

Trannor breezed into Tokh's home office and took Tokh's seat behind his desk, leaving the guest chairs for Tokh. There was no doubt who was in charge, and who would remain in charge.

"Sit. The incident with your emissary has sprung open a black hole of difficulty. First, the Emperor apologizes deeply for her assault. He's closed the palace for the next two days. No public events, no public meetings, nothing below his inner council. We've located the security footage of your emissary entering and leaving the room, and of the perpetrator's entrance and exit. Therein lies the problem."

Tokh was not impressed. "There are many problems right now."

Trannor sighed. "They're deeper than you know. This information is of highest secrecy, but as you have high clearance as an investigator as well as a General Four on the Senate, I will trust you with it at this time, but beware to keep it tightly sealed. The Emperor has been following an illegal weapons trade. We know your wife's stalker is involved with it, but he just delivers, using his business as disguise. He's paid by the buyers and suppliers, and they are the ones the Emperor seeks."

Tokh gave a small chuckle. "My sources have already uncovered that information. Hag Shinsuum. I know the trail goes all the way into the palace itself."

Trannor's face fell. "How? That information is of darkest secrecy. Not even all of the Inner Council knows. I was briefed on the details only today."

Tokh's amusement remained on his face. "You told me it was my problem, not yours. My men are the very best. Someone within the palace gave Major Masákh orders to block my investigation; the attack on his wife was retaliation for my capturing Emrehl, even though Masákh had nothing to do with that. That information came from you. The bigger question is, did the order come from Nadigh, or someone pretending to have his authority? If you will share your information with me, I will share what I know with you. It may be the same information, but we can confirm the validity of it."

Trannor's authority scaled back, and he sat quiet while he accepted the situation. "Very well. I did underestimate you, Tokh. I've known your ability to do the impossible for fifteen years; I apologize for my error. Nadigh's forces have been following them for quite some time, blocking just enough shipments to make it look random and accidental. The people fronting the money are hard to catch; even when apprehended, they have excellent lawyers and paper trails to make them seem clean. Nadigh has tried very hard to play this by public law, letting his men handle it so that the deeds are seen as the crime, not a vindictive squabble on his part, with their arrest being made into a personal grudge or abuse of power. He had hoped to have enough leverage to begin taking out Hag Shinsuum in the next few months.

"What no one counted on was your wife's stalker. Hag Shinsuum has tried to squash him, but he is obsessed. When you investigated him, you ran the risk of exposing them. They intercepted your transmissions, hoping to throw you off course. When that didn't work, they attempted to kidnap her outright and solve the issue, but your females are stronger than anyone imagined. When still you persisted, they went after the one wife whose abuse would likely derail you for a longer period."

"So it is tied to me," Tokh said.

"Indirectly. It's desperation on their part. The easiest thing to do would be to kill you," Trannor said. "With you out of the way, they can jump in and carry off your second wife, no questions asked. But you're too well connected. You're a Senator with strong ties to the Emperor and to global politics. Your death, in anything short of a very obvious accident, would send people looking for answers. It could draw the Emperor's eye. Therefore, you are still alive. Hag Shinsuum has no need for your wife; it's only one of their underlings squalling for her in a bloody tantrum, and they fear he'll trade information for acquiring her."

"So what action do we take?"

"That's the problem," Trannor sighed. "You'll have your revenge for your wife. That's set. However, no one considered they would move against the Emissary. That's created a very difficult situation if we're to avoid angering the Union. The Emperor's timeline has been cut from months to hours, and that's not easy to do. There are many targets that must be taken simultaneously or they'll have warning and disappear. There are spies within the palace; greatest secrecy must be observed. This will be a global attack, and that takes time to arrange. You must now lay low, play ignorant, be happy with your prey. The Emissary will have her head, but it may be several days. Be very, very careful what you say over the com until the palace moves; I'll send an imperial crew to refit your system. This is well above your head, Tokh, as I've cautioned you all along. You've succeeded in fouling up a year-long undercover investigation of highest government priority."

Tokh found no humor in the blame. He'd had to fight too hard to get around the roadblock; and just when he achieved victory, a second unnecessary catastrophe was dropped on his doorstep. "I've done nothing to bring this on myself. If you had merely given me my prey at the first request, it would have ended there and your surveillance would have continued unabated."

Trannor stood up, relinquishing the desk and his power. "No. It wouldn't. You would have had your prey and his head, and then they would have retaliated by taking yours. I need you alive."

Trannor refused Tokh's offer of dinner and slipped out as silently as he arrived. Tokh gulped his food without tasting it, then pulled his *aghát* into conference without waiting for dessert.

"At the Emissary's request, I sent a message to the palace via General Trannor requesting passage for a Union ship. General Trannor will be sending a team to check and clear my communications, but it won't be until morning. I don't expect a reply until then. That leaves me with the second of the Emissary's requests: recalling Masákh. I need to contact him now, but I don't dare because I don't know if he's compromised, nor do I know his present location. Messaging services will have closed by now."

Haghíde and Ráhnif had the chairs; Mátokhan leaned back against the door, hands in his pockets, too casual for a proper *aghát*. He cleared his throat. "I may know where he is. If we understood each other correctly, he's sought asylum at the Union Embassy. He was supposed to send a message if he was safe. With the state of communications, I don't know if he has or not. No one has received a word."

"I'll retrieve him," Haghíde said quickly. "He'll trust me, and so will Ambassador Halian."

"The question is, will he believe you," Mátokhan said. "He's convinced Tokh will kill him for not assisting him in his crisis. He believed it enough to be willing to abandon Kerasím forever. And even if Tokh doesn't, he believes the palace will kill him, and we're now aware that's a more certain threat."

"Whatever it is, I will swear to give him a three-day reprieve. I'll demand explanation, and should I feel the information warrant such justice, I won't act until the third day. He has my word, and I shall make a statement for him," Tokh said.

On paper, Tokh could demand Masákh's head, but a three-day head start would almost guarantee Masákh would never be caught and brought to justice. The order would simply stay open until he tried to return.

Haghíde bowed. "You're most kind, General. I'll be at their gates by daybreak."

Forty

Haghíde played it simple, requesting to speak to Halian, and he was granted entry. He left his weapons and even his jacket at the reception desk; if it wouldn't have broken Union decorum, he would have stripped to his underwear, or less, to prove to Masákh he carried no weapons.

"Haghíde!" Halian shook the hand that was offered. "How are you? What brings you to our embassy so early in the morning?"

"I've been waiting for your gates to open since suns-up. I wish to speak with Major Masákh."

Halian laughed. "This is a Union embassy, Haghíde. Masákh doesn't work here."

Haghíde expected the response, and stayed friendly. "I know for a fact he's here. It's not an issue. Communications cannot be trusted, therefore, I've come in person to bring him information and a message. I've surrendered my weapons, your staff have scanned me; I come in friendship and peace. My appearance is voluntary; I was not ordered to be here." That was truth.

"I wish I could help you, Major Haghíde, but we don't actually get many Kerasi just stopping by to say hello. In fact, none of you, actually, have ever just stopped by to be friendly and keep in contact. I spoke for you in Union court, I assisted you in making the right contacts, helped you integrate into Union society, you threw your voice behind my nomination for Ambassador, and you and your fellow *aghát* never even come by for a cup of *raffin* when you're in the city. I understand you're usually in the Union, but not all of you are stationed there anymore."

Haghíde's silence bore the truth. He'd never thought of it, never even considered it, and the dishonor shamed him. Halian was correct, and he had full reason to refuse hospitality. Haghíde bent his head. "My apologies. That is truth. It's a grave oversight on our part. No dishonor was ever intended. I shall see to it personally that the situation is corrected."

Halian gave a soft chuckle. "I'm messing with you, Haghíde. I'm not angry. Having a daily barrage of *aghát* dropping by for *raffin* would put a serious glitch in our work schedule. We don't have enough people for that. But once a month over a game of Tabs would be nice. So come, have a seat. We'll start today. Flais, could you bring us some *raffin*, please?" he said to an aide. "Come to my office."

Haghíde followed, but his impatience showed in his footsteps, sloppy behavior for an *aghát*. The aide entered with two cups and a carafe on a tray. "Truly, Major Halian, I'm here to speak to Masákh."

"And I told you, Major Haghíde, no one ever stops by to chat. Why would you think he would be here? What's going on?" He poured two cups and handed one over.

Haghíde took a taste to be polite, but was never a strong fan of *raffin* to start with. He played with the cup. "Truth: General Tokh's security has been breached and communications are suspect at the moment. I bring information for Masákh in a manner other parties may not overhear. If you wish, you may be witness when I speak to him. It's not classified. It's honorable for you to shield him, Major Halian, but this is his last known location, and that's unlikely to have changed." When he focused, Haghíde was as superb at negotiations as the rest of his team.

Halian sipped his cup in amusement. "I guess we're at a sort of stalemate, then."

"No. I will hear his words," said a third voice.

Halian turned his head, but Haghíde didn't flinch, as if he'd counted off the minutes and the script said it was time for entry stage right. Masákh stood in the back door of the office, out of uniform.

Haghíde didn't move a finger. "You may bind my hands to the chair if you desire. On my honor, I come with good intent; this is truth. If Ambassador Halian would assist, he will find a data chip in my shirt pocket. It's Tokh's message to you. It's safe for all ears."

Halian retrieved the chip, slipped it into the Kerasi interface at his desk, and let it play. Masákh entered the room.

When it was over, Haghíde spoke. "Mátokhan, Tótoghar, and I witnessed his words. Come back. Discuss the issue. You have a three-day reprieve. If Tokh feels your fear is warranted, you have three days before he will act. That's a very long head start. It could take weeks to locate someone after that. Tótoghar is waiting nearby."

Masákh sat, his forehead resting against his interlaced fingers, thinking out various scenarios. "If Mátokhan had told Aila my location, she would have demanded to come here, at the least demanded to accompany you. I'll consider it, after she's brought to me here and we discuss it. I will not have her made hostage."

"You need to come back," Haghíde said slowly. "Aila is at Tokh's, and you are free to speak to her there, or return here with her."

Masákh gave a soft snort and a flash of pained smile. "What's going on, Haghíde? You know information. Tell me why you won't bring my wife to me, or you'll know my wrath."

It was Haghíde's turn to smile in discomfort. "I have been expressly forbidden, by your wife, to discuss such information in any form with Union sources."

Halian crossed his legs and settled back, watching the drama. "Sorry, men. You're in my house, I'm host. My rules apply. Aila falls under my jurisdiction. I have every right to be informed."

Masákh's gaze grew cold and threatening. "I'm husband and I demand to know the information. Don't toy with me. You're now married; you should understand my anger. If you aren't my true brother, then your blood will be spilled today. My patience is thin, given the situations I face. What news does my wife hide?"

Haghíde didn't rise to the threat; instead, he seemed hurt by it. "I would never deceive you, Masákh. That's truth." He turned to Halian. "First you must swear you will keep the information inside this building. You mustn't act or even speak of the information to anyone, especially inside the Union, until Emissary Perrin – Emissary ghas Lil," he corrected, "gives approval that you may. She has expressly forbidden the information be given to the Union until such time as she wishes, including yourself."

Halian frowned. "She can't be pregnant. Hybrids can't happen." Haghíde waited. "All right. I promise. What you say will stay in this room as personal information, until she tells me to inform the government."

"On your honor," Haghíde confirmed. He turned back to Masákh, his closest friend, even without *aghát*. "Aila has taken refuge in her room and will not leave. She demands you be recalled immediately, and she demands immediate return to the Union. A message was delivered yesterday directly to the palace, and a ship should be coming. Tokh has now officially recalled you at her request. Two days ago, she was called to the palace on false pretense. Instead of being interviewed, she was assaulted by a former *bhísroti* who claimed to be a Senator, as a direct warning to you. The name does not match any known Senator. We are now tracking those leads as well. Tokh understands the threats against you may be very real; that's why he has granted you a reprieve to claim her. She is most angry and upset, and wishes your comfort and protection. It was our duty to protect her, and we failed. On behalf of the *aghát*, I apologize most deeply for our failure."

It was hard to tell who was more shocked, Masákh or Halian. Masákh paled and turned inward. Halian shot to the edge of his seat.

"She what? Is she all right? Was she hurt? Does she need medical attention? You need to bring her in to be looked at. How can I help?"

"She has minor bruising, but was not damaged. She has refused all medical attention. She wishes Masákh at her side. I don't know what help you can offer, other than demanding a ship for her return."

"I'll place a second request within the hour."

Masákh found his voice, empty and hollow, so very unlike him. "Who was with her?"

"Ráhnif," Haghíde said, "but she doesn't hold him responsible. She went into the room alone; he's ill with grief, knowing he stood guard at the door. He tried to turn in his commission, but Tokh won't accept it. He gave him four day's leave, but he won't leave her door. Don't blame him. He followed protocol. He had no more idea what would happen than she did. Neither you nor I would have done any different."

"'Don't go,' she asked. She claims every time I leave her side, something bad happens to her. And she is correct. Every bad thing to happen was in my absence. She'll be furious with me."

"Then come back with me now. She's the reason I'm here. She requires your comfort."

Masákh stood up. The *aghát* followed. "I will. I need to see her as much as she wishes me. Three days. If I can't fix my situation in two," he told Halian, "I will be here on the third day with Aila."

"I'll be expecting you," Halian said, and shook his hand. "And Masákh – don't leave me in the dark. I extended extra privilege to you; I expect you to keep me informed over those two days, even if you don't tell Aila. Let me know how she is, physically, mentally, and get her back here to see me in person as soon as you can."

Masákh bowed his head. "I thank you sincerely for your generous hospitality, Ambassador Halian. I will keep contact."

They were moving toward the door when Haghíde turned around. "I will make certain *raffin* days are scheduled."

Totoghar clapped Masákh on the shoulder as they approached the helicraft. "Masákh! About time you came back!"

Masákh clapped him in return. "It's an honor to see you, too." His foot was lifted toward the step when his com unit signaled. He glanced at the sender and his eyes widened with surprise, a serious mistake for an *aghát*. He strode to the tail of the craft and hit accept with a shaking finger.

The face on the screen was no one less than Emperor Nadigh himself. Masákh fought the urge to kneel before a comm unit. "Major Masákh gha Lil. I speak to you myself so there is no misunderstanding. It was brought to my attention that someone has given you false information in my name. I request your presence immediately to discuss the issue."

Masákh lifted his eyes. The worry on his teammates' faces mirrored his own. This could be his salvation; this could be his death. "If it would please the Emperor to grant my craft landing permission, I will be there in less than ten *fasím*."

"You will be met on landing." Nadigh closed his feed without any sign-off.

Masákh pocketed his com as he approached Haghíde and Totoghar. "It seems we will have a side trip first. I have been requested to the palace immediately, by his Majesty Emperor Nadigh himself. Take us to Derahl Nor."

Forty-one

Aila spent the day alone, save Ráhnif pacing outside in the hall and Mímihn and Fahni coming to check on her. Aila didn't think she was at any risk with Tokh home, but she understood having a personal guard for her was Haghíde's way of apologizing, and Ráhnif was so gutted by the knowledge he never heard her scream through two doors and a vestibule it was hard for him not to volunteer around the clock to make up for it. And in the late afternoon, a blessed afternoon with the Imahlva sun shining so bright and the sea-winds blowing a sweet scent of *lalimbad* flowers from the garden, one of her wishes came true.

Aila's door opened without warning and it was Masákh who stood there in strange clothes, looking as if he'd rushed across the world without stopping just to see her – which was quite possible, for all she knew. He stared, half in distress and half in longing.

If Aila had cried before, seeing him brought such a mix of pain and relief she started all over again. The tears poured forth as she pulled herself off the bed. His arms seized her and held her to him, and the world was right again.

After a minute he pulled back and wiped her eyes with his thumbs. Aila didn't think a Kerasi male was capable of the depth of feeling she saw in his face. *"Falahndi arihl!* They told me. Your grief is mine. Were you injured?"

Aila caught her breath and calmed a little. "Very minor. I was lucky."

"You were not." He pulled her over to the lounge seat, sat on it, and pulled her down onto his lap, holding her tight, nuzzling her hair and kissing her forehead. "I apologize most humbly. I thought you would be safe with Tokh. I'm used to thinking of you in Union terms; you have never before been my wife on Kerasím. I forget you can be called away just as I can. This won't work here. I can't worry about you and worry about my tasks at the same time. We must return to Union space, where you won't be such a target. I should have maintained contact; with open contact you could have sought my approval for the interview and I would have taken steps to assure it was appropriate."

Aila's head rested against his chest, her sobs softening. "Half of me is angry you'd think I'd stop to ask your permission before doing my job, but the other half is now well aware of why I should. Why, Masákh? At least have the courtesy to tell me why they did this. Don't tell me names or places. Just tell me what you were supposed to do that you didn't. If I have to suffer like this, I demand to know why."

Masákh held her close. His hand played with her hair, a soft mousy brown now streaked with highlights from the strong Imahlva sun. It seemed forever before he answered. "I wish I could tell you, but I'm as confused and betrayed as you were. I'm new to Inner Circle. I believed what was told to me, without double-checking like a cadet. I don't like to tell you things that may upset you, but I know the Union has strong laws against assault and that you're already quite upset, so I will tell my truth, though it may upset you more.

"I was given orders by someone whose name I didn't know. They knew mine, they knew my business, they knew I was Inner Circle; I had no reason to believe they weren't a contact. They gave me orders that went against my oaths. It bothered me greatly, but I was afraid it was a test, to prove my loyalty and worth. I tried to ask Mátokhan about it, but he wouldn't speak long enough to clarify my questions. He now knows he was wrong. He should have listened, then counseled me as needed. I was called to the palace this morning, where I met with the Emperor and then his council. From the mouth of Nadigh himself, he does not use liaisons. I would receive an encripted link requesting me to come to the palace, and any orders would be directly from Nadigh himself, in person, so there are no misunderstandings. I hadn't been told that yet. Nadigh appreciates the work I do behind Union lines and that reporting to him in person when I am on world will be sufficient. That was his only plan in making me Inner Circle, because of the people I know and thus information I may become aware of. He swore to me in person he gave no such orders. Now I must either accept the fact I allowed myself to be used against General Tokh by an enemy, or believe that the Emperor, the Emperor I have sworn my life to, who has granted me status and wealth and power above my caste, has lied to me. One of them is true and one is not, and I have no way to prove either."

Aila lifted her head. "You were ordered to cross General Tokh?"

She couldn't tell if Masákh was embarrassed or ashamed. "I was instructed to prevent Tokh's inquiry into Lady Mímihn's troubles. Because I knew General Trannor refused to assist him, I believed it was a palace directive. I had to choose between my loyalty to Tokh or to the Emperor. I was becoming ill with the conflict. I asked Tokh to send me into the field to track clues for him; it was a lie to both sides. I went so I didn't have to see Tokh every day and pretend to assist him. I continued to research the issue on my own initiative; I didn't give him the results until I felt I could no longer keep them from him. So I failed both directives."

"You can't fail a lie." Aila ached for him. No wonder he'd been so irritable. His loyalty to Tokh was unshakable. Cutting off his own fingers one by one would have been an easier choice. "Does Tokh know? What did he say?"

"He wasn't pleased that someone gave such an order, but understood I had no way to know if it was real or not. He thanked me for doing the least damage to him that I could. I took a great risk, and he knew it. The palace also understood my difficulty and relieved me of misconduct. I'm safe for the moment."

Aila dropped her head back onto his chest. "How did we get into such a mess, Masákh? And how the hell do we get out?"

Tokh called Aila into his office before dinner, Masákh by her side.

He called up several photos to his display screen. They were security photos, enlarged and enhanced for grainy detail. "Do either of you recognize him?"

"No," Masákh said.

Aila stared so long that both Tokh and Masákh turned to look at her. "That's the bastard. That's him. The *khatorahkt palabito ghinadín-tragayat ama-trixhoran*! He's the one who assaulted me. That's his chin. That's the shirt with the spade edging."

Masákh frowned at her. "You curse in Kerasi better than you speak."

"I have more reason."

308

"You are certain, beyond doubt?" Tokh asked. "You would risk executing an innocent man?"

"He's not innocent," Aila insisted. "I could tell him by voice alone. There's no mistake."

"So be it. You have identified former *bhisroti* Vanrish Yin Sintahl. He's no Senator, but friends with several. He runs a corporate finance company out of Lupagh Lura, a top-two hundred company world wide for income, which put him on the Financial Advisory Council, not the Senate. His name would be on file, and he could be granted limited access to the palace."

"That's not the same as Senate?"

"The Advisory Council is a panel of local experts who can report on trends within their region. Their reports go to the Senate Financial Council, which tracks situations based on the Advisory reports and then presents it to the Emperor," Tokh explained. "However, there is reasonable evidence that much of Vanrish Yin's business deals with spirit companies – they exist on paper only, perhaps an empty building somewhere. Money from illegal sources gets poured in, legal money flows out, and a portion of it goes to Vanrish Yin's pocket without seeing a tax note."

"We call it laundering," Aila said. "Soiled money goes in, clean money comes out. It's illegal in the Union."

"Here also," Tokh said. "The Emperor has requested your patience. He promises you your head, but it will take three to five days to get it. Vanrish Yin is well-invested in Hag Shinsuum, which makes it complicated to capture him. He has ears in the palace, as well as numerous body guards. It will take planning, or he will disappear before action can be taken."

"Have you received reply as to my request for a ship?" Aila asked, her clipped words straining to stay polite.

Masákh put his hands on her shoulders. "It will come. I myself requested Ambassador Halian for immediate return to the Union. Halian will not fail us."

"No," Tokh admitted. "Not yet. But this investigation has taken precedence, so I'm sure the date and time will be forthcoming later today."

* * *

Aila hadn't called home in a week, stretching the gaps between calls because she couldn't handle Leila's needling, but it would be worse if she never called. She was a bit surprised her mother even answered the call.

"My daughter? My daughter is calling me? I thought she was dead by now," Leila said in greeting.

"Hello, Mom. I'm sorry I didn't call you sooner. I don't have time or patience to call you every day. You know full well when I'll be calling."

"If you have to be there, I expect a call every day," Leila growled. "I don't want to have to wait three weeks to find you were murdered last Friday. I'm sorry if easing my anxiety because you're on a hostile world with almost no aid is such a burden on you. Masákh doesn't want you calling home?"

"Masákh is fine with it, Mom. Do you want to talk to him? I can get him."

"No. So you haven't been murdered yet. Are you afraid to leave the house? When are you going to stop all this nonsense and get back here?"

"I'm not afraid to leave the house, Mom. I was down at the palace this very week. I know you're going to be shocked, so I hope you're sitting down, but yesterday I did request permission from the Emperor to leave, so I expect to be out of here within the week. Masákh returned from assignment today, so he's just got to finish up a few things and we'll be set as soon as the ship arrives. Okay? Can you live with that?"

Leila paused in her blustering. "Well, imagine that. You're part of the Union after all. Don't forget, your marriage isn't legal here."

"I haven't forgotten, Mother. I'm well aware of it. You never let me forget. I will let you know as soon as my permission comes through."

"Hmph. I'm going to call Hhani's office and see what they can do to speed it up."

Aila rolled her eyes to the ceiling. "Please do, Mother. Go right ahead.

For the first time in days, Aila looked forward to sleep. Masákh would be next to her, Masákh whose presence always signaled safety. Now she could truly relax.

She changed into her nightwear while he meticulously removed his clothing, checked his weapons, arranged his communication devices, and made sure all his badges were lined up in proper order on the drawers. Aila sat on the side of the lounge to give her comm unit one last check for messages.

Masákh came up behind her and hugged her. His words bounced with charm and playfulness as he kissed and then whispered in her ear, "I am going to throw a *push* into you from one end of this house to the other, until you forget everything but me."

Aila twisted away in horror. She wrenched herself from his arms and stood up. "You're not going to do any such thing! Don't you touch me!"

Masákh frowned in confusion. "You cannot refuse to *push* me. I could beat you into submission and the law would support me. I know that's not your way, but we have been apart for days. I've looked forward to this night since I left. I know you were assaulted, but I will replace your bad memories with good ones. Are you denying I can do that?"

Aila stood in disbelief, her mouth open to speak but no sound coming out for the longest time. "You don't get it, Masákh. You really don't get it, do you. I was assaulted against my will. I was frightened half to death. It was every terror everyone ever filled me with for the last six years. I was held down and forced to submit to utter degradation at some psycho's whim. How could you expect me to want more of what I just went through, even with you?"

She searched her head for an example he could connect to. "You're Kerasi. You've told me it happens to men as well; that part of the high suicide rate among middle-caste males is from being humiliated. Were you ever humiliated? Do you have any idea what I feel like? Do you have any idea of how big a rock I feel in the middle of my stomach? Imagine just for a moment you were caught off guard and were grabbed by a superior and pinned down by his friends no matter how hard you fought, and humiliated when you least expected it. How would you feel? Would you want someone coming up to you afterward and telling you they were going to do the same thing to you over and over for the next six hours, until you enjoyed it?"

Masákh's face took on a far away gaze, and he fell silent. Aila's heart squeezed tight. She must have hit on something. Masákh always had a ready lecture to reply with.

He walked to the balcony doors and gazed out at the tiny lights outlining the rows of flowers in the gardens below, and the darker band of night where the land dropped over the cliff to the inlet and the black water surging with the tide. In the distance, the lights of boats shone like fireflies.

Damn Kerasi traditions! Aila followed him and stroked his arm. "I'm sorry. I just can't do that for you right now. I'll need a few more days to put my head together. It would help if I were back home, but I'm not. We'll get there again, but it's not going to be tonight."

Masákh stayed silent for another minute before speaking to the glass door. "As males, as officers, as Kerasi, we do not speak about such things. Sometimes things are known without saying, and sympathy and support can be given with a gesture or touch. Others you do not know and cannot assume either way. I... have been humiliated. Cadets wait for you to become fourteen, when you are legal to prey on, and there are those tormentors who hold lotteries to see which underling they will get. I was fifteen when a senior cadet caught me alone. He was *nhasarwharl*; as *whátaral*, I couldn't deny him. Even when I knew half the school was giving and half was receiving, I still felt deep shame, even though it was done privately. Now, twenty years later, I remember every unkind word he said to me, the pressure of each and every touch. My roommate saw my face when I returned, and surmised what had happened. Students are not allowed spirits in the dormitory, but he shared an illicit bottle of *flehdan* with me to celebrate my survival."

Aila wanted to cry, but was so horrified the tears wouldn't come. "I am so sorry."

Masákh wouldn't look at her. "As I said. You celebrate your survival." He put his arms around her again, comforting but not demanding, and he kissed her between her eyes. "If that is how you feel, then I understand your distress, and I apologize for distressing you further. Perhaps tonight we will simply drink to our survival, and plan what to do from here."

Aila smiled up at him, half-human looking, half-Kerasi looking, and the fuzzy comforting feeling overtook her. "I do love you."

312

"I have unfortunate news for you," Tokh said heavily. "Do not bring me your anger; I'm only the messenger. I've received word from the palace, from the office of the Emperor himself, specifically Chief Advisor Royal Brother Moragh. It was confirmed by General Trannor. Your request for a Union ship to retrieve you has been denied at this time. Emperor Nadigh requests your patience until he has finished his investigation into your incident and apprehended all who are involved. When his investigation is complete, your request will be approved."

Aila felt her insides go cold. "No! No! That is absolutely unacceptable. I demand to speak with Nadigh in person. I have his sworn testimony – he wrote it into law for me! – I can't be kept from leaving. I've been here more than six weeks! I need to go home! If I'd been able to leave on time, this whole situation wouldn't have happened! You're not keeping me here so something else can go wrong. It's just not going to happen. We'll see what the Union has to say about this!"

Aila's mouth pinched in tight and her eyes burned with fury. There was no mirror in Tokh's office, she didn't see it, but for moment she looked remarkably like her mother. Her fist shook at her side as if she wanted to punch something, but instead she spun on a heel and fled the room before Tokh could tell her otherwise.

She stormed from the office, through the kitchen, and out the patio doors to the gardens, far from the house, and hit the call button for the Embassy. Tokh insisted his new communication security was top of the line and clean, and Masákh had reinstalled the connection on her hand com, freeing her to use it. "Ross Halian, please. This is Aila Perrin, and it's urgent."

There was a brief pause while the call was transferred. Aila caught a deep breath. Ross barely had time to say "Hello?"

"What the hell kind of bullshit is this, Ross? What the hell do they mean they won't grant permission for a ship?"

On the tiny screen, Ross turned his head to the side as if to keep the words from hitting his face. "I knew you'd be calling. Stars above, you sound just like your mother."

"Not funny, Ross. They wrote it into law. I have to be allowed to leave. You have to get this resolved. Today. I've been trying to leave for weeks. *Weeks*, Ross."

"Let me speak, or you won't get any answers. I am aware of the situation. It pertains to everyone here, too, you know. Remember that part about being a diplomat, about negotiation and winning people over? This is where all of that comes into play. I spoke with Advisor Moragh, and he assures me it's temporary. The Emperor is involved with a restructuring of security, especially of trade routes, and promised me there would be approval within a week at the absolute most. I can keep checking every few days, but there isn't much I can do. It's their space."

Aila gave a hard sigh. Desperation, then pain crept into her voice. "Ross, that's not good enough. I've been here too long. I need to go home. Now. I need to get out of here for my own sanity."

"Are you okay?"

Indecision tore at Aila. Her bottom lip pressed into her top, her eyes darted side to side in an effort to escape, and her breath caught. "At the moment, yes, but I need to get out of here, as fast as possible. Don't tell my mother – PLEASE don't even give a hint to my mother, Ross, I beg you. I – I was assaulted on a trip to the palace several days ago. I won't go into details. Supposedly the Emperor didn't know about it, and that's what's behind that restructuring you were told about, while he goes after the perpetrator. Tokh's been really kind, but even the women are still Kerasi and they don't see things the same way I do, and I really, really need to get back to a sane universe for my own sake, if you know what I mean." Aila rubbed at her nose, but she didn't cry.

Halian's face filled with pain. "I'm so sorry to hear that. You should have come in immediately. What happens here is none of your mother's business; she has no access to our information, and no right to do so. Why don't you come in now. Have our medic check you over. Stay here and relax while you wait. You've gone native perhaps longer than any Union person ever has. I'm sure you've got plenty you can report on; getting back to work might take your mind off the wait. Is Masákh being supportive?"

The calmness of his words, the offer of a safe haven, helped Aila pull herself back from the brink. "Actually, yes. He's been far kinder and understanding than I ever imagined. But he feels the need to go back, too. He has no permanent duties here; he's just twiddling his thumbs. No. I'll stay here, but I have little patience left. Tokh promised me the head of my assaulter, as is my right, and he's working on that right now. I can't leave until he's done. Then I'll shake his hand and be out of here, while we're still on speaking terms."

Halian frowned, then shook his head as if he hadn't quite heard right. "Aila, you can't just take a man's head. You're not Kerasi; you're still bound by Union law, and capital punishment is against the law. Surely there's a Kerasi alternative."

Aila laughed. It had no humor whatsoever, a cold-blooded cackle that dared Halian to repeat himself. "Don't go there, Ross. Unless it's been done to you, don't even pretend to know what you're saying. As I keep getting reminded, I'm a Kerasi wife. I'm entitled to a head by Kerasi law, and that stinking son of a bitch is going to get what he deserves. You're the goddamned ambassador. This is what you were hired for. Get on your damned wave link and get me my ship. I don't want to hear a thing from you unless it's to tell me what day and time it will be here."

Aila closed out the link. Anger still had a tight grip, and for a mad moment she considered pitching the handcom as hard as she could and watching it sail to its death over the cliff wall, but reality wouldn't let her. Aila knew she was a lousy throw; it would never have the power to go out far enough to make the water, and with her luck would fall onto *dahneg* Oghil's front step and kill someone, adding to Tokh's woes. She pocketed the com and sat down in the farthest corner of the yard to sulk.

Forty-two

Investigators squeezed information from Emrehl the prisoner easier than expected. Tokh received approval to serve justice any way he saw fit, be it a tongue, a hand, or a head. He had far too many crises to deal with; he let Emrehl sit and stew in his prison cell one more night. Mímihn accompanied him back to Keranihn the next morning, without the baby.

Tokh picked up her hand and squeezed it. "You're sure about this? If you don't feel up to it, I'll do whatever you wish, and photograph the results for you."

Mímihn was quiet, so unlike her bubbly self. She didn't even smile as she nodded. "Yes. I'm scared. I'm scared even his dead body will come after me. But I must do this to put myself at rest. I'm afraid I'll become too angry. I might say or do something that won't be appropriate to my station as your *dahneg*-wife."

"We're going to the deepest, darkest depths of the building. Very few people are allowed there. You may be the first non-officer to enter it and leave on your own feet, certainly the first female. I'll be with you, Kassán, maybe one other. I give you permission to be angry. Say what you will. No one will object. Not me, not Kassán. You're there to pass judgment and order his death, not serve him rum."

Mímihn nodded once more, subdued and grim. "Only if it were on fire, and I spilled it on him."

Tokh led her through the halls of the S&I building, to the lifts, and then punched in his special code for the sub-basements. Down there, he handed over the signed permissions for Mímihn to access the floor. They waited in an office while the prisoner was brought from holding to a special room for medical interrogation. To that very day, Tokh got a sick feeling when he thought of Kassán working in such a room. Sometimes the set-up was simple – a combative prisoner was restrained, sedated, and interrogated under hypnotics to reveal information without the use of the mind scanners. Easy, straight-forward, and standard as a second-wave interrogation. Other times, however, more invasive measures could be used, such as force-feeding a prisoner who refused to eat, or punishments carried out, from castrations to unhandings, to physical incentives involving pain induction and psychological retraining. Things Kassán enjoyed too much.

Kassán greeted them while they waited. He bowed to Mímihn. "Lady Tokh. My apologies that you must be brought to such a place."

"Thank you."

He turned to Tokh. "Are you ready? Interrogation did nothing to change his temper. Be prepared."

"His is a fire that won't stop."

"Follow me."

Mímihn had dressed all in black, from her veil to her shoes. Black was not a mourning color on Kerasím, sky green was; the black was to hide behind. Black disappeared in dim light, blended into the shadows. She would be faceless, shapeless, a ghost of memory unless she chose to reveal herself. Black as her insides felt. Black as her vision would be if the room was dim. She didn't need vision to remember his face. Her nightmares never let her forget.

Tokh stopped at the door. Mímihn's veil was down, hiding her daffodil hair, but he tipped her head up for her to look at him. "He is in that room. He's angry at his capture. He's angry at me. He's going to say things to you, things meant to hurt you, to cause shame, to cause you as much pain as he can. Do you understand? None of that matters. You're there for one purpose only: to pass sentence on him and receive justice. You are the master now. He's restrained, tied fast to a table. He's helpless, except for his mouth. If you wish to speak to him, you're free to speak. You may reveal your hate to him. If you wish to hit him in the head with a rock, you may do that. If you choose to spit on him and leave, that's your choice. Do whatever you feel you must to set your heart free. But remember: no matter what he says, you are my wife, with value, and power, and the bearer of my son. That's something he can't change, and it makes him angrier. Don't let his words crush you; you are the power in there. You will order his death. Understand?"

"I think so," trembled the voice under the veil.

To Mímihn's relief, the room was surgically bright. In the center was an operating table, and bound to it under eight straps was her darkest demon, naked under the lights, struggling and cursing to himself. The voice alone made her stop in terror, the sight of his body almost unbearable. The door behind them shut with a click of finality, the sound of a trigger being pulled.

"The thief returns!" he shouted on seeing Tokh. "You haven't tortured me enough? My lawyers are marking down each and every grievance, have no fear. I'll bring down twice everything on you. *Push the Fortunes!* You didn't – you brought my property back? After all this, you're giving her back?" The rage turned to disbelief.

"No," Tokh said. "She is the one you wounded. She is the one you wronged. She is the one who will order your death."

He burst into laughter. "No, no. That worthless *lihx* doesn't have the nerve. I can command her to do anything right from here. What's my name, you filthy *trixahg*? Say it! Why don't you show these nice men what you can do. Show them. Get your mouth over here to me, *lihx*. You can start there and then move to the old one over there. Let your Thief watch. I'm sure he's put you through some paces of his own, but I'll make you forget all that."

Mímihn shook so hard she was suffocating; her lungs just could not pull in more than a fraction of air. And from somewhere, something stronger took over. Her lungs expanded, though her heart took refuge behind her stomach and shook enough for both. She stood up taller, anger filling her spine. She peeled back the veil.

"Oh ho! Look at that hair! You're certainly the center of attention now. What's my name, *trixahg*? Who owns you?"

Her smile was detached and cold, another person, another place, a *dahneg* wife of power and fury. "I'm aware of your name, Emrehl kasihn Garsuuhl, and it no longer holds power over me. I'm a hundred times the person you will ever be. I'm married to a *dahneg*, mother of his son. I have been to the palace of Derahl Nor, touched the hand of the Emperor, and lived more than a year in Union space. You, on the other hand, have no honor, and never will. You are the worst of Kerasím.

"I know I was a consort. I know what my job was. And I went to it with good spirit, determined to make the most of my position. I went with the intention to please, and the expectation I would be treated well for my efforts. But you could not be pleased. For every effort and kindness I gave, you treated me with cruelty and humiliation. When still I tried my best, you found more despicable ways to humiliate me. And when that still didn't break me, you took my sight. And I tried. Still, like the foolish child I was, I tried to please you. But I saw my death in that move. I planned to take my own life when I couldn't bear it any longer, before you could take it first. I wouldn't give you that pleasure. But Tokh stepped in like a Fortune of Mercy and saved me. For your ceaseless and unwarranted humiliation of me, and in the name of your wives, I sentence you to die, horribly and painfully. And yes, I can see again to watch."

Emrehl laughed at the ceiling. "Add that to my lawyer's list. I want my money back for the surgery. Next time, I'll make sure they take the eyes out. There's no fixing that. I should've had them taken out and fed to you, *trixahg*. What's my name, *lihx*? Have you told your precious thief just how many men you can take in a night?"

Mímihn shook, and her stomach wanted to crawl upward, but she held her ground. "You will not goad me. If you can't stop speaking to me like that, I will beat you, just like you beat me. I owe it to you for so many things, especially for the trouble you put my good husband through."

He laughed harder. "Oh, listen to her, all righteous like that!" He picked up his head and spoke to Kassán. "You hear that nerve? She couldn't hit a fly. She'd try and fight some of my friends, and she couldn't stop so much as a kiss."

Kassán's squinting stare would have sent rodents fleeing. "Do not expect sympathy from me. I see your kind all the time, and I reduce them to crying babies lying in their own *aaka*. It's easier than you think."

Mímihn's black-gloved hand shot out toward Tokh, palm up. Her face grew colder as the anger took over. Tokh realized what she wanted; he drew his incentive stick and placed it in her hand. Mímihn telescoped it open, and while Emrehl was still trying to engage Kassán, she brought the incentive stick down across his limp *hihvat* with all of her strength.

Emrehl screamed. "*Trixhor pan khar*! Holy Mother of Fortune! You worthless withered *trixahg lihx*!" He pulled up against the restraints, brown in the face and gasping in pain. "I'm going to kill you for that!"

Anger overtook Mímihn's fear. She replied with a swat across his face. "Speak politely!"

"Die, *lihx*. I'll *push* you to death this time. I will explode your *lihx*."

"That's not my name. It never was. You always found that amusing, didn't you. Let's see how amusing you find it now. What's my name?"

Emrehl's nostrils flared in and out with his anger. His head curled up off the table. "*Hihvat*-sucking, *aaka*-eating, fluid-leaking *trixahg*, that's your name."

"Not even close. Try again. What's my name, Emrehl? What's my name? I can't hear you," Mímihn crooned with a cold smile. She slammed him with the incentive stick so hard it broke the skin. He jerked and grunted.

"Filthy *lihx*! That's your name!"

"WHAT'S MY NAME!" Mímihn screeched, and she cracked the rod across his *khatas* three times until he screamed.

"Mímihn," he gasped. "Mímihn."

She cracked him again full force. "I CAN'T HEAR YOU!"

"MÍMIHN!" he shrieked.

"That's right. Mímihn daras-Giláhn, and don't you forget that. My, my, don't we look scared now. I love that sound of fear in your voice. You have no idea how much joy that sound gives me. Who has the power now, Emrehl?"

Emrehl lifted his head and spat at her. "Lousy worthless piece of consort trash! Worn out *pushing* oversized useless stinking *lihx*, not worth a *ghinadín's* turd."

Mímihn leaned down to his ear. "That's not what you said when you bought me. Or when you were grunting on me. Or what you told your friends when you invited them to sample. Or what your friends said to me. Or your father. Let's have truth: your father was better at *pushing* females than you were. He certainly knew how to make the ladies like him. Your wives certainly thought that way."

320

Emrehl wrenched against the restraints, ready to rip his limbs off if only to strangle her with his shoulder.

Tokh had listened to enough. His hand rested on the hilt of his sword. "It's your verdict. I'll take his head, unless you desire something else."

Mímihn grew wistful, watching her nightmare trying to rip through impossible bonds. "I've wanted this moment for so long, even if I never let myself think it. I want to know he's dead and gone, never to hurt anyone again. I want to know I can live a happy life and bury the bad forever. No one will ever look at me that way again. But inside, the hurt says that's not enough. The hurt says he needs to understand just what he did to me, how awful I felt, before he can die. Only then will I find peace. And I don't know which part of me is right."

"It's your choice."

"And if I listen to the hurt and let it sway me, what will you think of me then?"

Tokh's hands rubbed over her shoulders, and he kissed the side of her jaw. "You've been in pain far too long, and he is the cause. If his pain will ease your pain and make you joyous again, then I support your desire for revenge. Even a small reparation helped Zheníhda to feel better. You've had a much greater pain, so a greater payment is called for."

Mímihn nodded. "As long as you know it's the hurt that seeks revenge, and not my spirit. Not just for me, but for his wives as well. They were not bad ladies. I did feel sad for them."

"I will help you take his head."

"I will help you take his head," Emrehl parroted back. "Oh, big brave General, attacking a bound man. Cheating until the end."

She gave a huge sigh, staring at Emrehl with pity on her face. "I'm sorry, Tokh. I know you want his head, but I can't wish that. It's too simple. I want him blinded, I want his *hihvat* cut off and fed to him so it will weigh upon his stomach, I want his tongue cut out so he can't beg for help, and I want his hands cut off, so he's completely helpless and dependent on others. Then I want him put into a *ghinadín* prison for seventeen months, as long as I was his consort. And when they're done with him, I'll know he understands."

Kassán cackled from the other side of the table. "She's a vicious one, Tokh! You'd never know it from such a pretty face. Sometimes the faces distract you from the inside. Maybe we need her to pass judgment more often."

"It's tragedy she's in this room at all!" Tokh spat. "I find no amusement in her pain." He turned to Mímihn. "Do you wish to remove his *hihvat* yourself?"

Mímihn looked yellow and peaked, but she nodded. "Yes. I don't want to do it, but I've wished it for so long, I must make myself do it or I will regret it."

Emrehl laughed. "You don't have the *khatas, lihx*."

Kassán handed Tokh a surgical knife. He helped her, hand over hand, in one violent stroke, while Emrehl spouted a fountain of vile words and memories at her before he screamed.

She made it outside of the room before vomiting.

There was a little waiting area down below, used by officers transporting prisoners from the investigations. Mímihn sat there, alone without guard and unmolested. An officer brought her a cup of *raffin* with a silent bow. Sometimes she wept a little; sometimes she just sighed. It was over. Her nightmares were really over and would never come to haunt her again. Her son would grow up in peace, never knowing his mother's shame.

Tokh came into the sitting area. "They finished. He's force-fed, blinded, tongueless, and has lost his hands, as you wished. They're readying him for transport now. You might wish to wait here until he's been moved."

"No," Mímihn said softly. "I wish to see him one last time." Tokh gave a nod, and escorted her to the doors of the investigation lab.

Several minutes passed before Emrehl was brought out on a stretcher. Tokh was not Kassán; he insisted anesthesia be used. Emrehl was awake but groggy, and not yet in too much pain. The stumps of his arms were bandaged, but it was obvious there were no hands. Bloody spit trailed from his mouth and stained the sheet beneath him. His eyelids were half-open and leaking fluid, but the eyes saw nothing; Kassán was an expert at severing nerves, and the bruising would be minimal. Tokh made the stretcher-bearers pause.

Mímihn leaned down to his ear. "Emrehl? What's my name, Emrehl? What's my name? I own you. Don't you forget it." She clapped her hands with a loud report, the sound echoing down the stark empty hall, and he jerked and cried out at the noise.

Mímihn turned away. "He's all yours."

Forty-three

Operatives moved into position on four continents, silent and secreted, waiting for their signal. The logistics fell to four level-four generals operating under direct order from the Level Six Coordinator General of the Armies of Kerasím. There would be no delays due to location; everything would happen on the same mark, regardless of where or what the time of day. One mark, one movement. Twenty thousand men spread out as backup or as roadblocks to detain secondary targets. There was one chance only, one mark given, and no room for mistakes. Failure to subdue a prime target was not an option; alive was preferred but dead was acceptable.

On signal, commanders gave the order.

The Sword of Keranihn circled the globe in one swift stroke.

Former *bhísroti* Kinomir Ranopret was seized at a waterfront spa. *Bhísroti* Yanor gul Tan was seized as he exited a courthouse. Justice Shulbet Hass was seized mid-action at a party with twenty consorts; officers apologized for his premature uncoupling. Governor Isulbran Neril, barely able to walk after half a bottle of *dhurwah*, seized at home. Governor Kowhan Shanep, called from a meeting and seized, then shot dead by the Demi-Governor before he could be removed. The Demi-Governor was detained instead. Kallit Jinsoohr, owner of the largest metalworks company on the planet, seized sleeping from his bed; his three wives were not harmed. *Bhísroti* Nullan kir har Ghal, a direct cousin to the Emperor, seized at a race track. Senator Garben Smad of Kantandohr, pulled from a Temple of the Fortunes. He panicked and tried to run, resulting in a damaged building and a broken shoulder. Senator Urbesh Pesom of Holboth, seized at his son's wedding. Three guards were shot while interfering. Councilman Vanrish Yin Sintahl, seized from his private box at a pro *rahl*-ball game, along with four guests also on the list. *Bhísroti* Bish whar Korphat, owner of Twin Star Financial Investments, the third-largest bank of Kerasím, seized at work. Enraged beyond reason at the audaciousness of his public arrest, his heart blocked; he died before reaching treatment. *Dihnarwharl* palace aide Dakka tim Rau, seized at the palace.

The list went on for five pages. One hundred twenty were taken into custody; seventy others were executed immediately or in the process of trying to escape. Two hundred lesser targets remained wanted for questioning. Eight aircraft in flight were ordered to land by surrounding craft; twelve others were prevented from takeoff; one was shot down for attempted evasion. Checkpoints were set up at critical roadways and bridges; seventy four trucks carrying illegal contraband were detained. Bank assets for three hundred men and one hundred suspect businesses were frozen indefinitely, and all computer records seized for examination.

Hag Shinsuum collapsed like a volcano, two days before Emperor Nadigh would publicly declare the group illegal for crimes against the government, and any remaining members wanted men. Fighting in several key districts, including long-troubled Kanok Sohr, fell silent.

Forty-four

Tokh returned to Imahlva as the sun set, Ráhnif and Ghírandar accompanying him. He met Aila as she and Masákh descended the stairs for dinner.

He bowed in greeting. "I wish to tell you information you will not hear on the ComNet. One hundred twenty persons connected with Hag Shinsuum were apprehended in multiple simultaneous raids around the globe nine hours ago. Vanrish Yin Sintahl was among them. Due to the nature of his crimes against a foreign dignitary, he was processed immediately. Kassán himself ran the equipment and spared nothing. General Sil Pagh ran the interrogation; he is a highest-level interrogator and quite thorough. I was allowed to witness a portion of the interrogation. He admitted to your assault, and gave up the names of the guards who assisted him. They have also been seized. He's admitted to redirecting your calls to a private office. While you believed your calls came and went from the palace proper, they did not. Neither of us would have believed the information was falsified.

"The Emperor knows of Vanrish's arrest; he granted Trannor disciplinary rights according to law. You have requested his head. Assault of a female is now a crime, but not a capital offense. As he admitted to numerous crimes against the Emperor, including hacking palace communications and working to undermine the Emperor's credibility and power, those are a capital crime. General Trannor formally requested his head on your wish, though it would have been taken anyway. There will be a public execution of Vanrish and several other leaders of Hag Shinsuum in three days. You'll accompany me to Derahl Nor on that day to bear witness."

"I will accompany her," Masákh said.

"As is your right."

Aila's insides fluttered. She was glad the rat bastard had been caught, and hoped Kassán had worked him over with a special dose of brutality, but she hadn't counted on having to watch. One beheading was enough to last a lifetime, and if it was public, all eyes and cameras would be on her. Even with everything she'd seen and done, Aila wasn't sure she had the spine for that. She gripped Masákh's hand tight.

"I'll be there. And I will spit on his corpse."

She called Halian on his private line later that night.

"I just wanted to tell you they caught the guy."

Halian accepted the news as if she were discussing a bad grade that had already been anticipated. "Well, I'm glad for you, I guess. And their sentence?"

"He confessed to a long string of crimes, and was sentenced to death on fifteen of them, not including mine."

Halian bit his lip before answering. "I'll assume he was sent to a mind scanner to get that information. We both know a forced confession under torture isn't valid. No one can be held accountable for what they say under torture."

Aila's wistful sadness evaporated. "How can justice have eyes when it's supposed to be blind? Even Mímihn would have ruled the same. Even if he didn't confess – and he did easily, I was told, I know what he's guilty of, and because I'm under Emperor's Protection, his attack becomes a crime against the Emperor. That's all they need."

"I understand that. But act like a diplomat," Halian said. "That's supposed to be your job, isn't it? Isn't that what you've been taught to be, these last six years? Act like one for just a few minutes. The Union has a firm stance on capital punishment. You represent the Union. You represent Union law. Your job is to show them our way. This is one of those times."

Aila smiled. "Nice try, Ross. but I don't know who I am anymore. I honestly don't. I've been here so long, I don't know what I am or where I belong. In the Union, I'm told I'm nothing; I have no degree, I have no education, my opinion doesn't count, I'm just an intern who thinks she knows everything and all I do is get in trouble when I'm here because I don't know what I'm doing. I come to Kerasím, they treat me like a celebrity. Interviews, gifts, clothing, makeup, offers for film roles and high-level marriages that most Kerasi women would kill for. The government thinks I'm the best thing ever and would like my opinion on every meeting they have – you don't even have that. On Kerasím I'm now married to a Kerasi, which has taken away some of those special powers I used to have, as everyone now defers to my husband instead of me. So I don't know what or who I am anymore, Ross. I'm a Kerasi wife, following Kerasi law, by order of the Emperor, and the Union couldn't give a damn less. I could be gathering top secret information the Union would kill for but they'd never think to ask, because they give me no respect. So you tell me whose law I should care about right now. Have you gotten permission for a ship to get me home?"

Halian hung his head for a moment before meeting her on-camera gaze with a look of guilt. "I continue to plead, but no. No permission for a ship has been granted as of today."

"Then good night, Mr. Halian. I'll stop by next time I'm in Keranihn. Haghíde says your *raffin* would taste better if you used a higher-quality brand and allowed it to steep longer, but I'm willing to risk it in the name of friendship. Goodbye."

Forty-five

Three days went by way too fast when an execution loomed.

"What do you wear to an execution?" Aila asked Mímihn.

"I don't think there's any tradition," Mímihn replied. "If you're the widow to be, or the person's family, or you object, you might wear green for mourning, but that's all."

Aila was about to wear her black Union pants and a white Kerasi tunic, then remembered her tirade with Ross Halian. The Union stance was objection, and Aila herself claimed to be a Kerasi wife. She had a black Kerasi dress, but it seemed too frilly and fun for such an occasion. At last she chose a simple maroon skirt and tan shirt.

Aila'd had creeping willies as the days passed. Now, with hours, her spine was lashing around her back like an angry snake. Every death she'd seen had been unplanned and sudden: the beheading of the guard, Vanora, Omi Kel. Royal Son Turwheg's beheading had been over the ComNet, hundreds of miles away. It could have been a cinema, a simple special effect. Nothing pointed out it was occurring in real-time. This would be live, and broadcast cameras would be present. Aila chose her longest, darkest veil to complete her outfit, and pinned it firmly to her hair. Hiding was always the best policy.

She flew to Keranihn with Tokh, Masákh, and some of the *aghát* – Mátokhan and Haghíde were left in charge of the estate. Twenty-three of the highest ranking criminals would be put to death in a public ceremony. Nadigh would give a speech, his heir and advisors by his side. An area inside the main roadway was blocked off, the scaffoldings trucked in, and rows of bleacher seats for invited honorees were set up. One of them was meant for Aila.

They arrived an hour early; Tokh had access to the senatorial parlors but the *aghát* couldn't enter there, so they waited for Tokh's signal in a servant's waiting room, where Ambassador Halian caught up to Aila.

"This is really what you want to support?" Ross Halian counseled one final time. "You were horrified by that action during your captivity. This is against Union law. You're not asking for justice; you're asking for vengeance. You're asking the State to *murder* someone on your command. An injustice was done to you, but he didn't take your life, yet you're asking for a life in return. A *life*. Was this man's crime worth his life? You can rehabilitate a criminal, you can make them sorry for their crime, you can make them give restitution, you take their freedom, you can give someone back their freedom if you've made a mistake, but you can't give back a life once it's taken. You feel, deep down inside, this man's very existence should be forfeit? Think about that, Aila. Think about that hard." He wasn't quite pleading, and he wasn't quite telling her what to do. Aila knew what he wanted her to say, knew what her squirming spine wanted to avoid, but the words wouldn't come out.

"Funny that if I killed him during the assault, that would be okay," Aila replied. "Self-defense. It's the same result; why does a few days later make a difference? He's not repentant; he's still gloating. He has other crimes on top of mine. They're going to kill him even without my charges."

"And it could very well be in your power to stop that. Step up. Lead the way. Ask them not to take his head, sentence him to prison, sentence him to punishment. It's one life out of a mass execution, but one life can be a turning point."

"It's the same thing, Ross. A hundred lashes and castration? That will kill him. Send him back to the mind scanner, make him forget lust, make him cry every time he gets an urge? They can wipe his mind, turn him into an infant. Is that better? The Kerasi call a beheading a Mercy, because it avoids such fates. A beheading is more cruel than being beaten to death?"

"And what do you demonstrate, letting it happen? *This is your chance* – you, imagined leader of a feminist revolution – to show the Kerasi what it means to be a member of the Union, how we don't take lives. We take freedoms, we take rights, but we don't take *lives*. How does that make his family feel? How will they then channel their resentment over the death of their husband and father? Do you think they'll just accept the fact their loved one was a bad man and feel sorry? It doesn't happen that way, Aila. It increases the hatred of

330

Nadigh. You were an unfortunate pawn in this, but now you're also a willing participant. How will this play out back in the Union? You let a man be beheaded on your account without pleading on his behalf."

Aila rolled her eyes to glare at him. "Beheading a man on my account was my initiation into Kerasi society, and all he did was slap me for mouthing off. I hear your words, Ross, and I understand what you're saying. I do. 'There's a bigger picture here, and allowing capital punishment to continue without protesting against it allows the worst of their society to continue.' And I get that. And I understand that if I allow this in my name without saying something, it makes it impossible to ever stand up and say that afterward. 'Yeah, I know I said it was okay *that* time, but you really shouldn't be doing that now.' But you weren't the one assaulted, Ross. It wasn't you who was used in an attempt to control someone else. It was me. And maybe it will be a mark against my soul. Maybe it will. Maybe next week I'll wake up in a cold sweat, wondering how I let it happen. But I'm on Kerasím, and this is their law. At the moment, it's not in me to intervene."

"It remains her choice," Masákh said, "but for all purposes legal and otherwise, Aila is my wife here on Kerasím. It's her right to demand justice. However, I do understand the implications you have raised. I offer this: as husband, I have the right to witness justice for my wife. Therefore, I suggest she remain with you behind doors during the execution. As husband, I will insure justice does occur. She may witness the body in private following. It will not show objection to Kerasi law, but neither will it demonstrate approval, verbal or implied. That responsibility will be mine. She has seen enough death for her youth."

Ross Halian paused to think it through. He stared at Aila long and hard, but it held more pity than anger. "If we can't agree to stop it entirely, that's an acceptable compromise, as long as no hint of Union approval is given, because we very much do object. May God have Mercy on us."

Aila held his stare with quiet resolve. "May the Fortunes grant us peace."

It was strange, waiting in front of a morgue to receive a package. Aila wasn't sure where she stood on death anymore. Six years ago, Death was the most terrifying thing there was. It lurked under the bed, in dark corners, in empty corridors, and in Kassán's experiment rooms. It waited, ready to pounce, in the shadows of her prison cell back on Kye, but it never came for her. Now, Aila had met Death. She'd seen him standing on the other side of rooms, tattered black robes fluttering, skeletal hand pointing to the next victim like he was picking out a donut in a glass case. Death was out there, but he didn't scare her so much anymore; she knew how to fight him. While she waited, mouth dry, armpits damp, twitching at every tick she thought she heard, she thought back and counted. The beheaded guard, Sóghar, Nághtas, Vanora, Banukh the *fáhganid*, assorted people whose names she didn't know, that driver, Royal Son Turwheg's beheading, the recent deaths at Tokh's estate, and Death grinned with glee and guided her hand when she herself shot Omi Kel, traitor Secretary of State for the Planetary Union, when he attempted to kill Masákh just last year. Fifteen people? that she'd witnessed die, two by Tokh, two by Masákh, at least one by Haghíde, and one by herself, not counting those who might have died on her account but she didn't see. That was at least fourteen too many. Yeah, Vanrish Yin had greater crimes than those against her; the only reason he was still alive was she'd asked for his head, otherwise he would have been disposed of on capture. Did that make it her fault? Reason said no. And knowing the male Kerasi mind, she was just a gratuitous afterthought.

Ghírandar waited with her, to make sure nothing was left undone. "Have you ever killed someone?" she asked. It was starting to be an obsession. *Hello! How are you! Nice to meet you! Have you ever killed anyone?*

He nodded before answering. "I saw battle during my training. I don't know how many; I've never kept count. I doubt it's remarkable. I'm a good shot, not a great shot, and you don't get time to aim well in battle."

"Where was the battle?"

"A place called Nheir. It was an agricultural area in a drought and people were stealing from each other to survive, which had led to caste crimes and bloodshed. That much conflict is not common, but it does happen."

A door at the end of the corridor opened. Two men in coveralls pushed a gurney with a green plastic sheet over it; a large box sat on the end. Masákh followed. They stopped before her, and Aila felt the blood around her heart turn to frozen slush.

Masákh stepped forward, took her hand, and kissed her hair. "This is the body of Vanrish Yin Sintahl. You made a request for his head. You now have two choices: accept the head in its box and dispose of it as you choose, or acknowledge you have witnessed the head but decline to take possession, and they will dispose of it for you."

"I have no desire to take it with me." An army of squiggles scurried up Aila's back. That's all Mom needed: Aila asking to keep a dried Kerasi head on a shelf.

"Then you may witness the head, sign the paperwork, and you are free to go. Are you able to do that?"

Aila's eyes darted away from the sheet before her, and she swore she saw Death in the farthest corner of the hall, following the gurney but not too close. Five healthy people stood in the way of his prey, and he had to wait his turn. Fear seized her, and Aila felt an overwhelming urge to scream and cry and run away, but Death was between her and the exit. She took a fast, shaking breath and nodded.

Masákh opened the box. Aila peered inside. It was indeed a Kerasi head, eyes half open, jaw gaping, soaked in so much brown blood it was hard to make out the features, but the chin hank was still braided obscenely, and the laugh given by the open jaw made the face fit her memory.

Aila nodded. She swallowed hard, keeping her scream in her throat. "That's him. He's the one."

One of the orderlies handed her a lap pad and a stylus. Ghírandar took it, looked over the document for the important points. "If you feel justice has been served, sign here."

Masákh prompted, "Remember, your signature here is Aila ghas Lil."

Ooops. Forgot that detail. Aila nodded and signed her name in labored Kerasi letters, no different than any other Kerasi wife. The orderly took back the pad, printed Masákh a legal paper copy, and they moved the gurney to the morgue.

Masákh pocketed the papers, took her hand, and headed down the hall, Ghírandar behind. Death stepped to the side.

Aila felt the chill as he passed. She pulled free of Masákh's hand as she folded to her knees on the floor and wept.

Forty-six

Tokh was every bit as tired of the drama as Aila, and his patience was no better with the situation. With all his stresses, with the length of time he'd been forced to put up with her, he'd been far kinder than he had a right to be. In her heart Aila knew that, but it didn't stop her daily nagging.

"There is nothing I can do. The palace must give approval for Union ships to enter our space. I can fly you anywhere on the planet, but my access stops at the atmosphere. I have no control over space ships. I can't fly you to the border without prior approval. It is not possible."

"This is bullshit!" Aila raged. "This is exactly what I knew would happen when everyone demanded my marriage. I knew you people would trap me here. I will leave Kerasím, or there will be action."

"I have tried every source I know. The Emperor wishes you to remain here until his investigations are completed. He apologizes for the delay, but he wishes to make certain he has gotten all ends. Until the Emperor grants permission, you will stay."

"You really think so? We'll see about that," Aila snapped. "You aren't the only one who can move mountains."

Aila stormed back to her room, not waiting for Tokh to dismiss her. No doubt he'd chew her out for that later, and for going over his head, but she still had one contact he didn't. Aila'd kept it in greatest respect, never abused it at all, but now she was going to call in a favor. Seven weeks. Seven weeks she'd been on Kerasím, give or take half a week. At this rate, by the time a ship arrived, Baby Thoren would be able to escort her to it. Aila looked through her commlist and found the link she would bet cash Tokh didn't have, and she placed a request to meet with Greatest Lady Majesty Rimas herself.

And with the speed of snapping fingers, Rimas came through, agreeing to meet and finding room in her schedule just two days later. "Thank you, Rimas!" Aila said to her com when she saw the message, whether or not it was from Rimas herself or just her scheduler. Now all she needed was gumption, and Masákh to make certain it wasn't a false message.

Four of them flew into Keranihn that morning, Mátokhan and Ráhnif to check in at the palace for business of their own, and Masákh accompanying his wife, as a proper husband did. Aila and Masákh presented their credentials to the second security check point on the fourth floor, and again when they got to the proper room. They waited inside an overdecorated vestibule for a quarter hour.

Aila perched on an ornately carved wooden chair. "She's got to come through," she mumbled softly. "Otherwise my next call is straight to the Secretary of State."

"I understand your frustration," Masákh said, "but I'm not sure that would be a proper move yet. The correct sequence would be to go through your Embassy first."

"I've done that. Halian's been trying every day for more than a week."

"Then I would not waste a call on Secretary Hhani. He will need details and forms and a list of what you have tried; a lengthy, time-consuming call. Assume that you are indeed being held here, for whatever reason. If so, it is likely your calls to the Union may be monitored. If those listening don't like what you're saying, they may kill the call and block any future contact. If you have one chance at placing a call, the person you should contact would be your mother."

Aila was about to snap at him, but the logic hit her. Her mother would go straight to Hhani and drag him to the Kerasi border by his mustache if she had to. Mom would never let up with her badgering, and it wouldn't surprise Aila one bit if she called Tokh and screamed at him directly. Mom would start a war to get her home.

"Like always, you're right. That's a doomsday scenario though. I don't want to make that call until every last option has been tried. Once we do that, a war will start."

"Certainly."

The inner door opened, and they were ushered into the greeting room.

Aila and Masákh knelt low in the presence of the Royal Heir, but Rimas took Aila by the hands and pulled her to her feet. Masákh stood on his own. "Ahlo, Aila! Mai frehnd! I ham happy to see yu. Khome here! Yu bring house man?"

"Hello, Lady Majesty. Thank you for seeing me. You know my husband, Major Masákh." Aila spoke slow and clear; Rimas was making huge strides in learning Union, but anything beyond the simplest conversation was still lost on her. She switched to Emperor's Tongue.

"My husband insists on accompanying me after the incident with my last visit. It is his right."

"Khome, sit!" Rimas dragged her to a sofa. Masákh moved to stand against the wall with Rimas's guards. "What incident did you have?"

Aila tipped her head with a wry expression. Good. She had counted on Rimas being unaware. Now the question was, how much outrage would she have about it, and how much could Aila fan that flame into useful action. "Your father did not tell you? I would have thought that, it being an act of war between our people, and you being the Heir to Kerasím, he would have told you."

Rimas clouded up. "Tell me what? What act of war?"

"I was summoned to the palace scarcely a week ago on false premise. When I arrived here, I was most violently assaulted and informed it was to be a message to my husband. Your father was cooperative in tracking down the *bhísroti* who did it, and he did indeed send me a head, but I requested permission to allow ships to enter Kerasi space so I may leave Kerasím, which by his own law I must be allowed, and your father has denied me that permission. That's illegal, and that is also a dangerous act between our people. I don't wish to inform my people I'm being held against my will. I beg you, Heir Rimas, as a female, as Heir and leader of Kerasím, as my friend, let me go home to my people."

"Khit?" Rimas breathed in disbelief. "Slow – you say too many things. My Father-Emperor has been consumed this week with taking out seventy-nine members of a criminal organization undermining Kerasi financial securities, and two hundred of their associates. He

would not have time to deal with petty transportation requests. It's wrong of you to…"

"Hag Shinsuum," Aila interrupted. "Yes. I was sent the head of the Lupagh Lura cell. Vanrish Yin Sintahl. He was the *trixhor ghinadín* who assaulted me."

Rimas's boots gave a thud against the floor as she sat up. Her friendliness disappeared, and the irate glare that bored into Aila was going to serve Rimas well when she held the throne. "That information was of highest classification. How do you know it? Speak carefully, for if I sense deceit on the part of the Union you will not leave this palace."

If Aila could hold up against blustering General Trannor, she could outlast Rimas. Or so she hoped. *Deep breath.* "Because my assault and demand for a head made your father move his timeline from soon to immediate. Vanrish Yin Sintahl caused that massacre by assaulting me. I'm sorry if your father didn't tell you all the details, your Lady Majesty. My question to you would then be, Why would he not?"

"Why did you come here, then? What's the purpose of your visit, if not to create discord between my father and I?"

Aila softened. She bowed slowly from the waist, palms up, most respectful. "Your Lady Majesty, I came in friendship. You're the only one I can plead to for help. By your father's own law – I have the exact words you yourself sent me – no one is allowed to keep me from leaving Kerasím. That was a condition that was agreed upon before my marriage. Now your father won't let me leave. I'm trying to resolve this on the friendliest of terms, before my government gets involved. They won't be happy with me, and I fear it will be a third and final blow for the peace we've created. In any circumstances, I don't wish war with my husband's people. It leaves me with no homeland."

Rimas went silent. Aila couldn't begin to guess what she was thinking about, but she kept the momentum going. "If I may ask, have you ever been assaulted, My Lady Majesty?"

Rimas rolled a wary eye toward her. "I was *bhísroti*, eldest of the royal heir. No one would dare touch me in such a manner, not even the high-ranking sons." She thought a moment, then added, "Unless you count my wedding night. I didn't want to marry Shumar. He didn't want to marry me. I divorced him the day my father signed the law allowing me to, and never need to gaze upon his *eel*-face again."

"But you can imagine the fear and revulsion I had. You can understand why I want to leave to a place of safety, where I can feel comfort instead of fear."

"You speak of many topics," Rimas said curtly. "I can't answer all of them. You will wait here. I will speak with my father, confirm your statements, and I'll present your case for leaving." She stood up fast, mind made up.

"Guards! They are to remain here in the greeting room. You will grant them every courtesy until I return." Two of her guards bowed; the two outside the door followed her out of the vestibule.

Masákh crossed over to Aila. He had that old look from years ago, a warning that said she needed to watch herself. "You are walking a dangerous road. You are speaking with the Heir, and you need to show much more respect. Should her Lady Majesty take offense, there is nothing I can do to change a punishment. There's nothing Tokh can do. That's beyond anyone's ability to intervene. I won't address how your behavior reflects on me."

"I am not here as Kerasi. I am here as a Union diplomat who has made a tentative friendship with the first female heir to the throne of Kerasím. I have slight power over you in this case, and I am treading very carefully. You haven't seen anything yet," Aila warned. "Let's wait and see what she says when she comes back."

Aila and Masákh sat in Rimas's greeting room, mostly silent. If they spoke it was in Union, because it was most unlikely the guards spoke a word of it. This was it. Either Rimas would manage to get her off the planet, or Rimas was going to imprison her. Aila probably wouldn't lose her head, but it would be back to a cage and sleeping with the lights on, hoping her guards were honorable and weren't going to take advantage. Aila wasn't sure she could handle that again. Masákh would also be imprisoned, for allowing his wife to behave like that to royalty. It would bounce back to Tokh, and he would lose privilege, perhaps his coveted Senate seat. His star pupil would be a shame to the Emperor, and therefore her teacher would be toast, too.

Aila gave a monumental sigh and let her head fall back on the sofa. More than an hour passed before the door flung open, the guards stood straight, and Rimas came charging in.

"I have spoken with my father. We did not come to a compatible conclusion. Therefore, I have decided to act on my own authority. You speak of Union rights and Union laws, yet my father, despite his plans for progress, has no experience to draw upon. One cannot pass law, make decisions for their people, if they don't know of what they speak. I can't override my father's decision. He wishes you to remain in Royal safekeeping for the time being. However, if I have your honorable word you will remain in my custody, I will release you at the end of my journey."

"Journey, your Lady Majesty?" Aila was afraid to know. Would she be stuck at the palace until Rimas returned? If not, where were they going? How long would that take?

Rimas held her chin up in triumph. "I will accompany you back to the Union. You will remain with me, show me this great Union Empire you speak so highly of. I will see these females for myself, see how your society works, prove that you speak the truth. I will record this for my people to see for themselves. When I am done, you'll accompany me back to Kerasím for an honor ceremony, after which time you will be free to leave Kerasím, on my honor as Heir. If my father doesn't agree, you'll be allowed to turn back at the border, and I will deal with his wrath."

Aila's eyes felt as if they would fall from her head. *What?* No leader had ever crossed the border before. Aila had no power to barter such a deal. The best she could do was plead mercy to Secretary Hhani and hope he could pull something off in the next few months. Maybe Mom could get on him.

"I believe I can do that," Aila said cautiously. "I'll contact my government and find out when it could be arranged."

"When is eight hours from now," Rimas said. "That's when my ship will depart. Of course, you will need to make Union arrangements. I'll have several sisters who will accompany me, perhaps two children, six guards, and some advisors. General Tokh has *aghát* who work inside the Union; they may accompany me as translators. I will need protection. You are the law-daughter of a Kerasi General who is in charge of Union diplomacy; General Tokh may serve as commander of my guard. He may bring his wives, if he chooses, as they are among the females my father honored as Mothers of the Future. Whoever he wishes to bring may accompany him. We will need appropriate lodging for our castes, as well as transportation and food."

Eight hours? It couldn't be done. In anyone's wildest fantasies, it couldn't be done that fast. Aila wanted to cry. One did not just up and walk into a hostile territory with no record of presidential visits and expect it to work. This was going to fail beyond failure. They'd be living on the borderlands after this. She stared at Masákh with a growing pit of hopelessness in her stomach. This was the end of two dreams gone bad.

Masákh, her steadfast rock, reminded her of truth. He of all people knew how slow diplomacy worked. "You performed greater, harder feats of diplomacy when you were much younger. This is merely a building block on your success. You had no fear then; do not fear now. Be bold once more, and you will succeed. I cannot do this; only you." He tipped his head to her in encouragement.

Aila bowed to Rimas. "As you wish, Your Royal Lady Majesty. If it would please you, I think the orders to General Tokh would best come directly from you. He will have questions as to your safety I will not think of."

"You are probably correct. I will see to it. I've released transportation in your name back to Imahlva. My guard will take you there, then return you directly to my ship for immediate takeoff. Do not discuss a word of this to anyone not involved. The plan has yet to be presented to my father. If he has word before it's in place, you won't leave Kerasím."

Aila bowed again, as did Masákh. "Your word is my law, My Lady Heir."

Tokh was in a delicate situation when his comm went off: sitting on the toilet. He glanced at the identification, and was glad he was sitting where he was sitting. Then he realized where he was sitting, and was afraid to hit receive; surely it was beyond offensive to answer a call from the Emperor while relieving oneself. He glanced at the wall and the hanging artwork behind him. That background was better than when he sat. He stood up to answer, hoping to Space he had no need to shuffle to another room or aim the camera downward and reveal his condition. He hit receive.

Heir Rimas appeared on the screen. "General Tokh. I'm to understand you know how to operate with need-to-know orders?"

Tokh bowed his head. "Absolutely, My Royal Heir."

"I'm about to embark on a mission to the Union, with Aila Perrin by my side. You will accompany me as head of my guard, as you've been to the Union previously and can explain things to me. You will bring your *aghát* as translators. You may bring whichever wives, children, and servants you will need. I expect to spend one week in Union space, as well as however much travel time it will incur."

The Union Secretary Hhani had promised to have the price on Tokh's head removed; Tokh prayed it had been, or it would be a very ugly visit. "I would be most honored, Your Royal Majesty. When will the mission take place?"

"You'll present yourself and your entourage at half past the three-quarter mark at the royal hangar. Do not be late, and I warn you: in strictest confidence."

Tokh must have missed something. *"Tonight*, Your Lady Majesty?"

"Do not be late. If I am delayed, you will know my wrath."

"I shall be waiting, Your Lady Majesty."

Rimas ended the call. Tokh stood with his pants around his ankles for a full minute, then shook himself into action. He was still fastening his pants as he raced down the stairs.

"NIHDA! Mímihn! Where's Mímihn? Get the children. Get them now! We have no time. Thrit! I need you in here!" he bellowed out the kitchen door.

Zheníhda flew from her ComNet program; Fahni followed her. "What is it, Tokh? What's wrong?"

Mímihn stopped halfway down the stairs. Her voice was one step short of hysteria. "No! No, Tokh! I saw him! He's not a threat! Tell me he's not a threat!"

Tokh face was a pale tan and sweat had broken out across his forehead. "No, no threats. You're safe, I think. Good news, I guess. I've been requested to head the guard of the Heir on her next mission. I'm allowed to bring any family and servants I wish, as well as my *aghát*. She is touring the Union."

"The Planetary Union?" Zheníhda said with confusion.

"The Planetary Union," Tokh confirmed. "And you and the children may accompany me."

"Haghíde? Is Haghíde going?" Fahni asked.

"He's part of my *aghát*. I would think he'd be bringing you with him, since that's where he works."

Mímihn gave a scream. She held onto the railing and jumped up and down, then raced down the stairs to grab Tokh in a very undignified hug that nearly knocked him over. "YES! And I can see it this time! Where's Aila? Does she know? I can't wait to tell her!"

Tokh peeled her off his side. "She's already aware. There's no time. Rimas plans to leave in six hours. We have six hours to be at the Royal dock in Keranihn. You have three hours to pack for a two- or three-week trip."

Zheníhda stared at him. "Tokh! That's impossible!" She looked about in panic. "What clothing do we pack? What's the weather? Do we need to bring food? What will we eat? Do we need vaccinations? The house – what will we do with the house? We can't possibly be ready that fast! The Union is dangerous!"

"You can, and you will, and it's not." Tokh pushed her aside. "Thrit, I would like you to accompany me as my assistant. Shanohr, I'll leave you in charge of overseeing the house. I'll have Dalo and the children come stay during our absence, that way you won't be alone. I'll tell Khaním I'm taking everyone on holiday while I conduct some private business. He can check in for me to make sure the yard is kept up and all is well. And Wives – not a word! This is not public knowledge. You may tell the ladies I'm taking you on a long holiday, but I haven't told you where. That is truth – not even I know where we'll visit, but I expect there will be government functions, and Hhani knows I wish to tour schools, so that may happen. Now go! Go! There's no time! Thrit – go retrieve the children from school now, tell them we're leaving on a trip but you don't know where, then make sure your things are clean and pack them up. Don't forget Haghíde's boy."

"T'rit be ready whenever t'e General needs him," he said with a bow.

"The baby!" Mímihn realized. "What if he outgrows his things before we return? How can I pack enough for him? How will I have enough diapers?"

Tokh stared at her in disbelief. "They have babies in the Union, and I'm certain they don't shit on the floor. He can wear Union clothing until he returns." Mímihn blushed at the obvious.

Tokh rushed for his office. First he had to recall all of his *aghát*. Then he would call Aila Perrin and demand to know what she'd done.

* * *

Aila took a deep breath and entered the personal com address, tagging it highest priority. It needed time to get there, and time to get a reply. She started a second message before he could answer; better to get a head start and let him know immediately what was up rather than wait for him to respond, her to tell him, and him to reply. The closer they got to the Union, the faster the transmission would be, anyway.

"Hi, Secretary Hhani. Please don't kill me. I don't know how these things happen, they just do. I am en route back to the border; please let my mother know so she can change tantrums. Unfortunately… I am bringing a guest. I wasn't planning on it – trust me, it wasn't anywhere in my craziest imagination, but I didn't have any choice in the matter. I don't exactly have permission to leave Kerasím, and neither does she. I'm being escorted by none other than Her Lady Majesty Rimas, Heir to all Kerasím. She's decided she's going to see the Union for herself, and I don't have the power to tell her no. I will need permission for her to enter Union space, as well as a security detail fitting such a person. We need a destination, and we've got about a day or so, I figure, to come up with some sort of one-week itinerary for her – She'll do all the official government stuff you want, but mostly she wants to see normal Union life, and how our freedoms compare with theirs. And schools. They're very big on seeing our schools, because of female education. I'll send you our ship ID and coordinates."

Aila hit send, then started a new message. Let him catch up before he could scream. "And, unfortunately, she's going to need accommodations. She'll be bringing an entire entourage for security with her, including a camera crew. Not counting me and Masákh, there's eighteen or nineteen adults and about six children in tow. Also, you're going to need to make good on your promise to have erased all charges against General Tokh, because he's among her honor guard, along with his wives and the kids."

The replies started coming in.

"Aila! I'm so glad to hear from you. What's the urgency? Are you back in the Union yet?"

A little over half a minute later came the shriek over the parsecs. "Are you out of your ever-loving mind? Miss Perrin, you better be playing one hell of a joke on me. My heart can't take that kind of stress."

"What do you mean, she doesn't have permission to leave Kerasím? Aila, please explain! Is she a refugee? An asylum seeker? Are there war ships in pursuit that will cross our borders to bring her back? Aila, please explain the situation! What am I supposed to tell the President to prepare for?!" Hhani was looking a bit purple, made worse by the contrast of his white mustache. Now they could get down to meaningful conversation without propriety and polite nonsense getting in the way.

"No no no! Rimas already thought of that. That's what the camera crew is for – she's sending back everything to her father, to keep him from taking action. I'm a Kerasi celebrity; she's hoping to be the same, sending back victory and propaganda feeds for her father. If he does anything against her, all of Kerasím will see it and be angry. He has no choice; everything she will do will make him look better. What he'll do when she returns I don't know, but while she's here, everything should be quiet. To the best of my knowledge and belief, all she's truly after is a State-type tour of the Union, what it's like, how it works, what people do. It came together so fast there wasn't time to plan anything devious. I mean, literally, I went from having a meeting with her to eight hours later we were all on a flight to the border. She's putting an awful lot of trust in me and our friendship; I don't dare fail her."

This time it took the full four minutes for his reply. Hhani's head fell into his hand, stunned but trying to adapt. "Dear God, Aila. This can't be happening. We're nowhere prepared for this. Shit like this takes months, sometimes years to set up. I can't do this in four days. It just can't be done. Okay. Send me your ID, I'll get ships to the border who can escort you inward. Her party will have to change to a Union ship, and you'll fly directly to Centauri, no stops. I know she'll want to tour on the way in, but official things first. Make her aware you will be boarded and asked about your intentions. Make her aware she will be granted every courtesy and protection as a foreign official, the

344

hostilities between us neutralized for the moment in good will. I will inform the President immediately. Stay close to your com. I'll be calling you every fifteen minutes."

Aila apologized profusely again. "I will."

* * *

First Advisor Moragh checked his updates with half a glance. Nothing shattering had happened in the last day, though they remained on high alert as stragglers were located. The text on Moragh's com raised an added concern, and he dared mention it.

"My Emperor, there's a ship headed for our deep-space border, but it doesn't bear an authorization code from the Space Authority."

Nadigh frowned, intent on the document he was signing. "Incoming or outgoing? Whose authority does it claim?"

Moragh paused, desperate for a reason to back up the information. It didn't make sense. "Outgoing. Heir Rimas, your Majesty."

Nadigh's head jerked up. "What? Why? Get her, now! She'd better not have ignored my orders on the Emissary. I'll know what she's authorizing or else. Have Trannor check on her."

Moragh tapped through several message screens, spoke with one, two, three transfers. His face contorted through surprise, shock, and into fear. He kept the line open and spoke in a whisper. *"Heir Rimas is aboard the ship!"*

Nadigh blinked empty eyes. "What?"

"She's at the border now." He referenced his com again.

"Intercept!" Nadigh bellowed. The fury rose up his neck in a visible line, from copper to sienna to intense russet. "Seize the ship! I want her returned and here before me, right now!"

Moragh tried. He paled as he said, "I'm sorry, Majesty. They just crossed the line. There are Union ships waiting to escort them. We cannot move forward without their permission."

Nadigh's eyebrow rose and disappeared into his hair. His eyes darkened blacker than space as he growled, "Get me a direct line to that ship!"

Three *fasim* passed before the connection was made and Moragh threw the link onto the tactical wallscreen. Heir Rimas's face filled the screen. She acted as if nothing was unusual at all, that she was still in another room in the palace, though her eyes held a hint of amusement.

"You request me, Father-Emperor?"

"Rimas, what are you doing? Get back to me at once. I didn't give you permission to leave the palace, let alone authorize anyone to cross into Union space. Where is the Emissary?"

Rimas lost her innocence. "Under direct Imperial observation. You trained me twenty-five years to make strong decisions for the people of Kerasím, yet your entire staff keeps telling me I don't have the *khatas* to make strong decisions. I don't have *khatas*, but that doesn't mean that *burdaki* are not as strong as *khatas*. So I've made a decision to do something even you don't have the *khatas* for: I'm going to the Union, to meet with them directly on their worlds, see all these things the Union speaks of but I cannot imagine. If I'm to rule, I need to know for certain what I'm dealing with. The Emissary is with me under her own bond to be my guide and protector. In addition, I bear General Tokh and a crew of his men as advisors and guard. I'm no fool, *Bo*. I've brought a camera crew along to film all these wonders, true or false as they may be. I'll send the feeds directly to you, so you may edit them, take credit for them, and revel in the glory that they will provide for your wise decision to send me."

Nadigh's fury didn't diminish. "I gave you no permission to leave the palace, let alone the city, the region, the planet, or our space! Get back here! Rimas, not one step of this has been approved! We have no solid peace between us, just fumbled attempts that have resulted in repeated disasters! What will you do if you're taken prisoner? You are the Heir Apparent! If they insult you, it reflects directly on me and I'll have no choice but to declare war! A war we cannot win! You are delivering yourself to an enemy!"

Rimas held firm, the irony on her face making her seem more irreverent than she meant. "We had the Union's trust to send their people to us. We must give trust in return, or they will doubt us."

"And each time has wound up in disaster! Most of the diplomats died, Rimas, and the Emissary kidnapped and nearly assaulted. We let her back in and she was assaulted. They'll take their anger out on you, and you're not prepared to handle it."

Rimas chuckled. "They took my Wisefather in the same murder spree. We share the grief of that incident, a building block for

346

diplomacy. I have the promise of the Emissary, on her life, that I will not be harmed, and that she will return with me on her own will, to comment on the experience. I have the promise of the Secretary Hhani that we'll be kept secure. I've spoken to the Union President Rill, and he's given me his word that we are guaranteed safe passage in and out of the Union, with full honors. On the contrary, *Bo*. This is their greatest moment in proving their promise of peace.

"Now, I have much work to do. Most of my days will be before cameras. Let me go forge the peace we all desire. I'll be in frequent touch. Rimas, out."

Nadigh sat at the table, his face a dangerous shade of nausea. No words crossed his lips.

Moragh spoke quietly. "Shall I send direct word to the captain of the ship to cease flight, *tansohr Keralihn*?"

Nadigh's head bent until his forehead rested on the edge of the table. Another *fasim* passed before he spoke, defeated and desperate. "No. Let them go. They're in the hands of the Fortunes now. Great Fortunes of the Spirit, Fortune of Fate, guide my daughter, watch over her and protect her from harm. Let all her words be wise ones, and may they bring peace to our world and to the Union. Send a squadron to surround the Union Embassy. They will remain until the Heir returns. Send a private message to Major Halian: if my daughter is harmed, I will execute every person inside most painfully, without debate, without recourse."

Moragh bowed. "It will be done immediately, my Emperor."

Keeping It Straight

Castes

Thósikh – only the Emperor's immediate family and heir
(bhísroti – demoted under Nadigh to dáhneg)
(fáhganid – demoted under Nadigh to dáhneg)
dáhneg
díhnarwharl
nhásarwharl
whátaral
rhibáni
tághinet
tápatihn
soláhrin
ghinadín
(thanak tohr subclass)

Tokh's family:

Father: Talekh, wives Galisse, Filuhr
Siblings: Suntahr (G)
                 Kaloh   (G)
                 Nihren *f* (F)
                 Hamiran (F)
                 Filuhr is Tokh's mother
1st wife: **Zhenihda** Porenthal   (married 38 years)
                 Son – **Zénak**, wife Avalihn
                         Son – Khourbas (16)
                         Son – Zivas (15)
                 Son – **Kitras**, wife Dalo
                         Son – Lanag (11)
                         Daughter - Faelihn (9)
                         Son – Niboh (2)
2nd wife – **Umara** Gandarek (deceased, 10 years married)
                 Son – **Joralan** (12)
                 Daughter - **Kesseh** (9)
2nd wife - **Mímihn** rasas Invihral (married 4 years)
                 Son – **Thoren** (3 mos)

Tokh's servants: Thrit, Shanohr

Tokh's Officers:

Aghát

  Masákh gha Lil
  Haghíde Kitáhl
  Tótoghar Randán
  Gíhrandar Otta Paiéhr
  Mátokhan Mikhíristah
  Ráhnif Rihn

Command officers:

  General One Brinkh
  General Two Nevitahn
  Colonel Kassán kai-Imahr
  Colonel Khaním
  Colonel Dahven
  Major Khagan
  Captain Gifanan
  Captain Trihn

Neighbors in Imahlva:

Gilmaneg
Justice Wahtegahn Urdihn
  Wives: Arshmuhn and Gahna
Oghil, statistical analyst for Imahlva
Jália
Rakhnar, wife Pehris
Dammar
Tanoor

At the Palace of Derahl Nor

(former Emperor, Nághtas, murdered previous year)
Emperor Nadigh; six wives and fifteen daughters
  - chosen Heir, his eldest daughter Rimas
  - Her son and potential heir, Targha
Moragh, brother to Nadigh
Durghid, Uncle of Nadigh, Head of Empiric Senate
Yulghan, Director of Internal Affairs
General Trannor, Director of Union-Kerasi Relations
General Liehr, Director of the First Imperial Court
Nemutar, Minister of Foreign Affairs

Susan Olesen began publishing her own magazine at the age of fifteen and hasn't stopped writing since, authoring more than nine novels, two short story collections, an inexplicably viral blogpost on MP3 CD-books, as well as editing.

A graduate of Chase Collegiate School and Wells College, Susan has raised three children, four foster children, various unofficial adopted kids, a zoo of animals, and is now raising her granddaughter. If it's hungry or homeless, it will find her. Follow her on Facebook at Susan Olesen Author Page.

Watch for the conclusion of *Prisoner of the Mind* in 2020.

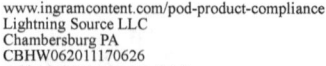